IRREGULARS

IRREGULARS

Kevin McCarthy

NEW ISLAND

IRREGULARS
First published 2013
by New Island
2 Brookside
Dundrum Road
Dublin 14

www.newisland.ie

PRINT ISBN: 978-184840-227-0
EPUB ISBN: 978-184840-228-7
MOBI ISBN: 978-184840-229-4

Typeset by JM InfoTech India
Cover design by Emma Barnes
Printed by TJ International Ltd, Padstow, Cornwall

New Island received financial assistance from
The Arts Council (An Comhairle Ealaíon), Dublin, Ireland

10 9 8 7 6 5 4 3 2 1

Times of unrest are always difficult for police and of course anyone who stands in the road of revolution is bound to get the wrong end of the stick. Contrary to what is thought generally, the Irish are a peaceable people, but when roused they can be ruthless.

David Nelligan
DMP man,
IRA spy,
National Army Director of Intelligence
The Spy in the Castle

He's mad that trusts in the tameness of a wolf, a horse's health, a boy's love, or a whore's oath.

William Shakespeare
King Lear

Acknowledgements

The author would like to thank the following: my agent, Jonathan Williams for his expert representation and editing; Eoin Purcell for his faith in the O'Keefe novels and his work on their behalf for both Mercier and New Island; Dr Justin Corfield for his editing, and all the staff at New Island for their tireless work and support; Emma Barnes for her once again wonderful cover design; my first reader and editor, my mother, Juliet McCarthy; John Dorney and Jim Herlihy for answering my many queries about the minutiae of life during the Civil War and the workings of the CID during the conflict; Colin McCarthy, Susan Dunne, Niall Hogan who generously read and offered comments on early drafts of the novel; my father, Geoffrey McCarthy, Breda Dunne, Geoffrey 'Jefe' McCarthy, Susannah and Jonathan Grimes, Mary McCarthy and Sergo Gabunya, Karen Fullenkamp and Gina McCarthy and all my friends and work colleagues who supported me during the writing of this book; most especially, the author would like to thank Regina, Áine and Eibhlin, without whom the writing of this novel would not have been possible.

This book is dedicated to my wife, Regina

OCTOBER 1922—DUBLIN

Prologue

Two boys enter Burton's Hotel on Lower Abbey Street and pause in the lobby as their eyes adjust to the bright, electric light. The young woman behind the reception desk watches as they share a quick word; watches as they settle something between them before the taller of the two approaches the desk, his companion stepping to the side of the lobby's entrance to wait.

The young woman notes that the approaching boy has clear skin and large, dark eyes; brown hair that hangs over his forehead from under his cap and is tightly cut around his ears and collar; that he is wearing long trousers and a well-cut jacket, polished black boots. She reckons him to be fourteen, perhaps fifteen, years old. He wears no telegraph boy's hat or badge and is too well-dressed for a messenger boy.

Smiling, revealing even, white teeth, the boy says, 'Mr Murphy from across the water, which room is he in?'

'And why would you be needing to know that?' the receptionist asks, smiling back at him not unkindly. A messenger boy after all, she thinks. Of a sort.

The boy blushes and takes off his cap, tapping it nervously against his thigh. The woman is used to this. She has a similar effect on many young men, causing them to blush and stammer and stumble over their words. It is not an effect she intends. She does not see herself as beautiful; though she is aware that her appearance—her green eyes, and the mass of red hair tamed in a demure French knot—is one of the reasons she was chosen above others to man the reception desk at Burton's Hotel.

'I've ... I need to see Mr Murphy. I've a message for him.'

'Why don't you give me the message? I'll have it taken up.' The young woman arranges the guest register on the mahogany counter, aligning it

perfectly with a stack of the previous day's newspapers and a booklet adver-tising train tours for the visitor to Ireland.

The boy shakes his head and says, 'No, I've to take it up meself … myself. It's important. It's …' He searches for help from his friend but none is forthcoming and he brings his gaze back to the woman. This time there is an exaggerated, youthful severity to his face, a seriousness in the boy's large, brown eyes that belies his age. 'Can you give me Mr Murphy's room number or have a porter call for him, Miss? He'd be cross with us both if he thinks I've been delayed.' He pauses for effect. 'And we can't be having that, can we?'

The woman nods at the veiled threat in the boy's words.

'Of course not,' she says. 'It's room thirty-four. You can take the lift. I'll get Michael to run it for you.'

'It's grand, Miss,' the boy says, appearing relieved by her acquiescence, smiling, his face young again, innocent. 'No need to bother your man. I'll take the stairs, sure.'

She watches as the boy turns away and crosses the lobby, checking the clock on the wall and her wrist-watch to be certain, and jots the time in a diary kept below the desk. When she hears the boy's footsteps ascending the stairs, she steps into the small closet behind the reception desk that houses the hotel's switchboard, closing the door behind her. First, she rings room thirty-four and speaks briefly with Mr Murphy from Southampton. Then she dials an outside line and consults with a man waiting in the Flowing Tide public house nearby.

Moments later, a man enters the hotel. Without acknowledging the receptionist or the lad waiting by the front door, he takes a seat in one of the lobby's armchairs and opens a newspaper.

The receptionist knows that this man's colleagues will soon be wait-ing—with a motor car, or perhaps on foot—in the darkened laneway that runs beside the hotel, for the boys to emerge.

Huddled in the laneway, hands jammed in the pockets of ill-fitting and threadbare jackets, are not the reading man's colleagues but two ragged, barefoot youths with caps pulled low on their foreheads.

The older of the two boys, a shock of long, white-blond hair riding his collar, does not plan on being barefoot for much longer. He has the fish-knife after all, and not many fellas—especially not jumped-up, jam-eating youngfellas like the ones they had spotted on Suffolk Street and followed to the hotel—put up much fight once they glommed an eyeful of the knife. No, the boy thinks, even if the youngfellas take ages inside, they are worth the wait. Worth a bob or two and a shiny, fine brace of black boots to land the toes in, in the offing, them two young buckos, strutting the streets this late at night like peacocks in their lovely smart jackets and white shirts. Asking for it, they are, he thinks and then says aloud: 'Fuckin' asking for it, wha?' His mate, smaller, younger, smiles and nods in the shadows beside him.

When the messenger boy returns to the lobby, the receptionist notes in her diary that it is four minutes to midnight, writing the time as '23:56' as she has been taught. She does not look up when he passes her post and is met by his waiting friend, nor does the man sitting across the lobby with the newspaper. She hears the front doors to the hotel open, feels a blast of cool evening air enter, bringing in with it the scent of coal smoke and diesel fumes, toasting hops and the low ebb of the Liffey.

A moment later she hears the man's newspaper crinkle and fold, hears the soft thap as he tosses it onto a side table and follows the boys out onto Lower Abbey Street.

She lights a cigarette in the empty lobby—holding it low below the counter out of a habit of secrecy—and takes furtive drags in silence. Waiting, wondering if she will ever know what has happened—if anything happens—outside.

1

Seán O'Keefe is on his fourth pint of stout in Slattery's of Rathmines. Relishing the silence—curling cigarette smoke winding in the shebeen light of late afternoon—he is drinking the day away, as he has done most days in the five months since he demobbed from the besieged and now disbanded Royal Irish Constabulary. What he had begun thinking of as an extended holiday from the incessant strife and danger of life as a Peeler has turned slowly, surely, to this: a Player's Navy Cut burning down in his fingers, a fairy mound of shredded betting slips in front of him on the bar, five or six pints in an afternoon and sometimes more of an evening. Not doing the dog on it, as the saying goes, but supping enough to damp down the nightmares that still come to him, even now, in his new life as a conscript in Dublin's vast army of thrifty, jobless bachelors. It is an army marching on bacon sandwiches, tinned stew and beans heated on single-ring gas burners in damp digs and back bedrooms; an army barracking in pubs and betting shops; convalescing in the Carnegie library, weary foot-soldiers obliterating the days and hours alongside snuffling, time-killing comrades.

Today, O'Keefe has had two winners—one a decent one, three bob at eight to one—and a fair place from Newmarket. He is up in pocket for his efforts, though it hardly matters to him if he wins or loses. He lifts the *Sporting Life* racing pages and wonders will he bother with another flutter.

'Michelle's Prize in the four-ten at Gowran Park,' an older man at the bar says, three stools away and the only other customer in the pub since O'Keefe entered, not looking at O'Keefe but staring at his own racing sheet, eyeglasses resting on a bulb of burst capillaries. 'I've been watching her—worth a look she is.'

'The ground's meant to be fierce hard going,' O'Keefe says, to be polite, not looking at the man in turn, 'but she'll have weight against her.'

The man beside him shrugs and pushes his spectacles up his nose.

Davey, the young barman's apprentice, stands over the day's *Freeman's Journal* opened out on the bar, his rag-wrapped hand idly polishing the inside of a pint glass. Sensing need—already proficient at the trade—he looks over, and O'Keefe nods for another pint, and as he does there is the unmistakable sound of gunfire from outside the pub. Four sharp cracks—pistol shots, O'Keefe knows from experience—and then a burst of what sounds like machine-gun fire. *Couldn't be*, he thinks. *No, it* could *be. It could be artillery next, the times that are in it*. As he thinks this, a stray round punches high through the pub's front window, carving the air above his head before shattering the nicotine-tinted mirror behind the bar. There is a moment of frozen silence before it is broken by a flurry of harried motion behind the counter, and O'Keefe watches young Davey wrench open the hatch to the keg cellar and leap below for cover.

O'Keefe turns in his chair but does not rise. *If it's for you, it won't go past you.* He listens, tossing his cigarette end to the floor. Two single shots follow, and again silence. Then a woman's high-pitched wailing, a whinnying horse and the urgent gurgle of male voices on the path outside the pub. The man on the stool beside him looks up from his newspaper, but not before circling something with a nub of pencil and jotting out several figures beside this.

'Safe enough for a shuffle 'cross the way, would you say? Wouldn't want to miss the off.'

O'Keefe knocks gently on the bar with his knuckles. 'You take your chances in this life.'

'That you do,' the man says, standing and draining the foamy dregs of his pint. 'Life, love, horses.' He smiles. 'Bullets. All a game of chance, wha'?'

Turning back to his pint, O'Keefe says, 'You're not wrong there, you're not.' He watches the man leave the pub, squinting against the momentary flare of raw daylight as the pub door swings open, and as he does, he thinks of his brother, Peter. *A game of chance ....* On the beaches of Turkey, bullets and luck. He had won and Peter had lost, and he had never felt like he'd won a thing since that day and the bloody days that followed. Guilt bucks inside him. *Lucky boy, you, O'Keefe.* He leans over the counter and looks down into the bar's cellar. 'Come up and pull my pint, Davey.'

The young barman's head appears in the hatch at floor level, red-faced with fear or shame or effort. On the smooth-worn boards around the hatch are shards of shattered mirror, a thousand tiny reflections of the end of an afternoon. 'Is it over?'

'It's over,' O'Keefe says.

Climbing the steps to stand behind the bar, letting the cellar hatch clap shut behind him, the barman looks up at the spidery bullet hole in the window and at the mess of glass crunching under his feet. 'Mr Slattery'll dock me wages for that mirror.'

'Only if the bullet was meant for you, Davey,' O'Keefe says. 'I'll tell him you did your best to catch it before it hit the mirror.'

'It's no lark, Mr O'Keefe. Those fuckin' ... feckin' ... *rebels*! And the Free Stater jaysus bastards. A shower of bullies ... all of them, both sides, God forgive me, but the English weren't half as bad. We could have been killed.'

'That'd stop Slattery docking your wages.'

The barman ignores him and collects a sweeping brush and dustpan from the end of the bar. 'What was it anyway? It's not often there's shooting around here. In town, fair enough, but Rathmines?

3

Sure, who's there to be shooting at? Surgeons and commercial travellers and bank managers, for the sake of holy God.'

'There's more than one who'd like a pop at his bank manager, mind,' O'Keefe says.

The young barman shakes his head and looks up from his sweeping. 'Will you not go out and see what happened, Mr O'Keefe?'

O'Keefe sighs. He has seen enough shooting in the past ten years to sate a lifetime's curiosity as to its causes and effects. Yet even now, since leaving the police and settling to his quiet life of pints and ponies, he cannot escape it. Gunfire is as common a sound as the tolling of church bells in his city now, but O'Keefe has stopped caring why, or how, or what has happened.

Once the bullets are not for him, he couldn't give a tupenny fuck. *Every bullet has its billet*—another saying he remembers from one of his wars. The billet this time: the mirror behind the wall, or some poor sap outside. He is about to say this to young Davey but is suddenly ashamed of the sentiment. *Once it's not got my name on it* …. There is something craven and cowardly in it. He searches for his reflection in the bar-room mirror and finds only the pocked and naked plaster.

He slumps off his stool. 'I'll go out and see. You pull me that pint.'

The young barman nods. 'Mind yourself, Mr O'Keefe. They could still be out there.'

'Life's a game of chance, Davey, were you not listening?'

On the footpath outside the pub, O'Keefe joins the usual crowd of onlookers that assembles at any accident as if to reassure itself of its continued good fortune relative to the hapless maimed or dying. 'Look-sees', he and his fellow constables in the RIC had called them.

The look-sees have clustered this time around the fresh corpse of a fallen dray horse, still bound in its traces, attached to the coal wagon it had pulled in life. The beast's legs are splayed unnaturally beneath it, its dead eyes wide and still behind blinkers, which have slipped in the tangled rigging of reins and bridle. A thickening pool of crimson soaks the road, grouting the gaps between the cobbles and the tram tracks.

Horse carts, motor cars and a tram halted on the obstructed tracks are blocking traffic behind the scene of the violence, and O'Keefe has an instinctive desire to enter the scene and bring it to order. He resists the urge, searching the crowd for any attending Dublin Metropolitan Police. There are none in sight, and O'Keefe is not surprised. Unarmed, the DMP are known to be scarce when the shooting starts. The new Free State government has allowed the DMP a continued existence, unlike his own disbanded Royal Irish Constabulary, but has not granted them any power to prevent or investigate crimes committed as part of the civil war. The new government has its own 'police' for such matters.

Several minutes have passed since the shooting, and O'Keefe's eyes are drawn to the sacks of coal stacked on the back of the wagon and to the street boys and haggard men beginning to take an interest in it. The coalman is lucky, he thinks, that his horse has been shot in Rathmines. Any closer to the city centre and there wouldn't be dust enough left on the coal wagon to raise a cough. He takes out a Player's and lights it, watching the wagon driver kneeling beside the horse. It takes O'Keefe a moment to decipher what the driver is shouting.

'Who will pay for this? Who will pay for me horse? Jaysus and all the fuckin' holy saints, I've had this horse for nine year and now look at her! Jaysus wept, how's a body to make a crust in this god-forsaken pit of a place at all?'

There are tears in the driver's eyes, rage or genuine grief for the horse, and O'Keefe feels a flash of pity for the man.

'Who indeed?' a man's voice next to him says, and O'Keefe turns to it.

It takes him a second to recognise the fellow. It is the thick, brown beard that has thrown O'Keefe, but there is no mistaking the voice, the gruff, jocular Dublin accent softened by the snowy steppes of his earliest childhood. 'Solly …'

'I heard you were back, Seáneen, and haunting the taverns. How're you keeping?'

'Better than some,' O'Keefe says, nodding at the coalman kneeling in the street and offering his hand to his old friend. 'Did you see it?'

'Heard it and ducked for cover like the coward I am. Chap over there said it was a car full of trenchcoats pulled up and started popping away at a lad on the opposite side of the road there. He claims it was the ever elusive Felim O'Hanley they were gunning for. The green pimpernel.'

'And the poor horse got it in the crossfire, along with Slattery's window and mirror. I nearly had a bullet with my pint.'

'Free State musketry leaves much to be desired, so I'm told.'

O'Keefe smiles. Harold 'Solly' Solomon had been eight years old when his father landed the Solomon clan in Dublin, renting the house two doors up from the O'Keefe's with another Ukrainian Jewish family fleeing the pogroms of central Europe for the poverty of Dublin. The poverty had not bothered the Solomons much, and they now own the house they had once rented. The three Solomon brothers are professional men, their sisters married well to upstanding Dublin Jews.

'Will you come inside for a glass or three, Solly?' O'Keefe asks.

Solly tugs a pocket watch from inside his coat. 'Seeing as I'm late already, sure, a quick one would be no harm.'

When they are settled at the bar with their pints of stout, Solly says, 'How is the father anyway, Seán? I've not been in since your mother called for me, what, two weeks ago now? I must stop in to him.'

O'Keefe is puzzled. He has been to see his mother only once since his return to Dublin. Five months of wilful negligence,

though his digs are hardly a mile from his home. This pub, a fif-
teen-minute walk to his front door. He feels heat rise to his face.

'I … I didn't know he wasn't well.'

Solly takes a sup and nods. 'I know things weren't good between
you and the Da, Seán. After Peter … God rest him. Jesus, don't I
know what fathers are like, having one of them myself?'

'Your auldfella's a sound man, Solly. Not like mine at all.'

'Different but the same. We go weeks without talking.'

'Not seven years, but …'

'No, not seven years. Jews have a harder time with begrudg-
ing silence than the likes of ye. If only for the chance of further
recrimination, my auldfella can't hold his tongue for long—you're
right there.' Solly laughs. 'He's always asking after you, Seán, Daddy
is. You should call in. The pot of borscht is still always on the go.
The mother as well would love to see you. She'd want to feed you
up, you know that.' He breaks into an imitation of his mother's
rudimentary English. '*Irish boy, only beer, need food for fat. No beer,
soup! Soup!* You're a fourth son to them, sure.'

'I'm too thick to be a Solomon.'

'Every house needs a heavy.'

O'Keefe laughs softly. 'Will you go another jar, Solly?'

Solly claps him on the shoulder. 'No, I've a patient to see in
Rathgar. I'll be hoofing it now that the tram's off. But we will,
Seán, soon, yes? Call in to me and we'll go for a gallon.'

O'Keefe realises what he must ask his old friend, and feels the
shame of asking. 'Solly? What's … wrong with the auldfella? He's
all right, isn't he?'

Solly's eyes darken under his homburg. 'You should go see him,
Seán. Go see him and then call in to me and we'll sit down for a
chat. But you'd do well to see him, right?' He squeezes O'Keefe's
shoulder, and O'Keefe shudders under the grip.

'All right, I will.'

'Good man, Seán.'

'Right so, Solly.'

O'Keefe walks his friend out of the pub, and watches him weave his way through the thinning crowd. On the street a DMP constable has finally arrived on the scene, and has enlisted some men standing on the path to help him shift the dead horse and the coal wagon off the tram tracks. O'Keefe turns momentarily north, instinct directing his heart homewards, but shame trumps instinct and he swivels about face—a parade ground pivot from his days of drill in the Peelers and the army—and heads back into Slattery's to the safety of the bar's daylight shadows.

For three days, O'Keefe drinks. He does not eat and does not play the horses and only vaguely remembers stumbling out of wherever he had finished the first night. There was whiskey involved and the heady miasma of perfume and sweat. The laughter of women and a crackling gramophone.

Noon or sometime after, O'Keefe rises and finds the bottle of Jameson on the desk beside his table. It is a bottle he has no recollection of buying but is glad he did. He pours stagnant water from a pitcher into a glass and adds whiskey, and in half an hour he starts again in Slattery's, and keeps at it until he falls down outside of Kehoe's on South Anne Street. He is lifted to his feet by a man he has met in the pub, and guided to a hack and driven back to his digs, stopping twice to be sick, once at the top of Stephen's Green and again at Harcourt Street. Shortly after this, a quarter mile from his family home, he tells the hackney man to stop. The driver waits in silence, his horse's breath a lazy billow in the night air. 'Fuck it, drive on,' O'Keefe says, before passing out.

He awakes early and is sick again, but blessedly back in his digs in the faded darkness of night on the cusp of morning. A darkness that will not grant sleep. He eyes the whiskey bottle, a quarter full, takes up the pitcher of water in shaking hands and pours it into his one glass and adds whiskey. And starts again. To help him sleep. Today, he thinks, he will see his father, his mother. But sleep first.

Again to Slattery's, where Davey asks him has he not had

enough, at half twelve in the afternoon, and from there in his memory he has only a dim, flickering reel of pubs and flashing blasts of conversation until a kindly constable and again a hack, and this time he gives the driver the address to his home instead of his digs.

His father answers his sloppy knocking and O'Keefe is dimly aware of the surprise on his father's face, and then a strange blankness as if he does not recognise his son, but it is gone in an instant, replaced by a smile and then his mother is there. And then he is aware of nothing until he awakes in the bed he had slept in as a boy, in the bed he had shared with his brother.

2

'So you're saying Detective Officer Kenny was dead before you got him to Jervis Street Infirmary in the taxi …?'

'Yes, he was,' the woman from the front desk of Burton's Hotel says.

Her interrogator looks up from the file he is reading. His gaze is unnerving because one of his eyes is made of glass, replacing the one that had been gouged out by Auxiliaries who'd captured and questioned him more than a year ago in a different and far simpler conflict. This man, she thinks, knows more than any man should about interrogation. As if reading her thoughts, he dons a pair of round spectacles under which the glass eye is less noticeable.

The woman, Nora Flynn, shakes her head and gazes out the second-floor window at the offices across the busy Westland Row thoroughfare. She can see men in shirtsleeves and ties, women at typewriters. The bustling business of a life assurance company, clacking and scribbling away in search of profit as if there was no way on earth men could be killing each other just a street or two away. *Bustling*, she thinks, liking the word, the innocent industry it implies.

These offices too are busy. There are men in shirtsleeves and women at typewriters, but over the shirtsleeves the men wear leather shoulder-holsters stuffed with pistols and in the typists' desk drawers, Nora knows, there are loaded Colt revolvers and files bearing the names of dead men and men marked for death. Bustling is not a word one would use, she decides, bringing her eyes back to the man with the file.

Nervous under the weight of her interrogator's silence, she continues. 'Sure, didn't they have a car? The Ford they were using. Why didn't they use it to take him to the hospital?'

Nora remembers running down Abbey Street, trailing a member of the surveillance squad whose name she does not know, an agent who moments earlier had burst through the hotel doors bellowing for Nora to help, that they had a man down injured. In her mind she sees the man pile through the open door of the Ford Tourer and the car leaving, roaring off in the direction of the Custom House, no instructions given to her other than to get the fallen man to a hospital. And she remembers the quiet that descended as the car's motor faded in the distance. She can almost feel the heft of Kenny's head in her lap and the warm blood on her hand as she pressed it to the wound, the knife handle still there, lodged between his ribs.

Her interrogator stares at her for a long moment, and Nora wonders if it would have been better to remain silent. She has worked with this man, and men like him, for the better part of two years, indirectly at first, but directly for the past nine months. This is, she thinks, her second war, and yet she feels little different, at times, than when she was a summer typist in her father's accountancy office.

'And all this happened at what time?'

She makes an effort to remember. 'It couldn't have been more than ten past midnight. You have my operations report. The boy passed by me and exited the hotel at … what did I write? Eleven fifty-six? Forty-six? And Detective Officer Kenny followed him.' She is growing angry, a flush of blood in her cheeks, her palms still sweating, but there is steel in her voice as she speaks. She has done her job. In no way is she to blame for the death of a man who should have known better.

Kenny, the man with the newspaper. An unlikely detective, she thinks, with his pinched, wan face, his thin body and quick-bitten fingernails. A man who, in reality, had looked every inch the Active Service Unit gunman he had been in the fight against the Crown. But they have called each other 'detective officers'—it is their rank and they are paid as such—ever since transforming from Michael Collins' handpicked squad of shooters to the Criminal Investigation Department in Oriel House. Detecting was not what men like Kenny had joined up for, Nora knows, though some of the newer members of CID, and some who had come to the unit from the Irish Republican Police or from IRA units in distant counties, are under the illusion that they are, in fact, detectives.

'And you've no idea who stabbed Kenny?' her interrogator asks, lighting a cigarette.

'No, no idea. You'll have to ask them when … when they come in,' she says, filling the silence as much as answering the question. Behind her low-burn anger, fear continues to smoulder. 'It's all in my report,' she adds. 'Did Dillon or O'Shea file theirs?'

Her interrogator watches her for a long moment. Then he closes the manila file on his desk and leans forward, holding out his packet of Sweet Aftons.

Finally: 'No. They've not come in yet, and when I rang Wellington barracks I was told they hadn't checked in there yet either.'

'So that leaves us where?' she asks, not sure if she should.

'It leaves us wanting to speak to them and catch whoever stabbed Detective Kenny. Finding O'Hanley seems secondary now, in a way, though we mustn't stop searching for him, or laying bait.'

Felim O'Hanley is the target of the hotel operation. Slippery as Collins—God rest him—had been to the British, and now running the Dublin Brigade for the anti-Treaty Irregulars. After another long silence, Nora meets her interrogator's eyes.

He says, 'There was nothing you could have done, Nora. You've been doing good work and you did what you were called on to do.'

She leans across the desk and takes a cigarette. Detective Superintendent Terence Carty, like Detective Officer Kenny, was a member of the Big Fella's special squad, one of his twelve apostles during the Tan War, but smarter, more nuanced than most of them. From fearing Carty to remembering now how he'd always respected the work she had done for the cause during that war; how he had personally recruited her into the Free State Army Intelligence Department and then into CID. He treated her as an agent, rather than just a mocked-up typist, like many of the others did. It was he who had suggested she man the desk at Burton's for this operation and had made sure she was included in the briefings pertaining to it.

It's as if Carty sees beyond the notion that women were suited only to the paperwork of war. Sophisticated, Nora thinks, but frightening in his own way. In his eyeglasses and shirtsleeves he might have appeared more at home in the assurance offices across the road, auditing claims for fire and theft. But Carty, Nora knows, had taken many lives as a gunman for Collins. He goes nowhere unarmed, wearing even now at his desk a Mauser C96 in a shoulder-holster instead of the standard issue Colt .45 revolver most of the men in the department carry. She wonders had he shot any of the men she had fingered during her time in the Castle with that same gun. How many men had he killed? More men than she herself had marked for death with a pen and carbon file copy? She pushes the line of thought from her mind. Silly questions. War possesses a mathematics all of its own.

'What do we do now?' she asks. Two minutes earlier she would not have dared.

Carty exhales a stream of smoke, stubs out his cigarette and removes his glasses to wipe them on his necktie. *Maybe not so sophisticated*, Nora thinks.

'We have to wait for Charlie and the rest of the boys to come in. Find out from them what happened. Find out if we'll be able to proceed with things or if the whole operation is scuppered. Charlie has his own way of doing things. He'll be back when he's ready.'

Carty speaks of Captain Charles Dillon as if of an eccentric uncle rather than a veteran gunman.

Nora is confused. 'But surely … I mean, Mr Murphy is blown. He can't be used. Not when the messengers failed to return to O'Hanley. At least we know from Murphy that it was O'Hanley who sent the boys.'

'*If* they failed to return,' Carty says.

'Something happened in that laneway, something involving the messenger boys. They weren't two minutes out the door when your man burst back into the hotel shouting they'd a man down stabbed. For all we know, Dillon could have the two messenger boys in custody at Wellington barracks, if not O'Hanley himself.'

Nora knows she is treading dangerously, making accusations she cannot substantiate, but she feels aggrieved. So what if Charlie Dillon has his own way of doing things? A man was dead, and an operation of many weeks' planning likely damaged beyond repair.

'If they'd plugged or pulled O'Hanley, we'd have heard about it by now,' Carty says, a vague smile at his lips.

'But what about Murphy? Is he not blown?'

'No, I think we'll keep him in his rooms for the time being. Until we see what happens. You'll continue to work the front desk, in shifts along with Detective Officers Malloy and Ring?'

'Of course.'

'And if our Mr Murphy *is*, in fact, blown,' Carty says, the smile blossoming now to a real one, 'our pals in the Crown can always lend us another one.'

'Their generosity knows no bounds.'

'You mean our pals in British Army intelligence aren't helping us for the good of an independent Ireland?'

Nora smiles for the first time in what feels like days. 'I rather doubt it, don't you?'

3

'**H**ow's the head, then?'

His father's voice. O'Keefe opens his eyes, convinced he is waking from one dream and slipping into another. A voice he has not heard in almost seven years. No. Dreaming. He closes his eyes again.

'There's tea for you. If you can keep it down.'

This time his eyes snap open. His father looms, sitting in a chair beside the bed, and a jolt of panic flashes through O'Keefe as he scans the room, realising now that it is his own room and, at once, not his at all. His gaze returns to his father—white hair in the years since he had seen him, the moustache that he has worn as long as O'Keefe has been alive and aware, now also white.

'What …?' O'Keefe says. 'What am I doing here?'

His father smiles, and the smile is a comfort to O'Keefe in his haze of waking. It has been so long since he has seen it, though his father smiled often when he and brother Peter and elder sister Sally had been children. O'Keefe's father had been a happy man once. A respected DMP detective, he had been a man proud of his work and his home and his ability to keep the O'Keefe family safe and secure; well-fed and schooled. Loved. And then Peter was killed in Turkey and his father had stopped smiling.

O'Keefe sits up, and as he does his vision blurs and sharp pain seizes his head and neck, nausea rising in his throat. Gingerly he lies back. 'Jaysus, my head. What happened to me?' He squeezes his eyes shut against the pain and senses, as much as hears, his father laugh. Smiling and now laughing.

O'Keefe wonders suddenly is Peter really dead or had he dreamed it all: the war and the water; the blood and the beach and the scattering death of a million Turkish rounds ripping through the men of the Dublin and Munster Fusiliers? And the wounds and the black winds of sadness that blew in when he let drop his guard? The hospital in Cork? His return to the police and the war in West Cork? His last parade in the Phoenix Park depot on his demob day five months before? All of it a dream, because he is in the bedroom of his childhood, in the bed he shared with his brother and his father is smiling, laughing.

'You really don't know, do yeh, son?'

O'Keefe says nothing but opens one eye. 'No,' he says. 'I've a feeling it's a good thing I don't.'

Again his father smiles. 'Well, Misters Guinness and Jameson thank you anyway.'

Closing his eyes again, O'Keefe dredges up a coherence of events as best he can.

A pub. A darkened laneway. A woman's laughter. Windmilling punches thrown and the smashing of glass. O'Keefe opens his eyes, checks his knuckles and breathes a sigh of relief to find them undamaged.

'What day is it?' he asks, and feels a dart of shame in the asking.

His father is reading *The Irish Times*, and he looks up over his reading glasses.

'Monday,' his father says, and in saying it, his face goes blank, in the same way it had when he'd opened the door to O'Keefe. He then holds the newspaper out at arm's length, as if it wondering at its purpose. There is a long moment of confounded silence before O'Keefe's father folds the paper with a flourish and scans the front page. 'Monday, yes. You've been here since yesterday early. Your mother nearly fainted when she saw the state of you.' He

17

smiles again as if this amuses him. 'We'd the doctor in—the young Jewish lad from up the road; a fine lad and knowledgeable about medicine from the Continent. He told us to watch over you, but that you'd live if you didn't die.'

'Solly, you mean, Da?' O'Keefe says, puzzled by his father's forgetfulness, but aware that his own thoughts are sluggish and slow in the aftermath of his spree.

His father's face returns the puzzlement. 'Solly?'

'Harold Solomon, Daddy. Solly …'

His father's brow buckles in sudden fury, and terror washes through O'Keefe. *What did I say?* And as quickly, his father's rage is gone and there is fear in his expression and then something else. Embarrassment, O'Keefe decides, closing his eyes against it, wishing his father would smile again.

After some moments of silence, O'Keefe asks, 'Where's Mam?'

'Your mother's sleeping now. She's the knees nearly worn off her with the praying.'

O'Keefe attempts a weak smile at the thought of his mother, on her knees in prayer, rosary beads hurtling through her fingers like the links of an anchor chain through a cat's eye. An image from his childhood as common as any other he has of her, his mother hard at the rosary. 'They seemed to have worked. The prayers …' O'Keefe says, and something in the corner of his mind darkens—a shadow passing through his memory—and he is no longer smiling.

'They do betimes,' his father replies, looking away to the window as if recalling all the times when prayers had gone unanswered.

In his reverie, his father's face goes slack and then brightens suddenly. 'Peter's due back from college soon, of course. And Sally, as well, with that friend of hers,' he says, smiling and nodding.

'But Peter is …' O'Keefe stops himself for a reason he does not understand. He studies his father's face and is unable to read it. It is as if a stranger is wearing a mask of gormless, glad perplexity that resembles his father but is not like his father at all. He decides he has misunderstood his father's words—that he is dreaming after all—and closes his eyes again to the mercy of sleep.

Some time later that night, O'Keefe awakens and it is dark in his room and his father is no longer there but he can hear his voice, deep and grave somewhere below in the house. And the voice of another man, something menacingly familiar in the tone of it, speaking with his father, his father's voice now raised in sudden anger. A door closing and then his father and the man speaking again, outside the house, and O'Keefe wonders if he is dreaming— hopes that he is—but knows that he is not and that his father has always taken guests outside when he wanted to speak of private matters. Of matters he did not want his wife to hear. But before long it is his mother's voice O'Keefe hears as well, outside with the men. He closes his eyes and prays that his father and the man are not speaking about him. He thinks of the blankness in his father's face, and remembers that he has come home to ask after his health. A dark shard of fear wedges itself beneath O'Keefe's ribs, and for the first time in as long as he can remember he prays, and does not feel a fool doing it.

The shadow of fear is still there, but it is mostly at bay because it is his mother who comes to him in the morning, bringing sweetened tea and scrambled eggs, bread and butter and a bowl of custard. He thinks of his father's words from the day before. He is certain now that he had heard him correctly. *And Peter's due back from college soon. And Sally.* The fear returns.

O'Keefe listens to his mother chatting, recounting street gossip—marriages, births, deaths, minor scandal—and he finds that if he closes his eyes and concentrates on her voice, he can fall under the comforting weight of the dream that has him still a boy; sick and off from school, his mother sitting beside him as she does now, Peter and Sally due home but not for a while yet; his father at the barracks and O'Keefe alone with his mother. Blessedly sick. A dream of times past so rare and precious and full of flat lemonade and scrambled eggs; bread and jam and Seville oranges and the sweet musk of his mother as she leans over to fluff his pillows, her hand on his forehead in search of fever.

His mother is oblivious to the fantasy, however, often mentioning the civil war that has ravaged Ireland these past months, flaring up in incidents of savagery almost unheard of in the fight for independence against the Crown that preceded it. His mother speaks of so-and-so's boy—*were you at school with him or was it Peter?*—gunned down in broad daylight. *Can you imagine?* Reading from the newspaper now. Another bank robbed. Limerick shelled by Free State troops. And other stories—*sotto voce* over garden walls or in the bakery or butcher's—that the newspapers were forbidden by the Free State government to tell. Tales of the bloody, vicious things Irishmen were doing to each other in the fight for a country to call their own. A Free State? A Republic? O'Keefe thinks, when he is lucid and in the present, that no notional nation state is worth the damage being done to the country and its people by the men who have claimed to be its liberators.

But now, as she speaks of these things, O'Keefe burrows deeper into the blankets and pretends that Peter and Sally will be home soon from school. Daddy home soon from the barracks for his tea. Mammy will be reading him *Oliver Twist* or *Great Irish Legends* and not newspaper stories about skirmishes and casualties and bloody-minded murder. Blessed illness.

Shame drives him up from the dream, and he rises to sitting in the bed. 'I'm sorry I took so long to come back here, Mam. And the state I came in …'

'Hush, Seán, don't mind. We're only happy to have you here, your father and I.'

O'Keefe is silent, and the guilt and relief he feels well up in him and his eyes brim with tears. 'Thanks, Mam.'

'Go 'way out of that, pet. Where can you come to when you need it but your home? Did you think we'd not have you?'

For a moment, O'Keefe does not answer. 'I thought Daddy might … I don't know.'

'Your father's different now, Seán,' his mother says, and even in his condition, he can sense that she wants to say more.

'I met Solly, in Rathmines last …' he cannot recall the day, and shame stabs at his ribs, '… last week. He asked after Da and said he'd been in to see him.'

'He was. Good auld Solly. And in to see you as well, saying how you were suffering from the most common of Irish illnesses and not to worry for you.'

O'Keefe smiles weakly, thinking of his father's reaction when he had mentioned Solly's name. The rage his father's face had shown at the mention of the old family friend. A rage directed at himself.

His mother continues, 'What a fine man he's become. And such a doctor. All the best of the Jews and Protestants attend his surgery, you know, Seán.'

O'Keefe laughs a little at his mother's casual snobbery. Only a doctor good enough for the wealthier of Dublin's Jews and Protestants would do her and her own. She is aware of this snobbery, of its general but necessary absurdity, and winks at her son.

'Is Da all right, Mam?' O'Keefe asks.

His mother is silent for a long moment and her eyes are suddenly sad and tired. Like his father, she has aged. It is he who should be looking after her and, again, shame and guilt course through his blood.

'You're father's not well, Seán, but not in his body. He's fit as a fiddle, his heart would do an ox proud.'

'What is it then?' But O'Keefe recalls the blankness that had visited his father's face, his need to consult the date on the newspaper's front page; his talk of Peter and Sally coming home from college, and he knows. 'He's not well in the head, Mam? Is that it?'

His mother nods. 'He forgets things. Simple things. And he gets frightened, at night …' She looks to the open doorway as if his father might enter at any moment. 'And gets so angry when he can't remember something, Seán.'

'What did Solly say?'

'He sent us to a surgeon, one of the masters in the Mater. He has your father on cannabis tincture and other pills.'

'And are they working?'

'They were.'

'Jesus, Mam.'

His mother smiles, and it is the saddest smile O'Keefe can remember her ever giving. 'He'll only get worse, the master says, until he'll have to be committed, for his own safety.'

O'Keefe says nothing, contemplating his father in an asylum. He had been to such places as a constable, and decides that he will not have his father in such a place. No place for any man, let alone his father. He wonders for a bitter second how his mother can even contemplate doing such a thing, but then decides that she wouldn't if she knew what they were like.

'And is he aware of it, Mam? Of how ill he is?'

'He is and he isn't, and half the time he forgets. Sometimes he goes out and I worry he'll be lost and never come back.'

'Where is he now?'

'He goes out with Maurice O'Toole most mornings. They go to train Mossy's greyhounds. I'd be lost without Maurice, I would. He's a saint, the man.'

Maurice 'Mossy' O'Toole, a retired G-Division detective, the same as his father.

'Jesus, Mam,' O'Keefe says. 'Look, I'll move back in and help you, let me do that at least. I've money, saved from my police wages. I'll help you here.'

'No,' his mother says, standing. 'Not that. You'll not be a nurse-maid. I've Mrs Devereaux and she's a great help all these years. Especially now. She's better with him than I am, still calling him "Sergeant". And when he gets in his rages, they just seem to run off her back like rain.'

Mrs Devereaux had been with the O'Keefe family since she was a young woman and O'Keefe a boy. She had married many years ago, but had continued to do washing and ironing, cooking the odd time and cleaning the fire grates for the O'Keefe family, coming each day, though there was hardly enough for her to do. O'Keefe had always been fond of her, never more so than now.

'Is she enough help for you, Mam?'

'She is of course. The most capable girl ... listen to me, *girl*, when the woman must be forty-five years old with grown children of her own. The most capable woman in Ireland and she's a true blessing with your father. And your sister comes some days and that's enough but sure, doesn't she have the babby now?'

His sister and her baby he's not yet seen. Guilt again beds down with the sadness in his heart. 'What can I do for you and Da then? I want to be of some help. However I can ...'

Again his mother is silent, as if deciding something. 'There is something you can do for me ... for your father. When you're better ...'

'What is it?'

'Not now. When you've your strength back, I'll tell you. You sleep, now, love,' his mother says, placing her warm hand on his brow. 'It's so good to have you home, Seán. Even if it was an ill wind that brought you.'

4

The messenger boy is no longer sobbing, but tears well in his eyes and run down his face when he blinks, his cheeks hot with shame because crying is not what proper soldiers of the Irish Republican Army do.

Nor do they wet themselves in terror, as he had done, in the back of the motor car as they brought him here, the man seated next to him letting out a roar when he felt the piss encroaching onto his side of the bench seat and driving his elbow into the boy's mouth, cutting the boy's lip against his teeth.

The messenger boy sniffs back blood and snot and tries to wipe the tears from his face with his shoulder. He cannot use his hands because they are cuffed so tightly behind him that he has lost all feeling in them. His legs are also bound with the belt from his own trousers, and the men have left him on the muddy floor with his back against the damp wall of this derelict cottage, the interior of which holds a cold darkness all its own, colder even, the boy imagines, than outside.

Shivering, unable to warm himself, he swallows back his fear and wonders how long he has been here, in the dark. And he wonders where the other boy has been taken. They had brought him in the car as well, the thief curled up on the floor of the Ford, resting their boots on him, digging their heels into his ribs, his balls, when he whimpered. The messenger wonders whether the other boy had pissed his trousers as well. Would serve him right if he had, the filthy, robbing gouger.

The enemy is everywhere, he thinks, Free State traitor bastards and street robbers; dippers and tenement scum like the lad with the fish-knife. When the Republic comes—the proper, goodo, decent republic the IRA had fought the Tans and Tommies for and not this half-arsed, cap-tipping Free State model sold to an ignorant people by Collins and Griffith and their mob of Crown stooges—they will clean up the streets right enough. No more dark lanes and mugger boys with knives. The streets are full of them, his mother has always said, and it flashes through his mind to tell his mother what has happened, how the two had tried to rob him. She was always on to him, when he was younger, about minding himself on the streets.

Tears well again in his eyes, and he swallows down the hard lump of sadness and fear in his throat. Another thing no proper soldier of the Republic would do: cry for his mammy when his prick is in the fire. Like his is now.

He sniffs again, and resolves to buck up and act like a soldier. No more tears, for the sake of all that's right and holy. *I'm fifteen years old*, he thinks. *Not some youngfella in short trousers mitching from school, but a scout, a messenger, a soldier of the IRA, Dublin Brigade, and now, a prisoner of war, no less.* He is momentarily pleased by this realisation. *I am a prisoner of war*, he tells himself, thinking of the letter he will write his mother. *Dear Mother, fear not for my safety. I am currently a prisoner of war* ....

And he resolves to say nothing to the men who have brought him here, no matter what they do to him. The message to Mr Murphy in Burton's Hotel had been delivered, as ordered, mouth to ear, and no evidence of this can be found on his person. So he will keep the head down, the mouth shut, no matter what they try on him. He is certain of this. He will make Commandant O'Hanley proud, he will, straightening his back against the wall and wishing he had a cigarette, though he has only recently begun smoking.

For some time he lets his mind wander in the dark, images of himself in the uniform of a soldier—in his fantasy it is a British Army uniform, as familiarity brings it to his mind first, and the army he fights for does not yet have one—of himself on a gallows, his eyes blindfolded, a rakish cigarette dangling from his lip, a fine, sweet weeping girleen dabbing at her eyes. He smiles to himself. *A prisoner of war, I am.* He only wishes his friend were with him. At least then he would not be alone in the dark. Even that thieving bastard of a robber would be company. Even him.

He wonders again what has become of the other boy, and as if his thoughts have provoked it, the thief boy begins to scream. The scream comes from outside the cottage and is piercing and girlish. One word is intelligible. The word is *No*.

The messenger boy shivers in the cold. The tears overflow his eyes and run down his cheeks, and this time he does nothing to try to staunch them. Different images now parade through his head.

5

Jeremiah Byrne awakes cold and wet with dew. In the grey light of morning he peers out from the high grass in which he had finally, several hours earlier, lain down to sleep. His stomach growls as if to wish him good morning and remind him that he has not eaten in more than a day.

Groggy, he searches his memory for the last food he has taken, and in this searching, the frantic action of the previous evening lurches into his conscious mind. He sits up abruptly and scans the field of grass where he has hidden. It is a smaller field than he'd thought when he stumbled upon it in the darkness, bordered by a low hedge and the Howth Road, he thinks, not having known for certain what road it was at the time, but only that it would take him far away from the men and the boys in the lane off the quays.

Jaysusfuck, he thinks. *Miles I must have run*. And as he thinks this, he looks at his right hand, and sees that it is stained with dried blood. Not his own blood, he remembers. Another fella's blood. *And thank fuck for that.*

Forced to cut the bastard, he thinks, when all he'd wanted was a root in the pockets and a pair of boots off the youngfellas they'd followed from the hotel.

Part of Jeremiah knows that he's in it neck deep now, whether the fella's dead or not, but another part of him can only hear the growling in his stomach, feel the parch in his throat. Giving the

27

field a final scan and reassuring himself there is no one about, he stands and brushes the dew from his clothing, beating his thighs and stomach with his palms to get the blood flowing.

Blood flowing. He thinks again of the fella in the laneway and decides that he doesn't mind if he had killed him. He's hardly eaten in two days and that bastard had come between Jeremiah Byrne and a fine, slap-up nosebag, courtesy of them young lads in the lane.

Time to find Tommo, he thinks, hoping his friend had made it away when the bother kicked off. Find Tommo first, get his side of things straight and make sure his mate keeps his cake-hole shut.

Then head back to the Ma and see if she'd used the two bob he'd given her two days ago—after dipping some gentleman swat's wallet on Grafton Street—to buy food for his sisters or gargle for herself. But he knows the answer already and sorrow wells up in him as he makes his way through the wet grass towards the road. And this sadness, like it always does, turns to anger as he walks, lest it overwhelm him. He has no choice in this. Anger he can use; sadness is useless. *So what, to fuck,* his anger says, *if I sliced the bastard, when that fella slept on a full belly every night and me and me sisters with nothing but grief to eat. Fuck him, the cunt. I'd stick him again.* If it would mean a hot meal, for himself, for his sisters. For them, he'd stick any bastard who crossed him.

Jeremiah hops a tram at Fairview Park, riding on the open back conductor's platform, hanging on to a handrail. He makes it three stops before the conductor comes down from the upper deck and ticketless Jeremiah leaps off. He has been making his way home for the better part of an hour now and will cover the last half mile on foot.

The night before seems strangely distant to him as he walks in the rare autumn sunlight, the cobbles and macadam warm and sticky with horse shit and motor oil and Indian summer-softened tar under his bare feet. Everything on Amiens Street—food stalls, fruit stands, shawlies selling holy medals and postcards, newspaper boys with the latest editions for the workers arriving by train from Amiens Street station, beer lorries and cart-horses and tinkers' scrap wagons—appears unchanged from any other day. Nothing has changed just because he had stabbed a fella. The world rolls on as if nothing has happened. Which means, he decides, that he must not have killed the man, because if he had, surely the world would be different somehow—the colours grander, brighter; the sounds louder and perhaps sweeter to his ear.

Of course, he's stabbed a fella once before, he has. An auld dosser in a lane who had half shocked the shite out of him, rising from the shadows like a ghost begging for coins, but that fella had lived to doss another day. Jeremiah had only carved up his arm, and that shielded by a heap of rags worn for warmth under a British Army greatcoat. As well as this, he recalls that he has cut youngfellas in fights the odd time, and taken the odd jab and slice himself from other fella's knives. But he knows that the world will be a different bleedin' spot alto-fuckin'-gether when auld Jerry gets round to snuffing a fella, and since the world today is just like it was on any other day, he decides he must not have snuffed that fella the night before.

Absently rubbing his palm on his trouser leg as he walks— though he had scrubbed it free of blood with dew-sodden grass at the side of the Howth Road—his stomach growls with hunger, twisting in on itself as he passes bakeries, cake shops, a working man's café where dockers and porters stand at a wooden counter, shovelling in the bacon and cabbage and washing them down with tea or buttermilk. *Another thing that hasn't changed*, he thinks, passing a man with a cart selling pig's trotters—*I'm still hungry*. Same as every day, with the stomach stuck to the ribs and scarce hope of a hot feed. He considers ordering a trotter with gherkins in newspaper and pulling a scarper, going so far as to loiter on the corner next to McCormack's early house pub to watch the vendor.

In the end, he moves on towards home. No sense getting lagged or shot. *Shot for a trotter.* Who knows which mob the vendor is paying protection tax to, or which fella idling on the corner has a rod in his pocket and a fierce yearning to use it. Too many lads hauling iron these days, and none of them would shy away from blasting the arse out of a youngfella.

No, no thieving for the moment, he thinks, and as he does, he sees a uniformed DMP man and thanks the god of gougers that the constable crosses the road to speak with a beggar-woman hassling passers-by.

Jeremiah stops, and in the reflection of a chemist's shop window he watches the policeman menace the beggar until she moves on. Studying his own reflection now, superimposed over the shop's wares—conventional medicines and ointments, but also herbal balms, tiger powders, curry paste and yearling's milk potions for superstitious sailors—he begins tucking his hair up under his rough, mushroom-shaped cap, as much of it as he can fit. His hair is the bane of his criminal existence. Even oiled, or unwashed for weeks as it mostly is, it falls out from under his cap in straws of golden light and makes him easy prey for even the blindest of coppers. He turns, instinctively scanning the quays around him. Sensing nothing out of the ordinary, he relaxes and carries on walking.

His hair is of some advantage, he will admit. Girls like it. Not that he is much bothered with them. His sisters are about the only ones he can tolerate. But it isn't girls he is thinking about—though a girl would do for a turn when the hare was in need of a hole. He is thinking about the other way he has discovered, in the past year, to score the odd bob. His blond hair helps him there and no joke. Fair hair a bonus, in the job of work that was this other way. A far easier way than robbing, he thinks. And, in ways, much harder.

6

O'Keefe's mother has told him that his father had been employed by a woman named Dolan. That his father had taken on the work to repay a debt that he would not disclose to wife or son, despite it driving him to wake in terror sweats, shouting, pleading with the darkness.

'*I didn't know ... she never told me, I couldn't have known ... please ...*'

'Told you what, Da?' O'Keefe had ventured the night before, but his father had responded to his question with the same blank look that O'Keefe had come to recognise, the vagueness in his features that spoke of shadows, voids, in his father's mind.

'You'll see to it, won't you, son?' his mother had asked. 'Your father's not able. It would shame him, it would, if the woman were to see him like he is ...'

'You know her?' O'Keefe had asked her in turn. 'This Dolan woman?'

'Not at all. Don't be daft,' his mother had said, turning away.

Now O'Keefe dresses in his freshly laundered suit of clothes. Civilian clothes marking the civilian he has become. A grey suit, white shirt and starched collar, though O'Keefe notices now that the shirt is not his own and must be his father's.

Even after five months as a civilian, he catches himself staring at this unfamiliar image in the mirror and, as he knots his tie, thinks back to the day he marched in the RIC's last parade before its disbandment, his polished black boots slapping the smooth cobbles of the Phoenix Park depot parade-ground. The lowering of the Union Jack and the raising of the Irish tricolour. He remembers the way he folded his bottle-green uniform trousers on the hanger with the coat and the hat, and how he had left them on the bunk there in the depot. Like a second skin, the armour of his past life shed, exchanged for this one suit of grey wool. The suit of everyman. Making him feel somehow less a man in the world now than he was before.

His childhood home behind him, O'Keefe turns onto Clanbrassil Street, slow-hoofs it to Patrick Street and past St Patrick's Cathedral, Foley's pub across the way, the public baths on his right, the address of the Dolan woman folded in his pocket. The streets are filled with the clatter and shriek of tram wheels on rails and the clanging of tram bells; the splutter and belch of coal lorries and motor cars; the clopping of cart-horses, movement and light assaulting O'Keefe's eyes. He starts, goose-pimples peppering his skin as barefooted boys scarper from an alleyway, fleeing some unseen misdemeanour.

Knock the booze on the head, he thinks. Too much of it altogether since he left the Peelers. He thinks again that he should have joined his barrack mates who signed on with the Palestinian Police after disbandment. The Greater Manchester Police as well was looking for experienced men. Or he could always go up north, to the six counties excluded from the Free State by the Treaty, as many other Peelers had done. Take a job at the very wellspring of the civil war now raging. Like the policing he had done in the Tan War, policing in Ulster—they had changed the name to the Royal *Ulster* Constabulary—would be little more than presiding over pogroms and sectarian bigots with their banners and sashes and such. *No thanks, pal.* Still, though he is wary, he is happy for this job, happy to repay his father's debt, whatever it may be. If only because nothing good comes of an Irishman with too much time on his hands.

A newspaper boy interrupts his reverie, hawking the dailies. *Read it he-ar! Free State Army crush Irregulars in Cork. Many dead*, the newsboy shouts, nearly singing. *Lo-ads reported dead. Read it he-ar!*

O'Keefe continues on up towards Christ Church Cathedral, passing young girls begging for coppers, clutching baby siblings to their scrawny chests or selling matches, some selling themselves. Common as rain in winter—women, girls hawking themselves in the laneways, doorways and cold water flats of the city. More whores than anywhere on earth, so it's said. Dublin, city of whores and angry men. Which is he? he thinks, and shakes his head at the routes taken by his mind when he lets it run.

He passes fruit and vegetable stalls. Thomas's bicycle repair shop—push-bikes upturned on the footpath like obstructions in no-man's land. O'Brien and Sons Butchers next, the coppery scent of blood from the open doorway suffusing the October air, seeping into O'Keefe's consciousness and turning his mind to memories of battle, but this time he does not let his thoughts wander. Instead he forces them down into the place on the sea-floor of his memory where he keeps them. The murder hole he has named it, and smiles sadly that he should have need of such a place, and wonders would there ever be a time when the smell of a butcher's shop would not remind him of the war.

In thinking this, O'Keefe considers how memory—experience—is locked into the meat of a body. He has no belief in a soul, or anything so elevated, but he does believe—he has read this recently during one of his long, clock-killing afternoons in the library and agrees with it—that memory becomes embedded in the physical self; that traces of all past action lay dormant in the muscle, in the sinew and tissue and blood of a man like some latent, malarial sickness and return to attack the mind and body in the form of recollection, unbidden, unexpected. *No better than beasts, we are,* he thinks as he continues walking, *as much slave to the senses as any butcher's dog seeking scraps at the sound of the knife on the strop.*

He hurries his pace for the sanctuary of a passing tram.

Leaving the tram at Amiens Street Station, O'Keefe walks less than three hundred yards before turning onto a quiet lane in the heart of the city. He consults the scrap of paper in his pocket.

He looks around him, taking in the long rows of two- and three-storey redbrick houses that line either side of the street. Autumn sunlight exposes grime that is invisible at night; the worn, crumbling brickwork stained black in places from gas-lamps and barrel fires that light the laneways and alleys and warm the hands of waiting hack drivers on cold nights. Rubbish spilling out of bins onto the cobbles. Dogs picking through the scraps, and cats, wary of the dogs, basking with eyes at half-mast on the sunny stone steps. The street is strangely absent of life, an oasis of silence in the otherwise roiling city. O'Keefe knows its residents exist at odds to the daylight.

Foley Street—formerly Montgomery Street—comes alive at night when it assumes the name most Dubliners know it by: *Monto*.

Also known as *The Kips*, it had once been the largest, most notorious red-light district in the Empire, and the street still thrives, despite the continuing departure of thousands of British Army troops from Ireland.

Memory stirs in his mind, of laughing women, sweet perfume and sour sweat. Of dancing at the edge of his balance. He cannot remember coming here on his binge—he is certain he would have been too drunk to get up to much bother and he's had none of the tell-tale itch or burning in his piss; his money had been in his wallet in his pocket upon waking in his digs—but he knows why he might have been tempted. Knowledge lodged in the meat of a body. Even turning the corner onto Foley Street he had felt it—a surge of loneliness strong enough to cut through the shame and the fear, a deep, liquid ache low in his chest. A catch in his throat. There are a multitude of reasons, O'Keefe knows, why a man could find himself in Monto, but the desperate need for the company of a woman was the most common. Men with jobs that would never pay enough to afford a wife. Men with no jobs. Soldiers or sailors hundreds, thousands of miles away from home. Monto served these men. And O'Keefe, the ache welling within him, realises he has become one of their number.

He searches the doors for the address.

7

... that this movement, that this moment in history follows from its birth in the fire-scorched womb of the GPO should not be smothered by the weakness and apostasy of its so-called leaders. To this end I have returned to Dublin from that green haven of Blessington—a refuge of idleness, corruption and cowardice in the face of the traitorous Free State scoundrels—in the foothills of the mountains that roll like a rebuke over this still fettered city of ours, in an effort to raise an army of men who will continue the struggle to cleanse this nation of the taint of occupation. To this end I have gathered around me young men of all classes and of the purest intent. It is the young of this nation, if guided correctly, who will tear from the blood-soaked soil the weeds of collaboration, wielding the scythes of our new, holy and Catholic Republic of Eire. To this end, our army will employ means that may seem cruel and lawless to a simple people who have grown so weary of war and stunted in their vision by centuries of subjugation. But it is my hope, and my prayer, that our Lord will guide me to enlighten these simple people, that the spilled blood of the corrupt will wash away the heretical apathy of the Irishman and raise him up as a proud, virtuous citizen of our holy republic. This virtue is displayed in the young men I have chosen for....

Commandant Felim O'Hanley rests his pen in the spine of his journal and rises from the small desk that fills a third of the space in his cramped attic quarters. Two steps take him across the room, where he climbs a wooden ladder to the skylight, lifting open the wood-framed light on its hinges, taking a mouthful of fresh air, the scent of autumn decay already in the windy essence of the autumn leaves on the trees surrounding the house where he has made his billet. The October sun is unseasonably warm, and O'Hanley turns his face to it, only his head visible against the sloped slate roof.

In his imagination, the republic he dreams of is one bathed in sun and light. It should not be like this as yet because this republic is still a long way from coming into being, and the way the Indian summer sun appears unashamed in the heavens over an Ireland still so mired in corruption makes him uneasy. As if God has let his guard down and the sun has defied Him. The soft *thwok* of tennis balls draw his attention to the fenced-in grass court in the garden below, and he looks down upon the fledgling soldiers of his army, wielding racquets instead of the weapons they so desperately need.

O'Hanley watches them fondly. He has every urge to be down there with them. He can't drill them as he would like to—the Haddington Road neighbours on either side of the grand house where they are billeted may believe the boys to be nephews and family friends from country towns availing of room and board at the moment, but certainly would not if he were to convert the suburban tennis court into a parade ground—but sport is good for the boys. O'Hanley smiles, the sunlight warm on his head as he watches his boys from his perch three stories above. Lithe and carefree movement, laughter and a curse as a tennis ball is *pfof-fed* out of the fenced court and into the garden proper. He will remind them about the cursing. It is not proper and right for soldiers of an army such as theirs to employ profanity.

A knock sounds below and beyond the walls of the room, and O'Hanley freezes on the ladder, waiting. He thinks of the Webley and the Mills bomb in his suit jacket hanging on the back of his chair. He will take his jacket and his journals from the desk and nothing else. There is nothing else for him to take if he must run. He has made it thus.

Silence. Then the knock in its full and recognisable sequence, and O'Hanley allows himself to relax.

Leaving the skylight propped open, he descends the ladder and goes to the heavy oak door, drawing back the deadlock and bar set into steel brackets on either side of the frame. He opens the door and steps into a small space between this door and another and pulls on a rope handle that opens the second door inwards. On the back of this door is shelving piled with folded jumpers and children's toys and riding boots and photographic albums—the detritus of family life. And standing in the closet that serves as entry to the house beyond, holding aside hangers full of old furs and overcoats, is Stephen Gilhooley.

'Stephen,' O'Hanley says, and allows the young man to pass by him and into his room.

'Jesus, Commandant, you'd never know there's a room through here, never.'

'Your language, Stephen. I will not tolerate swearing or the use of our Lord's name in vain. There is a discipline to language that regulates thought and a discipline to thought that guides language, and you'd do well to remember that.'

Stephen Gilhooley takes off his cap and looks sheepishly upwards at the skylight. He is dressed in a bloody white coat and heavy boots, a white, stiff cotton cap with a thumb smudge of blood on its brim. On the road outside the house is a Gilhooley Butchers delivery lorry. Stephen Gilhooley has, in fact, delivered several pounds of lamb chops and a rump roast to the matron of the house, Mrs Dempsey. Two stories below them in the kitchen, Mrs Dempsey and her spinster daughters unwrap and inspect the meat as if they had paid for it out of their own pockets.

'Sorry, Commandant. Only some of us aren't as used to talking like you are. Sure, I spend all day with my father and brothers and they do nothing but curse, even in front of the customers. I can't hardly help it.'

O'Hanley forces himself to smile. Without Stephen, he would be lost. Unlike some of the other volunteers, Stephen is not a former student. He is a boy of the lower orders, to be certain, but as with the finest legionaries in the armies of Rome, he is made of the noblest stuff. A young man of faith and courage, plying his father's trade with bonesaw and cleaver, amidst the blood and entrails of beasts, while waging war with a pistol or Thompson gun for O'Hanley and the scattered remnants of the First Dublin Brigade IRA. Such boys as Gilhooley, the butchers and blacksmiths, are forging a free, independent and holy nation of Ireland, subject, of course, to the guidance of a few remaining men like Felim O'Hanley and, at a stretch, de Valera. His smile darkens at the thought of Dev. Silent Dev, who has left him stranded and practically unarmed in this vast bog of traitors.

'Never mind. Sit down. We can't have the van outside longer than is necessary.'

'Sure I could be talking to one of the daughters, couldn't I? As far as the neighbours are to know.'

'Mrs Dempsey's daughters would hardly talk to the likes of you, Stephen,' O'Hanley says. He sits down on the single chair and indicates the bed with its tucked blankets and creased sheets. Like a monk's bed or a prisoner's.

'I only meant ...' Stephen stammers.

'... Never mind. What is the word from Murphy? The two lads I sent have yet to return. Have you seen Nicholas or Robert?'

'I waited at the meeting place but neither of them came.'

O'Hanley is silent for a long moment. 'No matter,' he says. 'They don't know where this house is, even if they've been lifted. We've been careful about that, haven't we?'

The Haddington Road house containing the hidden garret belongs to the Dempsey widow, and is shared by her daughters and, now, O'Hanley and his young charges in the anti-Treaty IRA. Mrs Dempsey is as radically anti-Treaty as any of them, motivated by the death of her son, an unfortunate Dublin Brigade Volunteer who'd been tortured and shot dead by Crown forces in the days following Bloody Sunday.

The manner of his death had ensured a closed-casket funeral for the lad and that Mrs Dempsey will never accept that her beautiful son had died for the flaccid capitulation that is the Treaty. Hers is now a safe house, the room purpose-built to hide her son in the Tan War and never used, now occupied by O'Hanley.

'Were you able to see Murphy yourself?'

Gilhooley frowns. 'Of course not. What if I was followed back here? When I learned Nicky and Robbo hadn't reported in, I telephoned his room and said only, "how much"? He asked could he not deal with you in person, and I told him "no" and that was that. He didn't like to do it by telephone at all.'

O'Hanley says, 'Which is why I sent the boys to arrange a meeting, but it can't be helped now. And how much does he want?'

'Thirteen thousand.'

'Robbery.'

'I know, but … he said the lot of it—guns, ammo, gelignite and detonators—is on a ship in Southampton waiting for us, but it's going to cost. He said he's people to pay.'

'Murphy said all of this on the telephone from his rooms? Surely he's aware that the switchboards are crawling with spies …?'

'He called them *units*. Like they were … I don't know. Chairs or sweeping brushes or something.'

O'Hanley thinks in silence for some time. 'And the other operation. We're certain about the train leaving tonight?'

'As certain as we can be. Mullen and Patterson are part of the guard, and I spoke with them only yesterday. That train's carrying more than thirteen grand by far. Borrowed off the English to pay the Northern lads. There must be five hundred of them, training out in the Curragh camp, and they have to be paid so's they don't jump ship and join us like half the fellas in the Free State army … Sure, it's several months' wages, so it won't be divvied out all at once. It was one of Collins' stunts before he was killed. He rigged it so them Ulster lads are kept on a long rope, paid over time for doing nothing rather than joining us in the real fight. They're the only lads in the whole of Ireland guaranteed to get their wages on time, just for staying *out* of the fight.'

Collins had brought a division of the IRA from the partitioned North down to the Curragh Camp to train under the Free State army when Ulster had become too hot for them. The northern volunteers would not agree to wage war as part of the Free State army against their former comrades in the anti-Treaty Irregulars, but had agreed to accept Free State army wages for promising to remain on the sidelines of the conflict until the IRA could once again unify and launch itself against the loyalist north as a whole. When Collins was shot dead in August, any such hopes of reunification seemed to die with him.

O'Hanley says, 'Your contacts, Mulally and Patterson, are they the only ones guarding the shipment who are sympathetic to our cause?'

'They wouldn't ask any others. But they'll sneak away and join us on the raid.'

'And you can trust these moonlighters? Serving in the Free State army and willing to help rob a Free State bank of Free State army wages?'

'Sure, neither of them has been paid in three weeks, and yet Mulcahy has come up quick enough with the scratch to pay them Ulster men to sit on their arses. Mully and Patto only joined the Free Staters for the wage, and since they've only got it now and again, they're more than willing to help. I'll have to throw them a few bob off the take, but they're game lads.'

'And tell me again why they are holding the money in a bank in Newbridge and not at the camp itself? It seems odd that they would risk holding it in a civilian bank when they could guard it more closely in a barracks safe?'

Stephen smiles. 'It's because they can't trust the Northern lads not to decide to advance themselves their wages and head back home to fight. Too many rifles around a camp like the Curragh, and the Free Staters don't trust the Ulster men, or even their own troops, not to up arms and rob the money themselves. So they keep it close enough that it's no bother getting it, but far enough away so's to be out of temptation to the lads in camp with guns and notions.'

O'Hanley's lips curl in a moue of distaste.

'All of them mired in corruption, dragged into it by the traitors of the Free State,' he says, though he knows in his heart that his own Irregular troops are often no better. There are more than a few hardened republicans among the ranks of the Free State Army, and just as many in the Irregulars, who don't mind or understand the Treaty, and many of them willing enough to change sides when it suits. O'Hanley has heard of men fighting one day for the Free State and the very next for the Irregulars at the battle for Kilmallock in County Limerick, switching teams and swapping tunics at the first rumour of better—or any—wages or hot food on the other side. Corruption and chaos, the twin ghosts haunting this war. *And here am I*, O'Hanley thinks, *consorting with them freely*.

'If you must have the moonlighters, have them, but I'd rather you used our own men.'

'Sure, we'll need more than myself and just those boys down there,' Gilhooley nods in the direction of the sound of swatted tennis balls through the open skylight. '… to take that bank.'

Those boys are only a few years younger than you, dear Stephen. And yet, Gilhooley is right. They are not experienced enough or large enough in numbers to hit even an unguarded bank on their own. A sick feeling wells in O'Hanley's gut. It has come to this. Using his boys for the kind of robbery that is as common as calving cows in the country. Like everyday brigands instead of the soldiers of destiny they aspire to be. He thinks back to what he has written in his journal. '… *means and methods that may seem cruel and lawless …*'

'Take whomever you need. Will your brothers go, do you think?'

Gilhooley shrugs. 'Dinnie has a babby now. Sure, he'd come along for some peace and quiet, if nothing else. And Ray will do it for the craic, never mind a few hours away from the auldfella and the shop.'

Stephen's father is staunchly sympathetic to the republican cause. He had fought in Bolands Mill with de Valera in 1916, and had escaped internment when the fighting ended, his knowledge of the back lanes of Dublin far better than any of his pursuers. He'd returned to his butcher shop and drifted away from the movement, but he supported the cause with food, funds and sons when he could spare them.

'You've guns enough, and your brothers at least have had some practice. And Mulally and Patterson?'

'They're grand lads. They can be trusted to do the job right if I tell 'em how.'

Gilhooley is little more than a boy himself, O'Hanley reflects. Eighteen, and yet so capable, loyal and brave. Rough, certainly, but a born leader.

'Hit the bank then, Stephen, and may God guide and protect you.'

Stephen Gilhooley blesses himself and replaces his white butcher's cap. 'And you, Commandant O'Hanley.' He holds out his hand and O'Hanley hesitates, inspecting the proffered hand for dried blood before he reluctantly takes it.

8

The Sheriff Street tenements where Jeremiah Byrne lives are two streets away from the Liffey quays. The buildings show grime-blackened brickwork and are hunched closely together, soaking up the daylight, forcing the autumn sun to fade its way up alleys, over chipped steps and onto the soft, grassless soil of fetid common yards. Jeremiah feels the chill of shadow as he shortcuts the warren of lanes leading to his home.

Like all Sheriff Street residents, Jeremiah knows every rat-run, every hidey-hole in the area. Residents pass through the open doors of neighbouring buildings and beat paths across what were once leafy gardens to access particular streets or dwellings. There is very little that is private in the tenements and, in this, Sheriff Street is no different from the rest of tenement Dublin. Outdoor toilets are shared, as are water pumps. Laundry lines are strung across lanes from building to building. Food, when it is scarce in one family and plentiful in another, is shared. Families of up to fifteen living in one room. Glass in less than half of all windows.

Jeremiah comes to the building that houses his family's flat, and climbs the cracked and hollow-worn front steps, entering through the doorway that has been without a door since before he was born. On the coldest, wettest days of winter, sheets of scrap wood from dock pallets are sometimes nailed together and propped in the empty doorframe against the wind and sleet, and this is guarded by residents so that it will not be taken by neighbouring tenants for firewood. The fanlight at the top of the doorway is free from any pane of glass, and serves only to funnel winter winds into the building more efficiently. Years before, some resident had vainly stuffed rags in several of the empty gaps where now they sag like oily clots, blackened by time and smoke and cooking grease.

Sixty odd people share the Georgian house that had once been home to a single, wealthy family and several servants. Jeremiah's flat was once a bedroom in this house. It is shared by his mother and her sister, his own four sisters and six male and female cousins and, occasionally, by his uncle. Of the children, Jeremiah is the oldest and the man of the family during times when his uncle, a carter, thief and opportunistic extortionist, is serving one of his numerous, if too short, prison sentences. Jeremiah knows that his uncle is free at the moment—has been for the past two weeks, though he has seen him only once briefly in that time—and says a small prayer. It is something he does rarely, and even then does it with the utter conviction that it is a useless practice, but he does it now; prays that his Uncle John Keegan has been lagged for something, anything and is not home and won't be for a long time. He mimes a sloppy sign of the cross as he mounts the patchwork wooden stairs to his flat.

He fears his Uncle John. There are few in the tenements who don't. But he fears more for his sisters when the man is around, and this is what has brought him home, if for only a few hours. It never occurs to him that it might not be safe to return home for any other reason.

'Jerry! Ma, Jerry's home!' One of his sisters greets him as he reaches the first floor landing outside the flat.

The girl is six years old, as blonde as her brother and she hugs him tightly. Jeremiah hugs her back, something warm and liquid flooding his insides; the first touch of another human being since he'd stuck the knife in the fella in the laneway.

'Sarah, pet. How's me dote?' he says, wondering briefly, as he has done in the past, if it was her hair, being so much like his own, that makes her his favourite. They are the only two of his mother's five children who have blond hair, and Jeremiah also wonders if they share the same father. It is a question that can never be answered, and so is never asked, though many times, on the docks or on the streets of the city, Jeremiah will see a man with hair like his own and wonder, *Is that me da? Mine and Sarah's da?*

'I'm grand, Jerry,' the girl says, pulling away from him and taking his hand. 'We got a flitch of bacon! Ma got it. I don't know how she got it, but she got it and she told me fuck off and don't be asking questions but we got it. Bacon, Jerry.'

Jeremiah knows how she'd got the bacon, and the butcher knows too, he thinks, and so will the butcher's missus when she gets the itch. He musses Sarah's hair and then smooths it back into place, his fingers lingering for a moment on the faded, frayed ribbon in her hair.

The poor thing could have a new ribbon, for jaysus sake, he tells himself. *Next time I'm out I'll reef it out of the hair of the first girl I see. A young girl could have a new fuckin' ribbon at least.*

He pulls his sister back by the hand before entering the flat. 'Is Uncle John Keegan in, Sarah? Tell us quick 'fore I go in.'

Sarah shakes her head, the joy of the coming meal and her brother's return washing from her features at the mention of her uncle's name. 'No, he's out, Jerry, but he'll be back, he will. He's carting on the quays. He's not in jail no more, Jerry.' She looks up at her brother, her grip tightening on his hand, fear and worry in her eyes. A lump rises in Jeremiah's throat at the thought of the man. The thought of him harming a hair on her head, the bastard. Her or any one of his sisters, nieces or nephews. The way he had harmed him. The beatings were only the half of it.

The bastard. His mother and aunty—Jeremiah couldn't give a ha' penny ride for either of them. But the little ones. He wishes now that he hadn't left his fish-knife stuck between the ribs of that fella in the lane the night before; thinking how he might have used it on his uncle, given half the chance.

He lets Sarah lead him through the tacked-up sheet that serves as a door into the one-room flat where his mother is sitting on the dwelling's single chair at a table fashioned from a packing crate. She is drinking tea—Jeremiah thinks it is tea—from a cup with no handle. She wears her hair tied back, a thick swatch of grey at her crown from where her hair has grown since she last had it dyed the shade of brown she favours when she has the money. In front of her on the packing crate table, blood seeping through its wrapping of day-old newspaper, is the lump of bacon.

His mother turns as he enters, watches him as his youngest sister and two of his nephews now hug him and hang from his legs and arms, asking what he has brought for them. He smiles and tells them he has nothing for them.

Without speaking, his mother returns to staring out the open window at drying clothes dangling in the soft autumn air on a line that bridges the building across from their own.

'Ma,' he says, 'I'm back and all, I am.'

His aunt emerges from behind a stained sheet hanging from a rope that divides the flat's sleeping and common space so that his mother and aunty might have a modicum of privacy when they have brought punters home. They usually work in the alleys and lanes, but sometimes they bring their work to the flat if the chap has paid for a warm roll instead of one up against a wall. His aunt delivers the greeting her sister has refused to give.

'And do you be wanting a medal, so? For your troubles?'

'Aunty Pauline,' Jeremiah says, lifting one of his sisters, Delilah, aged four, from where she is clinging to his leg. He nuzzles her hair with his face and, as he withdraws, spots a louse—one of many hundreds—clinging to an unwashed strand of the girl's hair. He takes it between his fingernails, drags it down the length of the strand and crushes it. He scratches the girl's head for her, serving only to awaken the remaining lice, causing the girl to begin scratching herself. He sighs—*Home*—scratches and feels the stirring of the lice in his own hair, under his arms, in his pubic hair.

'Gone how many days and come back with nothing but his goldilocks and no pot to piss in even,' his aunt says, not looking at him as she speaks, bending to feel the tea kettle hanging in the fireplace, feeling it cold. Then, to his mother: 'And you, it's my day for the chair, Madam Jump-up. You had it only bleedin' yesterday.'

'Fuck off away with you,' his mother says, not taking her eyes from the window. His mother is the younger of the sisters, but pays the bulk of the rent on the room, and is thus its mistress when Uncle John Keegan is away. When he is present, Aunt Pauline and her husband rule the roost.

'And you,' his mother says, finally turning to Jeremiah. 'You out gallivanting and see fit to come back skint as you left us. You think the world and her mother's here to put food in your gob? You may hump off with that hoor of an aunty of yours if you think so much as one hot drop of fat from this bacon will wet your lips.'

'You can keep your bacon. You didn't spend the money I brought in last week on bacon, I know bleedin' well, but.'

His mother looks at him now as if noticing him for the first time, some fear in her eyes that fades as quickly as it has come, thinking herself mistaken in fearing this boy she has reared. Not a man yet, still a youngfella, her Jerry. 'You'll not be minding what I spend on what, sonny buck. I'll skelp your arse soon as I did when you were a nipper, don't you think I fuckin' won't.'

'You'd want to rise up the lazy bones of your worn out arse first.'

His aunt raises her voice. 'The two of ye shut it. The racket of yis'd peel the paper from the walls, what's left of it. And it's my turn in the chair, Janey. You may get up off it, like the boy says.'

Jeremiah sighs and swallows and sets down his youngest sister, telling her to run out to Sarah. He wonders if his mother will leave the bacon alone long enough for him to snatch it before she can go out into the lane and swap it for drink. He doubts it.

'When are you boiling the bacon, Ma?'

'Never you mind when. When I've the notion to is when.'

He softens his tone. 'I'm only sayin' you should cook it before Uncle John comes in if yis want any for yiselves and the kids.' At times, Jeremiah has seen his uncle come in, a gallon of porter on board, and eat the family's entire meal of the day himself, the women and the children left to go hungry.

His aunt crosses the room in three strides and juts her chin out at Jeremiah. 'You'll not be talking of me husband like that, not in front of Pauline Byrne, you won't, you scut.' She raises an open hand as if to strike him and he laughs, a snigger that sounds to his own ears much the same as the laugh his Uncle John Keegan laughs when one of the women makes an idle threat against him; the laugh sounding like the one his uncle laughs just before he throws one or the other against the crumbling walls.

'Get up out of that,' he says to his aunt. 'It's only true and you know it.'

'You'll not talk like that about him,' she says again, and makes to strike him. As she does, she sees something in his eyes that is different to the last time she lashed out at him. Her hands stops halfway to his face.

Jeremiah's voice is low and calm when he speaks.

'I'll beat you worse than he does if you don't pack away that hand, Aunty Pauline. I will, by fuck.'

His aunt lowers her hand and steps away from him, muttering about her John and how he would see to youngfellas thinking they were lord muck of the manor and bullying poor Pauline Byrne about the place. The young cock-o-the-walk would see, so he would, what her man could do to a lad, when he got home.

Jeremiah ignores her, knowing she will be long drunk and the incident forgotten before his uncle returns.

His mother speaks up, still seated in the one chair, as if the confrontation between her son and sister has never happened. 'I'll cook it when I'm good and ready and no sooner. And no man will take it—no John Keegan and no Jeremiah Byrne who brings nothing to this house but empty fists and *queer* smiles.' She smiles at the insinuation and Jeremiah's face burns.

'Get the pox, y'auld bitch,' he says, turning to leave, shame flushing his cheeks, hatred roosting in his belly atop the hunger. Hatred for his mother. For his aunt. For his uncle. For the fact that he has no food or money to feed himself or the young ones and hatred for what his mother knows about him. Hatred for himself, the Molly, the *queer*. And this hatred bats its black wings and raids the place in his heart he keeps free for the love of his sisters.

Fuck all of them, every last one. He turns and leaves the flat, passing Sarah on the stairs, ignoring the hand she holds out to him and emerges onto the laneway, tears welling in his eyes. He needs to eat and he will swing it somehow on his own. He has done what he came to do. His sisters are alive, if not well. They will probably eat this evening. No, they *will* eat, because he decides now to ensure that they do, bacon or no bacon. He can do as much for them. Precious Sarah and his sisters. There are ways to scare up some coin. Ways. His face burns hot with the shame of it.

9

The door to forty-seven Foley Street is answered by a young girl in a pale blue dress and white apron. She is no more than twelve years old, O'Keefe reckons. He feels a hard bolt of anger in his gut, which fades only when he realises—taking in the apron and the damp rag in the girl's hand—that she is merely a serving maid or cleaner in the brothel. He cannot imagine his father owing anything to a woman who would employ so young a girl in such a place, though God knows there are enough girls of this age working in other knocking shops and in the lanes or on the quays.

'I'm here to see Mrs Dolan, if you please,' he says, smiling at the girl. 'My name is Seán O'Keefe. Dan O'Keefe's son, you can tell her.'

The girl nods, saying nothing, and holds the door open wider for him to enter. The house is quiet, like the street outside, and smells of stale smoke, perfume and whiskey. The scents invoke memory, and O'Keefe wonders has he been in this house before. He follows the girl through the short front hallway, down a flight of stairs and into a bright kitchen, then outside again, crossing a garden past an outdoor privy, a henhouse, a pigeon loft and small kitchen crop of vegetables. At the bottom of the garden they come to a steel door cut into the back wall of the yard. He follows the girl through the door and into another garden, across flagstones set

51

into the grass, arriving at a second redbrick house, identical to the one they have just left.

The girl enters the house, gesturing for O'Keefe to wait outside.

A moment later, another girl, older than the first, comes to the door. 'You're welcome, sir. Sorry about Maggie. She's deaf and dumb as a pillar but a great little worker all the same. Does a grand job reading lips, though with that stoat of a moustache on you, I wonder how she managed.' The girl smiles and O'Keefe smiles back. 'Mrs Dolan is in the parlour.'

He follows this girl upstairs and is met at the parlour door by an attractive woman clothed in a silk dress in a shade of dark yellow that complements her brown hair and eyes and her pale skin. She appears to O'Keefe to be in her forties, but could be older or younger. Older, he imagines, because his father had retired from the police almost ten years previously. Her hair is worn in an elaborate topknot, and O'Keefe wonders how much of it is a hairpiece and how much her own. She looks more like the wife of a judge or bank manager than a procuress, even if the dress appears to O'Keefe too elaborate for daytime wear.

'Thank you, Dolores,' the woman says, smiling brightly. 'Make us some tea, would you, dear? Or would the gentleman prefer something stronger?'

'Tea, please,' O'Keefe says with an urgency that makes his face redden.

The brothel madam laughs, and as she does, O'Keefe observes that she is missing most of her back teeth and that her laughter has a smoky rasp to it that is at once warm and vaguely menacing. The laughter of hard living, he thinks, much like his own rare laughter these days.

'Forgive me,' the woman says, extending her hand, her knuckles studded with emerald and ruby rings that O'Keefe guesses are not paste but real. 'My name is Ginny Dolan. I'm an old friend of your father's.'

'Seán O'Keefe, ma'm, pleased to meet you,' he says, taking her hand, but is wary of her suddenly, wondering again what hold a woman such as this could have over his father.

She studies O'Keefe, and under her gaze—dark eyes intent, intelligent and wholly separate from her smile—he feels the pull of fear again in his gut. 'I am given to understand that you were once a detective, like your father.'

'We didn't have a detective branch in the Peelers *per se*,' he says, thinking she must surely know this, in her line of work. 'Other than Crimes Special Branch, which looked after political crimes and such. But I worked my share of investigations, some plain-clothes, others in uniform.'

The Dolan woman smiles warmly at him and rests a hand on his forearm. 'Thank God for that then. You're just what I need, no offence to your father.'

'None taken,' O'Keefe says.

'Please, come through. How rude of me.'

Holding out her hand for him to enter, O'Keefe defers and allows the madam to enter the parlour first. As she passes in front of him, he notices that she walks with a pronounced limp and that her left leg appears to flay outwards, her spine canted in the opposing direction. A hobble more than a limp. Rickets, he thinks: the disease of the poor. He wonders how she had made her living as a whore with the disease, and decides that her ailment might have led to her rising from the shop floor to the director's office in some way.

O'Keefe knows, from his days in the police, that brothel madams can be callous creatures, every bit as brutal as their male counter-parts. Most, if not all, are former whores themselves—women so bludgeoned by life in the trade that nothing matters to them but the money they make off the backs of the girls they employ. But to O'Keefe, Ginny Dolan presents herself as a far more complex woman.

Perhaps it's her apparent wealth, O'Keefe thinks, realising that the house in which they stand is the madam's dwelling and not open for business. On the wall are photographs of a baby and young boy, along with a family photograph from some time in the last century. The hall tables are topped with vases holding fresh flowers. There is nothing of the stew house about this place. It is a home.

He waits until Ginny Dolan has lowered herself, painfully, onto her upholstered chair, and then takes a seat on a settee facing her across a low, cherrywood table. Smiling, he plumbs his imagination for what his father might have done to lead his son to this house—taking tea in a parlour room as if calling on an aunt or widowed family friend—and finds only the warp of shadow. Nothing good could have indebted his father to this woman, warm as she seems. As a G-man—a political detective in the DMP— Daniel O'Keefe would have been as familiar with whores and their pimps as with solicitors, priests or republicans. Good G-men had contacts and touts on every rung of society's ladder. But it was an axiom of the detectives' trade that these souls remained indebted to the detective, and not the other way round. Still, every copper makes mistakes and some mistakes could lead a man places where he wouldn't normally go. In thinking this, O'Keefe decides that he doesn't want to know what debt his father owes. He will repay it and that will be the end of it.

'I hope business is good for you,' he says, by way of saying something. He notes the sacred heart picture on the wall over the mantelpiece; the tended fire grate laid with turf and coal for the evening's fire; the stuffed chair in which the woman sits; the flowered wallpaper. And on the wall behind her, another posed photograph in an expensive frame—Ginny Dolan and a young boy of eight or nine years old. The same boy in the pictures in the hallway. He idly wonders who it is, assumes it is her son and wonders is she married.

'Ah well, you know yourself, Mr O'Keefe. Nothing's the same since all the trouble's started up again. Even when the boyos were fighting the Tommies and Tans, business was business and no politics was spoken in my house. Tommies and Tans and Shinners … Sure, gunmen of every stripe and hue …'—she gives O'Keefe a bold smile that makes her, for the first time since he has met her, appear the pimp she is—'… all of them need a taste now and again and, sure, what harm? Live and let live and let there be no ideologies under the counterpane.' She laughs and O'Keefe smiles politely.

'But now people are afraid to go out as much as they used to. No one's sure who's on whose side any more and who's carrying a gun and who's not. Times are hard, Mr O'Keefe, and only in Ireland, I think, can men let politics come between them and a screw.'

Despite himself, O'Keefe laughs at the truth of the woman's words.

'Now …', she continues, taking a cigarette from a silver case and waiting while O'Keefe leans across and lights it with an ornamental lighter from the table. Exhaling: '… now there's some who'd say auld upstairs girls like myself have no place in the new Free State, or whatever it is they're calling it. Can you imagine? A free and independent Ireland without her upstairs girls? And let me tell you, when the Dáil is sitting, Ginny Dolan's shop is still as busy as fleas on a fat man. Politicians are politicians no matter what colours they paint their posters. And the young gunmen do be just as bad for riding, for all their talk of God and independence. They'll happily take their cut of protection money from the likes of poor Ginny, a gratis poke at one of her girls and then turn round and curse her for a Free State spy or Republican whore or just plain bad for the morals of the country. Truth be told, since they shelled the Four Courts and started this blight of a civil war, I don't know who's the worst.'

It is not the first time O'Keefe has heard this said. Independence is a fine thing, if you can put bread on your table without being shot at for your troubles. And O'Keefe knows at first-hand how much the average gunman cares about the troubles of the common people of Ireland. About as much as the average politician, he thinks. 'It's hard to tell all right,' he says. 'Strange times.'

'Strange times indeed.'

The pair of them say nothing for the time it takes the girl to enter and pour tea.

They sip in silence for a moment, and O'Keefe sets down his teacup. 'Mrs Dolan, my father is in your debt.'

The woman's gaze is assessing but warm, and O'Keefe is confused by her scrutiny. Flattered but wary.

'You look like him, you do. So much like him when he was younger. He's not well, I hear.'

'No, but I'm prepared to fulfil any obligation he has to you.'

'I expect you are. Your father told me that you were a Peeler down in Cork. A fine one. A fine investigator.' She speaks as of a time long past, a different life, a different person. 'He was proud of you, as well he should be. A fine, strapping man like yourself. And doing right by his Da.'

O'Keefe's face reddens. 'I don't know how good I was, Mrs Dolan. I worked my share of investigations, as I said: any number of robberies and more than a handful of murders.'

'No, no … nothing like that,' Ginny Dolan says abruptly, and O'Keefe notices the woman's face change, her smile frozen. 'No … please God,' and in the common phrase—*please God*—O'Keefe hears a real prayer. 'Nothing so serious as that …'

'I didn't mean to imply anything, Mrs Dolan, sure. I'm not certain what you even want from me.'

'A job of work. You'll be well paid.'

'That's not necessary, Mrs Dolan. I'm here to repay what my father owes, whatever it is you need me for.' And as he says this, he regrets it. There are favours, he thinks, the madam of a brothel could ask for, that would test a man's morality at best. 'I'll try.'

'You'll take the job, Mr O'Keefe.' It is not a question.

'What is the job, Mrs Dolan?'

She takes another cigarette from her case and pauses while O'Keefe leans across and lights it.

'My son,' she says. 'I want you to find my son.'

'Your son?'

O'Keefe wishes he had a cigarette. He pats his pockets and realises he has not bought a packet since his binge.

Ginny Dolan holds out her open silver case and O'Keefe gratefully accepts one. He lights it and takes the smoke deep into his lungs, feeling light-headed and stronger for it.

'But why,' he asks, exhaling, 'do you not go to the police, Mrs Dolan, if your son is missing?'

The madam sets down her tea cup with a clatter. 'No police. Is that clear, Mr O'Keefe? I'll not have my son lagged by that shower, and they'd not be interested in finding him anyway. Your father,' she softens her tone, '... was a good man, Mr O'Keefe. We were great pals in our day ... I only wish him well, but I will have my Nicky found and no police.'

O'Keefe nods, unwilling to anger her further, finding himself slipping back into a role he thought he would never play again— that of investigator.

'No police then.' He pulls on his cigarette and begins. 'All right so, when was the last time you saw your son, Mrs Dolan?'

'Last month, more than a month really. Nicky slept here, like always, and then was off the next morning before I woke.' Her smile is gone now, fear etched into the pinched lines around her eyes, a filigree of worried years around her lips as she pulls on her cigarette.

'His name is Nicholas?' O'Keefe instinctively pats his pockets again, this time for the patrol diary that is no longer there. He feels unprepared and amateurish without one of the hardback notebooks he had carried all those years as a Peeler, resolving to commit what the woman says to memory and copy it down as soon as he is able.

She nods. 'Nicholas Dolan. And I should tell you, before we go any further, that he has been running with the anti-Treatyites. The

Irregulars as they're called now in the papers, so you see now why we cannot have the police looking for him. They'd hand him over to the Free Staters and he'd be banged up with the rest of them, or worse, shot.' She blesses herself as she says this, before continuing. 'Much though it breaks my heart, always having tried to rear the boy with a proper hatred for all politics—not politicians, mind, who are grand custom for a woman of my trade, but politics, ideas. This country is full of madmen and their mad ideas, and mad ideas never did anyone a lick of good, did they? But my Nicky up and joined them. Boys … men …' Her words ring with weary disgust. 'If there's a fight to be had somewhere, they'll seek it out. Peace and profit are just not good enough for them.'

O'Keefe groans inwardly. He wants to do right by this woman, for his father's sake. And in the past few minutes he has felt a spark of interest that he has not felt since he left the Constabulary—the instinct of the hunt, the search, that is every policeman's curse and blessing. But the boy could be anywhere in the country by now if he was fighting. And God knows, O'Keefe thinks, it will be hard enough scaring up a friendly contact among the Irregulars; someone who might be able to point to where the lad might be. It has been less than a year, after all, since a good number of them had been trying to kill him and his colleagues in the RIC.

'How do you know he joined the Irregulars, Mrs Dolan?'

'He told me. Fourteen years old, the cheek of him. And I forbade it, of course, but he's a headstrong boy, Mr O'Keefe. He was proud as punch. Said that he was running messages and other things he couldn't tell me. As if I'd spent years doting on him and educating him so that he could go out and join up with that army of eejits.' Ginny Dolan's voice cracks and she pulls a handkerchief from her dress sleeve and wipes her eyes. O'Keefe notes how the woman's speech shifts: from the delicate and refined one moment to the courser register of the streets where she runs her business the next.

She continues. 'And I blame his school mostly. It was there he learned all that independence nonsense that's about these days and even then they saw fit to throw him out. The masters there, and all their talk of the rights of man and republican heroes and indepen-dence. All well and good to a boy of fourteen until they cast him out for what his mother does for to put food in his mouth. To pay his school fees.'

Confused, O'Keefe holds up his hand. 'What school was it, Mrs Dolan? And why was he expelled?'

'Francis Xavier's, off North Great George's Street. Do you know it?'

'I do,' he says, sitting up, a slight dart of optimism piercing him, something he can use in this information. 'I went there myself. Me and my brother.'

'Of course you did. Sons of a respectable policeman.' There is bitterness in her voice now, a hardness that alerts O'Keefe to the danger a woman such as this could be. A woman of wealth like Ginny Dolan, in the trade that she plies, would not have got to where she is now in the world through kindness alone.

'But my Nicky? Turfed out when someone went to the Fathers with what kind of business I run. Some little turncoat. As if my money wasn't good enough for the mighty Jesuits and their fine school.' She roughly stubs her cigarette in the brass ashtray, exhal-ing a last blast of smoke. 'Fine and fucking dandy, Mr O'Keefe, for them Fathers teaching the sons of lawyers and bankers and … and politicians, all of them as bent as the bishop's crozier. But the son of a straight and true upstairs girl like myself isn't half good enough for them. As if it was Nicky's fault what his mammy does for a shil-ling. I run a good and honest business, Mr O'Keefe, and don't let any manjack tell you different. I'm good to my girls and I provide a service much needed in this city. And let me tell you, I know things about some of them holy Fathers that would curl your hair.'

O'Keefe nods, thinking just how much one's profession colours one's view of the world. In this way, coppers are the same as whores and their madams. Having seen so many times the worst the world can offer, they end up expecting it. First order of faith: everyone lies, trust no one. Second order: corruption is the rule, not the exception. Everyone, in their own way, is compromised. And yet how limiting a world view, O'Keefe thinks, feeling suddenly sorry for this woman. Feeling sorry for his father. For himself.

'When did he finish in the school?' he asks.

'Just before summer break—they asked him to leave. Very Christian of them too, it was. Jesus in heaven, I'd give an eye to know who played the Turk and told the Fathers. I'd have my Albert on him in a sweet minute, Mr O'Keefe, you can be sure of that.'

Again the anger, and with it, the recourse to Monto justice. He wonders who Albert is and remembers, vaguely, the name but not where or when he has heard it. He imagines the man to be Ginny Dolan's muscle. Every brothel-keeper has one or two, usually a husband or brother but just as often a disgraced policeman or demobbed soldier.

'And Nicholas gave you no indication of where he might have been going when he left to join the Irregulars?'

'No, none at all. Dolores saw him leave. I asked her and she was none the wiser.'

'And friends? Who are his friends, Mrs Dolan?'

'You can get all of that kind of thing from Albert. He knows all this as well as I do.'

O'Keefe nods, assuming he will meet this Albert sooner or later. He thinks of a final question. One that may be painful for the woman to consider.

'And what should I do, Mrs Dolan, if the boy refuses to come with me if I find him?'

'*When* you find him.'

'I'll try my best, Mrs Dolan, but the war ... will make it difficult. The Free State Army is having trouble enough hunting down the Irregulars as it is. And even if ...' he seeks to appease the woman but knows his odds are poor, '...*when* I find him, he might want to stay with his comrades. All the ideas, the uniforms, the guns … everything. It can be intoxicating to young lads. Fighting, scouting. Even running messages or splashing slogans onto walls.'

'You speak from experience, Mr O'Keefe?'

'I do,' he says, and does not tell her how quickly the camaraderie, the excitement, the sense of purpose could pall when you saw the life gouting out of men you knew and loved. All the pretty ideas, the craic and stories and barrack-room laughs—none of it worth a half-pint of a friend's—a brother's—blood. But still, men stayed and fought and died, even long after they had come to know better. He had himself. Because the flipside of bravery and camaraderie, every soldier knows, is cowardice and shame. Feared worse than death by most boys, most men.

'I just wonder,' O'Keefe continues, 'if you're prepared for the possibility that he might not want to come home.'

Ginny Dolan stares at him again for a long moment and O'Keefe fears he has angered her.

'I'm not as simple a woman as you might think, Mr O'Keefe. He may not come home for you, or even Albert …'

Again, O'Keefe wonders what role Albert plays in the household. The boy's father? Ginny's husband? There is no man in any of the photographs in the hallway or parlour.

'…but I need him found, and when you do find him, I'll decide what will be done.'

O'Keefe stands to leave, to start his search. Ginny Dolan rises with him in a rustle of silk and O'Keefe smells a faint scent of perfume—sickly sweet, corrupting—and unexpected fear judders through his senses.

'You might start by asking around Talbot Street,' she says, leading him to the front door. 'I know he was selling the anti-Treaty papers there some months back, before they shelled the Four Courts. The *Nationalist*. Some of the vendors there might know where he is. Of course, I had my Albert ask round, and didn't they tell him where to go with his questions? Not one bit afraid, they weren't, not even of my Albert. But you've more experience of asking questions. Albert, you see, he's not accustomed to asking for things. Not more than once, anyway.'

'Why would they be afraid of your Albert, Mrs Dolan?'

At this, the woman smiles. 'You've never met him, have you?'

'No, ma'm, I haven't.'

'Probably for the better, that, if you're to get along with him.'

'Get along with him?'

'Of course. You'll be working with him.'

O'Keefe frowns. 'I prefer to work on my own, Mrs Dolan.'

'I'm afraid,' she says, 'that you do not have a choice in this. You will be paid handsomely for your work, but my Albert will accompany you.' There is a steely menace in her voice, and behind her words O'Keefe senses the heavy price of the debt owed to this woman. Again he resists the urge to ask her what his father had done to incur it.

'I'll need to see Nicholas' room, Mrs Dolan, if I could.'

'Of course, upstairs, on the left.'

It takes O'Keefe less than ten minutes to search the room. He finds no diary or letters, though he sifts through the pages of countless adventure novels, war novels, cowboy books. There is a film poster for one of Valentino's recent flicks, *The Four Horsemen of the Apocalypse*, which O'Keefe has seen several times. Next to this is a yellowing poster copy of the 1916 Proclamation, and beside this a lithograph of the martyrs of 1916. It reminds O'Keefe of a soccer team's photo, a brief biography of each player—martyr—below each oval portrait. A scuffed, deflated football lies in a corner of the room. A desk piled high with school texts. Childhood toys and a stuffed bear on shelves in the closet, nothing in the pockets of any of the clothes hanging within. Nothing, all told, to give him any indication where the boy might be. He returns downstairs to where Ginny Dolan is waiting at the front door.

'Take this,' she says, the threat gone from her voice. She hands him a roll of pound notes and a recent photograph of her son— strikingly handsome, in his school jacket and tie, early teens with brown hair combed off his forehead, an open face, a boy on the edge of becoming a young man. O'Keefe senses something familiar about the lad, but decides it is the Xavier school jacket and tie. He and Peter had worn the same ones in their own school days.

'A handsome boy,' he says, attempting to hand her back the banknotes. 'I've no need for money, Mrs Dolan. I can manage.'

'Take it.' She closes his outstretched hand around the money. 'God only knows who you'll need to grease to find him.'

O'Keefe reluctantly puts the roll into his pocket, resolving to return it unspent, whatever the outcome of his investigations.

'You'll find Albert at the John of God's Boxing Club on Gardiner Street. He's expecting you,' Ginny Dolan says, holding her front door open for him to leave. 'And Mr O'Keefe … You won't disappoint me, will you not?'

10

O'Keefe finds the John of God's Boxing Club on Gardiner Street and enters, his eyes taking a moment to adjust to the dim light of a foyer plastered with yellowing fight bills. He follows the sound of clanking steel plates into a gym that is windowless and redolent of sweat and liniment, of leather and dust. He locates the source of the machine-like noise at the back of the gym. Under a dangling electric light-bulb, the sole occupant of the gym—the man O'Keefe assumes to be Ginny Dolan's doorman— is on his back on a bench, pressing an impossibly heavy stack of weights off his chest.

Standing by the empty boxing ring in a pale shaft of illumination from the gym's single skylight, O'Keefe watches as the man finishes his set of exercises, the weight bar crashing into the rack above the bench like the sound of trains coupling in a station.

'I can see your father in you,' the man says, sitting up, his bare chest and shoulders like slabs of quarried rock.

'Can you, now? Albert, is it?' O'Keefe says.

'I can and it is.'

O'Keefe says nothing, gazing at the man who returns his stare, unafraid.

'Look, I've been hired by Mrs Dolan to find her son, Nicholas. She wants you to help me or spy on me, I'm not sure which. Either way, I've come to tell you …'

'… That you're delighted to have me round as a minder.'

'That you shouldn't feel obliged.'

'I don't feel obliged, Mr O'Keefe,' Ginny Dolan's man says, standing and taking a pair of massive bowling-pin weights from a rack and beginning to swing them upwards and back down in a controlled motion. Grunting out the words: 'But Missus Dolan obliged me and she obliged you and that's all there is to say about it.'

'I'm well used to working on my own. I don't need your help, sir.'

'Your auldfella needs your help and you'll need mine. There's no sense in mithering on about it.'

'You'd do well to leave my auldfella out of it,' O'Keefe says, his face running hot.

'Don't worry yourself, Mr O'Keefe,' the doorman says, through the strain of his exercise. 'There'll be not another word about him. But I don't need to tell you he owes Mrs Dolan and it's my work to oversee the payment.'

Anger rises in O'Keefe, and he contemplates lunging for him, but there is too much that he does not know. About the debt. About his father.

'Are you nearly finished then, so we can get started?' he says.

Ginny Dolan's man does not reply, completing three sets of pin work. His wrists and forearms are as thick as the Latvian hemp rope tethering ships on the quays. He strips off his trousers and walks naked to a tap on the wall at the back of the gym. Over his shoulder, he says, 'Unless you want to wash me back, wait outside. I'll be all handsome and lovely in a flash.'

Some minutes later, O'Keefe is standing on the cobbled path in front of the gym with the doorman. Barefoot children in patched and ragged clothes gather around them, hands held out for copper coins. 'Please, mister, a ha'penny for a bit of grub. Please, mister, for me babby brother, he's fierce with the crooping coughs, so he is.'

Each child has a similar plea, and shouts it simultaneously so that soon they become indistinguishable to O'Keefe, but Ginny Dolan's man smiles at the children, his hand coming out of his pocket with a jangle of coins, which he carefully counts out, making sure each child gets two ha'pennies, no more no less, each an equal share of the spoils. As he dispenses his coins, more children approach and these are also given their share, each child responding with a loud and, to O'Keefe's ear, sincere belt of gratitude: 'Thanks mister. Blessing of God on yis, Mister Albert.' These children know him by name. Know him to be a soft touch.

O'Keefe studies Albert as he shoos away the children with a firm but kindly wave. The fact that he is a head shorter than O'Keefe is not unusual. O'Keefe is a constable's son and had been a constable himself. The height and girth requirements of the RIC and the Dublin Metropolitan Police have ensured that there are few men in the country bigger than policemen. Even so, Albert is shorter than average. O'Keefe puts him at five foot six in the raised boot heels he's wearing.

But, as he has seen in the gym, the man is built like an armoured car. His shoulders and biceps strain at the expensive light wool of his suit jacket—he wears no overcoat in the Indian summer weather—and the slabs of muscle that form his chest are like bodhráns under a crisp white shirt and pink and claret-striped tie, the wide chest tapering to a narrow waist and hips. His neck is freshly shaven, thick as the trunk of a young oak and a stiff white collar is drawn so tightly around it that O'Keefe imagines it would strangle the average man. A snap-brimmed black bowler tips low over pale blue eyes; a pale face—a night-worker's face—splashed with freckles, butted by a jutting jaw; a nose flattened like a boxer's. Or a doorman's, O'Keefe thinks, noting the small red moustache and devil's smeg of a beard at his clefted chin. He is roughly his own age—thirty odd—O'Keefe reckons.

'Are you finished?' O'Keefe says.

'I am,' Ginny Dolan's man replies, cocking his head to the right and closing one eye, casting his face in cynical, if not sinister, mien, as if because he is forced to look up at most men, he looks up to none. His voice is calm, however, and there is the flicker of a smile on his lips.

'Look,' O'Keefe says in one last effort to liberate himself. 'You feel free to look where you like. Mrs Dolan may have thought you could give me a dig-out but I'd say I'll be grand on my own.'

Ginny's man says nothing, and instead takes a thin cigar from inside his suit jacket and lingers over lighting it. Focusing on the tip of his cigar, he says, 'You weren't so grand on your own that you ended up in a drunk's bed at your auldfella's gaff.'

Heat rises to O'Keefe's face again, and he thinks he has probably blushed more in the past week than a wedding-night virgin. *So much for 'not another word about it'*. But there is anger melded to the shame he feels, and he holds his stare on Ginny Dolan's man for a long moment, much as he used to do to those who challenged him when he'd been a Peeler.

Ginny's man, head still cocked, meets this stare with one eye and holds it, unwavering, and O'Keefe realises that perhaps this Albert relishes a scrap as much as any policeman.

'You're a rare one, you are,' O'Keefe says.

'"Rare one" is right, Mr O'Keefe. Now you know.'

'Right so, now I know. And now I'll be off on my business for Mrs Dolan and you may shag off on yer own.'

The doorman does not appear offended. He pulls on his cigar and holds the smoke in his mouth, releasing it slowly, forming his lips into an O and conjuring a large ring of smoke. The wind catches the ring after a moment and snatches it away.

'Mrs Dolan says we work together, we work together. She's paying you. You do what she says and not one thing different.'

O'Keefe recalls the roll of notes Ginny Dolan had forced upon him for 'expenses'. He takes it out and tries to hand it to the doorman, who ignores it.

'Take it,' O'Keefe says.

'Put that back in your pocket before I get thick with you.'

O'Keefe realises there is no way he can force the money on the man and shoves it angrily back into his pocket. 'She obviously pays *you* well. Do you do everything she tells you *and not one thing different?*'

'That's a stupid bleedin' question.'

'Then bleedin' answer it.'

Albert sighs, as if speaking to a disappointingly dull pupil, and cocks his head again. 'The answer is that every fella from Foley Street to Amiens Street and down as far as the Custom House docks does exactly whatever Mrs Dolan does say, and so help them God they better. That's the answer and you'd do well to learn it. There's more men than me she can call on when she needs them. Not that she needs more than me more often than not.'

'Is that a threat then, Albert? Is that how I'm to take it?'

'You may take it any way you like, Mr O'Keefe, but you'll not cross me or Mrs Dolan.'

Again, O'Keefe resists the urge to lash out at the man, thinking of his father, his mother. What could his father possibly owe this man's madam? He feels a spark of resentment towards his father for landing him in this mess. Exhaling, he decides he will hold his fire; shrug off this thug of a doorman when the time is right.

Forcing himself, he says, 'So, Albert. You've a surname, Albert?'

'Just Albert does be grand.'

'Just Albert it is, so. I'm just Mr O'Keefe, then.'

'I'd say there's very little just about you, Mr O'Keefe, having once been a Peeler.'

O'Keefe smiles through his exasperation. 'Little enough, Just Albert, little enough.'

'So we're straight is all.'

'Straight as …' O'Keefe recalls a version of Ginny Dolan's words. '… straight as a bishop's …'

'... prick,' Just Albert says, 'when the Mass is finished.'

O'Keefe laughs despite himself. *Jackeens*, he thinks. *Dubs. Even men you hated could break your heart with a turn of phrase.*

11

'Smyth, you'll take the van to the house. Shouldn't need more than the one to manage the wife and kids,' Captain Hanson says, looking up from his plate of smoked salmon and brown bread. Only the best for Captain Hanson. 'And Tally. You'll drive the others and our friend the bank manager in the Ford, and I don't need to tell you, Tally, you don't so much as inch that motor forward until they come out and load up.'

Tally looks up blankly from his beans and rashers. The dining-room of the Athlone Arms hotel is empty, and the single waiter has disappeared into the kitchen. The gang has checked in to the hotel as a group of English journalists covering the civil conflict in Ireland, Bennett even showing the desk man the Box Brownie camera he'd purchased in Cork with his cut of the take from their first job. Finch had carried a notebook around for the first hour or two of their stay and then abandoned it, realising the hotel owner and staff do not mind what their business is, just so long as they are business for the hotel. A civil war is a hard time to run a hostelry, and there has been fighting in Athlone in recent weeks. The town is controlled by the Free State side at the moment, but no one knows when this might change and when the people of Ireland might once again begin staying in hotels.

'I'll be there. I was there last time and every time before, wasn't I?' Tally says.

Hanson stops chewing and swallows, his fork and knife held poised over his plate. Finch, Smyth, Bennett and Raney stop eating and look from Tally to Hanson. The silence seems to last a long minute.

'You weren't where I fucking told you to be,' Hanson says, his voice a rough, upper-class Scottish burr that is sometimes difficult to understand when he is speaking but utterly clear when he roars.

Tally blinks but says, 'I moved round the corner to get off the tram tracks. Wouldn't have been much of a getaway with the motor carved in two under the wheels of a bloody tram.'

Hanson again lets the silence hang heavy over the table and stares at Tally until Tally looks away. The Captain has that effect on men. There is something in his eyes—green, running to hazel, deep-set and thick-lidded like a reptile's. His waxed moustache like fangs on a viper. Finch wonders what it is about the Captain that makes him the leader of their little mob and not one of the others. Hard men all, veterans, and not easily led. Why not himself, for example, Jack Raymond Finch? A stout-hearted man, if he do say so himself, who has no love of taking orders from anyone.

Yes, Hanson had been an officer in the big war in Europe. Rising to captain and demobbing as one. But then so had Tally and Raney. Point of fact, Raney had been a captain as well and a major in the Auxiliaries whereas Hanson had remained a captain. Finch and Bennett and Smyth had been enlisted men and served as Black and Tan constables in the RIC, but all three had as much combat experience in the war and in the ditches and fields of Ireland as the others.

So it is not rank that makes Hanson the chief, nor is it physical size or toughness. Hanson is roughly the same size as Finch—five nine, eleven stone—and Finch imagines that they don't teach a man to scrap like a Shoreditch boy in the la-di-da schools and clubs, the likes of which Hanson had attended.

The same clubs—hunt clubs, golf clubs and débutante balls, that still thrive in Ireland despite the civil war—where Hanson dines and drinks, and meets people like the bank manager from Kildare town who has told him about the army payroll, which will be held for the Free State in his very own bank in Newbridge.

Or maybe, Finch reckons, tucking back into his roast chicken, it is merely because the whole lark, the strong-arm gang they had become, had been Hanson's idea in the first place. The idea being that, despite the truce and the Treaty and the disbandment of the RIC and Auxiliaries, there was still fun to be had in Ireland; that, having no coppers in the country, especially when you had recently served as one or something like one, could be a rare opportunity for a mob of men of certain experience and temperament.

And fair dues to the man, Finch thinks—dabbing at his lips with his linen serviette because this is what he has seen Hanson and Raney do. Sometimes it took a man with a bit of class, a touch of the book learning, to spot the main chance. Three pubs, two post offices, a bank and a creamery since they had started in May. Hitting them hard and then riding the pig's back until the money ran out and it was time to hit another one.

Bennett once told Finch that Captain Hanson had deposited his cut of their takings in various branches of the Ulster Bank throughout Ireland, intending to repatriate it to Scotland when he returned there. Finch and the others had spent theirs on the finest hotels, whores and whiskey.

'You just be where you're told to be, Tally,' Captain Hanson says, setting his knife and fork down on the side of his plate.

And Finch has no doubt that Tally, if he has any sense in the world, will be exactly where Hanson expects him to be when the job goes off.

Bennett raises his head. Good old Bennett. Finch's china plate from the muddy trenches of Flanders, they had also served as Black and Tans together in County Cork. Another East End boy, and the reason Finch is with the gang.

'And will we just release the woman and child there, when we've done? Or will we bring them back to town?' Bennett asks.

Hanson sighs deeply. He likes Bennett, Finch thinks, but even Finch knows what is coming.

'Why don't you drop the bank manager himself back at the house when we've done, Bennett, aye. That'll be just velvet. Have a chat with the Free State soldiers waiting for him while you're at it.'

Bennett smiles. He rarely takes offence at things, unless he's been drinking. 'And what then? I mean, right, what if the 'usband don't co-operate, go along with things? What if he won't leave his missus and kid with Smyth? I'd not like to leave my missus with 'im …'

'Fuck off, chum. She'd like it,' Smyth says.

'What would you do, Smyth, cough on her, mate?' Smyth's lungs had been damaged by mustard gas in the war.

'If he decides against travelling with us, Bennett, you're to put a bullet in the wife's knee. Then one in the kid's knee, and he'll get sense once he sees that.' Bennett nods and stays silent. He searches the dregs of his coffee cup and balls his napkin, then opens it up and folds it and sets it onto the tablecloth as Hanson has done. The others at the table watch Bennett, who waits until Hanson has risen from the table and made his way into the hotel lounge for his brandy and cigar. When the Captain has gone, Bennett turns to Finch.

'He's not serious, is he, Jack? About shooting the lady … and the kid?'

Finch sniggers. 'Don't be a mug all your life, Bennett, what do you think?'

But Bennett does not laugh or smile in return. 'That's the thing, Finchy. I don't know what to think. I'm not shooting no kid nor no bloody bint. I didn't even do that in the war. Or down in Cork, though God knows I would have liked to at times.'

Finch claps Bennett on the shoulder. 'You won't have to shoot a bint, Benny, or a kid. He's winding you up, mate.'

'I 'ope so, chum. I fucking 'ope he is …'

12

T hey make their way up Sackville Street—called O'Connell Street by Dubliners for many years—Just Albert worrying the multitude of coins in his pockets as he walks, O'Keefe taking in the shattered and burnt-out buildings that line what had once been one of the finer, more fashionable streets in the Empire.

This is not the first time O'Keefe has been on the street since the civil war started with the shelling of the Four Courts on the quays in late June and the fighting that spilled over onto O'Connell Street, but each time he walks it he experiences a sense of sadness and wonder. This is a street he'd walked since he was a boy, first with his hand tucked into his mother's or father's hand, strolling, window-shopping and watching Irish regiments of the British Army parade for the public on their return from foreign wars, eating fried bread with sugar, and Italian ices. Later, he had walked it on his way to school with his friends.

And now, along with the GPO, which is shrouded with scaffolding and only partially rebuilt, a number of hotels and grand stores on the street are charred shells—though Clerys, he notices, has reopened its ground floor. The street still functions in a makeshift, commercial way, but it is roughly patched and annexed, as if no owner wants to chance rebuilding until he is certain it won't be destroyed again.

He is surprised to find himself thinking of how his own city has become like the villages he had seen in Turkey. His Dublin, a town bludgeoned, scorched by war. O'Keefe still can't help but feeling that war is something that is supposed to happen elsewhere. He remembers again the returned Irish regiments parading when he was a boy in their splendid blue, red and green rigs. All of them back, he supposes now, from razing someone else's city, village, home. Even having fought in the Tan War—or at least having policed it—here in Ireland, in Cork albeit, he has difficulty believing the devastation that has visited his native city. Cork itself had been almost burned to the ground by raging Black and Tans and Auxiliaries and, unforgivable though that had been, O'Keefe had understood it. Cork was just another distant place to the men who had burned it. Another Ypres, Mons or Marne. Most of the damage here, on the streets of Dublin, had been done by Irishmen to their own capital city. He shakes his head sadly.

As if reading his thoughts, Albert says, 'Not even finished sweeping up the mess from the Rising and they go and try and blow the rest of it to smithereens.'

'They made a fair job of it,' O'Keefe says.

'Or a shite one.'

'How do you mean?'

Albert relights his cigar and hands a few coppers to a young girl in rags who has approached them from a side street. He smiles absently at her gratitude. 'Shite job because they were only trying to clear a few of the anti-Treaty lads out of them buildings. Same as in 1916. *Those* men of genius we once answered to—the Crown-bleedin'-forces—floated a battleship down the Liffey to chuck shells on a few loonies holed up in a poxy post office. I did be thinking the whole time they'd land one of them big shells on Mrs Dolan's gaff and we'd all be for it. 'Course, Mrs Dolan's a cool one. She said at the time that there was no chance sailors would ever shell a knocking shop, not even by accident.'

'True enough.'

Encouraged, Ginny Dolan's man continues. 'I mean, you're a man of the world, Mr O'Keefe, you tell me. How hard can it be to run a few buckos out of a building without blowing the jaysus thing up?'

O'Keefe looks at Just Albert in an effort to see if he is being sarcastic, and realises that he can't tell. He has a flashing memory of the village of Sedd El-Bahr, overlooking the beach on which he had landed in Gallipoli. There had been no artillery then, for the men who'd made it off the beach and through the Turkish guns and wire, up into the village. No. They had been forced to roust every sniper, from every house, with grenades, rifles and bayonets. He shudders at the memory and says, 'Hard is what it can be. Bloody hard and just plain bloody.'

Albert jingles the apparently endless supply of coins in his pockets. 'I don't know, Mr O'Keefe. When I tell fellas to shift, they fuckin' well shift.'

O'Keefe can smell the char from the destroyed buildings, and his wonder at the destruction of his city is overshadowed by the wonder he feels at having been landed with Mrs Dolan's doorman. He decides not to argue with the man. Decides it just isn't worth the breath. 'Well, that's just you, Just Albert. That's you all over.'

The doorman puffs his cigar and nods, as if O'Keefe has agreed with his line of argument. 'Right you are, Mr O'Keefe. Right you are.'

Turning right off O'Connell Street onto Parnell Street, they take a left onto North Great George's Street and arrive in front of Francis Xavier College where Nicholas Dolan had studied until he had been dismissed. The redbrick school runs a quarter length of the street, and O'Keefe sees now that some of its lower windows are boarded up. O'Keefe had imagined that the school would have been far enough away from O'Connell Street and the fighting to avoid damage, but perhaps not. Or perhaps the boarded windows were just a precaution against any further combat in the area.

In a way, the facts of the boy's expulsion, as relayed by Ginny Dolan, puzzle O'Keefe. He had attended this school, and he feels a wave of nostalgia wash over him just standing at its doors once again after so many years. He is surprised because he had thought that the Jesuits who run the school would be more understanding—more forgiving. Of course the Jesuits had always catered to the sons of the wealthy Catholics of the country—O'Keefe's own father had stretched his Sergeant's salary to pay the fees for himself and his brother—but they had always stressed to their charges a duty to the poor that the good fortune of their birth made obligatory. The men who had taught O'Keefe, not counting the odd lunatic, had been largely a forgiving and worldly cohort.

Nor were they snobs when it came to the backgrounds of the boys they taught. Scholarships were offered to bright boys from all walks of life. O'Keefe himself had never felt a lesser light than the barristers' or bankers' sons, or a brighter light than the scholarship boys, because he was the son of a policeman. But maybe things had changed.

He turns to Albert. 'Look, I think it might be better ...'

'No, it wouldn't,' the doorman says, dropping his cigar butt to the footpath and grinding it out with a shiny leather brogue.

'Wouldn't what? You don't even know what I was going to say.'

'I do, and it wouldn't. I'm to go with you, give you a hand when it's called for, mind I don't interfere, but stay with you all the same. You might think it's better I don't come in with you round all the holy fathers, but Mrs Dolan does think different.'

Anger again flares in O'Keefe. It has been a long time since he has been so freely contradicted by a sober or unarmed man. Since before he became a police constable, perhaps, and he realises that there is a great deal he will have to learn about life as a civilian. Still, Ginny Dolan's man is pushing him hard.

'Well, Mrs Dolan's not here and I'm telling you you're not helping me by running under my feet like some butcher's dog.'

'Well, I'm sorry to say, Mr O'Keefe, that I don't give a fuck what you're after telling me.'

O'Keefe takes a step forward now, jutting his chin, looming over Ginny Dolan's man.

Just Albert stands his ground, cocks his head to the side and squints through one eye. He is smiling. 'You'd want to mind your-self now. You'd be no good to Nicky or Mrs Dolan if I was to break you up here on the street, Mr O'Keefe.'

'Jesus, Mary and Joseph, who in the name of fuck do you think …?'

'Saying our prayers, are we?'

Albert steps back and touches the brim of his bowler. 'Hello, Father.'

O'Keefe spins around, feeling for a sudden moment like a schoolboy again.

'Father O'Dea? I …' The priest has aged, certainly, but has the same shock of rough, white hair and kindly, ruddy, farmer's face that O'Keefe remembers from his time in the school.

'Seán O'Keefe.' The priest smiles at O'Keefe's amazement.

'Yes, Father, how did you …?'

'You haven't changed really. I saw you from a short distance and remembered. Took me a wee second and then I had it.' He reaches out a hand and O'Keefe takes it. 'Hardly changed a bit but for the brush under your nose and the ding on your face there. I'd heard you'd gone off to fight. Heard about the brother as well, God rest him. I was sorry to hear it, Seán, so I was. He was a good lad, your brother.'

O'Keefe nods, his shock at having been recognised by the priest after more than twelve years turning to respect. Father O'Dea was a man who had kept tabs on the students he had taught for years after they had left his charge because he was a man who cared about what became of them. This had always been his way, and O'Keefe remembers again why he had liked the man so much when he had been a student.

'You're still teaching, Father?'

'No such luck, young Seán. They've gone and made me head-master for my sins. And your friend?'

O'Keefe snaps out of his reverie. 'I'm sorry, Father. My ...' he hesitates to say it and then does, '... my colleague Albert. Albert, Father O'Dea. The Father taught me Latin and Composition when I went to school here. For all the good it did me.' He smiles and the priest smiles back.

'It did you a world of good if you understand anything of the world, Seán. Pleased to meet you, Albert.' The Jesuit extends his hand and Albert takes it, though grudgingly it appears to O'Keefe. 'Albert ...?' The priest attempts, as if a surname would place the man better. Father O'Dea had always possessed an encyclopaedic knowledge of Dublin's northside, O'Keefe remembers, and taken delight in making connections between people if he didn't know them outright.

'Just Albert's grand, Father. No disrespect.'

'None taken. And you're from the area, Albert?'

'From the Kips, Father, again, no disrespect.'

But O'Keefe hears something in Just Albert's voice that runs against his words.

'I've many friends there,' the priest says, leaving Albert waiting for the judgement he had been expecting. 'Perhaps in the future I can count you another?'

Anxious to avoid a confrontation, O'Keefe says, 'Father, if it's no trouble to you, could we speak with you inside? I've been employed by a Mrs Ginny Dolan ...' he waits for the priest to acknowledge that he knows of the woman '... to find her son Nicholas. The boy has gone missing and Albert and myself have ...'

'... Albert and *I*,' the priest says, smiling.

O'Keefe smiles despite himself. '*We* were hoping to ask you a few questions, Father. I don't even know why, really, only that it seemed a good place to start. His school ... former school.'

79

'Certainly, please come in.'

Father O'Dea's office is all oak panelling, a large mahogany desk under a crucifix braced by paintings of St Francis Xavier and St Ignatius Loyola; the mingled scents of floor wax, pipe tobacco and incense. O'Keefe and Albert take chairs in front of the headmaster's desk, feeling like truants on the brink of chastisement.

'Tea, gentlemen? Or a drop of something stronger?'

Something stronger. O'Keefe would gladly die for a sup of the priest's whiskey. He decides to abstain, and is about to tell the priest that they would take tea if it was going when Just Albert intervenes. 'Nothing for us, Father. We need get down to business so we can find Nicholas.'

The man is now answering for the two of us, O'Keefe thinks, holding on to his anger in front of Father O'Dea. He will have it out with his 'colleague' when they leave. Until then he will direct the questioning, if they are to get anything useful to go on.

'Father,' he says, before the doorman can begin, 'if you don't mind my asking, do you remember Nicholas Dolan? He was expelled some time before the summer.'

'I do remember him, of course.'

'And can you tell me why Nicholas was actually asked to leave the college? By all accounts—well, by his mother's account—he was a bright boy and a fine student.'

'Oh, he was,' the priest says. 'He was a kind and clever lad. Always sticking up for the younger boys or the victims of bullies. He was a good boy who fell in with … with certain men both inside the school and out. Idealists, Seán. The kind of ideas that appeal to boys of a passionate nature.'

Just Albert shifts in his chair, and O'Keefe senses he has taken offence; that perhaps he feels the priest is implying that the boy was not supervised properly and, by implication, that streets of Monto were no place for a lad to be reared.

'So he was expelled before the summer holidays then,' O'Keefe prompts before Albert can give voice to any objections.

The headmaster takes time packing his pipe and lighting it. 'Late June, yes. I can check the date. But surely the lad hasn't been missing since then?'

'No, he's only been missing for the past month or so. And his mother knows of his involvement with the men you describe. The anti-Treatyites, the Irregulars. What I'm trying to get at is whether his dismissal might have led to his joining them. I mean …' O'Keefe wonders where to go next. He thinks it may have been a worthless venture coming here. What can the priest tell him, really, about the boy's whereabouts?

'It was quite the reverse, Seán.'

O'Keefe frowns. 'Pardon me, Father?'

'His dismissal. His dismissal was a result of his *being* a member of the anti-Treaty faction, a follower of Mellowes and O'Connor, that lot. A week, two weeks before the shooting started at the Four Courts, Nicholas was dismissed for bringing a pistol to school.'

'A what?' Just Albert says, leaning forward. 'I thought he was given the boot for … for how Missus Dolan makes a crust.'

Father O'Dea smiles and shakes his head. 'Is that what he told you?'

Just Albert nods, averting his eyes, as if embarrassed.

'I'm disappointed in the boy, but I can understand it,' the priest says. 'And is this the impression you were given as well, Seán?'

O'Keefe nods.

'Would you think such of us here, Seán?'

'No, Father, but I had no way of knowing. Things have changed in the country, Father. Things, people, are different.'

Father O'Dea puffs on his pipe. 'I don't think people are any different. They're not, in fact. Good people are good people and most people try to be good and oftentimes fail, but they're no different now. We've not changed much, I shouldn't think. Times, however, *are* different. What people think of as good has taken a strange road altogether. No doubt Nicholas thought that what he was doing was good, in its way. For the good of the country. *For a free and independent Ireland.*You hear that often, these days, to justify just about anything you care to mention.'

'I've heard it and seen it, Father,' O'Keefe says, vaguely ashamed that he had believed Mrs Dolan's version of events without question.

The priest continues: 'Nicholas was dismissed because he pointed a loaded weapon at a master and was leading a good number of other boys into actions that were disruptive to the functioning of this school, at best, and dangerous at worst. His mother's trade is of no concern to me.' His voice softens now. 'I was heartbroken to have to dismiss the boy, but I would have been negligent in my duties if I hadn't.'

'A loaded gun?' Just Albert says. 'Why? What in the name of Christ—begging your pardon, Father—was the lad doing with a loaded gun?'

'And why did he point it at one of the masters?' O'Keefe asks.

'You have to remember that the Irregulars were holding the Four Courts at the time. They were in need of weaponry and ammunition and had to get it into the Four Courts in some way. Nicholas told me that the gun was a sample from a shipment held by men on the docks. Men who had been smuggling arms for the IRA since the Tan War. These men had given him the gun to bring to one of our masters here, to see if the republicans would care to buy the whole shipment. It was a sample of merchandise, so to speak.'

'And was this the master he pointed it at?' O'Keefe says.

'No. The man he had brought it in for was absent that day, indeed, he never returned to the college, and he brought more than a few Xavier boys with him when he left to join his com-rades in the Four Courts. No, it was another master who had railed *against* the anti-Treatyites as traitors to the nation. As simple as that. Nicholas had the gun with him and could not help himself.Young boys are zealous creatures, gentlemen, as you both know.'

'And young boys make mistakes, Father,' O'Keefe says.

'They do. And I considered keeping him in school. I did.'

'Then why didn't you?' Just Albert asks.

'Because there were more than just Nicholas involved. The boys in the school, many of them, have … involved themselves politically. Boys are like that. And Nicholas was very influential. He was a leader of sorts. Even some of the older boys followed him. In the end, I asked himself and four others to go. I felt I had no choice in the matter. There were fistfights at break, in the hallways, over the national question. Class boycotts of teachers who supported the Treaty. Masters afraid to teach their classes for fear of saying the wrong thing and being threatened. It's not finished by any means, but the more radical actions have ceased. I'll say it again: it pained me to have to ask him to leave, of all the boys. But I felt it was for the safety of the other pupils, and indeed teachers here, that I had to do it. He sat in that very chair, Seán, and begged me not to. And then told me that he would do what he had done all over again, for the future of Ireland. An independent republic. I had high hopes for the boy. I've no doubt he'll go on to grand things, but this school cannot abide a boy who is a danger to it. If you want my opinion, Seán, the boy most likely joined O'Hanley and the other lads from the school.'

'Felim O'Hanley?'

'The very man. He was a fine master—one of our few lay teachers. An inspirational man when he wasn't away fighting, and the boys loved him. Loved him and his ideas. If I had known the trouble he would bring to the school, I would never have hired him, but he'd been a great friend to Patrick Pearse, had taught with the man, and I thought he would be good for the school at the time. If only as a balance to the pro-Crown contingent on the staff.'

O'Keefe remembers that O'Dea had always been a republican of sorts—rare enough for a priest in an order that educated the sires of the establishment.

'Jaysus,' Just Albert says. 'Sorry, Father, but jaysus, isn't O'Hanley only the most wanted man in the whole of Dublin after trying to blow up all the bridges?'

'He is.'

'But how do we know then,' O'Keefe says, 'that Nicholas wasn't lifted and interned after the attempt to blow the bridges into the city? Sure, weren't half the lads involved caught and locked up?'

'Or shot,' Father O'Dea adds.

'No, not that. He's not been shot or we would have heard. Or locked up…' There is worry in the doorman's voice, the first notes of fear O'Keefe has heard from him.

O'Keefe gathers his thoughts. Albert stares at the painting of Loyola.

'Is there any place you might suggest we look for the boy, Father?' he says finally.

The priest is silent for a moment. 'You might start with the man who gave him the gun.'

'You know who gave it to him?' Just Albert says.

'I asked, and Nicholas told me. He was an open boy, naïve in some ways and worldly in others.'

'He should have told me all this,' the doorman says, 'or Mrs Dolan. She would have forgiven him … anything, she would have. All of us would have. Will do … will forgive him.'

O'Keefe says, 'The men who gave him the gun … they wouldn't forgive him for telling you.'

'No they wouldn't, but they wouldn't hear of it from me. And as far as I know, the men who needed it got the gun anyway.'

'You mean he still had it when he left?'

'I was hardly the one to take it from him. In the times that are in it, I wished no harm to come to the boy.'

'You say some lad on the docks gave the gun to Nicky?' Just Albert says. 'Who was it then?'

'A man by the name of Dominic Mahon.'

Just Albert sits back in his chair as if he'd been shoved. 'Jaysus fuck,' he says. 'Domo Mahon.' He does not ask the Father to forgive his language this time.

The priest turns to O'Keefe. 'You've heard of him, Seán?'

O'Keefe nods. He has heard of the man and has heard of the family. Along with most of Dublin. 'I can see how they might have had the guns, the Mahons. There's not much of value that comes off a ship in this city that doesn't pass through Mahon hands at some time or another.'

'Sure, don't they control the quays and every docker on them?' Just Albert says. 'What in God's name was Nicky doing dealing with that mob, and me not knowing a thing about it?' It is as if, O'Keefe thinks, he is blaming himself for the boy's involvement with the Mahons.

The priest appears to sense this as well, and as if to humanise the Mahons says, 'One of their boys attended here some years back. A bright boy.'

'You'll take anyone here, Father,' Just Albert says.

Father O'Dea smiles and nods. '"Give us the boy at seven and we'll give you back the man." I wish Freddy Mahon had put his brains to better use, but there you are. You may tell him I said so if it doesn't implicate the boy.'

'So it's a trip down the docks for us, then,' O'Keefe says, rising from his chair. Albert stands with him.

'Not exactly,' Father O'Dea says.

'How do you mean, Father?'

'Dominic Mahon is interned in Gormanston Aerodrome, the last I heard. Himself and his many brothers and sons and one or two cousins I suspect.'

'Why there and not Mountjoy or Kilmainham?' O'Keefe says.

'Because they have too much influence in the prisons in Dublin, I'd imagine, with the ordinary criminals and warders. *And* they are not up on any formal charges as such. Free State intelligence knows, however, that they have sold, will sell, what arms they can get their hands on to the highest bidder and have decided to remove them from the picture.'

'Not unlike our former masters in the Crown would have done...' O'Keefe says.

Father O'Dea smiles. 'They're fast learners in the art of government, the Free Staters.'

'Where do you get all this ... information, Father,' Just Albert says, 'if you don't mind me asking?'

'We've more than one old boy who served in the IRA who is now in the Free State Army. Some visit, from time to time.'

'And old boys in the Irregulars as well, Father?' O'Keefe asks.

'Certainly. And then there are those like yourself and your friend Albert.'

'How so?'

'Serving the people themselves. People who have been harmed by the fighting of these past six years. People who have lost themselves and need to be found.'

Albert turns and opens the door. 'I serve Mrs Dolan and her only. Mr O'Keefe can serve dinner for all I care, once we find the boy.' He is ready to leave, a coiled tension in his muscled shoulders.

'I don't imagine a fella can just turn up at the gates of Gormanston and ask to visit whoever he likes,' O'Keefe says.

'*Whomever*,' the priest says, rising and extending a hand to O'Keefe.

Again O'Keefe smiles. Memories of innocent times, when grammar mattered more than bullet calibre or proclamations of intent.

Just Albert is impatient, tapping his bowler hat against his thigh in the doorway.

'No, I don't imagine one can, but there's a Xavier man, a commandant in the Free State Army—he was a senior warder in Mountjoy who helped the IRA from inside during the Tan War—who's in charge out at the camp. Another old boy ... of sorts. He'll ensure entry for you there if I ask him.'

'That'd be grand, Father. And thank you for your help today.'

'I'll give him a jingle, and if that fails, send a message, and tell him to expect the two of you, then?' Father O'Dea says, guiding O'Keefe to the door.

Just Albert answers. 'You do that, Father. The two of us. Until we find the boy, that's how it goes.'

O'Keefe shoots Albert a dark look. 'The sooner we find him the better.'

'I'll pray that you do, gentlemen. And I'll pray for the boy. And yourselves.'

'God helps the man who helps himself is how I see it, Father,' Just Albert says, giving the priest's hand a cursory grasp before turning and marching down the waxed parquet floor to the front door.

'I'm sorry for that ... for him, Father. I've been landed with him. The woman who's employed me has insisted ...'

'Mrs Dolan is an astute woman, Seán. I dare say she knew what she was doing, lending you Albert's services.'

O'Keefe is sceptical, but smiles all the same at his former teacher. 'I'd manage better on my own, I think.'

'Times have changed, Seán. You might find yourself more in need of the man than you'd imagine.'

'Please God, I won't.' He returns his trilby to his head and shakes the old Jesuit's hand.

On the footpath outside the school, the early evening sun has descended behind the buildings, casting the street in shade. O'Keefe stops and pats his jacket for a cigarette. Finding he has none, he thinks to ask Ginny Dolan's man for one of his cigars and then decides against it.

'Right,' Just Albert says, 'we'll pay your man a visit, so.'

O'Keefe is tired suddenly, his legs hollow, weak as if the day has chased him. He tries to remember when he had last eaten, and realises it was breakfast at his parents' house. Until this morning he had been an invalid. His own fault, he thinks, but he is paying for it now. The scar on his face begins to spasm, a sign that he needs to regather his strength, requires rest and food.

'Father O'Dea said he'd tell the fella to expect us tomorrow,' he says.

'We can make a start of it now.'

'We? Make a start of what, Albert? For fuck sake … *We* …' Exasperation melds with the tiredness O'Keefe feels, making him irritable and angry. This doorman is worse than some of the officers he had worked under in the RIC and the Army. Obstinate to the point of stupidity.

Puffing one of his thin cigars, Just Albert says, 'Yeah, *we*. If the Padre's man is not able, we could grease one of the guards and see the Mahons tonight.'

'Right, and end up walking around a camp full of angry fucking rebels and young Free State Army eejits armed to the teeth in the watchtowers, and all so we can meet one of the dodgiest mobs that ever walked the quays of Dublin. In the dark, mind.'

'You're not afraid of the dark, Mr O'Keefe, are you?'

O'Keefe remembers Father O'Dea's advice, but can't think of a single way this man's help might be worth the sheer frustration he embodies. He turns and begins walking towards Parnell Street and the tram stop at the monument. He does it before there is violence between them. 'I'll see you tomorrow, Just Albert. Ten a.m., I'll collect you at Mrs Dolan's shop. I'm for me tea and me bed.'

'You'll not find Nicholas from your bed.'

'And I won't find him at all unless I'm fit to do it. Tomorrow!' he calls out over his shoulder as he turns the corner, leaving Ginny Dolan's man behind.

13

O'Keefe steps off the tram in Rathmines. He thinks of a pint of stout, saliva flooding his mouth, and he wishes himself back in the cool, soothing gloom of Slattery's. The creak of the barstool as he sits, the hanging swirls of tobacco smoke in the odd shaft of evening sunlight admitted through a propped door. It takes him a long moment but he crosses the road and buys a quart bottle of barley water and a loaf of batch bread from Tumulty's Grocers and Hardware before making his way up the Leinster Road to the basement flat he rents from Mrs Cunningham.

Arriving at the two-storey redbrick house, he descends the steps to his basement room, checking first under the stairs that his Triumph Trusty is still safely tucked up under its oilskin cover. He finds that everything is as he had left it the week before: his towel hanging to dry on a wire rack before an empty fire grate, his wash-basin empty and dry, his few shirts, his trenchcoat and a single pair of heavy corduroy trousers hanging in the wardrobe. It occurs to him that he owns very few clothes for a man of his age, having spent most of his adult life in uniform. He had intended to buy a jumper some months ago, some casual wool trousers and stylish brown brogues that men were wearing now instead of boots, but had never bothered. It is as if the very act would sym-bolise the end of his life as a policeman, and he is not yet ready for that. Nearly six months a civilian and still not ready to believe it. He shakes his head, opening his dresser drawer, placing his wallet and keys within; his underwear and socks are neatly folded where Mrs Cunningham had placed them more than a week before. It reminds him that he must go upstairs to her and pay the rent he owes and for the laundry she has done.

Never once has he been so much as a day late with his rent, despite the aimless chaos of the past months, and here he is, he thinks, more than a week late. *You're a disgrace*, he thinks, feeling the word. *In this country, sure, better to be called a murderer than a disgrace.*

He sits down on the bed, however, exhaustion overcoming him. He will go up to Mrs Cunningham in a moment, he tells himself, shrugging off his suit jacket, tie and collar, hanging them on the chair, tossing his hat onto the desk beside the bed. His stomach rumbles, and he recalls the few tins of beef stew and beans he has stored in a press above the single-ring gas burner. He has to eat, he knows, and he tears off a hunk of the bread he's bought, washing it down with gulps of barley water. *Send one of the Cunningham boys back to the shops for a quarter pound of butter, heat the beef stew.* In a minute he will do this, but first lie down. *For a minute only ....*

Sleep gathers him in and opens its store of nightmares. The beach in Turkey and turquoise water running red. A man now, in a suit and flat cap, yards ahead of him, starting to run, as if in terror from O'Keefe, the hunter. Now the salon room in Ginny Dolan's kip, the contorted face of a woman, a wad of pound notes ....

Loud banging on the rear door of the flat that leads to the back garden. O'Keefe sits bolt upright and checks his watch, his heart pounding, the morass of his dreams leeching into his waking, fear driving him. He searches frantically for a gun he no longer carries before he gets his bearings, recognising his room, his hat on the desk. Heart slowing, he checks his watch. Seven twenty. In the evening? Morning? He thinks it is evening. He feels as if he has slept for only a short time, and the panic he feels begins to drain away. He stands and goes to the door. Nothing to fear now as he recognises the voices at the door.

'He *is* there. Ella saw him go in.'

'And how do you know?'

''Cause she said so is how, thick-as-a-plank.'

A sharp slap resounds, and O'Keefe pulls open the door to find the youngest Cunningham boy, Henry, returning the slap to his older brother Thomas.

'Lads,' he says.

The two boys leap back from the doorstep, startled. The younger regains his composure quickest and greets O'Keefe. 'You're back!' He turns to his brother. 'See, I told you he was bleedin' back.'

'It was Ella told *me* he was back, yeh sap!'

'What's the story, lads?' O'Keefe says, blinking away the last of his sleep.

The boys look up at him. 'Hiya, Mr O'Keefe. We done a show. You want to see our show, do yeh?'

'A show.' O'Keefe pats his pockets. He is an experienced audience to the Cunningham children's shows. He finds a few coppers in his trousers and thinks he will need to carry more—like his new associate Just Albert—if he is to continue living in the Cunningham house.

'It's a lovely show. Ella's in it and I'm in it and it's got songs.'

'And I'm in it!'

'Of course you are. Look,' O'Keefe says, taking three pennies from his pocket and handing them to the older of the boys. 'That's one each, right? I'm busy now but there's a penny each for you two and your sister. Well done on the show. I'd say it's only smash-ing.'

The boys appear crestfallen. 'But you haven't even seen it.'

'How do you know it's smashing if you haven't seen it?'

'Or heard the lovely songs?'

'Yeah, or heard them an' all?'

O'Keefe cannot help himself and smiles. A show, so.

A window slides open from above in the house. 'Boys, leave Mr O'Keefe alone and don't be bothering the man, for the love of God.'

The boys look up to see their mother, leaning from the kitchen window. Thomas acts as spokesman. 'But he already paid us money to see our show.'

Mrs Cunningham shows her own smile now. She is a handsome woman in her late thirties. She has dark hair worn in a bun and large, soft brown eyes and pale skin. Her sad smile is cut with good humour and O'Keefe wonders has it always been so, or is it the recent death of her husband that has sewn her every small joy with a thread of grief.

'Mr O'Keefe, you'll have those two ruined and you'll get no peace from them. Like feeding stray cats, giving the pair of them pennies every time they pester you.'

O'Keefe steps out of the flat into the garden and looks up at his landlady in the window. Hens peck at the gaps between flagstones. 'Sure, it's not every day, Mrs Cunningham, do you get to see a show for a penny in this town.'

The woman laughs. 'I wouldn't know, Mr O'Keefe. It's been so long since I've been to one.'

Too young to be a widow, O'Keefe thinks. But there are more young widows in Ireland now than at any other time since the Famine perhaps. Women like Mrs Cunningham, who'd lost her husband—an officer of the Leinster Rifles who had left his arm at the Somme—only two years before, in the last blast of the Spanish Flu to ravage the country. It is not an uncommon story—men surviving years of the worst fighting the world had ever seen, only to be snatched from life by the Spanish Lady on their return home. A disease that took the young and fit, those strong or lucky enough to survive the worst horrors of war, were some of the first to die. This is but another proof to O'Keefe, if any further proof were needed, that there can be no God in the heavens who would play such a terrible joke on the world of men.

Having lost her husband's handsome income—he had been a solicitor, before enlisting in Lansdowne Road with his rugby team-mates in a Pals Battalion—Mrs Cunningham has been forced to rent out the ground floor of the house that she and her husband had bought before the war. To supplement this meagre income the woman keeps hens and sells the eggs to local shops and neighbours, takes in ironing and laundry and makes dresses to order with her mother-in-law and ten-year-old daughter as helpmates.

'You've not missed much, from what I read in the papers,' O'Keefe says.

'I've enough drama in my life with those two, Mr O'Keefe, sure.'

He laughs. 'These two lads? I don't believe it for a minute.'

'You've been warned, sir. I'll leave you to it. Boys, leave the poor man alone now.'

'They're grand, Mrs Cunningham. And I'll be up shortly with last week's rent. I feel rotten being so late. I was laid up ... ill.'

'Sure, take your time, Mr O'Keefe. I've always known you were good for it. You're well now, I hope?'

Unconsciously, he touches the back of his head. 'Never better,' he says.

The rear kitchen door, next to the window out of which her mother is leaning, opens, and the oldest of the Cunningham children, a daughter, skips down the steps into the garden.

'Are you watching our show, Mr O'Keefe?' she asks.

'I am, of course, Ella. I wouldn't miss it.'

Smiling, the widow says, 'A short show, you lot. And then in and leave Mr O'Keefe in peace.'

The show has a pirate theme, O'Keefe suspects, though is not entirely certain. The two boys have swords made with slats from a packing crate—at one stage O'Keefe is forced to stop proceedings to remove a nail protruding from one of the swords—and Ella Cunningham sings *Green Grows the Rushes, O* in a high, sweet voice. When the song finishes, the boys return to scrapping, eventually abandoning their swords, ending up in the dirt, fighting for real until O'Keefe pulls them apart. Her role in the drama complete, Ella makes to go inside. The boys again begin fighting.

'That was a grand show, Ella,' O'Keefe says. 'Did you get your share of the ticket sales from your brother?'

For a moment, the girl appears confused before realisation dawns and she goes to the boys and wrenches them apart. 'Which of you has my penny?'

The youngest lad, Henry, points to his brother. 'Thomas does!'

The girl clips the older boy around the ear and jams her hand into his pocket, coming out with her spoils. 'You were going to filch it, you filthy caffler!' Another clip, the boy crying out this time. She turns now and smiles at O'Keefe.

'Thank you for the penny, Mr O'Keefe. I *sincerely* hope you enjoyed the show. We'll be doing another one tomorrow for you and Mammy. Perhaps you can watch it together?'

O'Keefe smiles at the girl. Ten years old and no flies on her. 'Well …'

'Lovely, we'll let you know what time in the morning. Ta ra!'

O'Keefe laughs and turns to go inside, the poison of his nightmares sluiced away by the manic, belligerent joy of these children. His father's illness. The job for Ginny Dolan. All gone for the moment. It has been months, he realises, since he has smiled as much as he has in the past half-hour. *Sincerely.* He is blessed, he thinks, in ways he'd not expected, to have a flat in the Cunningham house.

14

Jeremiah Byrne makes his way to the fruit and veg market behind the old distillery as darkness falls over Dublin. The last of the day's lorries and horse carts bearing the produce of Ireland to its capital are being unloaded by men who will work through the night. Gangs of children and a few old women wrapped in shawls against the evening chill scour the cobbled streets and footpaths around the market for vegetables that have fallen from the wagons.

A small onion, a fine, fat parsnip in his pocket, and still Jeremiah takes three carrots coated with the rich earth of County Meath from a smaller boy who cries for an older brother. The brother comes, eyes up Jeremiah then takes the smaller boy's hand and turns away. Even without a knife, Jeremiah Byrne has such an effect on other boys.

Around to the Smithfield side of the market and Jeremiah slips through a gap in the steel fencing that surrounds it and dodges behind a Bedford lorry to avoid a passing stockman. When the man passes, he reaches his hand between the slats of the Bedford's wagon bed and palms six large, pink Rooster potatoes into his shirt. He slips back out through the fence and turns for home, taking what he has gathered for his sisters and nephews so that he can be sure they have eaten. This way, foraging, stealing, he will not have to do the other thing. Not tonight.

From Hambone Lane—narrow, dark even during the day, a damp artery between tenements—onto Lower Sheriff Street, Jeremiah comes upon a group of lads his own age. The Sheriffer Boys, in short trousers, patched jackets, flat or bulbous caps and two pairs of shoes between them. Boys he has roamed with since he was old enough to walk; old enough to run. Himself and Tommo and the lads, robbing, scavenging the docks, dipping pockets and fighting fellas from other streets. They had been as close as brothers when they were younger, but in the past year things have changed.

They are all poor, their families forced to struggle and stroke for food, for work, for heat and light and luck. But Jeremiah knows, and the lads know as well, that the Byrne family is differ-ent from the others. Other mothers did not work the docks for drink money. Other families did not have an Uncle John Keegan and thank holy God for that. Poor they might be, but every one of the families had given money, food, blankets and beds to the poor Byrne women and their children until they had had it up to the back teeth with doing it. Up to the eye teeth with the Byrne sisters and Uncle John Keegan and their carry-on and God bless the children.

And with this, distance has grown between Jeremiah and the Sheriffer Boys. He has grown harder, tougher, in street fights unafraid to use a blade and his savagery putting the fear of God up the others. For these lads, scrapping in the lanes is a lark. A bit of broken timber over a fella's loaf, no bother. Hassling schoolboys for a few coppers, giving the odd one who baulks a bit of a hid-ing. But knives are a different story. No lad wants to kill a fella for living in a different lane. No few ha'pennies worth a hangman's rope or a stretch in industrial school. Nobody wanted to stick a youngfella. Nobody but Jeremiah.

Finally, they have stopped calling for him—as afraid of Jeremiah as they are of his uncle. They have stopped telling him where they are heading and with what gang they fix to scrap. Their mothers are still kind, on the whole, to his sisters, but they too have grown wary of Jeremiah. Old for his age—wiser and not in a right way at all—none of them wants a son banged up or dead on the cobbles on account of Jeremiah's madness. The blondie mad head on him. If handsome were manners, he'd be a gentleman. Not that any of it is the poor youngfella's fault at all, they say to each other sometimes as they hang out washing or gather on tenement steps fingering cloth in the wake of the Indian ribbon and fabric monger. What young lad *would* be right in the head with the strange doings under his mother's roof? The strange doings when Uncle John Keegan is about. But still and all, a mother can only look after her own as best she can, and Jeremiah Byrne is beyond looking after. Jeremiah knows this without ever having been told; senses it in the women and their boys.

Only Tommo—poor, soft-in-the-head, scared shitless and hungry—has stayed the course with Jeremiah. Loyal, like a beaten dog follows the boots that do the kicking.

'Wha's the story, boys?' Jeremiah says, noticing one of them, Paudge Mullen, take a sneaky drag off a fag end and then conceal it behind his back. Sly, tight bastard, Jeremiah thinks, ignoring the meanness for the moment, his own shirt and jacket bulging with produce he has no intention of sharing, though he might, if one of the lads asked. Might, or maybe fuck them and let them muster up their own nosebag.

'No story, Jerry, how's it hoppin'?'

'No bother at all, boys, not a bother on me.'

The boys' eyes stray in various directions, searching the ground, scanning the sky to avoid meeting Jeremiah's. Paudge Mullen has burned his fingers, Jeremiah sees, trying to pinch out the lit fag behind his back.

'Any of yis seen Tommo? Philly, you seen him?'

The oldest lad, Philip Beatty, speaks for the group. He has been called Philly for as long as anyone can remember. He is a year older and half a head taller than Jeremiah. In a straight scrap, Philly would have Jeremiah for his breakfast and tea, but it has been a long time since Jeremiah fought straight. Philly is as leery of Jeremiah as the rest of them, but has his face in front of the boys to think about.

'Haven't laid eye on him in days, Jerry,' he says. 'Sure, isn't his aul' one cryin' down the streets of town lookin' for his whelped arse as well.'

Jeremiah wonders on this for a moment. Tommo is soft on his mother; his father is as dead or gone as Jeremiah's own, but his mother is a kind-hearted, steady woman, rearing Tommo and his six siblings on her own, scrubbing bankers' floors at night and fretting on her children during the day. Tommo always checked in with her, without fail, never wanting her to worry about him.

As much to himself as to the lads, Jeremiah says, 'Musta been lagged, so.'

'How do yeh reckon?' Philly asks.

Jeremiah has an urge to tell the boys what has happened. He had been one of these lads once. The safety and warmth of their company like none he had ever had at home. He wants that now, suddenly, like hunger, but something inside him warns him not to tell them about the man he'd stabbed. No good will come of it.

'I don't reckon. Just he told me he was going on the rob is all.'

'On his own?' Doubt cuts through Philly's voice.

Jeremiah takes Philly's disbelief as a challenge. 'So fuckin' what of it?'

'Nothin' of it. Turn down the gas, Jerry. I was only sayin'.'

'Sayin' what, Philly? You don't believe me?' Jeremiah knows he should let the challenge die, but in his isolation he feels a sparking rage against the boys who had once been like his brothers.

''Course I believe yeh. So Tommo's gone on the rob on his tot. Grand. Fine. All God speed to him and may he only find purses stuffed with fuckin' gold. Don't take the hump, Jerry.' Philly smiles, palms out, smoothing things. He is the bossman of the Sheriffer Boys as much for his smarts as his fists. A fella who knows when to say when.

Jeremiah relaxes a little, and with this a sadness douses his anger. These had been his friends. Had been. Now they want him away. The spuds feel rough and lumpen against his skin inside his shirt.

'I swear he told me, lads, on me aul' fella's grave. He even asked for a lender of me blade.'

Philly's face shows nothing. 'Tommo the swordsman.'

Jeremiah smiles. 'I know.'

One of the younger lads speaks up. 'He's prolly up in bleedin' Jervis Street Hopsital with the point of it stuck up his arse.'

The gang laughs and Jeremiah joins them, a sad guffaw to cloak his lies. 'You're right, you are,' he says. 'So ...' He turns to go, awkward, his eyes avoiding theirs. 'I've to go bring some grub to the sisters.'

'Grand so,' Philly says, his face again betraying nothing.

Jeremiah steps away from the group and then wheels around. 'Mully,' he says to Paudge Mullen, startling the boy. 'You'd peel an orange in your pocket, you would. Gi's a bang off that burner you've got behind your back, yeh hungry cunt, yeh.' He smiles as he says it. Paudge Mullen's face blossoms bright red.

'Here, grand, Jerry. Take it, it's yours.'

Jeremiah takes the half-smoked fag. ''Course it is, Mully. 'Course it fuckin' is. What's yours is ours, Mully, right? And wha's mine is fuckin' mine, wha'?'

He feints a head-butt at the boy, and laughs as he crosses the street to his building. The Sheriffer Boys could run and fuck themselves. Every last one of them. Except Tommo—once he managed to keep his gob shut to those trenchcoated boyos, about who had gone and carved up their pal.

Entering his building, Jeremiah is halfway up the stairs, spuds bouncing against his chest, when he hears the voices of strange men. He stops, and above these voices hears the voice of his Uncle John Keegan. Fear electrifies his scalp under his cap.

His sister Sarah, hearing footsteps on the stairs, sticks her head through a broken gap in the banisters on the landing, her head emerging at eye level to Jeremiah. Her eyes are wide with panic.

'Jerry, don't go up! He's back and he's talking to some fellas.'

He puts his finger to his lips to shush his sister and listens, locking his gaze on the curtained doorway to the flat at the top of the stairs. The men's voices are raised now, cut with threat, and his Uncle John's words are angry at first in response before twisting to a plaintive mewl that sends a lance of pleasure jabbing through Jeremiah's fear. He has heard his uncle use this voice before, but only to Peelers who have come to arrest him.

He whispers to his sister. 'Are they going to lag Uncle John?'

Her eyes dart to the doorway of the flat and back to Jeremiah. She shakes her head and whispers back. 'They're wearin' suits. With ties and all and their hats tipped back on their heads.'

'But what do they want, Sarah, dote?' He feels the urge to flee, to be on the move. Part of him knows what Sarah will say before she says it.

'They're askin' about *you*, Jerry. They say you done something on a fella and they need to find you. And Uncle John ate all the bacon. It was only half cooked, and he ate it on us.'

Jeremiah's heart, already turning over at the sound of his uncle's voice, kicks up a gear, pistoning against his ribs like a diesel engine. He lifts his shirt and hands the vegetables and potatoes to his sister.

'Quiet now. Put them in your dress and take them to Mrs Fitz. She'll boil them up for you and the rest. Go now, and don't tell Mam or Uncle John you got them.' His whispered commands sound loud on the stairs, and he realises the men in the flat have stopped speaking. He quickly shoves the last of the spuds between the banisters at his sister, who hikes her dress to gather them. Jeremiah sees that the girl is naked under her dress.

'Where are your knickers, pet? You'll catch your death of a cold, Sarah, running round with no knickers.'

His sister's voice is matter of fact, and too loud on the landing, as if she has forgotten about the men in the flat. 'Uncle John Keegan told me I'm not allowed to wear them when he's home. He always says it …'

Revulsion, rage rises in Jeremiah's chest and overwhelms his fear. He is going to gut Uncle John Keegan if it is the last thing he ever does. His legs move involuntarily and he takes a step up, towards the flat. A stair creaks underneath his weight, and heavy boots shift on the bare floorboards of the flat.

His uncle's voice, a bellow: 'Who's out there, to fuck? Is that Jerry? Get your arse up here, you little …'

He does not hear the rest. 'Go to Mrs Fitz's, now, Sarah. Run!'

And he is gone, bolting down the stairs, leaping out into the light of day and slamming into a fishmonger as he lands, upending the man's basket of piled ray and plaice. The fishmonger goes down shouting, his flat catch of bottom fish slinging out in a salty arc onto the cobbles as Jeremiah keeps his feet and turns, left, then right. Kids on the lane are onto the fish like ravening gulls. Boots pound down the steps in pursuit, more shouting, barked orders. Jeremiah's bare feet slap the stones as he sprints across the street, vaulting the stone steps and into the dark hallway of another tenement, moving fast down the hallway and out, crossing the dead-grass garden and through a hole in the wall, onto Hambone Lane.

He does not see one of the hunters emerge from his building into the street, gun in hand; does not see him step on a stray plaice and slip, crashing down onto the cobbles amidst the grasping hands of tenement children reaping fish and the fish man's curses.

Breathless, Jeremiah reaches Talbot Street and slows to a fast walk, blending in with the crowd of late evening shoppers and travellers making their way to Amiens Street station. He ducks into a shop doorway and tucks his hair under his cap, leaning against the shop window to catch his wind.

Tommo, he thinks. *Tommo must have gabbed. The only loyal one of the whole shower of Sheriffer Boys not so bleedin' loyal after all.*

The owner of the shop comes to the door, a red-faced, white-haired man, and tells him to move off. Jeremiah holds the man's gaze for a long moment, thinking that if he still had his knife he might stab the bastard. Just to be stabbing somebody.

He makes his way back into the flow of pedestrians, his heartbeat slowing, breath returning, his stomach scorched with hunger and spent adrenaline as he walks. He knows now that he cannot allow himself to be caught. He doesn't think they would bother hanging a youngfella for a stabbing, though they might plug one. *Wouldn't even flinch to plug a youngfella who'd carved up one of their pals.* But even if they didn't hang or shoot him, they could lock him away in Artane Industrial School or, worse, send him down to the almost mythically distant Letterfrack in County Galway. Jeremiah knows boys who had been sent there, and he has not heard a word of them since. As if a lad is wiped off the earth, doing time in Letterfrack. For all he knows, those boys could be dead, so feared and far away is the 'Frack. And if this were to happen to him, Jeremiah knows, there would be no one around to feed his sisters. No one around, he thinks, to cut the guts out of his Uncle John Keegan.

All he needs now is a knife.

15

The Criminal Investigation Department offices in Oriel House, on Westland Row, may be spoken of in whispers by the people of Dublin, but they are offices like others in many respects, and Nora Flynn is officially employed by the CID as a 'typist,' as are the two other women on the staff. Her title is a cloak for her actual work, but she does, in fact, spend many of her days typing, filing and drafting intelligence reports. It is not unlike the work she had done in Dublin Castle as a typist and file girl for Crown intelligence, and later—from her position within the walls of the Castle—for the IRA.

As is common, Nora spends the afternoon at her desk, typing up intelligence reports and cross-referencing the files of anti-Treaty gunmen. She will resume her duties at the hotel desk the next day, in the morning, a rare day shift for which she is thankful.

'There's Nora,' a detective officer named Finnerty says, passing her desk in shirt sleeves and no tie, a Smith and Wesson .38 Long Special revolver in a shoulder-holster that is a notch too small for his portly frame.

She looks up from her typing. 'Here's me.'

The detective stops some feet away and turns back. 'You wouldn't know where the O'Malley files are hidden, Nora, would you?' He smiles and scratches the back of his neck, revealing a yellow bolt of dried sweat under his arm. Or perhaps it is staining from the leather of the shoulder holster, Nora thinks. Hopes.

'Have you tried looking under "O"?'

His smile fades. 'No, no, I suppose I didn't,' he says, shifting his weight from foot to foot, lingering. 'I … umm, you wouldn't mind if I dropped my surveillance diary down for you to knock out later …?'

Nora stares at him until his face flushes, as she had known would happen. Her colleagues in CID are hard men; men who had been gunmen in the Tan War. Killers and soldiers. But for all this, many of them had been no more than boys when they started fighting, some of them barely finishing school before joining the Volunteers, and their knowledge of women extends little beyond their mothers or sisters or some idealised sweetheart.

They are not all like this. Some are as bold and knowing as the English secret service or army intelligence officers who had propositioned her on an almost daily basis when she had worked in the Castle. But, to many, Nora's presence in the CID offices, in meetings or on jobs, is unsettling, a woman's place being rightfully at the cooker, the washboard, or waiting patiently for a late-arriving beau under Clerys' clock. If any of them knew— she sometimes thinks with a perverse kind of pride she regrets as soon as she becomes aware of it—how many dead Crown spies were on her conscience or how many men in this very office were still above ground rather than below it because of the work she had done for Michael Collins' boys, Broy and Nelligan, inside the Castle, they would soon stop asking her to type their reports. She returns to her typing without bothering to answer the man, slamming the carriage back as she reaches the end of a line.

'Ah sure, look …' Finnerty says, backing away from her desk, '… It's grand. I'll bang them out myself. No bother.'

Another typist—a former *Cumann na mBan* girl called Mary Whyte, who resents Nora's involvement in the Burton's Hotel surveillance—looks over at her and purses her lips, averting her eyes when Nora looks up. Nora knows what she is thinking: that Nora is some sort of Trucileer—a fair-weather patriot who, like many men and some women, joined the Free State cause only after the fighting with the English had ceased. Mary Whyte and the two other 'typists' had actively served in the women's auxiliary of the IRA during the Tan War, smuggling weapons under their skirts, delivering messages or tending the wounded. But Nora in turn cannot get over her prejudice that while she was risking her freedom—her life—as a double agent in the Castle, the likes of Mary Whyte and the other *Cumann na mBan* girls were busy baking bread and ironing shirts for the gunmen. And Nora knows that the *Cumann na mBan* girl will go later and ask Finnerty if he needs his report typed, her female colleague balancing her resentment of Nora with an ingratiating helpfulness towards the men in the office.

Nora would like a friend, a comrade in the CID—the other woman 'typist' is friendly in a reserved way—but Mary Whyte will never be that friend. Despite her envy of Nora's role in the Burton's Hotel surveillance, Nora thinks the woman would be more than happy to type the detective officers' reports all day, from the safety of the office.

Whipping the paper from the typewriter, Nora adds it to the file folder on the desk before shrouding the machine with its canvas cover and standing. 'I'm off,' she says to Mary Whyte, who does not look up or respond.

Nora shakes her head and pulls on her coat. *Have a lovely evening! And you too, Nora!* She descends the stairs to the building's basement, praying there is no one being held, and is relieved to find the interrogation rooms dark and silent.

The basement cells of Oriel House are what the people of Dublin fear most, Nora knows, with their blood-spattered walls and bolted-down chairs. Not really like other offices at all, she thinks, passing these rooms quickly, making for the steel door at the end of the short basement hallway. Through this and into the adjoining basement of the neighbouring building, which houses a travel agency, commercial bank and solicitors' offices. She will exit to the streets from this building, as if she were just another typist on her way home from just another job.

Home, though she does not think of it as such. A one-bedroom, kitchen and bathroom on the ground floor of a large house in Ballsbridge. A place to eat and sleep and bathe. A place no guest— not even her parents or siblings—has entered. No man, certainly. *Are you joking?*

Before turning the key, Nora runs her fingers along the edge of the door, finding the blade of grass she has wedged there when she'd left that morning. It is one of the tricks of her new trade, and has become habit.

Letting herself into the dark flat, she wonders, as she often does, on the turns her life has taken. From secretarial college to common typist girl, happily living at home, to this—fixing blades of grass between her door and jamb each day so that she will know if her flat has been entered, if an enemy is waiting there in the dark with a gun and a pillow. Instinctively, she feels in her handbag for the short-barrel Webley revolver she carries. She finds it a comforting weight.

Lights on, bag down, she realises that she is hungry and thinks of the cold ham in the ice chest. There is stale bread in the press. A hunk of mouldy cheddar. No. A bottle of lager beer? Her brother brings her a case of the German beer at her request every Monday, leaving it outside her door, and often it is gone by Friday—her brother who has never once seen the inside of this flat. Thinking this, Nora feels a sharp pang of guilt, but she finds a bottle opener, opens the beer and relishes its hoppy sourness. No whiskey tonight, she thinks, studiously avoiding the cupboard containing the bottle of Jameson. She pays a dosser who loiters outside the gates into Merrion Square to buy it for her in McSorley's pub, and often it too is gone by

Friday. Nora smiles wearily and takes another sup straight from the bottle of beer.

She had never considered herself to be a republican. She had become one eventually—or the Free State, pro-Treaty version of a republican, if such were even possible—but reluctantly, only after she had begun passing information to Ned Broy, DMP detective and one of the IRA's men inside the Castle, who would in turn pass her information on to Michael Collins and the volunteers who would use it against her employers in Crown intelligence. Two years ago. It seems a lifetime. A reluctant rebel now working for the most feared unit in the entire country. A 'typist' spy. A paper killer.

Nora had always been a good girl. Decent and kind and perhaps a bit spoiled. The daughter of an accountant father and piano teacher mother, she had finished her schooling in the Loreto convent on Stephen's Green at sixteen and entered the typist pool in the Dublin Corporation offices after attending secretarial college. Her older sisters had found fine husbands and Nora, it was assumed, would do the same after some years of light work.

She could be opinionated, as the nuns had noted in their reports—Nora has come to think of them now as intelligence reports when she allows herself to think of her past—but had been generally obedient and well-liked by the nuns and her classmates. A bright, mild-mannered girl who reflected her social class and rearing.

From Dublin Corporation to Dublin Castle after reading an advertisement in *The Irish Times* for skilled typists and filers. The pay had been better, and there was something the slightest bit thrilling about the idea of working behind the great walls of the Castle among the men in uniform and government. Three happy years there, in the Lord Lieutenant's offices, before the Tan War ignited in 1919 and she was transferred to the offices of the Chief of Combined Intelligence Services in Ireland as an epitomiser—a glorified reference librarian for the various networks of Crown spies in Ireland. Typing, filing and compiling like any other secretary in the country, except that it was intelligence reports and dossiers on IRA men she filed for the people whom many— including her own brothers—considered to be the enemy of the people of Ireland. She typed and filed and lunched in the Castle canteens or on benches on the parade ground with other girls from the typing pool. And in the evenings she went to dances with officers and intelligence men; even the odd RIC constable, up from the country on prison escorts or protection details. It had been a good life. The benighted contentment of a young, modern city girl.

She had enjoyed the work at first. From the cold, bureaucratic distance of the Castle 'I Division' offices, she did a thorough and efficient job of absorbing intelligence from disparate sources, surprising herself with her ability to remember aliases and names gleaned from various reports and documentation. She proved equally adept at scouring old photographs collected in raids of suspects' houses and matching them to custody photographs to prove identity. This ability was noted by her superiors, and soon she was asked to work on specific cases, assigned by agents of the secret service, British Army intelligence and RIC Crimes Special Branch to consolidate, or *epitomise* as it was called in I-Division, information on men requiring 'urgent attention' from their services.

Nora slumps into the single, hard-backed chair at the table, the table's surface bare but for a half-full ashtray bristling with dog-ends. She laughs through her nose and takes out a Murad Turkish from her handbag. The Crown had been masters of euphemism. How naïve she had been. 'Urgent Attention' when what they meant was murder.

And now, she thinks, lighting her cigarette, the Free State Army and Dáil are becoming as bad as their past masters. The anti-Treatyites, no longer to be called Republicans in the newspapers, by order of the Free State Director of Communications, but instead, 'Irregulars' or 'rebels'. No longer will the Irregulars 'attack' or 'commandeer' or 'arrest' but now 'fire at' or 'loot' or 'kidnap' like common criminals. Her colleagues in the CID 'attend' to their targets. Nobody says 'kill.' 'Shoot.' 'Dispatch.' But this is what she had abetted in the Castle, and it is what she does now: picks targets and sources routes for the shooters. Puts names to faces. A pointer bitch, she thinks. A gundog in her second war now. A proper veteran spook. Like some of the Crown men she had worked for and then, later, fingered for Ned Broy and the IRA.

It had taken Nora some time to discover this, however. During most of her time working in the Castle she had agreed with the newspapers who branded the IRA as corner boys and common murderers, and viewed her work as helping to restore order to the country. It would be some time before she came to see her Crown masters as every bit as murderous as the men of the IRA.

Slowly, as the weeks and war rolled on, it dawned that there were real, flesh and blood men at the end of the information she had helped compile, and that these men—weeks, months or sometimes only days after she had delivered the files, tidy, chronological and clipped together just so—were ending up dead, their files returned to 'I' Division, 'Deceased' stamped in bright red letters on the covers. And she came to realise that somewhere in Ireland, outside the cold stone walls of the Castle, the dossiers she compiled had bullets attached to them.

Slow dawning, until one day came a request from an Auxiliary captain out of the Beggar's Bush barracks for anything they had on a gunman by the name of Owen Hannigan.

When she allows herself now, she remembers how she had smiled at the officer, standing at her desk with his ridiculous Glengarry cap clutched in front of him, automatic pistols in holsters that hung down on his thighs, a handsome man in his thirties with eyes that made him look sad rather than savage, as the Auxies were usually portrayed in certain newspapers. She remembers how she told him that she recognised the name and would see what she could dig up on the man. A local, the Auxie had stressed. From the Ranelagh Road, word was, but they did not have much on him.

Nora could have told the agent the exact house without moving from her desk, but she smiled and told him she would have a gander at the files.

'Good girl,' the Auxie had said, smiling with his sad eyes.

Owen Hannigan. Not only a name and grainy photograph to Nora, but a face and a voice. She knew his mother and father well. She skipped lunch that day, and decided there was no way she could allow Owen Hannigan's file to reach the Auxiliaries and be returned to her some future day stamped in bloody red letters.

Nora finishes her bottle of lager and thinks again of the Jameson. *What harm a small drop? No. Not tonight.*

When two years before she had told her brother's friend, Denis Murphy of the Fourth Battalion, Dublin Brigade, IRA, to warn Owen Hannigan, she could hardly have imagined where her resolve would take her.

No mere typist and file girl now, in this new war, and in her loneliness she wonders whether she is able for her new role. Out of the ante-room and into the shadowed halls of the fray. Where men die in your arms and not only on paper. Where your part in a man's death is questioned; where men like Dillon and O'Shea are still in the wind and only God knows what has happened to the messenger boys they had been following.

Nora has a dread feeling that things are unfinished. She decides she must be fresh for the days ahead. Uncertain days. She sets the beer bottle on the sink and, instead of the whiskey, chooses a bath, knowing she should eat but too tired to fix something.

She goes into the bathroom—an indoor toilet, hot-water tap and claw-footed tub being what had drawn her to the flat, along with its general anonymity—and runs the water. As she takes off her dress, hanging it on a hook on the back of the door, she thinks of her purse on the table and the gun inside it. In her underclothes, she dashes into the kitchen and retrieves her bag, bringing it with her into the bathroom and setting it on the floor beside the tub. Crime is rampant in the city and country, the civilian police unable to serve or protect the newly independent Irish amidst the anarchy of civil war. No sense leaving her bag on a table as an invitation to a housebreaker. Not with a Webley revolver in it. It would be a shame, she thinks, to have to shoot her first visitor.

16

'Gi's a go on the Trusty, Mr O'Keefe, please! Please!'

The Cunningham boys are waiting on the footpath in school uniforms of grey jumpers and short trousers as O'Keefe wheels his Trusty up the steps to the street, wondering, as he does, if the boys do anything other than chart his movements. Still, they are a hard pair to dislike. Thomas has his hands jammed in his pockets and young Henry's hair appears to have resisted the comb, but there is a look of bright, youthful anticipation on their faces as if to say that nothing starts a schoolboy's Tuesday autumn morning better than an auld gallop on a Triumph motorcycle.

O'Keefe lifts the bike onto its stand and checks his wristwatch. It is one of the few things he has kept from the war besides his scars and nightmares. A quarter to nine. It will take him an hour at least to get to the Free State Army internment camp at Gormanston Aerodrome, barring any obstacles on the road or checkpoints. At the best of times, road travel in Ireland can take longer than it may appear on a map, but for the past three and a half years of war in the country, trenching and blocking roads have become a favoured tactic of guerrilla warfare, meaning an hour's trip could take a day.

There is no rush, however. Father O'Dea had given no specific time when his man in the prison camp would be expecting their visit, and O'Keefe has no intention of collecting Just Albert. If Ginny Dolan's man wants to be there, he can make his own way.

But anxiety niggles behind his bravado. He tries to suppress thoughts of his father's illness, unable to stop himself from wondering if his father even remembers his debt to the madam, whatever it might be. Would it matter if he did? He resolves to view his search for the brothel madam's son as a normal job of work, a case like any other he'd worked in the past.

At very least, the trip is the excuse he needs to drop in on his sister Sally in Balbriggan. He is not sure what good may come of questioning Dominic Mahon, the head of the docker family, or any other Irregular he may stumble across in the camp in his quest to find Nicholas, but it will do his heart good to see his older sister and her new baby. His spirits lift as he lowers his tinted goggles against the morning sun.

'Please, Mr O'Keefe, gi's a backer on the bike, would yeh?' the younger boy says, unable to contain himself.

'Right, lads,' he says, swinging a leg over the Trusty. 'Who's first?'

He should have known better than to ask, he thinks, carrying both boys now on the back of the bike for a spin up and down Leinster Road, their laughter—proud shouts of 'Look at us!' to their schoolmates on the footpath—pitched high above the growl of the Trusty's four-stroke. O'Keefe is smiling as he brings the bike to a stop in front of the Cunningham house, drops off his pillion passengers and roars away again with a crisp salute to the boys, determined to enjoy the ride out to Gormanston.

It is the one thing that will always make him happy. Speed. Motion. He must get more of it, he thinks, as he moves through the gears. Abandon the paralysis of the pub. Take the Trusty out more often. Up into the Wicklow Mountains. Trips to the country with a bedroll and fishing rod. Once this job is done, it is what he will do.

He is still smiling when he comes upon a manned checkpoint on the Drumcondra Road.

17

Nora Flynn is reading the log of the previous night's work at her desk in the CID offices when she hears her name. She turns and sees Carty, the head of CID, standing at his open door, his small, round spectacles reflecting light from a window.

'You couldn't join us for a moment, Nora, could you?'

She closes the log. *Us?* She should have gone directly to the hotel for her shift but had always reported in to read the logs, noting active surveillances, contacts with the enemy and captures—occasionally kills—made while she was off duty. Rarely is there anything in the logs to directly affect the surveillance she is presently overseeing, but coming into the offices, despite the risk, is a way of setting her mind to the job of work that is intelligence. Like an actress, she has come to think, putting on her greasepaint: coming into the office to read the duty logs before taking on her role as a desk clerk in a hotel.

Nora clears her throat. 'I was ... I'm on shift at Burton's, in ...'

'I've rung and you'll be covered. If the gun merchant leaves between now and then, you can catch up with the boys tailing him. There's no hurry. Please,' he opens the door to his office wider, 'join us.'

Inside the office, seated in chairs in front of Carty's desk are Captain Charlie Dillon, Free State Army Intelligence, and Micka O'Shea, who Nora assumes is CID like herself, having seen him before in the office—a detective officer, like herself, though no more of one than she is.

'You know the lads, of course,' Carty says by way of introduction. 'Coyle's not here. He's still out hunting down the lad … the lads who did for Detective Kenny.'

'Mary,' Dillon says, turning in his seat to watch her enter the room.

'Nora,' she says. 'Lieutenant Nora Flynn.'

'Of course, Nora. Lieutenant Flynn. Our girl in the Castle.' He smiles, referring to the role that had brought her into the IRA. And referring to something else perhaps. Nora blushes and swallows. She knows the stories some of the men tell about her. Stories of how she had enjoyed luring the young English Secret Service man from the safety of his quarters in Dublin Castle to his death. Stories of how she had gone about it; of what she had done to get him to meet her outside the Castle gates, against all protocol and good sense. She can picture Charlie Dillon, winking, nudging a comrade. *I'd imagine she was fierce persuasive, your one, the Flynn girleen. Like putty, the English lad, like a lamb to the slaughter ….*

Stop it, Nora. Stop it now. She swallows down the memory. She'd done her job, followed orders. What choice had she had?

O'Shea says nothing, but turns in his seat too. He has a flat labourer's cap resting on his knee, a bulbous, misshapen nose, thick, unruly brown hair. He holds a cigarette to his lips and does not let it down until he has inhaled half of it. Nora watches as he releases the smoke in two long streams from his nose.

There is something sinister about these men, unsavoury. Nora's stomach tightens and her heart begins to run hard against her breastbone. She feels hot, suddenly, cold sweat breaking on her forehead. They are her colleagues, she must remind herself, and she is a Detective Officer. And yet there is something predatory in their gaze, their eyes surveying her like a cat would a mouse; her body, she feels more than thinks, like meat to carnivores. She swallows and smiles and hates herself a little for smiling.

Dillon is a handsome man, his grey suit sharp, a strong jaw and the youthful, pink white skin of a clerk or Protestant clergyman— but there is something wrong with his appearance, something off. It is his eyes, she thinks, looking away. The man's eyes are pale blue; vacant and amused at the same time. Carty passes behind her and takes a seat at his desk.

'Oh,' Carty says now, realising there is no place for her to sit. 'I'll have a chair brought in … I'm sorry, Nora …'

'There's no need,' she says.

'Really, I'll …'

'No,' she says, sharper than she intends to. 'I'm grand standing. I've sat the whole way in on the tram.'

Carty sits back behind the desk as if unsure of the set-up. Unsure of things in his own office, Nora realises, and wonders is he afraid of these two men? They are Free State Army Intelligence and do not, as such, answer to Carty.

Dillon and Carty had worked together in Michael Collins' Squad during the Tan War. Possibly O'Shea as well, though he might be from Cork. She is not certain because she has never spoken to him or heard him speak. But Dillon and Carty. They had surely killed together. How much more intimately could you know a man? And Carty could put the fear of God in men—in women, as she had experienced herself, sitting where Dillon is now—with his ever-staring eye and his questions. But there is something about Dillon that Carty lacks. *Or perhaps Carty has what Dillon lacks?* A sense of the horror of things. Dillon, still smiling, a slim version of the cocky corner boy's grin, as if reading her thoughts, says, 'Sure, she'll be grand. If she's able for a man's work, she's able to stand for the short minute we'll all be here.'

Nora shows him a smile that stops at her eyes. A riposte rises to her lips and dies there; her loathing too cut with apprehension to loose it. 'I'm grand.'

'Well then,' Carty says. 'I just wanted to keep you informed of events, Nora.' He nods at the two Army Intel men. 'Charlie and

Micka have dropped in their report on the night … on Kenny's killing, God rest him, and the pursuit that followed. It's here and it matches yours.' He smiles as he says this, as if Nora should be reassured somehow by this fact. *What?* she thinks. *Did you think I lied in mine? Got it wrong somehow?* Her loathing now turns to Carty. Pandering to these two. The pals brigade.

'That's good to hear. And you two couldn't have turned it in a day or two ago and saved us the waiting?' she hears herself say.

Dillon laughs and O'Shea takes another endless pull on his cigarette, lowering it to tap a finger of ash into the dish on Carty's desk.

'Seeing as we were tracking the little fu … the little so-and-sos from hither to yonder and back again for the past days, that might have been difficult,' Dillon says. 'I've had four hours sleep since it happened. Your man, Kenny, remember, was CID and a good man. Reports wait. Murderers don't.'

Nora says nothing, waiting for Carty to interject, but when he does not, she says, 'I appreciate … we appreciate your trying to find the killer. We could have helped if you'd kept us abreast of … events. You didn't find the one who did it, did you?'

'No,' Carty says now, 'but they gave it a fair shot and are still looking, aren't ye, lads?'

'Sure, Eddie's still at it, and we've a sniff or two left to run down, on the boy with the knife anyway.'

'And the other two. Surely they'd have given him up by now?' Nora says.

Still smiling, Dillon says, 'If we had them. Didn't the other two scarper in the mêlée as well? Like rats, slipped away when we turned to grab the knifeman.'

'And no sign of them?' Nora asks, wondering at her own outspokenness; as if this were her operation. Realising now that she'd been granted the right to boldness when she'd been left holding the dying Kenny in her arms. When she'd scrubbed his blood from her dress in water gone cold in her sink that night and then, finally, when she'd thrown the blouse and skirt into the bin so she would not be reminded of the weight of the dead man on her lap every time she wore them. She thinks: *Scarpered in the mêlée?* Why then had she seen Mick O'Shea and another detective, Eddie Coyle, raining punches down at someone in the rear seat of the Ford as she held Kenny? She had been on the ground, and the motor car had been several yards away, but she is certain she saw this. She wonders why she had not remembered this when she'd written her report. The car had roared away moments later and she had been concentrating on Kenny's laboured breathing, his last breaths. Perhaps it hadn't seemed important at the time.

'No sign at all. Nor of O'Hanley,' Dillon says.

'Nor will there be …' Nora says, less surprised by her boldness now, '… Not if the young lad's made it back to tell him Murphy is blown.'

'And why would Murphy be blown, sure?' O'Shea says, speaking for the first time. His accent is Cork, Nora confirms, and there is none of Dillon's faux comradely warmth in it. 'Sure, the two lads we stopped with the messenger boy were robbing him. The messenger boy's not to know we were on to him alone. And where to fuck else will O'Hanley and the lads get their guns? They need field pieces now or we'll mop them up in weeks. Murphy is the only one who can source them and sure, didn't O'Hanley use him himself in the Tan War? They're bosom chums, them two, so why would a missing messenger boy put him off?'

Nora catches the look Dillon gives O'Shea but cannot read it. It passes from his eyes as quickly as it had come and he smiles again. Dillon says, 'And even if O'Hanley is spooked, sure there's others won't be. Deasy had dealings with Murphy down in Cork as well, as far as I know, and we've got the word out that he's here and has artillery and gelignite to sell. One of them will bite.' He appears cheerful, Nora thinks, as if this is all a grand game.

'Of course, which is why we should get you back to the hotel, Nora, and …'

There is a knock on Carty's office door, and it is opened without waiting for a reply by a CID man in shirtsleeves. Words rush out of the man.

'We've got a lead on Kavanagh. He's been holed up in Swords and is heading for town by pushbike. We've a lad on him but he's staying back out of sight. Our lad thinks he's heading for Drumcondra.'

Nora does not recognise the name of the wanted man—Kavanagh—but this is not unusual. CID have hundreds of names on file. Hundreds of targets.

Carty stands now. 'Dillon and O'Shea will go with you. Take two motors and set up a roadblock. Who's our lad tailing him?'

'Duggan,' the man at the door says.

'Grand, one of the cars goes back and meets Duggan on the road while the other can set up the checkpoint. Get the word off Duggan on what Kavanagh looks like and what he's wearing, then head back to the checkpoint before he gets there.'

'And do we pull him or tail him?' O'Shea says, standing and ramming his cap onto his head, looking to Nora more like a labourer than a soldier or agent.

'Or shoot him?' Dillon says, smiling, standing, donning his trilby at the rakish tilt that all the gunmen seemed to affect.

Carty pauses. 'Look, make the decision as you need to. If you think you can tail him, tail him. If you have to pull him …'

'He shot Dessie, you know, Terence,' Dillon says, no light or humour in his smile. Dessie Galvin had been a fine Volunteer during the Tan War. The first CID man to die, some two months back, gunned down entering a vacant building off Henry Street. Nora thinks that Dillon had been there that day. Possibly O'Shea.

For the first time, Carty's voice is short with Dillon. 'I know who he is and who he shot.'

'So?'

'So play the game the way the ball falls.'

A chill washes over Nora's back and she stands aside as Dillon and O'Shea leave the office.

'Will that be all, sir?' she says to Carty, who is staring after the men as if he has forgotten she is there.

'What? Oh, yes,' he looks down at his desk and will not meet her eyes. 'Yes, you'd better move out, hadn't you?'

18

Shifting down, O'Keefe slows the Trusty to a halt. A Talbot Tourer motorcar is parked diagonally across the tram tracks in the middle of the road, with just enough space on either side for cars to squeeze past, some one hundred yards north of the gates to St Patrick's Teacher Training College. Four men work the checkpoint, all of them in mufti-suits and trenchcoats despite the Indian summer morning's warmth; sharp trilbys and polished black shoes. All are armed, O'Keefe knows, though he sees only one man holding a stubby rifle with a drum magazine. One of the new Thompson hand-held machine-guns, he realises, having read reports of the gun being shipped into Ireland by the IRA when he had still been in the RIC. One of the men, holding a clipboard with a sheaf of papers attached to it, shouts a question over his shoulder and O'Keefe turns and follows the man's gaze to the reason for the checkpoint.

To O'Keefe's left on the footpath, underneath one of the large oak trees that loom over this stretch of road, is a body. A dead man in canvas work trousers and scuffed brown boots is entangled in a bicycle, his legs asprawl through the frame as if the push-bike were a trap, head thrown back, eyes staring lifelessly up at the yellowing leaves, a thickening pool of blood on the footpath under the body. A flat cap lies some feet away. Blood on the white, collarless shirt. A fifth man, also in civilian clothes much like the ones worn by the dead man—rough woollen jacket, heavy boots and flat cap—is squatting and rummaging through the dead man's pockets. O'Keefe watches as he stands, finding nothing, and wipes the blood from his hands on his trousers. He lights a cigarette, and even from fifteen feet away O'Keefe can see that his hands are shaking.

O'Keefe wonders if the cycling man was killed having tried to run the checkpoint, or if the checkpoint was mounted as a result of the killing. However it happened, he thinks, they should at least afford the dead man the dignity of covering his face, closing his eyes. No crowd gathers around the body, terrified no doubt by the men in the trilbys and trenchcoats. Instead, O'Keefe sees that people are crossing the road to pass on the far side.

He turns back to the checkpoint, idling the Trusty behind an ass cart driven by an elderly man. The men holding up traffic and questioning drivers are Free State men, O'Keefe reckons—army intelligence or special detectives from the new and much-feared Criminal Investigation Department recently established in Oriel House. They are too open about the killing and the checkpoint to be anything else. The Irregulars also man their own roadblocks, but rarely in Free State controlled areas, and even then rarely in daylight. And generally, Irregular checkpoints are set up with the intent to commandeer transport.

O'Keefe feels some comfort in knowing who is asking the questions. It allows him to formulate the correct answers.

The man with the Thompson gun waves a car through on the opposite side of the road now and points at O'Keefe to approach. He raises the machine-gun and brings it across his chest, finger resting on the trigger guard. It is not an aggressive move, but one of readiness, and O'Keefe recognises it for what it is. He has manned checkpoints in the past himself.

Despite this awareness, O'Keefe's mouth is dry and his heart-beat begins to jog against his ribs. And with this, a dull sense of anger swells in his throat at these gunmen on the streets of his city.

Yes, he thinks, he has always wanted an Ireland free from British rule—as long as no one had to die for it. And yes, these men are likely members of an army under the mandate of the new, democratically elected Free State government of Ireland. But still he cannot help but wonder what these very men had been up to a year ago. He wonders how many of his friends in the RIC these heavily armed and strutting peacocks had assassinated in the name of liberty.

O'Keefe knows that these men are fighting a war against their former comrades in the IRA—rebels, Irregulars—who oppose the Treaty guaranteeing Free State status to Ireland in exchange for the six counties in the north. The whole thing a mire of accusations, recriminations, as former comrades hurl lethal insult and increasingly heavy weaponry over the widening ideological divide.

The dead man on the footpath is most likely one of these staunch, violent Irregulars, though his face has taken on the innocent mien that death lends to every man. He could well be a bloody-minded gunman of the worst sort, O'Keefe thinks. But still there is something sad about the scene. Perhaps it's the gormless, everyday tangle of limbs and push-bike.

Of the two sides—Free State army or Republican Irregular—O'Keefe supposes he sides with the Free Staters, with the government and its army, of which these men are members. Best of a bad lot, he supposes. The people of Ireland want freedom from Crown rule, but more than that, they want peace. They want to work, to raise their families, to raise a glass without the constant menace of gunmen at the door; without having to shield their children's eyes from the bodies and blood on the streets of their towns. The Irish people, O'Keefe believes along with many others, had not so much voted in favour of the Treaty, a flawed and flaccid compromise, as much as they had voted for an end to violence. And these men at this checkpoint are charged with achieving that peace, even if it means gunning down men on bicycles on a sunny autumn morning.

So they are Free State soldiers or detectives, but that does not make them any less dangerous. These trenchcoated men appear calm enough to O'Keefe, none of the jumpy, paranoid shouting and high-pitched laughter, the waving of guns and desperately smoked cigarettes that often follow an action in wartime, a killing. But O'Keefe's palms are sweating in his leather gloves because he knows what can happen at checkpoints manned by men with guns, democratic mandate or no. The man with the clip-board approaches him under the watchful gaze of the Thompson gunner.

O'Keefe lifts his goggles onto his forehead and removes his leather helmet, showing he has nothing to hide from them, that he presents no threat.

'Step off the bike,' says the man from the footpath, approaching now from across the road.

O'Keefe turns back to look at him and does what he says, shutting down the Trusty and lifting it onto its stand. He raises his arms.

'What are you doing?' the man with the clipboard says.

'Making it easier for you to search me,' O'Keefe says, know-ing this is coming. He has been searched before on the streets of Dublin and had, as a policeman, searched many men himself. 'I can put them down if you like.'

'You're the kind to cut it clever, are you?'

The man with the flat cap approaches from behind and slaps O'Keefe roughly under the armpits with open palms before he can reply. He then pats down his back, sides, arms and between his legs, tugging O'Keefe's balls and then running his hands down his legs to his boots. He digs his fingers into the boots before stand-ing and searching the saddle-bags on the Trusty. Throughout this, O'Keefe says nothing.

'Clean,' the flat capped man says, before walking back to the footpath.

'Can I drop my arms now?'

The man with the clipboard does not respond, but O'Keefe lowers his arms, considers lighting a cigarette and then decides against it. *Don't provoke them or you won't make Gormanston today. Or ever*, he thinks, his eyes darting over to the dead man on the footpath.

The man ruffles through the pages on his clipboard, the tell-tale bulge of a revolver grip visible beneath his tan trenchcoat. After a long moment, he says, 'Name?'

Jesus, O'Keefe thinks, *what cost a few manners?* The RIC had had its faults, O'Keefe is the first to admit, but lack of professional courtesy was not one of them. He says nothing until the man with the clipboard looks up and repeats his question.

O'Keefe does his best to keep the anger from his voice. 'O'Keefe. Seán O'Keefe.'

The man with the clipboard holds his gaze on O'Keefe, who tries to keep his expression neutral.

'Address?' The man shuffles through the pages on his board.

O'Keefe tells him, wondering as he does if it is wise, and then decides there is no reason not to tell the truth. He has a flashing realisation that this must be exactly how innumerable men had felt when he'd questioned them during his time in the police. The instant, instinctive urge to lie, often for no reason, in the face of authority. Some latent guilt inside all men driving the lie. *I've nothing to hide.* But his memory sparks, ignites with images of Turks he had killed in the war, too many to remember all of them, but he recalls one he'd done with a bayonet and another—hardly older than Nicholas Dolan—with a trenching tool. Images of IRA men he had shot in Cork as a copper. Men like these men in front of him. He'd been the hunter and the hunted then. He swallows and regrets telling the man his correct address.

'And what line of work are you in, O'Keefe, Seán?'

There is an edge to the question and O'Keefe's disquiet tilts back to anger. He is suddenly pleased with himself for neglecting to vote in the May election. *Shower of bullies, thugs, the lot of them.*

'I'm unemployed at the moment.'

The man smiles over at his colleague with the Thompson gun and then turns back to O'Keefe. 'Fine motorbike for an unemployed man. How did you come about it?'

'I bought it.'

'You bought it, did you? With what?'

'With money I'd saved.'

'So you were employed before you were unemployed then?'

O'Keefe breathes through clenched teeth. 'I was.'

'At what?'

O'Keefe cannot help himself. He could have been anything—a house painter, a teacher; a shop clerk or hod carrier.

'I was a Peeler.'

The man's eyes—watery blue under the brim of his hat—narrow and his smile widens. 'Lads,' he calls back to his colleagues, 'we've a rusty copper here. Says he's unemployed.'

The Thompson gunner laughs. ''Course he is. Sure, you've his job now, Charlie.'

The third man at the checkpoint does not laugh, O'Keefe notices. He stares for a moment at O'Keefe and then looks away, something furtive, fearful in his eyes, and O'Keefe wonders if maybe it is remorse or shame he is seeing. Had he been the one who had shot down the cycling man? Or had he perhaps murdered RIC men in the past and now, confronted by one still living, feels the weight of guilt for it? O'Keefe doubts it. Shoot a man down over a card game or a woman and you're a criminal, he thinks. Shoot a man down over an idea and they make you a detective in the new Free State. He looks back to the man with the clipboard.

'Can I go now?'

'Twenty-three Leinster Road, Rathmines is your current address?'

'I told you it was. Can I go?'

'You in a hurry, are you? Surely an out-of-work Peeler's got no place to be going quickly?'

O'Keefe says nothing but holds the man's gaze until the sound of a tram's clanging bell breaks the impasse. The man with the clipboard turns and tells the Thompson gunner to let O'Keefe through.

Keeping his rage in check, O'Keefe replaces his helmet and goggles, kick-starts the bike and eases his way around the Talbot. As he passes it, the third man at the checkpoint—holding his hand out to halt traffic in the opposite direction—looks at O'Keefe quickly and then looks away. The man in the flat cap is standing over the cycling man's body again, but this time the dead man's face is covered with his cap.

O'Keefe wonders was it a friend, a former comrade whom these men have shot dead on this sunny autumn morning.

19

There are five men in the Ford Tourer and four of them sweat because they are wearing heavy trenchcoats. It is unseasonably warm for an October day in Kildare. The fifth man's sweat is born of terror.

'Please don't harm my child. I'll do anything you say ...' begs the bank manager, a Mr Anthony Roche, captive on the rear bench seat between Finch and Raney.

In the end, only one man—Smyth, with his mustard-gas-abraded lungs—had been needed to mind the banker's wife, housemaid and child.

'What about the wife?' Raney says, in his flat Ulster accent. 'You don't mind what happens to the auld doll?'

The banker shakes his head. 'Of course. Jesus, what do you take me for?' There is some of the high-handedness one expects of a bank manager in his tone, and Raney elbows the man harder than he has to in the ribs.

'I'm only ragging you, Mr Moneybags. Our chum won't lay a finger on her once you do what you're told. Unless she wants him to, aye?' Again the digging elbow in the ribs. A Winchester pump shotgun rests on the floor of the Ford beside Raney's feet.

Jack Finch, seated on the other side of the banker, smiles. *Serves the stuffed cunt right, him with his airs and graces.* Finch decides he does not mind robbing this man's bank and will be happy to leave him unsure about his wife's safety. Smyth's a pukka lad and won't hurt a kid, and probably won't try to get up on the wife. Not with the maid and kid watching anyway. Smyth can be prissy like that, but the wife is an all right bit of mutton—no lamb—and Finch would not have minded a poke at her himself. But such is life. He promises himself the nicest, fattest whore he can afford when the job's done and they're away to Dublin. *Now keep the mind on the job.* They turn onto Edward Street, coming to a halt behind a beer lorry that has stopped to allow a squad of uniformed Free State soldiers to cross in front of it.

'Don't get no ideas, chum,' Finch says, jabbing one of his two Webleys into the soft flesh of the banker's armpit. 'Bunch of kids just learning the trade, them lot. More likely to shoot you or each other, them wet boys.'

'He's no fool,' says Tally, from behind the wheel. 'He knows what's good for the missus and the kid, don't you, mate?' He turns to watch the banker nod, the haughtiness gone now, his face pale under his bowler, sweat beading on his cheeks. Tally turns back and watches as the Free State troops march to the opposite side of the road, passing the Ford less than ten feet away. He has a Colt .1911 held on his lap under the folds of his trenchcoat.

The beer lorry moves forward. The men in the car release a collective breath and Tally follows the lorry until he comes to the bank where Hanson and Bennett are waiting, parked at the curb in a hardtop Chevrolet Sedan Captain Hanson had won in Cobh in a game of cards.

'Anything else you like to tell us, chum?' Finch says.

The banker swallows. 'No ... I've told you about the two soldiers guarding the safe.'

'You told us about them. Nothing else?'

The banker shakes his head.

Finch says, 'You know it's not *you* I'll shoot if something goes sour. It's your wife and kid who roll sevens if you're fucking us about. Nothing funny?'

'No, no …'

'Good stuff. Let's hop it, gents,' Raney says, stepping out of the Ford and holding the door open for the banker and Finch to exit. He carries an empty leather holdall in one hand, the Winchester against his leg in the folds of his long coat in the other. Bennett gets out of the Chevy to join them.

Finch notices Captain Hanson behind the wheel of the Chevrolet, a newspaper opened to hide his face as the bank manager passes. No sense in their hostage learning it was the Captain—that fine man he'd met in the Hermitage golf club bar and shared more than several tumblers of Bushmills with over an afternoon—who had turned a banker's drunken blather into a cushy payday. Hanson would be hard to catch even if there were any coppers in the country to try it, but there is no gain in taking chances.

They mount the steps, and Finch, also carrying an empty leather travel bag, says to the banker, 'Right, you call them two guards into your office like it's important business. You do things proper and no one gets 'urt—not them guards, not your customers, not your tellers, right?' He rests his hand on the door and waits for the banker to nod. *Handy number, this*, Finch thinks as they enter the bank, leaving the bustle of the market town street for the hush of country commerce inside. *Be nice to do a job where, for once, there's no shooting.*

Commandant O'Hanley's man, young Stephen Gilhooley and his two older brothers ride in one car, smelling faintly of meat and blood, cuticles claret-stained after a morning's work for their father at Gilhooley's Butchers and Purveyors of Fine Meats. The four others—Stephen's two inside men from the Free State army and two of O'Hanley's young Irregular charges—ride in the second. They pull up to the bank at the corner of the Dublin Road and Edward Street. Raymond Gilhooley gets out of the car and walks to the corner, glancing both ways up Edward Street and then at the bank itself. He walks back to the cars and taps the bonnet.

'Grand so. No troops or coppers I can see.'

'There's hardly a copper left in the whole of Ireland,' Stephen says, smiling. 'And good fuckin' riddance.'

They get out of their battered, stolen Willys–Overland 90, each with an empty coal-sack bunched in his jacket pocket, throwing down half-smoked cigarettes. The others climb out of their Ford Tourer, which had been requisitioned for the job at a hastily drummed up checkpoint in the village of Tallaght. Webleys bulge in waistbands under the younger boys' shirttails; sawn off shotguns beneath overcoats for the older Gilhooley brothers and, for Stephen Gilhooley, a Thompson sub-machine-gun dangles on a strap under his coat.

Finch stays close to the hostage as they cross the Bank of Ireland's small atrium, and then nudges him with his Webley barrel. 'Call them,' he says.

Bennett is on the opposite side of the banker, a chopped-down Winchester pump gun nestled close to his leg, and Raney is behind them with his full-length Winchester. All three wear low-dipped trilbys and, as one witness would later remember, expensive brogues polished to army standard shine.

The banker clears his throat, removing his bowler to reveal thinning hair sweat-matted to his scalp. 'Gentlemen,' he calls to the two uniformed Free State guards at the locked walk-in safe to the right of the teller's windows. 'Come in to my office, please. I need an urgent word …'

The two guards look at each other, and the larger of the two says, 'We're not meant move til we're relieved, sir.' His words are authoritative, and Finch gives the man a long look as the banker stops. He does not like what he sees in the guard's eyes, and swiftly decides there will be no fannying round with him. The shorter guard is younger and looks to the older for his lead. *No bother there.* Finch's finger moves from the Webley's trigger guard to its trigger. He scans the barred teller windows and counts three customers waiting—two older farmers and a young woman—as the single middle-aged male teller serves a woman wrapped in a black shawl. A second teller, a young man just out of his teens by the look of him, sits at a desk behind the cage filling in forms.

Finch says, without moving his lips, 'The big lad.'

Raney, behind Finch, says, 'Clocked him, aye.'

The banker's skin is a shade of white that indicates only fear or illness. His voice is thinner than it had been in the car. 'Gentlemen, these men have been sent on urgent business from Dublin, sent by …' the banker stops, as if thinking of a name or title to suitably impress the guards, but more likely he cannot recall who is in charge of what department, '… by Headquarters Staff in relation to matters pertaining to … your duties. I should not like to have them report you for insubordination or obstructing the orders of the Free State government …'

'Move into your office,' Finch mumbles. 'They follow or I'll shoot the both of them.'

'Please, gentlemen, time is against us,' the banker says, a crack in his voice that Finch hopes the guards don't hear.

They move as a group of four to the banker's office, situated to the left of the tellers' cages, and enter.

'Sit,' Bennett says, pointing to the banker's chair behind the desk. The banker sits and Bennett stands behind him with the cut-down shotgun to his temple.

Finch stands behind the door, and when the guard's knock comes, Bennett says, 'Come in.'

The door opens and the bigger guard walks his face into Raney's shotgun barrel, his own Enfield rifle still slung on his shoulder.

'Call your mate,' Finch says, levelling his Webley at the man, 'or I'll put a bullet in your nog and then I'll go out and put one in his. Call him.'

'Fuck sake.' The guard's face darkens, he balls his fists. 'For fuck sake.'

'Try it,' Raney says, shoving the gaping up-and-under Winchester barrels closer to the guard's eyes. 'I'll paint that wall with you, big man.'

Finch watches the guard's fists unclench. 'Call him.'

'Gareth,' the big guard says, clearing his throat, and then louder out of the open office door. 'Get over here now, boy.' He does not look at the men, but fixes his gaze on the window behind the seated banker, and does not react when Raney slips the Enfield rifle from his shoulder, ejecting the round from its chamber and detaching the box magazine, pocketing both. Raney waves the shotgun barrel at the man and he follows it across the room. Finch decides not to wait for the younger guard and slams the butt of his Webley into the back of the guard's skull as he passes, the guard collapsing forward with a grunt. Finch moves back to the door, then and as the second guard enters, he closes it. He steps from behind him and delivers an expert uppercut, his punch landing just below the young man's ribs. Raney grabs the lad's rifle before he falls and Finch takes two sets of handcuffs—souvenirs from his time in the constabulary—and cuffs the guards behind their backs.

'Right, you,' he says to the banker, 'up and open the safe and we'll be off.' Bennett lifts the banker to standing, the man having seemingly lost the power to do so himself.

'Don't faint, Shylock,' Bennett says. 'You open that safe or I'll kill every cunt in this bank and then your wife and kid, right?'

The banker nods. 'Please … I'm all right.'

The men leave the office, passing behind the short queue for the teller, and Finch watches the young man filling forms look up, a question in his eyes. They reach the safe and the bank manager begins to spin the dial, his fingers sweating, stopping to wipe them on his trousers. Four numbers in, an audible click and the banker lifts the lever below the dial and begins to spin the wheel lock counter-clockwise. Twenty seconds later, the heavy door is swung open and the men walk in.

'Take him back to the office and cuff him, mate,' Finch says to Bennett, beginning to shove packets of pound notes into his leather bag, Raney working the opposite side of the safe.

'Right-o, you, let's go,' Bennett says to the banker before smiling and winking at Finch. 'Piece of piss, innit, mate?'

'Here we go, lads,' Stephen Gilhooley says, moving towards the street corner with the others in his wake, 'try not to shoot the two guards …' he stops and turns back to the six men, '… unless you have to.'

'We won't have to,' Mullen, one of the moonlighting Free Staters says. 'I know the one of them, and he's as windy as a March day that fella. Just shout at him and he'll shite himself.' He scans the street and pulls a pair of motorcycle goggles down over his eyes, raises a neck scarf to cover his mouth while his Free State comrade does the same. A drover taps the hind of the last cow in his milking herd as it passes up Edward Street in front of the bank, studiously ignoring the masked men moving with purpose towards the bank's stone steps.

Gilhooley tips his cap lower and his brothers quickly knot kerchiefs over their mouths as they walk, passing two parked cars in front of the bank, Gilhooley dismissing the man in the Chevy reading a paper. He is oblivious as the drover, it appears, to their passing.

They mount the short flight of stone steps, beginning to jog halfway up, one of O'Hanley's young lads holding open the door as they pass one by one. The lad remains outside the bank, his face uncovered, to keep sketch.

From inside the bank comes the sound of bellowing voices and a woman's scream.

'Everyone, down on the floor, *now!*' Stephen Gilhooley shouts, waving the Thompson at the three customers and the wide-mouthed teller and his partner behind the cage. 'This is a stick up!'

The shawled woman, having completed her business, has turned and faces the masked men. She screams and drops her handbag, screams again before one of the Free State moonlighters crosses to her and forces her to the floor with the others.

'The payroll!' Stephen says, rushing the counter. 'Where is it, the Army payroll?'

The terrified teller is unable to speak, but points to the open vault.

Gilhooley and his brothers take the coal-sacks from their pockets and turn to the safe.

Finch freezes when he hears the shouting. Raney begins to speak, and when he does so Finch signals for silence. He hears the words 'payroll' and 'Army payroll' and shoves a last packet of notes into his bag, hanging the bag's straps on the crook of his arm. He takes a second Webley from the holster on his thigh, holding one in each hand. Raney does likewise with his bag and clutches the Winchester in both hands.

'Would you fuckin' believe it, mate? We're being *robbed*.' Finch smiles at Raney. He has known the man for these many months and has enjoyed his company. A good skin, Raney, if a touch on the mad side.

'I'd believe anything, aye, after some of the things I seen in the war. Good luck, Jack,' Raney says. 'See you in Dublin if I don't see you in hell first.'

'I'll see you in the Ford in thirty seconds time, chum. Don't you facking fret about it.'

Raney smiles. 'Time for the fireworks.' He moves towards the vault's open door.

The first to the vault is the moonlighting Free State soldier named Mulally. As he reaches it, his Enfield rifle held in loosely across his body, he is met by the smiling face of a trilby-hatted man. His brow furrows in confusion and he has not had time to register the

Winchester when fire erupts from its barrel, ripping into his chest, killing him instantly.

Gilhooley, six feet behind Mulally, watches as the moonlighter's trenchcoat billows at the back, the heavy shot passing through the soldier's body in a spray of blood, the body collapsing as if it is nothing more than a suit of clothes tossed in a heap to the floor. He raises the Thompson gun and watches as Patterson brings up his own Enfield, but too late. He watches as Patterson is hit by pistol fire coming from behind the Winchester; watches as a second man steps out of the vault, two Webleys raised and watches the first man, still smiling, rack another round into the shotgun and swing it towards him and his brothers.

All this in an instant, and Gilhooley reacts, loosing off a burst from the Thompson before turning and diving to the side of the tellers' cages, his brothers following, scrambling, boots slipping on the polished floor for the tight cover where the counter extends out from beside the bank manager's office.

It is the Thompson gun that rouses Captain Hanson. He had watched the men enter and decided to wait, to see if his men could handle things without him. The Thompson gun is the kicker. Captain Hanson, for all his faults, will not abandon these men who have chosen to follow him. He leaves the Chevrolet and mounts the steps, not bothering to conceal the Colt automatics he draws from their low-slung holsters.

He is three steps from the young scout at the top, and the scout begins to tug at the small pistol in his belt, the gun's hammer catching on a belt loop, and Hanson raises a Colt and shoots the boy in the face, the back of the boy's head blown onto the grey stone of the bank's façade.

Bennett, in Roche's office, hears the shooting, fumbles with the handcuffs but cannot latch them. He settles for slamming the banker face first into the wall and kicking him twice in the ribs as he falls. He opens his cut-down shotgun, checks its load and takes his back-up Webley from his coat pocket. He tips his hat back on his head and throws open the office door.

Hanson sees the men huddled at one end of the teller's counter, registering the Thompson gun, the cut-down shotguns, and begins firing.

The office door is flung open and he directs his fire there, seeing Bennett too late as two of his heavy .45 calibre rounds hit the Londoner high in the chest. He winces and turns his fire to the Gilhooley brothers. He does not notice the boy—the youngest of the Irregulars—behind him, to his left, three feet away, his arm outstretched, shaking, his knuckles white on his pistol's grip.

The boy yanks at the trigger, his eyes squeezed shut, and continues jerking it until it is empty, and he opens his eyes to see the dead man at his feet, two shiny Colts in either hand, their barrels smoking, blood spreading in a pool on the marble floor, the man's eyes wide and surprised in sudden death.

Raney fires a round at the men cowering at the counter, and Finch begins to sprint for the bank door, passing the paralysed boy clutching an empty revolver. Raising his own Webley, Finch thinks to shoot the boy but decides against it, saving his rounds.

Pumping the Winchester, Raney fires another horror of buckshot, splintering the wooden counter above the huddled men, blasting chunks of plaster from the wall beside them. He walks as he shoots, racking the pump, smiling, but his aim is awkward, not adjusting for the heavy bag on his arm and the high prime of the shells. He has not kept count of how many rounds he has fired and, as he thinks this, the Winchester's chamber sounds with a hollow *thack* of the hammer striking hot nothing.

He is still smiling as Finch, standing in the doorway of the bank, turns and shouts for him and watches as the Thompson gunner rises from his cover and begins to spray the bank with lead. Finch watches as Raney goes down in a foamy haze of blood and pulverised bone. He sees Bennett, dead, and Hanson. *Last man standing, naughty Jack Finch.*

Finch turns, flinging open the bank's door, and he is flying, leaping down the bank steps when the single, stray .45 round strikes him in the meat of his lower back. He lands hard on the path beside the Chevrolet, his breath blown from his body, his pistol and the leather bag flung out and away from him, packets of notes tumbling onto the rough cobbled street. He looks at the sky and waits for the shots to come. He turns his head and notices that Tally has scarpered in the Ford. *The windy toerag.* Ten seconds pass and Finch counts another. He thinks of his mother, whom he would have liked to see again. When the shot does not come, he pushes thoughts of his mother away, rises to his feet and finds, by the mercy of Mars, the Chevrolet is still running, idling quietly at the curb as if expecting him. Warm blood runs down his leg and spills out of the cuff of his trousers. He does not bother stopping for the bag.

Ears ringing in the sudden silence, gun smoke snaking in window light, Gilhooley waits for almost a minute before rising, then runs to the leather tote on the dead man's arm.

'Get the guns, lads. All of them.' His voice is calm, as if repeating a customer's order in his father's shop.

His two brothers and the surviving youth edge past Gilhooley, arms full of weapons, coming into the shocking afternoon light outside the bank to see a lone Chevrolet pulling away, turning the corner for the Dublin road.

'The others,' Dinnie, the eldest Gilhooley brother says, as if only remembering, 'we have to go back in to get …'

'They're dead, yeh slow shite,' younger brother Stephen says, passing him on the steps, the leather bag over his arm. 'We need to move, unless you want to shoot your way back to fuckin' Dublin.'

The elder Gilhooley brothers glance at young Stephen and then bound down the stairs after him. Each of them wonders how it has come to pass that the baby of the family had become the bossman, and both deciding, as they bundle into the Overland 90, that they don't care how or why, once they get home in one piece. The boy has mettle, sure as fuck, and that is why they are still standing, still running for Dublin. And may God rest them dead lads back in the bank.

20

O'Keefe passes several lorry loads of Free State troops on the Belfast road, near Swords, and a foot patrol at Blake's Cross in Lusk, but neither bothers to stop him. His anger at the checkpoint fades as he nears Gormanston.

Two miles after passing through Balbriggan—where he plans to stop later and visit his sister—he turns off the Belfast road at the mossy thatch of the Cock Tavern, a pub reputed to be the oldest existing in Ireland among a hundred others claiming the same. He makes his way down the long, crushed gravel track running between farmers' fields before coming to the main gate of Gormanston Free State Army Camp. Formerly an aerodrome for training wartime pilots for the British Royal Flying Corps, it had served as an induction depot for Auxiliary and Black and Tan police constables during the Tan War. Lately, it had been re-commissioned as a transport depot for the Free State Army and internment camp for captured Irregulars.

He stops at the gates—reinforced steel topped with barbed wire, with sandbagged sentry posts on either side—and dismounts. The sentry posts are manned by two young soldiers in Free State Army olive green, and around the gates are gathered a number of women and children, the women holding baskets covered with dish towels, some of them laughing and chatting. Others, O'Keefe notes, are tearful, tense, pleading with the blank-faced sentries who look over their heads at nothing.

A few older men are also among the small crowd, smoking pipes and speaking solemnly out of the sides of their mouths. They are oblivious of the children who dart out from behind them in desultory games of chase. An older boy of ten or eleven silently approaches O'Keefe and stares at the Trusty. O'Keefe smiles, but the boy does not smile back. His father, O'Keefe imagines, is one of the men behind the barbed wire of the camp. Some of these families are coping while others are going hungry for a husband's—a father's—fidelity to the ideal of a great republic. O'Keefe wonders are there any ideas worth the bloated belly of one single child and decides he doesn't know the answer.

He makes his way over to the sentry to the left of the gate, and tells him he has an appointment to see the camp commandant. The sentry asks him his name, nods and retreats behind the sandbags into the hut. O'Keefe can hear him cranking the telephone when he feels a presence at his shoulder, closer than is comfortable.

'You took your sweet time about coming, Mr O'Keefe.'

O'Keefe relaxes his guard but curses inwardly. 'Just Albert. Fancy meeting you here.'

'We'd an appointment. I made my way here without you. Hope you didn't mind.'

Turning now, O'Keefe sees that Albert is smiling. He reminds O'Keefe of a heavily muscled imp. ''Course I don't. Only glad you found the place. Fair way out of the Big Smoke for a man like yerself, Albert. All the grass and cows and sea air not too hard on the constitution, wha?'

Just Albert tilts his head and squints, still smiling. 'Not at all. Does a body good, a day in the country.'

The sentry comes out of the guard hut and motions for O'Keefe to follow.

'He's with me,' O'Keefe tells the sentry, and the sentry nods.

'I already rang in about him. The commandant is expecting both of you.'

'Grand, so. After you then, Just Albert.'

'Dirt before the brush, Mr O'Keefe,' Albert says, squinting, smiling.

O'Keefe shakes his head and follows the sentry through the open gate, thinking that he'd had lice in the war that had been easier to shake off than Ginny Dolan's man.

The commandant's office and camp administration were housed in a Nissen hut some fifty yards inside the main gate. To its left and right, forming a U shape, were two further huts with signs designating them as 'Visits' and 'Infirmary.' O'Keefe wonders at the wisdom of locating the camp hospital so close to the commandant's office in case of an outbreak of TB or dysentery, but imagines there is a reason for it. As he crosses the yard now, with Just Albert at his heels, he notes that the camp proper is set within a second, inner fence of heavy razor and barbed wire. Every hundred yards or so is a watchtower looming over the wire. In the one closest to the commandant's hut, O'Keefe can see a guard in olive green, pacing the platform outside the tower with a rifle in the crook of his elbow.

The commandant meets them at the door to the hut.

'Gentlemen, welcome, you're very welcome! I'm Commandant Michael Quinn. Father O'Dea told me to be expecting you.' He holds out his hand, and O'Keefe and Just Albert shake it in turn.

'Thank you for seeing us, Commandant,' O'Keefe says. 'I'm Seán O'Keefe and this is … Albert. Father O'Dea said you might help us if you were able.'

The commandant shoots a roguish grin. 'Sure, for the good Father I'll do what I can for yis lads. Please, come in.'

He leads them inside the hut, and down to the end farthest from the infirmary and closest to the main gate. For a quick getaway, in case of a rising in the prison camp, O'Keefe thinks, and then chastises himself for his cynicism. It is a tired habit from his days in the constabulary: assuming a darker motive for every action.

The commandant's office has been walled off from the rest of the hut with a plywood partition and thick curtains for a door, highlighting the makeshift, hurried establishment of the prison camp. Once inside, the commandant takes a seat behind his desk and indicates two chairs placed in front of it. O'Keefe notes a cast-iron stove in a corner with a tin chimney pipe rising to a rough cut hole in the Nissen hut's roof. The stove gives off a low heat, but the inside of the office is damp and cool despite the mild weather outside. There is one window, behind the commandant's desk, and files are stacked on an army cot and a camp table in the corner.

When they are settled, Commandant Quinn says, 'Pardon the state of the place, lads. I'm to be moving into the old British Army officers' quarters any day now, once they figure out what's what out here. It's fierce at the moment, but fuck it, they say it's pure murder here in winter. The bollix do be froze off you of a cold night even now—when the wind's from the east, off the sea. Jaysus, lads. Mind you,' he says, smiling wickedly, 'the job does have its pleasures. Watch this.'

Quinn bellows without warning, causing O'Keefe to start slightly in his chair. Just Albert, O'Keefe notices, hasn't flinched.

'Bring us a pot of tea, lads! And don't forget the cream biscuits this time!'

From farther down the hut there is the sound of scraping chairs and boots on the rough floorboards.

Quinn turns and winks at his visitors. 'I fuckin' love doing that, I do. Those two lads, college fellas, both of them. One, his auldfella's a doctor.' The commandant laughs. 'And any jaysus time I let out a roar, they jump and then jump higher and bring in the biscuits and tea. I'm tellin' you, when I was in the 'Joy, I had a chief who done the same thing on me for years. *Tea, Quinn! And move your arse!* And where is he now, I ask you?'

O'Keefe, unsure of whether or not the commandant's question is rhetorical, smiles neutrally.

Rhetorical it is. 'Not fuckin' here is where he's not! Not commandant of his own fuckin' camp, he's not!' Quinn's face is flushed red with laughter, and again he roars, 'What's taking ye two jinnies with the tea?'

Half mad, this fella, O'Keefe decides, wondering about his connection to Xavier College, considering his disdain for 'college fellas' and doctors' sons.

As if reading O'Keefe's thoughts, Commandant Quinn says, 'So, are yis auld Xavier boys yerselves or what, lads?'

'I am,' O'Keefe says. 'What year did you finish there, Commandant?'

'Finish?' Quinn says. 'You must be joking. Poor auld Father O'Dea done every-bleedin'-thing he could to keep me in the place, but finally even he knew I needed the boot. Thick as two planks, I was. Still am!' He laughs again.

Quinn is a portly man in his mid-thirties, his face dusted with red stubble and his eyes flashing with mirth. A man more at home telling ribald yarns in a public house than commanding an internment camp maybe, but O'Keefe had seen less likely looking officers than this one during his time in the army, and looks are, he knows, often deceptive when it comes to good soldiering or leadership.

'You mustn't have been too thick to pass the entrance exams,' O'Keefe says.

'Exams? Not on yer life, Mr O'Keefe. Sure, me auld-one was a cleaner in the residence where the Jesuits lived, and wasn't I always under her feet when she cleaned, her with no one to mind me. The priests took a shine to me, God only knows why, and they let me into Xavier free and gratis—exams be fucked. I couldn't have spelt "exams", let alone sat one. Father O'Dea, though, a grand fella and no mistake. Felt fierce awful about giving me the shove and looked out for me ever after. Got me the job as a warder in Mountjoy when I turned eighteen. Best job I ever had til I got this one!'

'And how did yeh get this one?' Just Albert asks, the sarcasm in his voice barely disguised. O'Keefe can guess what Ginny

Dolan's man feels about prison warders and their Free State equivalents. More than one filthy song is sung in Monto kips heralding the misdeeds of prison warders and ending in their almighty comeuppances.

But Quinn appears to have missed the jibe behind the words. As he is about to speak, the tea arrives. 'You tell them,' the commandant says, 'tell them, Fiachna … Fiachra … whatever your name is. You tell them how I got this job of work.' He is beaming, and as the young subaltern sets the tea tray on the table, Quinn again winks at O'Keefe. 'Tell them, Fiach.' The commandant makes the young man's name sound vaguely obscene.

'Fiachna,' the young man says, contempt on his face.

'Tell them.'

The subaltern sighs, and says, as if reciting it, 'You got the job, Commandant, in honour of your loyal and dutiful service to the just cause of liberty during your time as a warder in Mountjoy. Michael Collins himself, God rest him, promoted you to the post.'

'Right you are, sonny buck. The Big Fella himself, may he rest in eternal peace.' Quinn turns back to O'Keefe and Albert. 'I was the inside man when the Dillon boys dollied themselves up in Tommy uniforms and tried to break out Seán Mac Eoin. I was meant to go out with them in the armoured car, only some plank in the party decided to light up the governor's office with his Enfield. Still and all, I done my service for the cause …'

'Will there be anything else, Commandant?'

'We're grand now, Frank. Thank you.'

'Fiachna.'

'*Fiachna.* What kind of name is that at all? Your mother mustn't have liked you much, giving you a name like that.'

The subaltern brushes through the curtains and is gone.

'I love winding them two toffs up, I do,' Quinn says.

O'Keefe smiles. 'It'd make the day shorter, sure.'

'That it does, Mr O'Keefe, that it does. Now, you're here to see some fellas, Father O'Dea tells me, about a missing boy?'

'Yes,' O'Keefe says, looking over to see if Just Albert will let him take the lead. Albert is impassive, so O'Keefe continues. 'The woman I'm … we're … working for has hired us to find her son. He's missing, and we believe the Mahon brothers might know something about it. Dominic Mahon, more specifically. We're not sure what he can tell us, but we'll give it a bash and see what we get.'

The commandant pours out the tea and then lights a cigarette, holding the box of Gold Flake out to his visitors. O'Keefe realises he has again forgotten to buy cigarettes and takes one, nodding his thanks. Just Albert lights one of his small cigars with a brass lighter.

'The Mahons. Right. Take your tea there, men, before it goes cold,' Quinn says, lifting his cup and slurping loudly.

They take the mugs from the tray, O'Keefe wondering what young Fiachna might have doctored it with, but deciding it would be rude not to chance it.

Quinn sets down his cup and picks up a manila file from his desk. 'I had this pulled when Father O'Dea jingled and said who yis wanted to see. A terrible shower, the Mahons. Are you lads sure yis need speak with the likes of them? They're not even proper republicans at all. A mob of dirty dockers who got us some guns in the Tan War and now sell to Dev's Irregulars on the other side. They'd sell their own mother if you wanted to buy her, I'm telling you. They've a hut all to themselves because none of the other republican lads will bunk up with them. I'd have one of me guards take you out there if he'd agree to go, but none of them will. And I don't imagine any would know where their hut was anyway.'

'What?' O'Keefe says. 'Your guards don't know which hut is the Mahons'?'

'And what do you mean by '*if*' they'd take us out?' Just Albert says. 'This is the mighty Free State army, isn't it? Can't you order them to take us?'

This time, O'Keefe does not mind Albert's question. He had been wondering the same thing.

Quinn takes a long drag on his cigarette and a sup of tea. 'Look, lads, I'm not proud to say this, but this camp is not run by me or by the Free State Army or any of my guards, and don't let no one tell you any different. All prisons are the same to some degree. The warders only run a jail with the consent of the men in their charge, if you get me. Sure, every warder wants to go home at night in one piece, and every lag wants what he thinks he's a right to, and the two come to a reasonable accommodation. But this place ...' Quinn shakes his head sadly. 'It's not at all easy being jailer to them that were your friends and comrades before this war started.'

The commandant slurps at his tea. 'These lot're hard men, soldiers, gunmen. Not a bit like your normal lag, I tell you. Your common and garden lags, most of the time, couldn't be arsed trying to escape because they're happy with three meals, a cot and a candle, which is more than most of them have on the outside.' He inhales on his cigarette, then points with it at the small, grime-streaked window.

'But these fellas? No. We control the outside here, but inside that wire, the republican boys say what's what and who's who, and that's that. Some of my guards, sure, they won't go in there for love or money, for fear of their lives. We're outnumbered for one. We need more guards than they've given us, and they've stuck me with too many prisoners, by jaysus. Only a week ago, didn't two of my lads venture in—and they can't go in armed, not on your life, not unless we send in a company of them—and didn't we find them two guards, two days later, mind, and they were stripped stark bollix naked and trussed up in an empty hut. And in the meantime two of the prisoners had kitted themselves up in the guards' gear and strolled out them front gates, cool as you please. Can't say it impressed the bossmen much. What the Big Fella—God rest him—would have said, for the love of Mary, if he was alive to see such a thing.'

Quinn stubs out his cigarette and continues. 'But them two guards were treated fair. They weren't beaten too bad, and they were given blankets at night and were fed and watered. But the rest of my men now, they won't set foot inside the wire since. It's a great big, poxy balls-up, lads, I'll be the first to admit. They sent too many Irregulars here and now there's no managing them. I can contain them, just about, but I can't manage them. Not at the moment. All them fellas, see, inside the wire—most of them anyway—they spent these last years fighting the Tans and Peelers … no offence, Mr O'Keefe, the Father told me you'd been a copper, and fair dues, I knew many fine ones in my days in the Joy.'

'None taken,' O'Keefe says, and drags on his cigarette, relishing the bite of the smoke at the back of his throat.

'Like I was saying, them lads, they all fought alongside the likes of me and some of my guards in the IRA, and we think they're traitors now and they think we're traitors and who knows who's right? But this is no normal prison at all. There's one lad, one of my guards, a youngfella just joined up—only last August mustered into the Free State Army, like most lads, for the wage, and who can blame him?—and wasn't he, a few weeks back, on one of the watchtowers? And didn't he look down, and who does he see?'

The commandant waits, as if his guests might venture a guess.

O'Keefe fills the silence. 'Who was it?'

Quinn smiles with satisfaction. 'Only his own shaggin' brother, down there inside the wire. And the brother, of course, sees my man, *his* brother, on the tower! And doesn't he start shouting up at him, *"Mickey, you traitorous bastard, you soup-takin' whore of the Crown, fuckin' bastard, come down from that tower and I'll sort your Turk cabbage out for good. Our mother never loved the sleeveen shite of you, she didn't."'*

Even Just Albert smiles at this.

'And didn't the brother wait down there every day for his brother to be on the tower so he could stand and abuse him, telling all his republican mates that that pig-shagger in the tower was once his brother, but is dead to him now as any scrap-rooting rat should be.' Quinn smiles and shakes his head. 'Lads, if this isn't the most loony shop of a prison, I don't know what is.'

'And what happened to your man in the tower?' Just Albert asks.

'I had him transferred out to the Curragh Camp. Sure, he wasn't himself, listening to that all day. Even his mother, who was happy with the wages he brought in, mind you, wouldn't speak to him once she found out he was standing guard over his brother. There were favourites in that family and no joke!'

O'Keefe shakes his head. Like everyone else in the country, he has heard stories of families divided by the Treaty—brothers, fathers, sons fighting on opposite sides. *There's no war like civil war, so the saying goes.*

'So that's just by way of letting you in on things, lads. I'll give you the number of the hut the Mahon boys are *supposed* to be in, but that doesn't mean they're still in it. Sure, half the names in the camp are false ones, and when we get notice to release a fella, we've rarely any idea if it's the actual fella being sent out under that name! The leaders inside there decide who gets released, and if we can't stand up, hand on heart, and say, "You're not the lad of this name", then, fuck it, men, we just cut them loose.'

O'Keefe nods. 'What else can you do?'

'Not a lot, Mr O'Keefe. Not a bleedin' lot, but it makes for bad jailing. I'm not proud of it, but then who knows if them fellas inside there aren't in the right about the Treaty? And here am I, locking them up, the same lads I fought with only a year ago.'

'We will be escorted then, inside the wire?' Just Albert asks, as if he cannot be bothered either way.

Quinn laughs. 'Will you fuck. Look, I can give you ten men or no men, but you'll be better on your own. If you've a mob of armed guards 'round you inside there, they'll only take you for Free Stater spooks and you'll get nothing from no man. If yis go in on your own, they'll know you're something different. My advice, once inside, is find Séamus Brennan. A Cork lad. A ranking general, apparently. He was a bossman when he was on our side against the Tans. Anyway, he seems to be in charge of things behind the wire. If he likes what you have to say, then yis're in. If not, we'll see you in a few minutes. Or next week, please God. You're not armed, are you?'

O'Keefe tells him they are not, thinking: *Séamus Brennan.* Where does he know that name from? There. He has it. *If it is the same man. A stroke of luck?* They'll soon see.

They leave the office and cross to the set of internal gates that leads into the camp proper. Quinn orders the pair of sentries to open the gates.

'Mind yourselves, lads. Take care you don't cause offence. Hard enough not to, though. Fellas are fierce touchy, all the same, these days.' He is smiling as he says this, but O'Keefe knows that he's serious behind the smile. *A prison governor afraid to enter his own prison.*

O'Keefe hopes the Brennan that Commandant Quinn has spoken of is the same man he thinks him to be.

21

Inside the wire, O'Keefe and Just Albert walk a worn dirt path that is, no doubt, a slick track of mud when it rains. Flimsy wooden huts are arrayed in rows on either side of the path, the smell of salt in the air from the sea a few hundred yards beyond the eastern-most stretch of wire. O'Keefe can hear the shushing of waves over the murmur and chat of men gathered outside the huts in loose groups. Some are perched on wooden pallets that serve as steps up to the huts, others sprawled on the dry grass; some read books and look up as the two men pass. Another group sits in a circle in the warm sun reciting phrases in Irish, while in front of a different hut the men play cards, but without the usual banter one might expect of sol-diers passing time. There is bitterness in the men's faces, their voices, and O'Keefe finds himself avoiding their eyes, as if one look might incite violence. He knows that he should stop at one of these huts close to the front gate to ask where he might find Séamus Brennan, but instead he finds himself moving deeper into the camp, furtively searching for a man or group of men who appear approachable. Behind him, Just Albert follows, hands in his pockets, coins clink-ing loudly over the hushed mumble of the interned, sounding out of place on this windswept wasteland of beach and prison. O'Keefe gathers his courage and turns off the path.

Smoke rises lazily from the tin chimney of the hut, and the men loitering in front of it go silent at their approach. O'Keefe gets the smell of boiled cabbage and bacon coming from the open door of the dwelling, and his stomach, independent of his fear, growls with hunger.

'Lads,' he says, unable to think of a more apt greeting. Something tells him that commenting on the weather will not be taken kindly by these men. They are tough-looking, variously sized, but lean and angry, skin roughened brown by wind and sun. They are much like the men O'Keefe remembers from his time in the army, lacking only the kit and uniform, but there is a silent rage that he can sense among them, smouldering just beneath their silence. None of them responds to his greeting.

'We're looking to speak with Séamus Brennan, if we could,' he tries, as their menace thickens in the humid sea air. The sound of waves and Albert's jingling coins. O'Keefe turns back to the doorman and stares until he ceases bothering the copper in his pockets. When he brings his gaze back to the men, Just Albert resumes it again, a smirk on his face that O'Keefe can feel but not see.

O'Keefe controls the bite of ire he feels towards Ginny's man, and this anger is replaced by a dawning fear. He wonders suddenly if he has arrested any of these men in the past. Shot at them? Had he, God forbid, killed one of their brothers or friends? It is not beyond the possible.

He swallows, his mouth dry. 'We're not police or Free State intelligence or any of the other things you're probably thinking. I've met Mr Brennan before and helped him once and I'm hoping he can help me now with a matter that's nothing to do with your being in here or with the war outside.'

'Everything has to do with the war going on outside if you've come to see a man who's inside,' one of the men says. He is in his twenties, with light green eyes and blond hair worn oiled and combed back off his forehead. He wears woollen army uniform trousers and braces over a cotton undershirt.

O'Keefe considers the man's words before speaking. Then: 'Fair enough. Maybe it does have to do with the war. It probably does. But I've no truck with your enemies, if that's a better way of putting it. If you could point me to Séamus Brennan's hut, I can explain it to him.'

'Why don't you explain it to us first,' the same man says.

'Because he just fuckin' told yis he'd rather explain it to the man himself is why,' Just Albert says from behind O'Keefe.

The words are spoken without rancour, but O'Keefe cringes inwardly. What had started as oblique negotiation, Ginny Dolan's man has given a shove towards confrontation. A confrontation they will not win.

'Look,' O'Keefe says, 'can one of you give him a message that Seán O'Keefe, out of Ballycarleton once, is here to see him? And then let him make up his own mind to see me or not. If he says to take the road out, we'll take it. That's all I'm asking.'

One of the group steps forward, big, his shirt sleeves rolled over thick forearms. 'I'll show ye the fucking road, I will,' he says.

The green-eyed man intervenes. 'Leave off. I'll take them to Brennan and see what he says. Follow me,' he says to O'Keefe and Albert, stepping past them. O'Keefe turns to follow, and after a long moment staring at the men, so does Just Albert. As they trail their guide between the maze of huts, deeper into the camp, O'Keefe wonders how close they had just come to a serious beating or worse.

After a few minutes they come to a hut in what O'Keefe takes to be the centre of the camp. It appears to be the farthest away from any of the guard towers and has purpose-built steps of scrap wood leading up to its doorway. Green-eyes disappears inside, leaving O'Keefe and Albert waiting in stilted silence and subject to wary, menacing interest from prisoners loitering in front of a neighbouring hut.

'Sergeant O'Keefe,' Séamus Brennan says, looking down from the doorway, and O'Keefe thanks a God he has ceased to believe in that it is the man he had hoped for.

Séamus Brennan had been the OIC of Brigade Intelligence of the West Cork Thirds, IRA, during the Tan War. O'Keefe had heard, or read in a file sometime before his demobilisation from the RIC, that Brennan had been promoted to OIC of Intelligence for the Southern Division, IRA, and had held that post until he'd sided with de Valera and the anti-Treaty Irregulars. O'Keefe had met him while investigating the murder of a young woman whose body had been left on a hillside outside of Drumdoolin in West Cork. He had found Brennan to be a ruthless, though personable, professional officer who had seemed to respect O'Keefe's detective work and had tried to recruit O'Keefe into the ranks of the IRA. O'Keefe had declined his offer, his loyalty having always been to his comrades in the RIC, but he had respected Brennan in return.

'Just plain Seán, now, Mr Brennan. General Brennan? It's been some time since I've held rank in any service at all.'

Brennan smiles. 'Haven't joined the Civic Guard then? I understand they're looking for men like yerself, boy. Men with policing experience.'

'I've done enough policing to last a man a lifetime, General. I'm doing a favour for … for a friend, is all. Could I speak with you privately, sir?'

There is a quiet, cunning charisma about Brennan that had impressed O'Keefe the first time they met, and it is still there now, though it is dimmed somewhat—by age, O'Keefe imagines, and by disillusionment. By captivity. Older than the average IRA man even then, Brennan has aged harshly in the three years since O'Keefe had seen him last. The intelligence man's hair has gone white and his face is drawn—sharp, haggard lines grid his eyes and mouth, and his hand appears clenched in a painful, awkward way. Brennan notices O'Keefe's attention to his hand and holds it up.

'Courtesy of our friends in the Auxiliaries, who kindly held it down and stamped on it until it became useless altogether. My claw of war.' Brennan laughs quietly. 'I've fresher wounds, sure, courtesy of former friends now working for the Free State. Some of them I trained in myself, boy. Imagine.'

'Nothing's too difficult to imagine these days, sir,' O'Keefe says.

'Sure, you said it before, the time I met you. *War makes strange bedfellows.* Strange enemies too.' There is a sadness in Brennnan's voice, but little of the rage O'Keefe senses in the younger men in the camp. 'Come inside, so, and I'll see if I can help ye. And then I'll try again to convince you to join us in our struggle.'

O'Keefe returns his smile. 'Thanks again for the offer, sir, but I've done my share of fighting. I don't think I'll take it up again.'

They follow him inside, where Brennan sits down at a table of sanded boards. He indicates two stools across from him at the table, and pours out tea from a pot heating on an army field stove. 'I was just having some myself lads, I hope you'll join me. I'd offer you a cigarette but we've not had a package in a week. The boys are convinced the guards are smoking their fags and spreading their mothers' jams on their Free State toast back in barracks, though it's likely our own boys have cut the rail lines or burned out a post office here and there, delaying deliveries.'

O'Keefe's face flushes with embarrassment. He should have brought an offering of some sort to the camp. When, he thinks, did a man ever visit a prison without bringing something in as a gift for the prisoner? Albert seems to read his thoughts—not for the first time, O'Keefe realises—and reaches into his pocket, coming out with a packet of the thin cigars he smokes. He hands them across to Brennan who takes them, laughing with surprise.

'That's kind of you, sir,' he says to Albert, who nods and lights one of his own. 'Now, boys, what can I help you with?'

O'Keefe explains it to him while Brennan relishes his cigar and sips tea, nodding occasionally.

When O'Keefe has finished, Brennan pinches out his quarter-smoked cigar and sets it on the table. 'The Mahons. Well, boy, it'd want to be a fairly close friend you're doing this favour for, to meet up with that mob for your troubles.'

'It is,' Just Albert says, and Brennan looks at him and then back to O'Keefe.

'I've heard stories about them,' O'Keefe says.

Brennan claps O'Keefe on the shoulder with his good hand. 'Wait til ye meet them, then. Sure, the stories haven't a patch on the real thing ...'

To O'Keefe's surprise, Just Albert has managed to ply their green-eyed escort with one of his cigars while O'Keefe had been saying his goodbyes to Brennan, and now they chat as they walk, the three men. They learn that his name is Eamonn Dunne, a Kerryman who had been captured after his column had been ambushed by Free State troops while sleeping in what they had thought to be a safe house. Dunne's brother, he tells them, had been shot down in his stockinged feet in the raid and is in Mountjoy Jail now, having only just survived his wounds. Dunne tells them that he is more concerned about getting a transfer to Mountjoy himself so that he might tend to his brother than he is in escaping and continuing the fight for the freedom of Ireland.

'Sure, fuck, lads,' he says, as they follow him between the huts towards the eastern, beach side of the camp, 'this whole lark'll be done with soon enough, and between yourselves and meself and the four walls—the wire, anyway,' he smiles, 'there's no way we'll win it. The Free State bastards know every hidey hole, every safe house in the country and every fucking trick in the book, I tell you. There's only so many ways you can fight a war like ours, and sure didn't the Free State fellas help *write* the bloody book.'

'The sooner it's done the better, I say,' Albert says. 'Too many fellas thinking they're top dogs, just because they're carrying a pistol and wearing a funny hat.'

'I'm telling you, it'll be over before you know it,' Dunne says, 'but not before it gets a whole shagging lot bloodier. There's boys in here so angry they'd rip the throat from your neck for talking like I'm talking now, and the Free Staters have got fierce savage since Mick Collins was shot. Before, sure, it could be like they were windy about shooting fellas they'd fought the Tans with, but not any more; not after they put the Big Fella in the ground. No, this war won't be won by us … or by them, really, when you think about it. But that never stopped lads from keeping on shooting each other just for spite.'

O'Keefe finds himself agreeing. He had fought in just such a futile, needless war. He had lost his own brother in it. For what? For fuck all. He tells this to Dunne, and also tells him that he is better off locked up and out of it.

'If I can get the brother back to his health, please God, then I'll be better off altogether and damn the rest. I'm sick of the whole thing, I am.'

'You and the rest of the bleedin' country,' Just Albert says.

'The rest of the country don't matter a shite to most of the boys in this camp once they've a chance to plug some fucker who's called them traitors.' They come to a stop in front of a relatively isolated hut. 'Here you are, and I'll leave you to it. And thanks for the cigar, friend. Sure, I knew I'd come upon a kind-hearted Jackeen one day, I did.' He smiles at the men and leaves them.

The hut is in the farthest, northeast corner of the camp, close to the inner perimeter fence. Through the two sets of wire and just beyond the tracks of the Dublin–Belfast railway line, O'Keefe can view the sea. The beach before it is long with low tide, the wet sand reflecting sunlight as if it had been varnished. Nature has been rough with the dwelling and sea wind has sandblasted the outer walls, scouring paint from the door.

Two men sit on a sea trunk that serves as a bench to the left of the pallet steps. One of them is smoking a needle-thin cigarette rolled in newsprint. They are smaller, thinner than most of the men they have seen in the camp. Dublin men, O'Keefe thinks, remembering the whippet-like lads he had served with in the army, many of them tenement-reared, and weighing little more than the kit and rifle they were made to carry, but carried nonetheless.

The IRA had been for many years the preserve of middle-class men and rural farm labourers; of intellectuals and the sons of generations of dispossessed and evicted subsistence farmers. But the civil war had widened the pool of fighting men on both sides of the Treaty and this, inevitably, included men like the ones seated on the sea trunk.

O'Keefe does not bother with formalities. 'Is the bossman in?'

The man on the left—in his twenties, his flat cap pulled low over his eyes, black razor-shadow on his angled features—takes a pull on his roll-up.

'Who wants to know?'

Before O'Keefe can answer, Just Albert steps in front of O'Keefe and leans down until he is at eye level with the man. He says something in a low voice that O'Keefe cannot hear and then stands back, allowing the man to stand and enter the hut. The second man watches but says nothing, avoiding Just Albert's eyes.

The man in the cap returns to the doorway. 'He's inside.'

Just Albert indicates for O'Keefe to lead the way, and O'Keefe nods his thanks for having their passage smoothed. He is growing weary of the jousting this day has required. He had forgotten how difficult investigating anything in Ireland could be; forgotten just how guarded and suspicious of intent eight hundred years of foreign rule could make a people. And the recent years of war had made things worse. When he had been in uniform, there had been people in any town who would discreetly aid an investigation, if it were thought to be morally right. There were also those who were happy to put the finger on another man so long as their names were left out of any testimony, thus, at very least, providing the intelligence that any investigating police require. But there were few who would willingly volunteer anything to a common man in a suit. Ireland had never had great success with plain-clothes police detectives since they were thought to be little more than informants or spies when out of uniform. So O'Keefe expects little from the Mahons. *A common man in a common suit is what I am now and nothing more*, O'Keefe thinks, and he feels a great distance between his life now and his past life as an RIC man.

He enters the hut, Just Albert behind him, and slowly his eyes adjust to the dim interior light. Three men are seated at a table in the centre of the room, and through an open doorway behind them O'Keefe can see a room housing bunks, all of them neatly made with turned-down sheets that would not have been out of place in a police or army barracks. Or a prison, he thinks, noticing how everything in the room in which he stands is tidied or hung away on hooks or displayed on purpose-built shelves. The military discipline of the men in the other huts could hardly be more rigorous than the penal tidiness these men had embraced during various spells in Dublin's jails.

'Gentlemen,' O'Keefe says. 'I was hoping to speak with Dominic Mahon if I could.' As he speaks, he realises there are two other men in the room besides those at the table. They are young and big and one of them has a flat, smashed nose like a boxer's. They move now and take up a place on either side of the entry door behind O'Keefe and Just Albert.

'If you could, who would you be?' one of the men at the table says. O'Keefe judges the speaker to be Mahon himself because the other two look at him when he speaks, as if to take their lead.

'My name is Seán O'Keefe. I've been hired by …'

'What'd you call yourself?' a second man asks. He has oiled, black hair, a pencil-thin moustache and a pile of newsprint roll-ups on the table in front of him.

'Seán O'Keefe …'

The third man speaks to his mates at the table. He is stocky and fit, shoulders and biceps straining his shirt fabric. Built like Just Albert, O'Keefe briefly thinks, only from slinging crates off ships rather than dumbbells. 'It looks the same, it does.'

It? O'Keefe frowns.

'Couldn't be …' The black-haired man squints with concentration, focusing on O'Keefe's face.

'He's the cut of him, I'm fuckin' tellin' yeh,' the stocky man says now. 'Why don't yeh ask him?'

'Ask him what?' Just Albert says, and O'Keefe can hear the smirk in his voice.

'You're no relation to Daniel O'Keefe are you? Big, strapping G-Division copper?' the first man says, the one O'Keefe assumes to be Dominic Mahon.

'I … well, I am.'

'Holy jaysus, the chances of it …' the stocky man says, smiling in a way O'Keefe does not like.

O'Keefe sees Dominic Mahon nod. Sensing movement behind him, he turns, into the arms of one of the men behind him, who links his hands together in front of O'Keefe, squeezing him tightly in a bear hug and lifting him off his feet.

'What in the name of Jesus…?' O'Keefe says, before his breath is viced from his lungs. He writhes against the man's grip and sees Just Albert move now, skipping for the doorway, towards the big man still stationed there. For a moment, O'Keefe thinks Albert is fleeing the hut, and the man at the door thinks the same, taking two steps forward as if to cut off his escape.

'Albert!' O'Keefe manages, but Just Albert ignores him, his hand going inside his suit coat and coming out with a stunted club the length of his forearm, stepping inside the big man's lunge and using his wrist to swing the club in a short arc. Lightning quick, the sound of the club on skull is like cracking wood, and the man's stunned momentum takes him forward past the grappling O'Keefe and face down onto the table where the three men sit, its legs collapsing, the three men shoving back and standing to enter the fray.

The stocky docker is closest to the captive O'Keefe, and he moves forward and throws a telegraphed, windmill right. O'Keefe sees it, his arms still pinned at his sides, and lowers his head into the punch, the fist slamming into his forehead. An explosion of white stars erupts in O'Keefe's eyes, and he hears bones snap in the man's hand, but the man brings his fist back to swing again. As he does, Just Albert feints a headshot with the club, and instead swings it low and up into the man's groin with a sickening *thud*. The man doubles as if hinged, his punch dying in the air, and vomits in a cascade that splatters O'Keefe's legs and boots.

Stars clearing in his eyes now, O'Keefe senses that the man holding him has turned his head to follow Albert's progress, tracking Ginny's man as he moves with his club to the black-haired man with the moustache. This man has a knife but Just Albert advances, as if oblivious, with a relentless, practiced aggression.

As if unconscious, O'Keefe lolls his head forward and then hurls it back with all the force he can bring to bear. The back of his skull connects with the right side of his captor's face and O'Keefe can feel the the big man's cheek shatter and collapse. Yellow bolts of pain shoot through O'Keefe's head and neck and he nearly faints as the man releases him, vertigo claiming him, falling, falling.

O'Keefe hits the duckboard floor hard on his hands and knees, the hut spinning around him. Holding his face, the big man lifts a leg to swing a kick at O'Keefe, who sees it but cannot move. The boot is halfway to his ribs when Albert's spit-shined brogues dance past on the floor under O'Keefe's pain-blurred gaze and there is a resounding crack and the sound of a heavy body dropping.

From O'Keefe's vantage point on the floor, Ginny Dolan's man is a whir of fluid, violent motion, feinting again with the club as the black-haired man swings his knife, allowing Albert inside the arc of the blade to jab his club into the man's throat, stopping the knifeman's breath on its way out, a sucking gawp in place of the breath as the assailant drops to his knees. The knife clanks to the floor and the man's hands scrabble at his neck, face going bright red and then just as quickly, death-pale grey. Just Albert kicks the blade away to a corner of the room and swings the club into the man's face, obliterating his nose in a mist of blood.

O'Keefe raises himself to his knees, nausea welling in his own throat. As he rises, his eyes catch movement in the doorway and register the two men from outside entering. He stumbles forward and lifts an upturned chair from the floor. On his knees, he swings the chair, splintering it across the chest and shoulders of the first of the two to enter the hut. Without pause, he brings the remains of the chair to bear on the second man, swinging wildly and catching him in the stomach. He brings it back over his head to swing again when it is taken from his hands from behind. Instinctively, he covers his head, but the blow he is expecting does not come.

'A hand up, Mr O'Keefe?'

Just Albert stands over him with his hand extended, his face glowing with the healthy flush of moderate exercise, as if he had just returned from a country walk. The club is nowhere to be seen and O'Keefe assumes he has returned it to its place inside his jacket. He takes Albert's hand and allows himself to be pulled to his feet.

Surveying the scene, O'Keefe sees the man who had held him sitting with his back to the wall of the hut, his hands pressed to his shattered cheek-bone. Three other men lay on the hut's duck-boards, the short, stocky man rolling from side to side, clutching his hands between his legs, a high-pitched moan, like a wounded dog's, emanating from deep in his throat. The two others lie on the floor unmoving, and O'Keefe says a silent prayer that Ginny Dolan's man has not killed them. The two men they had encountered outside stand with their palms held out, looking across the room to their boss for guidance. To O'Keefe they appear as if they are pleading for mercy. O'Keefe follows their eyes to where Dominic Mahon has sat down and watches him light one of the needle-thin fags.

Exhaling, Dominic Mahon tells the two to move the wounded men. 'They need see the sawbones. Take Jimmy first …' Mahon prods his unmoving comrade with his boot, '… and then come back for the others, but don't disturb us here. We've things to discuss it seems, wha?' He smiles now at O'Keefe, and indicates the one remaining chair.

O'Keefe rights the chair and sits down, the pain in his head beginning to throb as adrenaline surges and ebbs in his veins. Just

Albert takes up a place behind his chair, standing like a sentinel over his shoulder.

'You're Dominic Mahon, aren't you?' O'Keefe says, suddenly worrying that the man they had come to see might be among the unconscious. And then, the words emerging unbidden: 'And if you say *"who wants to know?"* I'll kick your teeth in.'

'No doubting you were a Peeler, so, and your father's son,' Dominic Mahon says.

O'Keefe leans forward in his chair. 'What do you mean by that?'

'If you don't know, then I'm hardly the one to tell you.'

His fists balling instinctively, O'Keefe repeats his question. 'Are you Dominic Mahon?'

'Of course I fuckin' am. Who'd you think I was? You only need ask your gorilla, Albert there. He's known me for how long, Al?'

'Too long,' Just Albert says.

'Now, now, no way to speak to an auld buddy who sends every sea captain, every dirty deckhand and ship's passenger the way of Mrs Dolan's shop for nothing but kindness's sake.'

'And ten pound a year at Christmas.'

'One good turn deserves another, me auld flower.'

O'Keefe cuts in. 'This needn't have happened. Look, all we need is to ask you a few questions. Nothing to incriminate you. We're looking for a boy is all …'

'Sure, Ginny Dolan can find you one of them any time you've the fancy …'

'Keep it up, to fuck,' Just Albert says, 'and you'll be sipping your dinner, Dominic.'

'And always so cordial, we were, in the past, Albert.'

'Past is past,' Just Albert says. 'We're looking for Mrs Dolan's Nicky. You've to tell us what we need to know.' Albert reaches down and drags one of the supine men to the door of the hut by his collar and drops him outside. He does the same with the second, each unconscious body dropping like a sack of spuds onto the hard ground. Then he closes the hut door. 'Or I will hurt you like you've never been hurt, Dominic. So stop taking the piss and listen to what the man says.'

Dominic Mahon locks eyes with Just Albert for a long moment. He does not appear frightened. Finally, he turns to O'Keefe and smiles. 'Cigarette, gentlemen?'

O'Keefe reaches across, accepts one and takes a light. He is not as big as O'Keefe had imagined, Dominic Mahon. Mid-forties, he reckons, with cold blue eyes and red hair oiled back off his freckled forehead. An expensive white shirt and collar with cufflinks in the shape of anchors at his wrists. It has been a long time, O'Keefe thinks, since this man has slung a gaff.

'Now, first off, why didn't yis tell me yis were working for Ginny Dolan? We needn't have cracked any heads at all.' He smiles again. 'Sure, I've known Ginny for years, so yis can save your hard talk, Albert, for your Saturday sweetheart. Any problem of Ginny's, I'm happy to help with.'

O'Keefe turns to look at Just Albert, gauging his response. He is relieved when Ginny's man laughs. 'You just answer Mr O'Keefe's questions here and there'll be no more hard talk.'

'Grand so.'

'Grand,' Albert says, taking out one of his cigars and lighting it.

Turning back to Mahon, O'Keefe slips the recent photograph of Nicholas Dolan from his jacket and hands it to the docker. 'Mrs Dolan's son,' he says. 'You knew him, I take it. He's missing now. Fifteen years old, looks young for his age. You supplied him with a gun some months ago. I need the name of his contact in the Irregulars.'

Dominic Mahon exhales smoke and laughs. 'You don't want much, do yeh?'

'It will never come back to you, Mr Mahon. You have my word on that.'

Mahon shakes his head. 'I couldn't give a tinker's bollix if it does. Them poxy *Irregular* ...' Mahon says the word with a disdain

O'Keefe recognises from his time in the police; the same way some men once called him *Peeler*, '... bastards cut me and the lads loose as quick as did their mates in the Free State army. After all the blasters and barkers we got them in the Tan War. Ungrateful bla'guards. That boy was the end of it for us Mahons on the docks, as far as guns went. I was stupid to use him. I could get hold of nobody and I thought maybe he could tempt his bosses into paying out for a few crates of Webleys and Lee–Enfields we'd liberated from an English boat. The shipment meant for the Free Staters and all, but that lad ...'

O'Keefe senses Just Albert tense behind him, and so does Dominic Mahon, who changes his tone mid-sentence.

'He was a grand youngfella. That's why I used him. You say he looks young for his age, but he was older than his years in more ways than one.'

'Is,' Just Albert says.

'Wha'?'

'*Is* older than his years. Not *was*.'

Exasperation sharpens his words. The docker king is not used to being so freely contradicted. 'For fuck sake, Al. I didn't mean nothing by it. Jesus, since when did you become such a sore prick? You used to be a good auld skin, good for a giggle, Albert.'

'Since Nicky went missing and I found out you had something to do with it.'

'Now, look here. I had nothin' to do with his going where-in-fuckin'-ever he's bunked off to. I told you. I shouldn't have given him the gun, fair enough; shouldn't have used him as a runner neither, but I gave him the gun and that was the last I seen of him. I'd never want any harm come to him, for jaysus sake. Ginny and I have been pals for years, so we have.'

O'Keefe attempts to bring Mahon back to his story. He knows how easy it is to accidentally slip into the past tense when speaking of missing persons. He has done it himself. 'It's all right, Albert.' He turns back to Dominic. 'And did Nicky get the gun to his bosses in the Irregulars then, Mr Mahon? Did you hear from them about the shipment?'

'I did not. Sure, didn't the youngfella take it into school with him?'

'He did.'

Mahon smiles ruefully. 'And he gave my name to the priest, didn't he?'

'He did. How did you find out?'

'You just told me. But not to worry. There's no way I would have harmed a hair on that boy's head, even if I had known. You'd never have time for anything else anyway, if you spent all your time plugging touts in Dublin. They're thick as fleas in a knacker's horse blanket these days, young O'Keefe. And he only a boy like any of me own.' Mahon nods in a sentimental manner.

'Lucky for you, you didn't,' Just Albert says.

'Give it a rest, Al. I'm heartscalded with all your threats. I know you're in a tither about Ginny's boy, but you know as well as I do you won't touch a hair of me head ...'

'You sure of that?' Albert says.

'... for fear of what I could do, even from here, to Ginny's business, so leave out the rough talk, I'm telling you. I'm weary of it. And yes I'm fuckin' sure of it, so leave it out. Even dead, I'm dangerous to you and Ginny.'

O'Keefe says, 'There's no possibility of any of your people having done something to the boy?'

'Jaysus, do yeh listen or not? I told you I didn't know for certain he shopped us up to the padre—who no doubt then gave us up to the Free Staters—til you just told me. I did suspect, mind. But I'm a fair man and I'd never have hurt a man—a boy—on the basis of a sniff only. And none of my people would. Sure, they'd be dead men themselves if they done something like that on a mere notion. I'll say it again: I never hurt nobody on a rumour or a feeling in me gut. Not often, anyway. And no young boy, surely.'

'Why did you suspect that he'd told Father O'Dea?' O'Keefe asks.

'Look, everybody knows how cozy that padre does be with the Free Staters, and weren't we raided by Free State intelligence not long after I'd heard about Nicholas bringing the gun to school? Just put two and two together. They chucked us off the docks first and in here shortly after. Sure, the Free State boys think they don't need the likes of us any more on the docks. Think they've gone legitimate all of a sudden, when two year ago there was nothing those pompous gits now sitting in the government wouldn't buy off us Mahons. They call us criminals when the only difference between ourselves and the gun merchants they do be dealing with now instead of us is volume.'

'Who did you want Nicky to give the gun to, Mr Mahon?'

Dominic Mahon speaks as if he has stopped caring. He looks old suddenly to O'Keefe. Things, O'Keefe suspects, have not gone the way they were supposed to for Dominic.

From his father and grandfather Mahon had inherited an empire of easy profit and power that extended far beyond the docks. An empire that had thrived on the bureaucratic labyrinth of port customs and an ancient resentment of a foreign power ruling Ireland. It was a corruption justified by British rule and enforced by thuggery and graft. O'Keefe suspects that Dominic Mahon had not counted on the idealists in either camp, Free State or Irregular, and that he couldn't imagine anyone doing anything if it wasn't for personal profit. Idealists were dangerous to Mahon because he could not predict what they might do. His high times on the docks are done, O'Keefe thinks, and he appears to know this.

Mahon says, 'O'Hanley. Good auld Felim O'Hanley, the last of the rebel schoolmaster gunmen, thank fuck. The rest are mostly banged up in here or in the Joy. But yis'll never find him. The Free Staters have been looking for ages and haven't had a nibble. He might be out of the country for all I know.'

'Not when there's a war on, surely,' O'Keefe says. He has heard about O'Hanley. A grainy photograph of the rebel's face had graced the cork notice-board in O'Keefe's RIC barracks for most of the Tan War, O'Hanley having been wanted for the kill-ings of several men in the army and police, all the time continuing to teach in various schools around Dublin, including Xavier for a time. A lethal operator, but one apparently cultured and intelligent. Now O'Hanley was gaining a reputation for being even more elusive than Michael Collins, and O'Keefe imagines that this does not sit well with the likes of Free State army intelligence. He can-not imagine a gunman as ideologically motivated, as highly skilled and widely feared as O'Hanley, sitting out the war in Boston or Glasgow.

'Ah, who knows?' Mahon says. 'Sure, O'Hanley was already courting the big gunrunners before all this with Nicky anyway. Try asking one of them. There's a fella works out of Burton's Hotel, used to work for the British Army Disposal Board selling on the surplus from the war in Europe. He ran some of his guns through us on the docks, but then cut us out as well when Collins and the lads told him to. Now there's soldiers unloading ships my family's unloaded for years. I know for a fact that Nicky used to run mes-sages for O'Hanley to that fucker.'

'This man, this gun dealer. He's in Dublin now?' O'Keefe says.

'Far as I know. He's meant to be organising something big for the Irregulars, though fuck knows where O'Hanley'll get the shekels. But then I've heard this fella's supplying the Free Staters as well, so don't listen to me. Playing both sides against the middle of his purse. Like something I'd have done meself once.' Mahon smiles and drops another tiny cigarette end onto the floor.

'And have you a name for him?' O'Keefe asks.

'Happy to give it. *Murphy*. No one knows his first name, and everyone thinks it's gas that this proper English squire is called Murphy, but that's what he goes by. It might even be his real name, who knows, but?'

'Who knows …'? O'Keefe says, standing, feeling suddenly light-headed and weak. 'Thank you for your help, Mr Mahon.'

'Not a bother, young O'Keefe. But I'll say this and say no more. Them fellas Albert put down with his club? Them fellas aren't half as forgiving as I am. I'd mind they don't get released out of here any time soon…' Dominic Mahon looks at Just Albert now, '… and if they do I'd not want to be round town to meet them. No telling what they might do.' He turns his attention back to O'Keefe. 'And you, Mr O'Keefe. You're not as hard a man as your father, so take care where you stick your boot in. Albert's not your shadow. He mightn't be around every time you've need of him …'

O'Keefe chooses to ignore Mahon, thinking he is trying to salvage some residual dignity from the sad shambles of his day. A king, his army routed, forced to bow to two spear-throwers.

'Mind we don't wet ourselves,' Just Albert says, turning and leaving the hut.

They make their way in the general direction of the inner camp gate through the maze of huts, O'Keefe's head throbbing, Albert jingling coins in his pockets and drawing hard stares from the men outside the huts. The doorman seems to enjoy this and smiles, throwing out the odd wink to any man whose face shows particular menace. As if he owns the place, O'Keefe thinks, wondering if such an attitude of invincibility comes from confidence or complete disregard for one's life and health.

But O'Keefe does not have the energy to be annoyed with him. He feels hollow and deflated, unlike how he would have felt in his past life as a constable when he received information that might further an investigation. It is another sign, he thinks, of how distant is his life now from that life. Like another man had lived it altogether.

'Thanks, anyway, Albert,' he says, as much to stop himself thinking as anything. 'For stepping in, back there. I never saw it coming.'

'I could've told you we'd be scrapping all right. Could have told you yesterday.'

'And why didn't you then?'

'Would you have listened?'

O'Keefe shrugs. 'Probably not. How did you know?'

Just Albert smiles. 'You're the cut off your auldfella is how I knew. I reckoned they'd clock it soon enough and there'd be bother then.'

'Clock what?'

'That you're your father's son.'

'And why would that matter to the Mahons?' O'Keefe stops as they reach the inner gates of the camp.

''Cause your auldfella couldn't abide them Mahons one bit. He ...' Albert pauses as if considering what to say.

'What?'

'Look, there's a load we don't know about our fathers and more we don't want to. Your father's a decent auld skin, for a copper, and let's leave it at that. If it's anything to you, Mr O'Keefe, I don't even know who *my* father was ...'

22

The town of Balbriggan, where O'Keefe's sister Sally had been a teacher until she'd had her first baby, is a fishing and mill town on the Irish Sea, some two miles south of Gormanston camp. As O'Keefe enters the town—Albert riding pillion—he takes note of the rebuilding on both sides of the road and of the new whitewashed cottages down one of the lanes. By the harbour, he has heard, are the scorched shells of the hosiery mills torched two years previously when Auxiliaries and Black and Tans had run amok after the shooting of an RIC man and his brother in a local pub. O'Keefe had heard that the incident had more to do with too much drink and too many guns in one small room than any kind of political assassination of the sort suffered by so many of his former RIC colleagues but the result had been the same. A town sacked, two local men tortured and bayoneted to death by Crown forces and left in the ashes of the town square while Balbriggan's inhabitants had fled to the countryside in terror. Hundreds jobless. Hundreds homeless. O'Keefe knows that similar things are still happening throughout the country, but it is Irishmen doing it this time.

His sister lives in a small cottage off Chapel Street, and she cries joyfully and hugs O'Keefe when she sees him. She has filled out some in her face and bust—the baby, he imagines—but with this appears younger to O'Keefe. Her hair is the same shade of brown as his own and she is tall like he is, but she resembles Peter more than him, the lines around her eyes, like Peter's, the etchings of a natural disposition to laughter.

He thinks back to when he had last seen her. *Five years ago? Six?* He had been laid up in the Army hospital at Victoria Barracks in Cork and she had taken the train down to visit him. At the time he'd hardly been able to speak, so ill had he been with blood poisoning; so numb with grief and guilt over their brother's death. And then, after returning to his duties in the RIC, he had received a regretful letter from Sally telling him that since he was a police-man he could not attend her wedding. Her husband hailed from a large, republican family and, as a member of the 'Crown forces', he would not have been welcome. The letter had angered O'Keefe. But Sally is a mother now—eager to show off her baby—and he is no longer a Peeler. *Bygones be bygones*, he thinks, feeling at ease for the first time in days, taking tender comfort in the warmth of his sister's embrace. How long has it been since he'd been held in another's arms? It's like food, he is suddenly certain, food or drink. Any kind of affection at all. And he is starved of it.

'Come in, come in,' Sally says, taking her brother by the arm. 'You don't know how happy you've made me calling like this. There's not a day goes by I don't pray for you and wish you well. And your friend, please ...' She takes Albert's arm in her other hand. 'Please come in. You're very welcome, Mr ...?'

'Albert. Just Albert's grand, Missus.'

'Mister Albert then,' Sally says, leading the two men into the cottage. 'You're very welcome to our home, Mr Albert.'

Just Albert sits with Sally's baby, Matilda, in his arms by the low turf fire. The cottage is neat, clean and modern—there is fresh, piped water and a large Belfast sink; a modern cooking range where Sally labours over boiling spuds, vegetables and a silverside of corned beef. She chats to O'Keefe as she works, turning now and again to smile at him, as if she cannot believe he is there. He is aware that she does not speak of their father in front of a stranger, and also neatly dodges any talk about his time as an RIC man, but he does not mind this. She talks mainly of herself, the baby and her husband, calling her husband 'himself' as if not yet ready to name him to O'Keefe, until he has met him; until they have shaken hands and seen that each are men loved by Sally and must, therefore, accommodate one another. O'Keefe, seated at the oilclothed table, steaming tea mug in front of him, is willing.

His own conversation is as loose and easy as it has been for months as he chats about the Cunningham family, and the Daly family in Cork, whom she has met, and how they now number six children and that Sally would want to be getting on with things if she hoped to catch them up. He tells her how Jim Daly, his oldest friend from the RIC, has taken a job with the Civic Guard down in Cork, and could they not see what trouble they were letting themselves in for, the Free Staters, admitting a known labour agitator and malingerer like Daly into the ranks of their newly formed national police force? Even Just Albert laughs at this, a wry chuckle, as he jogs the baby on his knee.

In the brief silence that follows their laughter, O'Keefe notices how contented the baby appears in Albert's care, smiling up into the doorman's mug—the red jag of beard under his bottom lip, the flattened nose that ends in a point, the knife-sharp cheek-bones, like those of a prizefighter. The baby gurgles and grips the doorman's scarred knuckles, trying to raise herself up on bowed legs.

'You're a natural there, Albert. I'd never have thought,' O'Keefe says.

Just Albert smiles, but at the baby. 'Sure, she's not the first babby I've bounced on me knee, Mr O'Keefe.'

'Minding brothers and sisters?' Sally asks.

O'Keefe waits for Albert's response, interested to hear the answer. He knows nothing of the man, thinking that he was as likely to have been hewn from the rubble of old Montgomery

Street as anything else. And in a way, he learns that he is not entirely wrong in this thinking.

'No, I've no brothers or sisters, not that I know of. Though loads over the years that were like brothers and sisters to me. No, more's the time I've sat up with the babbies while their mothers worked. Once it was quiet enough in me own work I was happy to do it.'

'And what work is it you do, Mr Albert?' Sally asks, straining the water from the boiled potatoes and leaving them under a towel to steam, a kindly lilt in the question that masks an Irish woman's intrusion into another's affairs.

O'Keefe cringes inwardly, embarrassed suddenly for Albert, though the man himself appears unconcerned.

'I work for Mrs Dolan,' he says, and O'Keefe realises that Albert assumes that his employer is known to all and any.

'A fine house, it's said,' Sally tells Albert, and it surprises O'Keefe that his sister has heard of the woman.

'It is. I mind the shop for Mrs Dolan, keep things ticking over. I could be doing anything. Minding the nippers can be one of them jobs comes along with it, given the number of girls in Mrs Dolan's employ. You might've heard tell of Monto Babies …'

Just Albert stops and waits for Sally's response. Monto Babies, the children born to prostitutes in the district and raised communally by the madams and working girls alike. Some—*many*, O'Keefe imagines—end up in the trade themselves, or on the fringes of it, acting as cleaners, doormen or cooks in the brothels. Other move in the criminal half-light of the city as pocket-gougers, housebreakers or strong-arm robbers. The fortunate among these, however, leave the morning-quiet Monto lanes for school each day or are bought apprenticeships with the pooled earnings of their many 'mothers' and 'aunties', becoming skilled workers in the various trades, and even professions, Dublin offers.

Dubliners are oddly compassionate towards the Monto children, seeing them as native sons and daughters of their city, little

different in many ways from their own except for their parent-
age. They are poorer, certainly, the strange Dublin logic goes,
and it is sad that they are bastards, but they are loved by somebody, most of the time, and by Holy God and Our Lady all the
time and, sure, isn't that enough? Others, of course, view them
as the scum tide of the night-time streets, criminal, illegitimate
and barely human. But these people, O'Keefe imagines, are in
the minority.

Sally says, 'I have heard of them, Mr Albert, and I've always
heard they're well-loved and minded.'

'Not all of them,' the doorman says, 'but most. I was one meself,
sure. Mrs Dolan took me in when I was three years of age, though
I hardly remember it. She tells the story herself, now and again, of
how I was running wild in all the weathers with only a strip of a
shirt on me back and riddled with nits. Fighting dogs in the lanes
for scraps of grub. Me own mother, God knows what became of
her. Maybe she left Monto, got out of it, or maybe she died, but the
best thing ever happened me was Mrs Dolan coming along. She
was working herself then …'

He looks up to gauge Sally's reaction, and Sally smiles kindly at
him. '… But she took me into the house where she worked: Mrs
McDowell's house. And she and the other girls fed and reared me.
When she set herself up, she brought me with her and there I've
been ever since.'

Sally nods. 'She sounds a fine woman, Mr Albert.'

'She is.'

'And Nicholas, Albert. Is he a Monto baby as well?' O'Keefe
asks, thinking it might matter somehow.

'No, he's her own.' Just Albert looks over at O'Keefe now, his
face serious again, the hardness emerging like something solid and
malign floating to the surface of a calm sea. 'Her only natural child.
And that's why we must find him.'

O'Keefe nods, showing Albert he understands. Nicholas is Mrs
Dolan's son. So, in his own way, is Just Albert. For Albert, O'Keefe

realises, the search for Nicholas is no mere job for the madam. It is the search for a brother.

At the door of the cottage, Sally hugs O'Keefe and takes the baby from Just Albert, shaking his hand warmly.

'If you're ever passing through Balbriggan, Mr Albert, don't be a stranger. Matilda and I would love to see you again. And John, my husband. Wouldn't we Tildy?' The baby curls a loose strand of Sally's hair in her fist.

'And you, Seáneen,' she says, 'you must come out and stay. And meet John. There's more than one fine public house in this town. You'd like him ... despite past things. And he'd like you, I know he would.'

O'Keefe looks away, for the first time since he had arrived. 'He's not ... involved any more, then?'

Sally puts her hand on his forearm. 'No, thank God. He works every hour the Lord sends him. Carpenters are in demand, putting the town back together, so there's no shortage of work for the moment. His brother Danny is in the Free State Army now, down in Limerick we think. There's other brothers of his who lean strongly to the anti-Treaty side. John's hardly sure what he believes these days, but that Irishmen killing Irishmen is not the way to go about things.'

'Wise man,' O'Keefe says.

'And a good man. You must come, really. You can swim down at the baths on the beach. You'd like him, Seán, you would.'

There is a small desperation in his sister's voice, and O'Keefe knows that whether he comes to like the man or not, for Sally's sake he will act as if he does.

'Promise you'll come and stay when you finish your work with Mr Albert,' she says.

O'Keefe kisses her on the cheek and then kisses his niece.

'I promise,' he says, neither brother nor sister once making any mention of their father or his illness.

23

O'Keefe and Just Albert enter Burton's Hotel just after six that evening, stopping at the reception desk where an attractive, red-haired woman smiles and asks if she can help them.

O'Keefe smiles back. He cannot help himself and it does not feel forced. 'We're looking to speak with Mr Murphy, please. He's staying here, we believe. If you could give us his room number ...'

At the mention of Murphy's name, the woman brightens. 'Oh, of course, Mr Murphy is a guest here. And who can I say is asking for him?'

'If you could give us his room number, we could make our own way up.' O'Keefe notices a hotel porter loitering by the lift, listening in on the exchange at the desk.

'Of course,' the woman says, still smiling, 'let me get your names and then I'll send Michael up with a message.'

'We wouldn't want to be any trouble to yourself or your porter, Miss,' O'Keefe says, unable to stop himself from casting a quick glance down at the woman's ring finger. It is bare and O'Keefe is oddly pleased by this, though he should be annoyed with her for impeding their progress. It hardly matters anyway, he thinks. A woman as pretty as this receptionist surely has a fella somewhere—some earnest bank clerk or student with fine prospects to take her to dances. She is beautiful, though not in a conventional way, he muses, possessing a certain maturity. *Poise?*

O'Keefe cannot come up with a word for it. Depth, perhaps, and he leaves it at that.

'It's no trouble at all, if you'd just give your names here ...'

'Or you could just give us the room number.'

'Well,' she says, 'actually, he's just gone into the dining-room for his evening meal. If you'd give me your name, I could ask ...'

'We'll find him there then.' Just Albert cuts across the woman, startling her for a second, her rich green eyes widening, the smile freezing on her face and then settling on Albert as if assessing him. Her eyes go to the porter who is standing by the lift, and the porter turns nervously away.

O'Keefe feels the heat rise to his face, realising what a pair they must make—the muscled, dandified Monto thug and himself—constabulary-tall with the knotted ridge of bayonet scar running down the side of his face and the thick moustache he wears in a vain effort to distract from the injury. In uniform he'd never worried about what physical impression he made upon people, his bottle-green tunic and peaked cap, baton and side-arm serving as a form of disguise and armour, lending a comforting anonymity to all his interactions. But here he is now, a battered nothing of a man in a road-dusty trenchcoat and trilby, conning for a room number with a whore madam's headbreaker behind him.

'It's just that he's having his tea ...'

'That's grand, Miss,' O'Keefe says. 'We'll find him ourselves. It's grand ...'

He turns and follows Just Albert into the hotel dining-room, noting the white tablecloths, the heavy silver cutlery and crystal goblets. Burton's is known throughout Ireland for putting on a fine feed for a reasonable price. It is the kind of hotel used by wealthy cattle dealers, bank officials, creamery owners up from the country. The IRA had used it for years as safe haven and staging point in their fight against the Crown in Dublin as much for the food, O'Keefe imagines, as for its sympathetic, republican-minded owner. It had suffered some damage during the battle for

O'Connell Street at the start of the civil war, but of this damage there is no sign now.

'There,' Just Albert says.

There are few diners and, at first, O'Keefe does not think that the gun merchant is among them, though he is uncertain what a British gun dealer might look like. *Piratical, a docker type like the Mahons?* He lets his eyes scan the room—an older couple, several pairs of women in Georgette dresses and fur-trimmed suit jackets; a group of what appear to be country businessmen—and not seeing any single male diners, he turns to Albert.

'Where?' he says.

'In the far corner by the kitchen. The small fella tucked nicely in between the two lads.'

'I see them now.'

'You'd want smaller dinner guests,' Just Albert says. 'Them two'd cost you in grub, wha'?'

'Those boys are no guests, Albert.'

'You're joking.'

'I'm …' O'Keefe catches the sarcasm and begins to move through the tables towards the small man and his two companions, neither of whom are eating.

They have chosen the table for its clear view of the whole room, and for its access to a quick exit through the kitchen. Like he would have done himself, O'Keefe thinks.

'Mr Murphy?'

The man is short and slight, with pale skin and average features, thinning brown hair combed back from his forehead like potato drills in a sloping field. He is dressed in a conservative, blue pinstriped suit with a tie that matches the wine on the table in front of him.

'Yes,' the man says, looking up without smiling, but without rancour either. 'What may I help you with?' His voice, pleasant, Home Counties.

O'Keefe relaxes a little and thinks that, for once, this could be simple. 'A quiet word is all. In private, if possible.'

The big man to Murphy's left, O'Keefe notices—blond, clean-shaven—is staring at him while his colleague focuses on Just Albert. Neither has his hands inside his jacket, but both wear their jackets open and loose. Professionals. Ex-army or police.

Murphy spoons soup into his mouth, and then butters a slice of bread, setting the bread back onto the plate and cutting it into four equal squares. He takes one square up and eats it, chewing methodically, taking his time before responding.

'Roger and Arnold are trustworthy men, Mr …?'

'O'Keefe,' he says, 'Seán O'Keefe. And this is Mr Albert.'

The arms dealer smiles politely. 'Trustworthy and necessary men, Mr O'Keefe, in my line of business. Any words you have with me, you'll have with them. We haven't met before, have we?'

'No, sir, we haven't,' O'Keefe says, accepting that Roger and Arnold are to be party to their chat. 'May I sit down?'

Indicating the empty place at the table, Murphy says, 'Of course, please. You'll excuse me, I shall continue to dine.'

With Just Albert remaining standing behind him, O'Keefe takes the proffered chair and reaches into his trenchcoat for the photograph of Nicholas Dolan. As he does, Roger and Arnold mimic his action, hands sliding into their own coats in readiness. O'Keefe smiles. 'A picture, lads. I'm taking out a photograph is all,' he says, and one of the big men returns his smile but his hand remains inside his jacket until O'Keefe produces the photo.

As O'Keefe attempts to hand the picture to Murphy, the arms trader raises a finger to stop him before taking up another small square of bread and beginning again his regimented mastication, appearing to silently count out an even number of chews before swallowing. When he has done this he takes two careful spoonfuls of soup, then wipes his lips on the corner of a linen napkin.

'Now,' he says, 'what might you be in the market for, Mr O'Keefe?'

'Information. Nothing more. I'm employed by a local woman to find her son, Nicholas.' He places the boy's picture on the table in front of Murphy. 'He's been missing for over a week and his mother's frantic with worry about him.'

O'Keefe watches as Murphy picks up the photo and examines it. He waits for some response from the man before he continues, hoping the gun merchant might show a sign of recognition. But Murphy's face remains neutral, betraying nothing.

'I've been told that the boy runs errands, messages for men you might be doing business with …'

'And what business might that be, Mr O'Keefe?' The arms merchant smiles, and O'Keefe notes how small and even are his teeth, as if ground down to a bureaucratic standard.

'Your business is no concern of mine, Mr Murphy. I'm looking for the boy, nothing more.'

Again the gun dealer interrupts. 'Who exactly are you working for, Mr O'Keefe? Out of curiosity. Professional curiosity, let's say.'

'I told you. I've been employed by a woman to find her son.'

Murphy raises the soup spoon to his mouth twice, and then another square of buttered bread. He holds his eyes on O'Keefe as he takes his time chewing.

Anger stirs in O'Keefe's gut. Either this man knows something about the boy or he doesn't, but O'Keefe senses that he will not say either way. And his heavies, sitting on either side of him like rough centurions—bored with being confined by their work to this staid hotel—appear easily amused by mugs asking after lost boys, no doubt hoping for the chance to leaven the boredom with their fists.

O'Keefe swallows down his anger as it rises to his throat, realising just how weary he has become of hard men. Thugs who hire out their violence to the likes of Murphy—a soft man making his living from the instruments of death. Irony compounded by vicious, bloody irony. He is weary of men like the Mahons and the soldiers on either side of the civil war raging around them. Gunmen and bullies making up the laws of Ireland as they go along, making them up to suit themselves. *How had this happened?* Ireland had been a peaceful place when he was growing up. Subjugated, conquered, but peaceful for a child, for a family, to live in. *Or had it been?* Perhaps it had only been that way for him and his family, his father a copper—one of the subjugators. There had always been a bad, red streak of violence running in the blood of Ireland's men. It is in himself, he knows, and his mind begins to reel a little and the anger shunts again into his throat. Irony of ironies. Bone tired of violent men, he is on the edge of violence himself. He clenches his fists in his lap and breathes out through his nose.

Murphy finishes chewing and swallows. 'So I take it you are neither employed by Free State nor Irregular. Correct?'

'Yes, I …'

'And the woman's name who employs you? You can't be too careful, you know, in my line.' Murphy's bland smile has returned to his lips but there is a trace of mockery in his voice.

O'Keefe reins in his urge to upturn the table and hopes that Albert might have missed the man's tone. Whatever his own urge to mayhem, there would be no reining in Albert's. 'Her name is Mrs Dolan. Ginny Dolan. She's a local merchant woman here.'

The larger of the guards turns to his employer, smiling. '*Local merchant?* Fucking fanny merchant what she is. Runs a stew in Monto, not ten minutes' walk from here. Arnold and me have been. Local merchant, my arse! My prick's still stinging for that old doll's merchandise.'

Just Albert moves for the man and O'Keefe stands, knocking his chair over behind him, holding out an arm to obstruct Albert's lunge. Two Colt automatic pistols are slipped silently from jackets, barrels levelled, one at O'Keefe, one at Albert.

O'Keefe turns back to Murphy. 'Mr Murphy, have you or your men had any contact with the boy or not?'

Murphy holds his gaze for a long moment, his smile perfectly bland, his teeth small and neat. 'Not,' he says finally. He puts the last square of buttered bread into his mouth and begins to chew.

O'Keefe takes up the photograph from the table and turns to leave, hoping Just Albert will follow.

In the hotel lobby, O'Keefe tips his hat to the receptionist at the desk and slips Nicholas' photo into his jacket pocket. He tries to think of something to say to the woman, wondering if she has seen what transpired in the dining-room. He hopes she hasn't, and then thinks how little it would matter if she had. On impulse, he turns and goes over to the desk, taking out the photo again.

'Miss, if you'd be so kind. Would you mind looking at this picture? We're looking for this boy, and were told he'd been to see a man in this hotel …'

'Mr Murphy?' the woman says, taking the picture, concern in her eyes now.

'Yes, Mr Murphy.'

'Nothing untoward, I hope. Here at Burton's …'

O'Keefe smiles. 'No. Nothing like that I don't think. The young lad's missing. We've been asked by his mother to find him. You didn't see him by chance?'

Slowly, the woman shakes her head. 'His mother …' she says, looking up at O'Keefe. There is concern in her eyes. He smiles, wanting to reassure her somehow.

'I'm sure he's grand,' O'Keefe says. 'You know youngfellas.'

She smiles and nods. 'I've four brothers.'

O'Keefe smiles back, and wonders is there something in the look she gives him, her eyes holding his, briefly, before going back to the photo. After a long moment, she hands it back to him.

'I'm sorry,' she says, not meeting his eyes this time. 'I don't think I've ever seen him. We do have a good few boys, in and out with messages. I can ask some of the other staff if you've a copy of the photograph to leave us …?'

O'Keefe feels foolish suddenly, realising he should have had copies made of the photograph so that he could leave them with people. It is a basic error, but then he'd hardly thought that finding the lad would be so difficult. Or perhaps he'd thought it wouldn't be possible to find him at all. Either way, he had not taken the job as seriously as he should have. And as he thinks this, a thread of fear for Ginny Dolan's boy unspools in his blood. And he *is* a boy, he thinks, running in a world of wolves like the Mahon men in Gormanston, or those in the dining-room he has just left.

'I'd be much obliged if you would. I can come back with copies and you could show them around.'

'Yes, please do. I'll be working tomorrow from nine. You can drop them by any time, Mr …?'

'O'Keefe. Seán O'Keefe,' he says, suddenly glad that he has told her. Glad that she will register his name at the very least and is now aware, however slightly, of his existence in the world. 'That'd be grand, Miss. Thank you.'

'Not a bother, Mr O'Keefe. I only hope you find him.' She smiles again and O'Keefe's heart feels light, weightless for a passing moment.

'And who should I ask for, then, when I drop off the pictures?'

'You can ask for me. Nora Flynn.'

'Lovely to meet you, Miss Flynn.'

'And you, Mr O'Keefe. And have you an address or a telephone where you can be reached? If I hear anything?'

'Of course,' he says, taking the proffered pen and jotting his name and address on to a page of hotel stationery.

'Grand so, Mr O'Keefe.'

O'Keefe leaves the lobby smiling.

On the footpath outside the hotel, Just Albert lights one of his cigars. The Indian summer's warmth is fleeing the concrete at their feet, chill descending from above.

Just Albert says, 'You think now's a good time for mottin', Mr O'Keefe?'

O'Keefe frowns. 'What are you blathering about, Albert?'

'Your one. The foxy-haired girleen at the desk. I've eyes, Mr O'Keefe, and you've a job to do. You worry about the bints when the job's done.'

Rage ignites in O'Keefe, like a smashed paraffin lamp on bedding hay, scorching the small joy he'd felt on meeting the woman. He takes a step towards Albert. 'You mind what you say to me, Albert, I'm telling you.'

'Or what?' Just Albert gives him the same dismissive smile he gives to all men.

'Or ... Fuck it, Albert. You'd try the patience of a saint.' O'Keefe turns away, exhaustion claiming his anger, an oily slick of despondency settling over him.

Albert appears to sense this and shuts down his smirk. 'Nicholas is only a boy, Mr O'Keefe. We need find him before he comes to harm.'

'I know that, Albert, and I'm trying to help you and Mrs Dolan find Nicky. I *want* to find him, by God I do. But you have to let me do it the way I know how.'

Just Albert's face darkens. 'Them cunts inside know something.'

'They might, but we'll never hear it now after you going for your man in there.'

'He shouldn't have run his mouth about Mrs Dolan.'

O'Keefe sighs. It was like talking to a child, sometimes, explaining things to Just Albert.

'I know he shouldn't have, Albert. But he was sending up a balloon ... a test. Like was done in the war. He was trying to see how far he could push us. Probably because he was bored, fecked off with listening to rubbish all day. Who knows? And didn't you give him the response he wanted? Brightened up his bleedin' day and got us nothing. Look ... sometimes, when you're working a case, interviewing a fella, you have to eat things you normally wouldn't. It's the way the world works, Albert.'

Just Albert ponders this for a moment. 'Not my world.'

'We're not *in* your world at the moment. Neither is Nicholas, and we're not going to find him if we don't ask the right questions in the right way. That girl in there might be a grand help to us if one of the other staff at the hotel has seen Nicholas. That's how investigations work … how they break open. The offhand comment. The odd sighting. The last person you expect to know something, knows something.'

Ginny Dolan's man drops his cigar to the ground and crushes it under his boot. 'I'll get what we need to know out of them fuckers in there.'

'You'll get killed, Albert, and Mrs Dolan doesn't need that, does she?'

'Them? Kill me?'

'Yes, Albert. Those two are more than just docker muscle or drunken punters. They know how to hurt people and have done it before.'

Just Albert shakes his head and smiles his smile, squinting up at O'Keefe under his hat brim. 'And here I thought you were getting to know me better, Mr O'Keefe.'

'You're a hard man to know, Albert.'

'Hard men are good to know in this town, Mr O'Keefe.'

'You're right about that, and that's what's wrong with the place.'

'You're hurting me feelings.'

'Jesus, give us peace,' O'Keefe says, smiling again despite himself. He needs food, cigarettes. A drink, sleep. 'Don't go near them again until I think over what to do. Nine tomorrow I'll call for you.'

'Don't be late, Mr O'Keefe.'

'God forbid.'

'It's not God you need worry about.'

O'Keefe smiles wearily. For the love of all that's holy. Dublin. You could lose sleep trying to get the last word in.

Nora Flynn watches the two men on the footpath in front of the hotel from behind a curtained window in the lobby. The shorter man is smiling and shaking his head, and the taller man,

Mr O'Keefe, removes his hat and rubs the back of his head as if he is exasperated or tired.

An urge to go out to this Seán O'Keefe comes to her, rising up in her chest on a swell of something like guilt; redeem her lies by confessing to him that she *has* seen the boy, Nicholas Dolan. The man is working for the boy's mother. *Stop, now, Nora. It does no soldier any good at all, thinking on the mothers who have been left at home.* The urge to confess passes and the cruel, handsome face of Charlie Dillon comes into her mind. She pushes it away. *Do your work, Nora. The boy's a soldier. A runner for O'Hanley. Old enough to know better*, she thinks, but she is not convinced.

She watches as O'Keefe turns and mounts a motorbike. Without waiting for him to ride off or stopping to think of the consequences, she moves quickly to the hotel switchboard and rings the men on duty in the Flowing Tide pub, different ones this time but assigned the same duties.

As she sets the receiver back in its cradle, she hopes that these duties will extend only as far as shadowing this Mr Seán O'Keefe. There is something about him that interests her—a warmth in his tired eyes. A certain strength tempered by kindness. *Don't be daft, Nora, you've hardly spoken hardly two words to him.* But she had seen, watching from the doorway to the dining-room, how he had handled the scene with Mr Murphy and his men. He had not been afraid of them or what they represent. Perhaps in this he is a fool. *You should be afraid, Mr O'Keefe, if you've any sense at all.*

Nora says a small prayer for the man's safety and that he will find the boy he seeks—and blesses herself before she returns to the reception desk, hoping no one has seen her in the act.

Silly superstition, she thinks, knowing in her heart that such prayers are rarely answered by a God who seems to have stopped listening.

24

No more than two miles from Burton's Hotel, just off the North Circular Road, Jack Finch pulls up—the Chevrolet's engine spluttering, radiator steaming—in front of a house with a plaque reading 'Doctor's Surgery' beside its front door. Holding his side, his trouser leg and trenchcoat tail saturated, he slides off the blood-slick bench seat and out of the car.

He stumbles on the footpath, vision blurring, and lunges a hand out for the support of an iron fence that fronts the redbrick surgery. It takes more than a minute to right himself before he is able to mount the steps to the doctor's door, fragments of thought coupling, shattering in his head as he shuffles, his boot leaving a snail's wake of blood on the flagstones. One thought only snags his consciousness: *If the doctor's out, ol' chum, you're for the common grave ....*

He thumps on the door, oblivious to its brass knocker, and his fist leaves a bloody imprint. After a short wait, a young woman answers the door.

'Yes? Oh, Jesus, sir ...'

'I'm shot, Miss. Is the doctor in?' Finch manages before he collapses on the doctor's doorstep.

Dr Stephen Hyland examines his insentient patient and cleans and staunches the wound as best he can before sitting back and examining his conscience.

There is a simple way to avoid bother, he knows. Simple as undressing the wound and letting the man bleed out and die and say nothing more about it. The man was dead on arrival at his surgery, he could easily enough say, and there had been nothing he could do to save him. Anyone would understand that surely. Neither Irregular nor Free Stater could blame him for the man's death. If he *were* to save him and ring the army or police, however, there is no telling who would come looking for an explanation; the same if he simply brought the man to the hospital. This man had come to his humble and unsuitable surgery because a hospital is off limits to him. Hyland has no illusions about this. The wounded man is not a patient of his, nor has the doctor ever seen his face before. Sheer dumb luck has brought him, and he owes this man nothing. But at the same time the doctor knows there is nothing to be gained, in the days that are in it, from making enemies on either side of the conflict. Keeping the head down is the only way, and Hyland has been good at it thus far. Simpler, for all concerned, if this man should die here now.

But is it in him to will a man to die when he can, at very least, attempt to save him? A bullet wound does not speak well for a man's character, but there are innocent men shot, and can he live with letting a man who might be innocent die?

The doctor thinks of the lethal weight in the pocket of the man's bloodied trenchcoat and decides that innocence is less than likely, whomever he is fighting for.

Dr Hyland lights his pipe and watches the patient's slow, laboured breathing. He then sets down his pipe and rifles the wounded man's trouser and suit jacket pockets, his billfold.

Bloodstained but legible, behind a solid sheaf of pound notes in the billfold, the doctor finds a scrap of paper and on the paper is an address and a name. *Seán O'Keefe, 24 Fumbally Lane, Blackpitts, Dublin.*

Realising he will not have to let this man bleed out in his surgery, Dr Hyland smiles, relieved to think that the man can now bleed out somewhere else.

'Janey,' he calls out of the surgery door to the young nurse receptionist who had answered the door. 'Ring for a motor cab, will you? Our patient is in need of transport.'

25

O'Keefe awakes to steady hammering on the rear, garden access door of his flat. A bar of October morning sun cuts through a gap in the curtains and carves light across his blanket.

The black tide of despondency laps at his consciousness and he forces it back for the second time in as many days, knowing he is riding his luck, aware that when the tide chooses to rise and wash in, it will come, and there will be nothing he can do about it, even if he cared to try.

He sits up and checks his watch—half past seven—and rubs sleep from his eyes. The knocking resumes and then stops. O'Keefe can hear the whispered conversation from behind the door, and relaxes as he rises from his bed, pulling on a pair of corduroy trousers and a cotton vest.

'His bike is under the front steps, so he has to be in.'

'His bike was here last week and he wasn't feckin' in.'

'You said "feck", I'm tellin Ma.'

'Yeh rat. *Informer!* You wake the Ma and *you'll* get a clatter, you will, yeh thick shite.'

O'Keefe can hear the sound of a slap and another given in return. 'Lads,' he says, opening the door. 'It's fierce early for visits, isn't it?'

The younger Cunningham boy, Henry, his school uniform shirt misbuttoned so that one end of it hangs low over his short trousers and the other rides up over his pale belly, says, 'I know. Ma would reef us out of it if she knew. Come here, look ...' Henry nudges his brother, who takes out a deck of cards. 'We learned how to play Twenty-five off Granny.'

'Did you now?'

'We did.'

'And?'

The elder brother, Thomas, takes over. 'And ...' the boy has large, brown eyes and hair that will not stay combed if it were glued down and varnished, '... will you give us a game? We can't play each other 'cause Henry's always cheatin'.'

'*You're* always feckin' cheatin'.'

'Lads ...'

'You are!'

O'Keefe smiles, helpless. He wonders was he and his own brother like this pair, the best of friends and never not fighting. 'All right, lads, one game and then I'm off for work. Let me make tea and some beans.'

'Can we have some?' Henry says.

'See, I told yeh he was awake,' Thomas says.

O'Keefe loses four hands of Twenty-five to the boys. He is, he thinks, the world's worst card player. Or perhaps Henry had been cheating. He smiles a little as he dresses and shaves.

As he mounts the Trusty, patting his trenchcoat pocket for the photo of Nicholas Dolan, he hears his name called. He turns, startled, to see the woman from the reception desk at Burton's Hotel coming towards him on the footpath. He summons her name. Nora Flynn.

'Mr O'Keefe,' she says, stopping on the path in front of him. 'What a coincidence. Do you live here? I'm only up Leinster Road myself. Up at the top in digs.'

'Yes, the basement rooms here. *Room*, really,' O'Keefe says. Unconsciously he removes his leather helmet and smooths his hair with his fingers. Lost for words, he repeats hers. 'What a coincidence. I was just on my way to get the photograph copied. I was going to call in at the hotel with copies on the way to collect my friend.'

The woman smiles, and something wells in O'Keefe's chest. She is wearing a long, blue linen skirt and white blouse under a navy jacket, and carries a worn leather satchel bag. The simplicity of the outfit highlights her beauty, O'Keefe thinks, his eyes fixed on the woman's voluminous red hair, which is gathered into a neat French roll. There is a smattering of freckles on her nose and O'Keefe restrains his gaze from lingering on her shapely figure. He concentrates on her eyes—sea-green he notes, framed by thick, dark red lashes. She is tall, but she carries her height with grace and confidence.

There is a momentary but not unpleasant silence between them, as if both are thinking that whatever either one of them says next will be of some significance. Nora looks thoughtful, as if deliberating the wisdom of befriending this stranger. Then she smiles and nods at the Trusty.

'Is it yours?'

'It is. I bought her in Cork. After the war ...' O'Keefe stops, suddenly feeling he has said too much. As if he has admitted something shameful. Nora looks at him and appears to sense this, her eyes settling briefly on the scar on his face.

'It's lovely. You must give us a spin some time. I've never been on a motorbike before. My brothers are mad about them.'

O'Keefe smiles. 'I am as well. She's my one true love, she is.' He stops. How ridiculous he must sound—how pathetic—to a woman as poised and lovely as this Nora Flynn. Another rootless, jobless war veteran on the make.

But Nora laughs and her cheeks bloom with colour. 'Surely that can't be true, Mr O'Keefe.'

'Sad but true, Miss Flynn,' he says, trying to make light of his awkwardness. Somehow, he has lost his easy way with women. The war, he thinks. He knows.

Again there is silence but this time neither of them glances away.

'Would you …' O'Keefe feels he should stop himself before he goes on but finds he is unable, '… Would you like a lift into work? I've only to stop at the printer's … there's one on Camden Street, and then I could drop you. Only if you'd like. If …'

'I'd like that very much, Mr O'Keefe. Thank you.'

They smile at each other and Nora mounts the bike side-saddle, taking a tentative hold of O'Keefe's waist.

'Here,' he says, handing her the goggles. 'Wear these. Just in case.'

'Just in case of what, Mr O'Keefe?' she asks, but smiles, and there is something lovely and wicked in the smile that O'Keefe is meant to see and does. 'Am I in danger?'

He shakes his head as he kick-starts the bike.

'Not too fast!' she shouts.

O'Keefe laughs. 'Not too fast, so.'

Nora Flynn watches the smiling Seán O'Keefe roar away from the hotel, swinging left onto O'Connell Street. Her own smile in return is genuine. She has enjoyed the jaunt on the motorbike despite herself, but her smile fades when she remembers the duty to which she has been assigned. *A job of work, girl, and no summer holiday.*

Her 'chance' meeting with Seán O'Keefe; the small, safe-house room she had been moved into in the middle of the night in the home of a family with a son in the Free State army—all of it possible, necessary, because she had rung her colleagues waiting in the Flowing Tide. What she had not imagined when she rang them was that O'Keefe would become her work. *Her* target.

It had come to Carty that O'Keefe, in his hunt for the boy, might lead them to O'Hanley, and was thus worth marking. And she would be the marker. She catches herself using the language of football in her mind, and recalls how she has only started doing this since joining CID. In sport, men employ the terms of war; in war, the words of sport. And in a war, women fall into the same habits, talking, thinking like men. *Yet still treated as women, sure as God*.

But female detectives have their uses, Nora knows well. Much of her work in CID involves the tracking of women aiding and abetting the Irregulars. Active ones, carrying messages or even weapons to the gunmen. Passive ones she searches on the streets or minds on silent raids, when she and her CID or Army Intelligence colleagues take over the houses of known Irregulars and wait— *schtum*—with their families as hostage, in the hope of snaring a returning gunman come home for a mother's feed. In these raids, Nora is mostly tasked with tending to the women and children, and many of these women call her a Free State whore, traitor bitch. Others are resigned and silent, and their silence digs at her conscience more than the harsh words. Why their dignified acquiescence bothers her is a mystery. Her conscience is clean. She has done her work and no more, no less.

And this Seán O'Keefe will not be a burden or threat to her conscience. He will be easy. The way he looks at her—even she can see it. *A dandy-doddle, this job of work that is Seán O'Keefe*, she thinks, the unexpected thrill of the motorbike ride giving way to something harder, darker inside her.

At the hotel switchboard, she rings and reports her morning's progress to a fellow detective officer at Oriel House, knowing Carty will be pleased when he hears of it.

26

O'Keefe and Just Albert make little progress.

After dropping the photograph of Nicholas Dolan at the Fine Print shop on Camden Street and delivering Nora to the hotel, he'd collected Albert at Ginny Dolan's house. The woman herself had been out, and O'Keefe had been glad not to have to report their lack of headway in person, though no doubt Just Albert had already done so.

They pass the rest of the morning and afternoon questioning newsboys who sell or hand out republican news sheets, learning only that it had been some months since Nicholas had done anything on the papers—selling or postering for the anti-Treaty side was punishable by imprisonment—and that rumour has it he had moved up to working for O'Hanley himself, since the wily brigade commandant had returned to Dublin. Nothing in it they don't know already.

O'Keefe remarks to Just Albert just how much it would mean for a boy of Nicholas's age to serve under a hero like O'Hanley.

Albert spits on the cobbles. 'And I give a ha'penny fuck about the fella? This O'Hanley puts Nicky in harm's way and he'll be a hero floating face down in the Liffey.'

They move on down Talbot Street and receive hard looks from some men on the corner of Marlborough Street as they question another newsboy. One of the men approaches them, as the boy shakes his head and moves on, and demands to know what their business is. Just Albert tells him, and asks the man does he know anything about the missing boy, seeing as he is so alight with knowledge of what transpires on Talbot Street from his perch on the corner. The man huffs, offended, and asks the staring Just Albert who he thinks he is to be asking questions of people. He glances back at his friends, who avoid his eyes, and then says he knows nothing before skulking away. O'Keefe wonders does the bold cornerboy realise how lucky he is to depart a confrontation with Just Albert with only his pride wounded.

Albert stews in silence for the rest of the afternoon. O'Keefe can sense the raging thrum of tension in the man's posture, in his movements. Nothing will satisfy him except finding the boy, but he will settle for a ruck.

Just Albert says, 'Two fuckin' streets away from Monto we are, standing here with our pricks in our hands and not a drop of piss to show for it. You're the copper, Mr O'Keefe. What should we be doing next?' He looks up at O'Keefe, squinting, head cocked.

In his face, O'Keefe now sees something more than just anger or frustration. He sees worry. Fear.

'*Former* copper, Albert,' he says evenly. 'And even if I was still a copper, I'm not sure there's anything the whole of the DMP or Civic Guard—or whatever they're calling it now—could do to find the lad if he doesn't want to be found. He's in deep, obviously, if he's running with O'Hanley. Sure, the whole Free State army and every one of its spooks is looking for the commandant and can't find him. What does that say about our chances?'

The doorman lights a short cigar. 'I don't care a shite what it says. We need find Nicky.'

O'Keefe recalls the urgency, the worry, he had felt for the boy the previous evening when they had met the gun dealer, but he does not feel it now. He lights a Navy Cut, strange happiness simmering in his heart. It is the rare light of the October sun, perhaps, but more likely it is the prospect of meeting Nora Flynn again. A glowing anticipation as warm as the sun on his back, like he hasn't felt in years. Dropping her at the hotel that morning, they had agreed that he'd call in that evening to deliver the copies of the photograph, and she'd hinted that she might like to go for another spin. *Maybe*, she had said, but she'd smiled when she said it.

Just Albert squints up at him as if trying to read his thoughts. 'Did you hear me?'

'Of course I heard you, Albert. I'm only thinking that maybe Mrs Dolan needn't be so worried. There's no one would harm a youngfella if they can help it, war be damned.'

But as he says this he knows it's not true, and guilt snags on the lie—guilt that his own heart is lighter today than it has been in months while Albert's and Ginny Dolan's are heavy with concern. But such is the way of things. Around every corner, in every tenement and cottage, every hospital and battlefield, someone, somewhere is dying, some tragedy is being wrought, and yet the world goes on. Men and women meet. Babies are born and pints sunk and horses run; books read and children fed and socks darned. Men are killed and he himself has killed his share of them. His brother cut to ribbons. Boys are lost and boys are found. But the world carries on, O'Keefe thinks, and sometimes the sun shines and a woman smiles at you. *Enjoy when you can, endure when you must.* Where had he read that?

He takes a long pull on his Player's. 'You know I want to find him, and maybe we will. But we might have to accept as well … Mrs Dolan might have to accept … that the boy made a choice to go off with the Irregulars and that he'll come back in his own time. When the fighting is finished or he's pulled by the Free Staters.'

'Or shot,' Just Albert says, tossing down his cigar. 'They're shooting lads they find carrying weapons. Doing it on the sly at the moment but there's talk of making it law. Nicky was carrying guns for them boys.'

'He was carrying a gun *because* he's a boy, Albert. That's why. Because they'll *not* shoot a youngfella for carrying. The people won't stand for the likes of it.'

Just Albert lowers his head and stares at his boots. 'You've been around Monto as long as I have, you learn there's not a lot that people won't stand for, once it doesn't happen to them.'

Evening lowers, and before it closes O'Keefe and Just Albert collect the two hundred printed posters of the boy's photograph. O'Keefe pays for them out of his own pocket, insistent that Ginny Dolan get every penny of her expense roll returned to her because, more than likely, he feels he will have little or nothing to show for it. The posters are of good quality, and O'Keefe's address, as well as Ginny Dolan's, is printed at the bottom of the page. A reward is offered for any information leading to the boy's whereabouts. O'Keefe had debated the wisdom of doing this, knowing that the prospect of payment brings out the loonies, increasing the possibility of chasing ghost boys conjured by the crooked or greedy or mad. But Albert approves, thinking it better than nothing and telling O'Keefe that Ginny Dolan will pay more than he might imagine for Nicky's return. They make their way on the Trusty back to Talbot Street and employ a dozen newsboys to poster the city.

Job done, Just Albert looks at the sky, then at O'Keefe. 'We should be doing something else. Talking to people.'

'We are doing something, Albert. Posting the photograph around town is a good thing. If anyone knows anything, the reward might tempt them to tell us.'

'Fishing for touts.'

'You could say that. In the meantime, I'll see if I can drum up a contact in the Irregulars who might be able to get a message to the boy at least.'

'Good luck with that. They'll be eager to speak with a copper.' There is bitterness in his voice.

'*Former* copper, Albert. I was only thinking aloud.' O'Keefe is silent for a moment before speaking again. 'We could go to the DMP. They might …'

'No police. Mrs Dolan was clear on that. We find him, not them.'

'They might be better able …'

'And then Nicky eats a bullet for a rat? Imagine they did find him and found other rebel lads along with him. He'd be shot by his mates in the Irregulars or live his life with the shame of fellas thinking him an informer. No police.' Just Albert squints up at O'Keefe, his face set in a way that says there will be no more discussion of the matter.

27

The reception hall of the Achill Guest House and Baths is all exposed brickwork, holy statues and cold, parquet tile floor. A sagging line of half-drunk and hungry men extends out of the front door and Jeremiah Byrne is amongst them, waiting until the man behind the wire cage of the cashier's desk is occupied by one of the sots in the queue.

'You,' the man in the cage says. 'You know I'll extend you no favours, McPhail. No favours at all unless you've the scratch to warrant them, and since you haven't had a ship since the war, I know you've nothing and may shove off with yourself.'

'What, here's me only arriving in and already you're slandering me? You fuckin' goat's poxed cunt of a bastard son of a tinker bitch.' The drunk, McPhail, raises his arms, grabbing the wire mesh of the cage with hands like claws, as if to wrench the cage from its frame. He continues his rant, as Jeremiah had hoped he would, raising himself to his full height, a large man in a tattered black overcoat and sailor's cap, the coat open now like bat's wings, blocking the cashier's view of the foyer.

Jeremiah ducks low and darts across the reception hall as the drunken man calls the cashier every common slur and curse, including some that Jerry has never heard before. *Sailors are like that*, he thinks, hearing the drunk call the cashier a 'whore's rusted seed pipe' as he turns into the main hallway of the doss-house.

Others in the queue may have seen him, but fuck them. Few of them had never pinched a free doss somewhere, and they would rather sleep with both eyes shut than spend the night waiting for a youngfella like himself to creep up on them in the dark and slit their throats for a touting, Turk informer. Jeremiah isn't half worth wasting their own sad, few coppers of kip on.

He can still be unlucky, he knows, if he bumps into another of the house's workers who gives enough of a toss to ask to see his rooming chit—the small paper ticket that changes colours each night of the week, indicating payment of doss fees. But there are ways around them if it happens, and most of the staff—kitchen women, mop men or coal boys—are known to care about as much as Jeremiah himself does, who has paid for what, once a fella doesn't make more work for a body.

He stops in the dim, gas-lit hallway, letting his eyes adjust. The Achill is located on a laneway off the Smithfield markets, not far from where he pilfered the potatoes and onions for his sisters, what …? *Yesterday? The day before?* He has lost track of the days since he fled Uncle John Keegan and the suited men at his tenement. Since then, he has been sleeping rough, going with punters behind the market pubs for a bob or two, doing things he had thought he was finished doing when he'd discovered what could be done with a knife. With the few coins he earned he had eaten fish and chipped potatoes wrapped in newspaper from an Italian shop, using the rest for a bottle of fortified wine to drink against the autumn night. Now he is stiff and tired, craving proper rest and in need of money. And a knife.

The Achill is nothing like its beautiful Mayo island namesake. A doss-house, plain and simple—one step up from the poorhouse— a former lying-in hospital for women. It is one of the meaner of such establishments in the city, catering to single men who pay nightly for a dormitory bed and flea-sparked blanket. Clean sheets, when available, cost extra. A meal in the canteen, also extra, knife and fork available for a rental charge. Showers, located in the basement, extra again. But it is warm and dry and Jeremiah knows he can kip safely here. Once he's inside, he need not pay for a bed and cozying around one of the coal stoves in the common rooms is free. A fella is meant to be eighteen years of age to bed down here, Jeremiah well knows, but he looks old enough if he wants to and has seen younger lads than himself behind these walls. More often than not, down in the showers.

He delays thinking of this and approaches a group of men gathered against the wall under one of the gas jets. His stomach growls. There are four men, one of them sitting on a bench built into the wall, the other three standing around him. Jeremiah takes out a cigarette as he approaches. He had dipped the packet from a man he'd serviced the night before, and now he has a flaring memory of the scent of sour beer, stale vomit and the bleachy taste of the man's goo, his hand rummaging the punter's pockets, coming out with half a box of Player's and a broken-toothed comb. The cigarettes cost nearly as much as the punter had paid him for his suck.

'Any yis have a light?' he asks, sidling up, the cigarette dangling from his mouth. The men are mostly old enough not to be dangerous—broken-down dipsos, men in their thirties and forties, muscle eaten away and withered by drink, making them slump in on themselves, looking ancient and worn. Too slow by half to be a hassle, Jerry thinks, even without a blade on him. Yet.

'Who's the youngfella then?' the seated man asks, looking up at him, and Jeremiah corrects himself. *This fella could do harm. Go easy with him, so.*

'Thomas,' he says. 'Tommy Fallon's the name.'

The man on the bench smiles, and Jeremiah can smell the reek of waning stout and whiskey rising from him.

'A light is all. Have me an auld puff and then head down for a wash. Let the smoke take the edge off the hunger before me kip.'

'No scratch for grub, youngfella?' the seated man says, still smiling but something dark in his eyes under his dirty cap, heavy brows.

'Not a bean,' Jeremiah says. He has used this story before. It is his way of innocently announcing where he will be and what he needs, to the kind of men who might like to find him. It is safer this way. Courting fellas who might not want it could be ropey, some of them hating a lad for what he's offering, others hating him for maybe wanting what he offers but despising themselves more for wanting it. And there are always those who hate a lad for charging for what they think is their right to take for free. No matter the reason, getting it wrong could earn a youngfella a bad beating or worse. Jeremiah had once seen a boy in the basement, a fella younger than himself, badly pulped for kneeling in front of a man who'd been eying him through the steam. That lad had read the signals wrong and paid for it with pints of his claret, spinning down the hair-gnarled drain of the doss-house showers.

'No bean for a feed, so,' the seated man says, striking a match off the stone bench seat and offering it to Jeremiah, holding Jeremiah's eyes with his own until understanding has passed between them. 'I may have a wash meself,' he says, letting the match burn down to his thick, calloused fingers before blowing it out.

'Nothing like a wash,' Jeremiah says, as he moves off from the men, 'for to keep a body clean.'

28

The house below his attic bolthole is quiet—the Dempsey women gone visiting, he assumes, his young soldiers in bed or yet to return from their duties with Gilhooley—and O'Hanley scratches in his journal by candlelight. The silence here at the top of the Haddington Road house is unnerving. It is as if he is alone in the city of Dublin—like Christ might have felt, midway through his forty days in the desert, he thinks—and he would welcome the company of one of the young men. Just to sit beside him on the bed while he writes here at his desk, exuding the musky smell of tennis sweat and stolen cigarettes. He has banned the boys from smoking as well as swearing, but he knows they do it anyway.

His mind conjures a memory of his favourite soldier; a time when the lad had ascended to the attic to report some trivial matter and O'Hanley had asked him to stay. The memory is rich and vivid, with the soft sussing of the boy's breath, strong on it the scent of tobacco; the boy's arms thrown back and hands clasped behind the head in repose, pale skin under his arms ....

O'Hanley closes his eyes and forces the image away, shame welling in his belly.

He envies men who smoke, he thinks, as he gnaws at the skin around his thumb nail, a ruby pearl of blood rising up from the cuticle. Many of the priests in Maynooth had smoked when he was there, so surely it is a venal sin at most. There must be comfort in the searing balm of tobacco. A comfort he needs now. And he should let the boys smoke. They are doing the work of men for the country. He has often envied men who drink as well; envies them the easy laughter, the warm brotherhood and loosening of cares, though he knows an eight by ten foot attic room is no place for spirits or beer. Certainly he will court-martial any boy he finds drinking. Drink is the bane of revolution. Ireland locked in fetters for centuries, soaked in whiskey and the cause betrayed, time and time again, by men in their cups. No, he is blessed that he does not know even the taste of it. He inks his pen and returns to his journal.

... that our Lord works in ways we cannot fathom. Even in writing this I recall the verse from my days in the seminary though it gives me little comfort. "What man can know the intentions of God? And who can comprehend the will of the Lord? For the reasoning of mortals is inadequate, our attitudes of mind unstable, for a perishable body presses down on the soul, and this tent of clay weighs down the mind with its many cares."

And don't I have many cares? Thus, while I never waver, while my faith in Christ's workings on behalf of a true and sovereign Irish republic can never be in doubt, it is in times such as this that I succumb to the temptation to question His means. This is not doubt. I have utter faith that He sees the rightness of our cause and that He has blessed me with the will and mettle of His holy spirit so that I, like my martyred brother Pádraig Pearse, may he rest in the arms of our Lord, might wage a war of purification and liberation for my country. But to my shame, I do doubt the ways in which He works. How am I supposed to wage this war from the confines of this safe house attic room where I have been ordered to stay? How am I to battle Mulcahy and O'Higgins and their Free State treachery when men of my own army are unwilling to fight for the cause because they are loathe to raise a hand in anger against their former comrades as was, apparently, the case in Limerick? I should be in Limerick now, presiding over a holy and liberated city, the first city of the new, blessed Republic of Ireland when instead Limerick is in filthy Free State hands and I am sentenced to what seems an eternity of waiting in this room. Unable to contact but a handful of my comrades, most having fled this city in shameful capitulation, I await news from Newbridge like the planner of any common robbery. His means are a mystery to me and I can only beg forgiveness for the means I am forced to employ.

Could I ever have imagined, seven years ago, teaching each day alongside Master Pearse, may he rest in God's mercy, that I would be party to such deeds? That the young men I have chosen might shed precious blood robbing payrolls so that the sword of liberation might be purchased from the very hands of the oppressor? I ...

Again, the knock on the closet door that disguises the room. O'Hanley takes up the revolver from beside his journal. But the knock is correct, and he holds the pistol by his leg as he unbolts the two doors leading into his room.

Smiling, Stephen Gilhooley enters and drops a leather travel bag at O'Hanley's feet before slumping down onto the bed.

O'Hanley crouches and loosens the leather straps binding the bag. 'You came by foot I take it? The butcher's lorry is hardly parked in front of the house at this hour?' His voice is flat and dry.

'I'm no fool, for fuck sake.'

'Your language, Stephen ...'

Gilhooley ignores him. He is still riding the heist's adrenaline and is giddy with his survival and success. 'I hopped a tram and then hoofed it. I was even stopped by a clatter of Free State troops and blagged my way out of bother. Staying with me auntie, I told them. Kicked out the gaff by the auldfella, says I. They never even searched me or the bag, the shower of bogtrotting bastards. They'd be leaking out on the Baggot Street footpath if they had.'

O'Hanley silently forgives the young man his uncouth ways and opens the bag. Inside, bound in butcher's string and packed under a selection of shirts and smalls are twenty odd wedges of sterling banknotes. The smell of it hits O'Hanley and he blesses himself. He feels a momentary flash of shame at his earlier doubts.

This, he thinks, is how the Lord works. A surge of confidence rises in his chest.

'How much is it?'

'More than enough for Murphy's gear. Fourteen thousand and a bit.'

Gilhooley does not tell O'Hanley of the four thousand he has given his father from the take to pay off loans to suppliers to his shop and for a new refrigeration unit. His father has done his bit for the cause, and can use the few quid for the times that are in it. His brothers, too, have taken a taste but not so much as you'd know. Sure, Dinnie has a baby to feed and Ray needs his cut to pay the mothers of his now dead Free State army mates who tipped them to the job in the first place. Robbery costs, though no hope of Commandant O'Hanley understanding the notion.

'And the boys?'

Gilhooley leans forward on the bed now, his smile fading. 'Dinnie and Rayo, the brothers, they're grand. They made it back grand. The two lads I took from here ...'

'Yes?' O'Hanley's eyes cloud with concern.

'One's all right. He's staying with the McKinneys in Inchicore for tonight. He'll be fed and bedded down and make his own way back to the rendezvous point late tomorrow where I'll collect him.' The boys are taken to and from the Dempsey house in the back of the butcher's van, so that if they are captured they cannot locate the house for Free State intelligence.

'Who didn't make it?' O'Hanley asks. All his boys are precious to him, but he has lost two already this week. Robert and Nicholas and now another. He does not want to hear it but as ranking officer he must.

'Little Alan Fenlon. He ate a bullet keeping sketch in front of the bank. We'd some bother on the job.'

'Free Staters?'

And here, Gilhooley laughs, little Alan Fenlon forgotten for the moment. 'You'd not believe it if I told yeh.'

O'Hanley closes the bag and sits back in his chair at the desk. He inks his pen again and scratches the date onto the top left corner of a separate journal entitled *Operations*. 'Tell me,' he says.

'Seems like we weren't the only fellas looking to knock off that bank. Bunch of English boys with rifles and shotguns were at it first.'

'And?'

'And we plugged the lot of 'em, but Alan caught one in all the shooting. We got their Winchesters and two Colt automatics, you'll be happy to know. One of them might have made it out but I hit him, sure as God. He won't make it far.'

O'Hanley says a silent prayer for the repose of the soul of little Alan Fenlon. Sixteen years old, the boy was. No matter, O'Hanley thinks, blessing himself again. The young soldier died in the service of his country and will take his place at the right hand of the holy Father in heaven.

'I am happy, Stephen. Tomorrow, then, you'll take the money to Murphy. Once we can arm them, our army will rise from their torpor and stagnation and ...'

Stephen Gilhooley listens for a minute to O'Hanley's speech. He has heard it any number of times before. It is the one about the corruption that takes its seat in the hearts of Irishmen. Of demon drink and cowardly merchants dipping fingers in the smooth rubbed tills of petty shops but never finding a ha'pence for the cause of Irish independence.

O'Hanley is a quare one, no mistake. Gilhooley has thought this since he watched the older man fight in the GPO and spotted targets for him during his days in the Tan War. O'Hanley is a killer, a patriot, a leader of men. But he is a strange bird. All the same, he keeps things lively, Gilhooley thinks, and he's no man for half-measures; for surrendering half the country under the terms of a Treaty that any proper republican wouldn't bother wiping his arse on. Gilhooley is no man for half-measures himself, and this is what he likes about O'Hanley, strange bird and all that he is.

29

Nora Flynn says yes. She tells O'Keefe she'd only be delighted to share a drink with him and isn't she dying with the thirst and gumming for a nail? She appears to regret saying this, and O'Keefe catches her sudden shyness and tells her that he is of the same mind himself.

They decide on the Shelbourne Hotel bar, O'Keefe sipping Jameson and Nora Bombay gin and tonic water with a slice of lime. It is a nice touch, the lime, O'Keefe thinks, and is glad they have come here. The Shelbourne has been all but taken over by members of the new Free State government—Dáil representatives from country constituencies holed up in Dublin as much for their own safety, O'Keefe imagines, as for any legislative purpose—but the hotel retains its grandeur. O'Keefe wonders will it continue to be Mecca for the Protestant Ascendancy in this newly independent Ireland—hosting its débutante balls, hunt club dinners and wedding parties for the former ruling class of the country—as it has been for the past hundred years. He wonders will there even be an ascendancy any longer. He has heard of Protestants burnt out of their homes, some murdered. Many, he has heard, are selling up—or are trying to—and heading home to England. O'Keefe catches himself. *Home.* Many of these families had been in Ireland for centuries and are no more English than he is. Yes, many may have kept flats in London and married into families across the water. But not all of them, and not all Irish Protestants are wealthy landowners. He remembers the small farmers he would meet in West Cork when he served there in the RIC, poor as any of their Catholic neighbours. And how many regular coppers who had served alongside him had been Protestant? Many, and many fine men. He hopes the new Free State government will remember this, despite the treatment being meted out to Catholics in Belfast and the newly partitioned northern counties.

Nora returns to her seat across from O'Keefe. 'Marble!' she says. 'The whole of it, from the stairs to the sinks is all marble.' She smiles as she speaks. 'I can't believe I've never been in here before.'

They have already spoken of Nicholas, and O'Keefe's difficulty in finding the boy, O'Keefe omitting details of his employer and her business, and Nora agrees with him—*though what would I know?*—that the boy will most likely turn up when he tires of the hard bread, the strange beds and damp ditches of the guerrilla fighter. Or when he misses his mother enough. She asks him if he has discovered anything about where he might be and he tells her no. He lowers his voice when he says it, and tells her that the boy is reputed to be working for Felim O'Hanley. The very man himself. Her eyes widen, and he is pleased with himself for sharing this vaguely scandalous nugget with her. Taking her into his confidence.

'He'll turn up,' she tells him again, 'please God, none for the worse, when he's good and ready.' They raise their glasses to it.

O'Keefe smiles back at her. 'I've only been in here myself once before, for a friend's wedding.'

'A happy union?' Nora says, taking a sip of her drink.

O'Keefe turns away. 'He … died. He was killed at the Somme. God knows why he went at all. Why anyone did.'

'At least he had the happiness of a fine wedding here. And a fine wife, I'm sure.'

O'Keefe senses the effort she makes to be cheerful and smiles. 'He did. He had that.'

They speak now of other hotels, of weddings they have attended. Of meals served and speeches made by drunken fathers and best men. Of the dresses and the cost of things. They smile and laugh as they speak.

She tells O'Keefe when he asks her that she has worked in Burton's Hotel for the past year and a bit, and before that as a typist in Dublin Castle. Nothing interesting about it but it's paying work, she tells him, and O'Keefe tells her about his life in the RIC and how he is unsure of what to do now. He had taken the job of finding Nicholas, he tells her, as much for something to do as anything. He does not speak of his father's illness. Instead, he tells her he has plenty of savings, because it feels important to him that she knows this. More than enough to tide him over until he finds proper work, whatever that will be, when he finishes this job for Mrs Dolan. 'And I could always hire myself out,' he says, 'to people who don't want somebody found.'

Nora laughs at this. 'A Pinkerton man who helps you stay lost!'

But O'Keefe is not listening. His eyes are tracking a group of men as they enter the bar and take several tables against the back wall, facing the entrance. One of them eyes O'Keefe, staring at him for a long moment before O'Keefe looks away, not wanting a challenge from the man to spoil his time with Nora.

'You look like you're miles away.'

He smiles. 'Only as far as the back of the bar.'

'Who are those men?' she asks, taking a cigarette from her bag and allowing O'Keefe to light it. It is the third time he has done so, and he feels now an easy familiarity in the act.

'They're protection of some sort. For the nobs from the Dáil staying here, I imagine. Protective Corps from Oriel House, maybe. Keeping an eye out for anyone who might not wish the best for the men in the Free State government.'

'Who could that be?' she says, a cynical edge under the music of her voice.

O'Keefe shrugs. 'I've never much liked politicians myself.'

'But you hardly support the Irregulars, do you?'

O'Keefe drinks. 'No, of course not. I'd support the Quakers and pacifists if they were in the running, I suppose, though I hardly imagine any of them would be much better if they were to get a taste of power.'

Nora sighs. 'Even in the hotel bar of the Shelbourne, imagine. It feels sometimes as if there's no place you can go where the war isn't.'

'This table here,' he says.

'How do you mean?'

'We'll declare this table to be a ceasefire zone. We'll officially banish belligerence of any kind from here. You did leave your weapon at the door?'

Nora smiles and thinks of the Webley in her bag. 'Did you?'

'I've come unarmed this evening, madam. I'm at your mercy.'

'You're mad, Mr O'Keefe,' she says.

O'Keefe agrees and sips more whiskey, smiling again at Nora, unable to help himself, and she smiles back.

'What?' she says.

'What do you mean, "what?"'

'You're smiling at me.'

And O'Keefe wonders how long it has been since he has smiled as much or as easily.

'I like the look of you. But I'll stop if you like.'

'It's better you smiling than frowning at me.'

'Much better, altogether.'

And O'Keefe keeps smiling at her as she sips her drink, and for the moment, he feels, their table in the Shelbourne is the one place in Ireland where the war is not.

'This is it,' Nora says, stepping off the Trusty and smoothing her skirt. Her hair has come loose on the short ride from Stephen's

Green to Rathmines and she gathers it back and holds it to her head before giving up, letting it fall free.

'So it is,' O'Keefe replies. A two-story redbrick house at the top of Leinster Road. Hardly three hundred yards from his own. Blessed coincidence? Fate? He smiles. *Jesus, listen to yourself, Seán.*

'I've had a lovely evening. You're a gent to stand for the drinks. The Shelbourne is the dearest place in the city.'

'My pleasure,' he says, unsure of whether to dismount or stay on the bike. Nora stands close by on the footpath, close enough to reach out and touch. He lowers his goggles and lets them hang around his neck.

'I'd ask you in for a cup of tea but ...' Nora looks away, brushes red curls from her face and then looks back at O'Keefe.

'I know,' O'Keefe says, hearing how daft he sounds, the nervous longing in his own voice. 'Sure, it's late.'

'And my landlord, he's terribly old-fashioned about ... visitors. Even a cup of tea would set his mind turning over.' She smiles, and in the light from the street lamps, O'Keefe imagines she is blushing.

'Some people are like that. Always thinking the worst.'

Nora laughs lightly, and it is a beautiful sound to O'Keefe. She says, '"Nothing good ever happens after midnight." One of my father's favourite sayings.'

'And do you believe him?' he asks. 'Your father?'

'I don't know, Mr O'Keefe. Should I?'

'I'm not sure, Miss Flynn. Should you?'

Nora takes a step closer to him. Standing above him on the footpath, a head taller than he is on the Trusty.

'Well ...' she says.

'Well.'

'I should be getting in. I've work tomorrow.'

'I have as well.'

'Well then.'

'Well ...'

She leans into him and presses her lips against his. O'Keefe is as surprised as he is happy, feeling Nora's heart beating fast under the soft press of her breasts against his chest. They kiss for a long minute, O'Keefe breathing in the lavender smell of her clothes, her hair, the sweet tartness of lime and gin on her lips.

30

Minutes later, O'Keefe rounds the corner, anticipating sleep, the heat of Nora's body is still with him after seeing her into her digs, the scent of her hair still rich in his senses. He slows his bike and sees Just Albert, leaning against the bonnet of a Bentley motor car parked in front of the Cunningham house.

Shutting down the Trusty, O'Keefe says, 'Jesus, Albert. Has me watch stopped or didn't we say nine tomorrow morning?'

Ginny Dolan's man indicates the car. All thought of Nora evaporates into the cool night air, the taste of her gone, suddenly, from O'Keefe's lips.

'Get in the car. Now. Mrs Dolan is waiting for us.'

'Waiting? Where?'

'The morgue. They think they found Nicholas.'

'What do you mean? Who's found him?'

'Some farmer. The bodies of two youngfellas, in a field out in Clondalkin.'

'It might not be him,' O'Keefe says, unable to believe that the boy is dead. There is something so unreconciled about this that it seems untrue.

'A Murder Man came by the shop. He described him to Mrs Dolan. He'd seen the posters.'

'It might not be him.'

'His name is on the collar of his jacket.'

Like a schoolboy, O'Keefe thinks.
'Still …'
'Get in the car.'

Oh, Jesus, what are you at, girl?
Leaving the light off, Nora crosses her small room to the thick, musty drapes and parts them an inch. Surely, they hadn't been followed. Had they? Carty hadn't said anything about a tail. She *was* the tail. They'd hardly spare more men to shadow someone like O'Keefe. A bit player. Nor would they put eyes on his basement flat. On her room. No, of course not. Why would they be watching *her* room? CID is overstretched as it is, men dispatched throughout the country, hunting proper Irregulars. Fighting men. Carty thinks it's important to know what O'Keefe knows about the Dolan boy and if the boy's connected to O'Hanley like they think, but there are far bigger fish to fry than a jobless, war-weary ex-Peeler. O'Hanley himself had been spotted and fired on, supposedly, crossing Leeson Street bridge only yesterday. *They can't be sparing men to spy on the likes of me …*—Nora corrects herself—*… to spy on the likes of O'Keefe. No.*

But what if she is wrong? What if one of them has seen her kissing O'Keefe? What if one of the stuffed turkeys living in this house has seen them? A safe house in the Tan War—so Spartan and cold it makes her long for her lonely rooms in Ballsbridge—and now used by Free State forces; located conveniently close to O'Keefe's flat. The owner, a prig of a schoolmaster with a son in the Free State army, would tell his contact in CID, whomever it is, what he had seen through his front window—the embrace, the kiss. *Jesus*. A phrase from her childhood rises unbidden in her mind. *Eating the face off him.* She groans audibly. *Nora, you foolish, stupid woman.*

It had been part of her cover only. *Yes. Part of the job. Like with the Englishman before ….* She stops herself from remembering. *No.*

Yes. It is what she will tell them. He had wanted to kiss her and she'd let him. But she had leaned into him, hadn't she? That is the truth of it. He had wanted to kiss her and she had wanted to kiss him back.

She lets the drapes fall closed over the night-quiet street, saying a small prayer that she has not been seen with O'Keefe. She turns on the electric light and the shabby room is cast in harsh glare. A sunken single bed and fraying counterpane. An ashtray with a stubbed-out cigarette standing up like a finger raised to hospitality. A faded hunting print askew on the smoke-yellow wall. A safe house room.

There is a full-length mirror on the back of the door, and Nora avoids looking at it as she undresses. Then, in her undergarments, she cannot help herself and looks. Too tall, too Irish-looking somehow, with her round hips and full breasts and unruly red hair. More country girl than spy, she thinks. A female agent should be cigarillo-thin, black-haired, dark-eyed. Every country had used them during the war in Europe, she had learned in her training. Worldly, well-travelled and world-weary women, she imagines. Nora feels only weary. Mata Hari. *Jesus, girl, you're no Mata Hari.* Nora angrily opens the overnight bag she has brought, pulls her nightdress from it and throws it over her head, taking off her bra and panties underneath it, unable to face her own nakedness in the mirror.

Disgust wells up in her belly and she crawls into bed, the sour smell of some other guest's sweat in the sheets as she peels them back. She reaches down into her purse by the bed, takes out a cigarette and lights it. The owner of the house has told her expressly not to smoke in bed. This is why she does it, thinking, *It's not only the look of you, Nora, that's putting the dark clouds over your head.*

No. You're taken with this O'Keefe. It's wrong, but there it is, and Nora can still feel the heat of his lips from when she had kissed him. Let him kiss her. There is something about him, she thinks, blowing smoke at the jaundiced paint on the wall. A sadness, a kindness, that masks something rougher, darker. Even the smell of him. Cigarettes, whiskey and shaving soap and oil from the Triumph. She realises that she has learned nothing of note to report to Carty about O'Keefe's investigation into the boy's whereabouts.

31

Just Albert turns the Bentley off Amiens Street and into Foley Street. O'Keefe checks his wristwatch. Twenty past one in the morning. The busiest time of day in Monto.

Foot traffic slows their progress, weaving gentlemen in half-mast neckties and open jackets, university students and labouring men in flat caps. A uniformed DMP constable, idly swinging his baton from a leather thong on his wrist. Doors to most of the houses on the street are open, light pouring out onto the paving stones from within. Lamps in front windows are draped with red kerchiefs or scarves. Working girls stand on the steps of the houses and shout at groups of passing men. Some of the groups stop and banter back at the girls before continuing on their way while others follow the girls into the houses. A fire burning in an oil drum on the corner of Foley Street. A queue stretching five people long from the door of Mossy Morrison's shop to buy his famous pigs' trotters and mushy peas. Horse-drawn hacks and the odd motor car, idling, girls climbing in and out of the cars, men stepping gingerly down from the hackneys. Children running barefoot in the night street, in and out of the gas light, carrying cigarettes and messages from house to house. Monto babies, keeping the same hours as their guardians. Children of the night. Like Just Albert had been but Nicholas had not. O'Keefe recalls the photograph in his pocket and the one on the wall in Ginny Dolan's parlour of a fresh-faced school boy, well-rested, well-fed. Loved.

From the open car window, O'Keefe hears raised voices, gramophone music, shrieks of laughter. The echolalia of Monto. What kind of desperation brings men here? Men like his father? No, he can't conceive of it. The debt to Ginny Dolan must be something different altogether. A debt, O'Keefe thinks, that will remain unpaid if the boy on the mortuary slab is her son.

'Wait here,' Just Albert says, pulling up in front of Ginny Dolan's brothel.

O'Keefe assents in silence. Hers is the only house on the street with its door closed to the night, no light in its windows, no music or laughter in this house. Nor will there be, he imagines, for a long while to come, and feels a stab of pity for the madam.

Moments pass and the brothel door opens. Just Albert holds Ginny Dolan's arm at the crook of her elbow, gently, tenderly as any loving son, escorting her limping figure down the steps to the car. O'Keefe is moved at the sight of them, feeling as if he is intruding upon an intimacy he was never meant to witness. He wonders then at his presence here. Why has Albert insisted he accompany them for the identification of the body? A grim awareness rises within O'Keefe as he gets out of the car and opens the rear door for the woman. His work for Ginny Dolan is far from finished.

'Mrs Dolan,' he says.

The woman eases herself into the car and stares at him without speaking and there is something so terrible in her face, in her eyes, that O'Keefe shudders. It appears that she has been weeping but has made a conscious effort to disguise it, her eyes lined with kohl and mascara, her face powdered. And under the grief O'Keefe senses rage as yet held in check. Her only natural son. And O'Keefe has failed to find him, has failed this woman, and now people will pay for his failure. There is something so savage beneath her sorrow that O'Keefe is frightened by the power of it. He closes the door and turns away. Just Albert shakes his head and sits behind the wheel while O'Keefe hand cranks the Bentley's starter.

The Dublin Coroner's Court and City Morgue is a redbrick building on Store Street with a green painted wooden gate at its side large enough for ambulance or horse and cart to pass through. The public entrance is located to the right of the gate and here O'Keefe, Just Albert and Ginny Dolan are met by a priest and a tall, gaunt man in a wool suit and dark tie. The man, in his late thirties, is a detective, O'Keefe decides, the Murder Man Albert had spoken of.

'Mrs Dolan,' the priest says. 'This may be difficult, but with the love of Our Holy Father in heaven …'

Ginny Dolan shrugs free from Albert's supporting hand and draws herself up to her full height. She is not tall but presents a formidable figure. Noble, O'Keefe cannot help but thinking. Fierce.

'We will not be needing you tonight, Father. Or any other night, for that matter. Your lot had no time for my Nicky when he was alive, you'll not roost over him or me now.'

The priest takes a breath as if to counter or reassure, but stops and retreats a step behind the other man. There is a flash of fear in the priest's eyes. Instinctive, primal. O'Keefe pities him a little.

The detective says, 'Mrs Dolan, I know how you must feel, but there's no harm having …'

'You've no idea how I must be feeling, Detective. Now take me to my son.'

'This way, please,' the detective says, leading Ginny Dolan down the hallway. O'Keefe and Just Albert follow and the detective stops. 'These gentlemen, Mrs Dolan …'

'These gentlemen work for me, Detective. They will accompany me through.'

The detective gives each of them a long, assessing look, pausing longest to lock eyes with Albert. It is a look O'Keefe recognises. He had used it himself as a copper—used it to gauge and weigh and intimidate, all at the same time. The detective shakes his head almost imperceptibly and turns, continuing on through a set of swinging doors.

Through a second set of doors to a third, these marked simply 'Morgue.' A wooden crucifix hangs above the door and O'Keefe wonders if it has always been there or is it a recent Free State addition.

The detective comes to a halt and clears his throat, looking more at the wall above her head than at Ginny Dolan herself. 'This will be difficult, Mrs Dolan. I will have to ask you if the body I'm to show you is your son. It requires that you say "yes" or "no" aloud. Do you think …'—the detective looks at O'Keefe, appearing to study the scar on his face, as if only aware of it now—'… will you be able for that, Mrs Dolan?'

There is an intense light in Ginny Dolan's eyes and steel in her voice. 'I am able, Detective. Let me in.'

Nodding once, the detective opens the door, stepping through and holding it open from inside. Just Albert guides Ginny Dolan, a hand on the small of her back, and O'Keefe follows behind, uneasy amidst the scents of mould and bleach, the faint tang of decay. *I should not be here*, he thinks. *I should not see this.*

One body lies covered with a sheet on a dissection table in the middle of the room and a second is sheeted on a gurney against the wall. Ginny Dolan stumps across the tiled floor, her breath billowing in the unnaturally cool air. She stops at the head of the nearest corpse. Just Albert stands beside her, his hand on her shoulder.

'Is it this one?' she asks, her voice neutral.

'It is, ma'm.' The speaker is an older man in a white coat. He rises from a desk in the near corner of the room, taking up a manila file and opening it in front of him. He removes a pen from behind his ear and dips it into the ink-well set into the desk, readying himself in a discreet, practised manner. The detective lets the doors swing shut behind him and approaches Ginny Dolan and Just Albert.

'Lift the sheet, Albert,' she says, and O'Keefe watches her swallow, her jaw flex and clench.

The detective reaches over Just Albert. 'It's all right, Mrs Dolan. I can …'

'Lift the sheet, Albert. And do it now, when I tell you.'

Just Albert looks at the detective, and though O'Keefe cannot see his eyes he knows what is in them because the detective stops and backs away two steps from the table. Albert looks to his mistress and she nods. He lifts back the sheet down to the corpse's shoulders.

Ginny Dolan leans over the boy's body and stares at the face for a long, silent moment. She then leans down and kisses the corpse's cheek. O'Keefe watches the detective nod to the man in the white coat, who scratches something into the file and then closes it.

The detective turns back to Ginny Dolan, who has risen and replaced the sheet over the dead boy's face herself. 'Mrs Dolan, is this your son? Nicholas Dolan?'

A hard knot rises in O'Keefe's throat as he waits for the answer he knows is coming.

It is then that he sees Just Albert's face, his eyes.

'No,' Ginny Dolan says. 'This is not my son. Show me the other body.'

The detective's eyes flare in disbelief. 'Not your son? But his name … he was wearing a coat, a jacket with *Nicholas Dolan* written on the tag …'

Ginny ignores him and hobbles across the room to the corpse on the gurney, not waiting, lifting up the sheet. Albert follows and so now does O'Keefe and the detective. She pauses and considers the face, and this time kisses the dead boy on the forehead.

There is a slight catch in her voice as she begins to speak. 'This … this is not my Nicholas either, Detective.'

The detective frowns. There is a trace of annoyance in his voice, as if he has been caught out at something. 'But the jacket … and these bills posted around the city …' He takes one of the posters from inside his coat and unfolds it. 'He …' Crossing back to the first body, the detective looks at the photo and then lifts the sheet and looks at the corpse's face. 'I could have sworn. We have the jacket …. He … this one, was wearing it when he was found …'

A simple enough mistake, O'Keefe thinks. He might have made it himself. The boy is missing—his face on posters all over the city—and then a boy's body turns up dressed in a jacket with that same missing boy's name stitched onto its label; a boy of the same age. Any investigator might have made it. O'Keefe looks over the shoulder of the detective and thinks that there is some resemblance to Nicholas in the swollen features of the dead boy. Close enough to convince a detective it was the same lad.

'Please,' the detective says. 'In the office here I have the jacket. Could you tell me if it is your son's?' He is all motion now, taking the manila file from the morgue assistant and scratching something into its pages. He takes out his patrol diary and scribbles something else.

Ginny Dolan and Just Albert follow the detective through the swinging doors, leaving O'Keefe, for the moment, alone with the white-coated attendant and the bodies.

Without thinking, O'Keefe approaches the first body on the table. He gently lifts back the sheet and begins to examine the body. The attendant says, 'Who are you then to be looking?'

'I'm working for Mrs Dolan. Trying to find her son. I was a Peeler and I've investigated murders before. How did they die?' He does not look up as he speaks, but delves into his pocket and comes out with a pound note. He holds the note up for the attendant to see, all the while letting his eyes take in the destruction of the body on the table. The attendant goes silent.

There is heavy bruising on the torso and face, angry black-and-blue mottling that stands out against the corpse's death pallor. The bruises are there on the thighs as well. 'Cause of death?' he asks, moving now, stopping at the bottom of the table, his attention drawn to the soles of the dead boy's feet.

The attendant is silent for a moment. 'Shot. Two rounds, back of the skull. Same gun used on both bodies as far as we can tell. Same sized wounds it looks. The surgeon hasn't been in yet for the autopsies.'

O'Keefe nods. He is staring at the soles of the feet, which are dirty and calloused, as if the boy was used to running city streets barefoot. His eyes move up the body, stopping at the boy's midsection. There are the same angry, red, circular welts on the boy's penis and scrotum as there are on the feet. 'Cigar burns,' he says aloud.

The attendant looks at the swing-doors, which remain closed. 'Not the first we've seen. Tortured first, the poor youngfella. Other bodies have had them but they were older lads. Most of bodies are claimed by one side or the other and are taken to the barracks rather than here, but when they're not claimed, they become sudden reportable deaths like any other. But not like any other at all, really.' He looks to the door and then back at O'Keefe and lowers his voice. 'Like these two, burns on the bottom of the feet and on the tackle. Soldiers some of them, rebels. Others, touts maybe. But …'

'But what?' O'Keefe says, drawing the sheet back over the body. He has seen enough.

The attendant pauses and looks to the doors again. O'Keefe adds another pound note to the one in his hand.

'It seems to be the same marks every time. The cigar burns and the two bullets to the back of the head. The surgeon thinks …'

'Thinks what?'

'… Thinks it's the same fella or fellas doing it to all of them.'

'Any idea who it might be?'

The attendant shrugs. 'Sure, most of the bodies brought here are Irregulars, which means the fellas killing them are officially "persons unknown".'

'How do you mean?'

'You've heard there's inquests into all deaths now, since the fighting on O'Connell Street? Any deaths not in proper combat, any like this, right?'

'And?'

'And nothing. The inquests are as bent as a nine-bob note. Dogs know that if you're a dead Free Stater, your death is ruled "unlawful murder"; if you're a dead anti-Treaty man, an Irregular, well, then you've officially had your ticket punched by "persons unknown".'

O'Keefe considers this for a moment. 'And these two young-fellas?'

'Likely to remain persons unknown, killed by "persons unknown." The same persons who've been battering and burning and plugging the others we've seen.'

The swing doors open and the detective enters. The attendant's face flushes bright red. The detective stops and looks first at the morgue attendant and then at O'Keefe.

'Find what you were looking for?'

'Will you be able to find who killed these two lads?' O'Keefe asks.

The detective shrugs. 'I doubt it. They were executed for some reason or other. We'll ask around but, sure, you know yourself. Don't you?'

'I do.'

'I can see it in you. What happened?'

'I demobbed from the Peelers and now …'

'… Now you're some kind of Pinkerton man?'

'No, just helping the woman find her boy is all.'

The detective holds open the doors for him. 'They're waiting for you.'

'Was it Nicky's jacket he was wearing?'

'It was. His mother confirmed it.'

'How did this youngfella get it? He's not had a pair of shoes in his life by the state of his feet.'

'You mean you didn't ask him?' The detective cracks a grim smile as O'Keefe passes through the doors into the hallway, where he is met by another man—larger, dark-eyed, jowly and wearing a trilby.

Thick eyebrows and a bruiser's scowl. Another detective, O'Keefe realises. Behind him is a woman—small, poor, a black knitted shawl covering her hair and shoulders. Mrs Dolan has stopped her at the door. She has a hand on her forearm and is nodding and whispering to the woman. Just Albert stares at O'Keefe and the two detectives.

Castle men, O'Keefe reckons, using the name by which plain-clothes detectives are still known to most Dubliners. Their other collective name is *G-men*. The Dublin Metropolitan Police has been allowed by the Free State to continue to police the city and its detective squad, G Division, is based as it always had been, in Dublin Castle. Originally assigned to political crimes, Michael Collins' gunmen had eliminated most of G Division during the Tan War. So these must be new lads, O'Keefe thinks. Recently promoted and in no hurry to stick their snouts into the business of civil war and its waging.

'Who's this?' the new detective says to his partner.

'He's been hired by Mrs Dolan to find her son. He was with the Peelers.'

The larger detective talks over his partner as if the fact of O'Keefe's former career is of no importance to him. 'And we know for certain that's not her son in there?'

'It's not him.'

O'Keefe can picture this detective in an interview room in a city barracks, his sleeves rolled up, looming over some poor bastard. Instinctively, O'Keefe's eyes drop to the man's knuckles, to the scarring he knows he will find there.

'What's your name? Have you any identification on you?'

'No.'

'So you've no way of proving who you are, so.'

'I'm doing the woman a good turn. Nothing more.'

'Not much of one so far. How much she paying you? More than I'm fucking paid no doubt.'

O'Keefe ignores the big man. Policemen in Ireland complain about their wages the way cocks crow the morning sun up. He'd been no different himself. 'How long have those boys been dead?' he asks.

The big man leans into O'Keefe and O'Keefe can smell onions and meat and stout on his breath. 'And I ask you again. Who in the name of fuck are you to be asking questions? How do I know you weren't the one who's after scorching them boys' mickeys and putting two in the back of their heads? How am I to know?'

The first detective intervenes. 'Give it a rest, Pat. It's not like we're going to be asking anyone any questions ourselves, you know as well as I do.' He holds out his hand to O'Keefe and O'Keefe takes it. 'I'm Mulligan and this is Wynn.'

'Seán O'Keefe.'

'For fuck sake,' Wynn says.

'You were a Murder Man yourself weren't you?' Mulligan continues.

'No, but I investigated my share of them.'

'You've the cut of a Peeler. The way you examined the body ...'

'You saw that then?'

'I see what I want to see. What I'm allowed see, now'days.'

O'Keefe nods. 'I was in Cork, during the Tan War. I know how that is. Still, I managed to lag the odd fella. War doesn't give a man an excuse to do what was done to those boys.'

'A lecture now. You're not in the Peelers any more,' Wynn says.

'I'm only trying to find the boy for Mrs Dolan. Is that the mother of the other lad?' O'Keefe asks, nodding at the figure down the hallway.

Mulligan shrugs. 'She might be. She reported her boy missing a week ago. A gurrier, the youngfella is. Has a record for robberies, dipping bags and the like. For all I know, she's mother to the one we thought was Nicholas.'

'Was he known to be with the Irregulars? Or the youth wing ... what are they called? The Fianna ... Na Fianna?' O'Keefe says.

'The lad you're looking for ... he's with them?'

O'Keefe nods.'And you've no idea who the other boy is?'

'No, and we've no record in any of the Divisions of any other boys reported missing. Being in the Irregulars might explain that.'

'It could,' O'Keefe says. 'You wouldn't, by any chance, know where I might find Felim O'Hanley?'

Both detectives smile at this.'Jesus, I hope she's paying you well if you're looking for him.'

'It's not the money, believe me.'

'Kind hearts are easily broken,'Wynn says, shaking his head.

'Happy hunting, gentlemen.'

'To you too, Mr O'Keefe. Let us know if you find anything.'

Over his shoulder O'Keefe hears the big detective call to the woman he has brought. His voice is surprisingly gentle. 'Mrs Fallon. It's time now.'

The woman takes her arm from Mrs Dolan and passes O'Keefe on her way down the hallway.

O'Keefe, Ginny Dolan and Just Albert wait at the entrance while the woman goes through the first and second sets of swing-doors. O'Keefe moves to step outside, but Ginny Dolan stops him. 'Wait.'

Moments later a keening cry rends the silence of the morgue, and Ginny Dolan nods and pushes through the entrance door to the outside.

Again, they wait, this time on the street—Ginny Dolan smoking a cigarette in a long holder—letting the cool night air wash over them, listening to the night sounds of the city. A goods train clattering through Amiens Street station nearby. Faint shouting and laughter from Monto.

Some minutes pass and the woman emerges from the Morgue, no sign of the detective with her this time. Tears streak down her cheeks and O'Keefe thinks of an expression his mother used. *The tears cutting ditches in her face.* Ginny Dolan once again takes the woman's arm, and this time hugs her close.

'I'm sorry for your troubles, Mrs Fallon,' O'Keefe hears her say. 'Take this.' Ginny Dolan presses what O'Keefe assumes to be a roll of banknotes into the woman's hand. 'For the funeral.'

The woman says something and Ginny nods and says, 'Of course. My men will find them. They'll be taken care of.'

Finally, the woman pulls away, saying that she will not accept a lift and needs to walk, to think of her baby, Thomas. Her oldest boy. A good boy she says, but for that bastard Jeremiah Byrne. She'd always known it would be that Jerry who would be the death of her son ....

'And do you know where this Jeremiah Byrne lives?' Ginny Dolan asks.

'Of course I do, sure isn't it across the road from my own lodgings?' And with this she begins to weep.

Thanking the woman and turning to O'Keefe, Ginny Dolan says to him, 'Come in the back of the car with me, Mr O'Keefe.'

O'Keefe has known this was coming and feels powerless to avoid it. He wants to help the woman, more now than ever, but is afraid of what this will entail. This is no longer the simple search for a missing boy. He climbs into the back of the Bentley with the madam while Just Albert cranks the car's starter.

The woman says nothing for a long moment. He senses the depth of her worry, her fear, and under these, the mass of her rage. At him perhaps, for not finding her boy. At the men her boy has left her to join in revolt. At the man or men who tortured and killed those two boys in the morgue. She had kissed those boys like they were her own. There was none of the joy O'Keefe had expected when she discovered that her Nicholas was not one of them. There had been only relief, and then with it, a new terror.

Finally: 'How did those boys die, Mr O'Keefe?'

'They were shot. Executed. Two bullets in the back of the head.'

'Was that all?'

O'Keefe pauses. 'Yes, that was all.'

'You're lying to me, Mr O'Keefe. I can smell it.'

He looks at her now. 'They were ...'

'They were hurt before they died, weren't they?'

O'Keefe nods, wondering how she knows this. As if reading his thoughts, she says, 'I saw the bottom of that boy's feet.'

'We've no way of knowing if Nicholas even knows those lads, Mrs Dolan.'

'That boy was wearing his jacket.'

'Still.'

'You'll continue to look for my Nicky, Mr O'Keefe.'

It is not a question.

'I will of course, Mrs Dolan. I'll do what I can, but...' He pauses.

'Yes?'

O'Keefe does not speak for a moment. 'I think the police need to be kept in this, Mrs Dolan. They can help us find Nicholas.'

Ginny Dolan laughs bitterly. 'They've no notion nor means to look for Nicky, and you know it as well as I do. Nor have they any notion of finding who killed those two boys. They'll write it off to the Irregulars or the Free Staters and be done with it. And even if they did find Nicholas, they'd have him up in front of a judge charged with treason or some such and hauled off to industrial school before you could say boo. They'd love to do that to a son of mine, the bastards, and I'll not give them the pleasure. I hired you to find Nicholas, Mr O'Keefe. And now I want you to find who killed those two boys.'

O'Keefe has a strong urge to do just this, but knows what his chances are. 'I'll do my best, if it's possible. But you must know, that things happen in war and sometimes, there's no one brought to book.'

'Torturing a young boy, two young boys, is an act of war, Mr O'Keefe? Is that what you're telling me?' There is a hard edge to her voice.

'No, not at all. Not to you or me or any civilised soul. But there are men who do things in war and use war as an excuse for doing things they wouldn't otherwise do. And there is something about this war, a civil war, that makes people *more* ashamed of what's being done, I reckon. Of all of it. On both sides. I just don't think …'

He feels he is talking in circles. Why can't he come out and say it? He will try to find the killers because he does not think anyone else will. But there has been so much murder in Ireland in the past few years that the deaths of two boys could very likely pass unnoticed by a people, by institutions, inured to murder and wanting only peace. Free State or Republic, O'Keefe knows, the people of Ireland do not care one way or the other which one comes to pass once the shooting stops and they can go about raising their families again, making a wage. In a way, he thinks, this makes the people of Ireland more willing to tolerate outrages of violence in the name of achieving that peace. A whore's son involved with the Irregulars would warrant little sympathy, even one as well-bred and educated as Nicholas, let alone the street robber on the table inside the morgue. As for the other boy, it wouldn't matter. Normal rules have been suspended and all is fair in this civil war, once a peace is somehow achieved.

'You sound like a civilised soul yourself, Mr O'Keefe, with all your fine ideas about war and peace. Your father had the same pretty way with words. A civilised man, your father, in his own manner. Are you such a man, Mr O'Keefe?'

He is stumped for the moment, and then catches the warning. His father owes a debt to this woman and it is O'Keefe's to pay.

'I try to be,' he says.

'Then you find my Nicky your own way. Find those killers if you can.' Ginny Dolan's eyes shine in the darkness. 'But mind you, my Albert … he's not so civilised as you claim to be.'

There is nothing he can say to this.

32

They park the Bentley on George's Dock and walk the war-ren of lanes that lead away from the river. Just Albert appears to know them well.

'You lads, come here, you,' Just Albert says. He waits as a ruck of boys, lounging with youthful menace on crumbling tenement steps, rises and makes its way over. There is an autumn evening chill in the air, bolstered by the seep of fog from the river.

'Which building does Jeremiah Byrne live in?' O'Keefe asks as Just Albert moves off into the shadows of the laneway.

'Who wants to know?' one of the boys says.

'Never you mind. Which building?'

'I was only sayin', mister, don't be gettin' the hump on yeh.'

Just Albert returns and stares hard at the lad before handing him a shilling. The boys smiles and pockets the coin.

'Third on yis'r right, first floor, the one with no windies in it. And by all means, tell the cunt I sent yis. Me brother's gonna have the bastard for his tea when he finds him.'

As they approach the building, curious children in the lane gather and follow them at a safe distance, holding out their hands before moving away, seeing something in Just Albert's eyes that frightens them. The coins are silent in his pockets as he walks, his fists clenched and held at his sides as he mounts the steps of the tenement.

'First floor the youngfella said.'

'I heard him.'

A man sitting halfway up the steps and clutching a bottle of cheap sherry looks up at them and then looks away. Albert notices and stops.

'You've something to say, have you?' he says to the man.

O'Keefe stops with him and takes the girder of his arm in his hand. 'He said nothing, Albert, leave it. Sure, we know where the boy lives.'

'He wants to tell us something, he does. Don't you, pal?' It is not a question. Light from one of the few unbroken lamps on the street is reflected in the man's eyes, bloodshot and afraid. 'Don't you?' Just Albert says again and his voice is nearer the growl of an animal than the speech of a man.

The man nods slowly and O'Keefe wonders if he understands. Then: 'Only that yis are not the first come looking here for young Jerry Byrne.'

'And how do you know we're looking for him?'

'Sure, ye're wearing suits aren't ye? And in my experience …'—the man burps and winces, something hot and painful in his throat—'… anyone wearing a suit round here is looking for that young lad lately, for good or bad.'

Just Albert hands the man a coin, and the man takes it without thanks. 'See?' Albert says to O'Keefe. He looks down at O'Keefe's hand on his arm and O'Keefe releases it.

'It could be those detectives, the ones from the morgue. The Fallon boy's mother told them the same she told us, no doubt. That this Jeremiah Byrne is involved … somehow. But we can't assume he's guilty of something, Albert.'

Ginny Dolan's man ignores him for a moment, standing on the top step in the open door of the tenement building. He looks up and down the row of tenements and then back up at the dimly lit windows. There is no electricity in the flats, and rarely on the landings or hallways either, so the residents use tallow candles or oil-lamps when there is money enough, living in stygian darkness or going to bed early when there is none. The doorman says, 'This Byrne lad would want to be praying no harm's come to Nicky.'

'More flies with honey, Albert,' O'Keefe says, and feels a fool saying it.

'Where'd you learn that, Mr O'Keefe, in the Peelers was it?' They enter the building.

The entrance hallway is a sea of warped floorboards, the original tiles long stripped and sold or reused, and O'Keefe's senses are struck by the smells of boiled cabbage, paraffin oil, scorched dripping; of black mould and crumbling brick and sweat and cheap tobacco. The walls and landing sing with the sounds of a baby's crying and a man's deep, hacking cough; the stuttering burst of a woman's laughter; footsteps on the rotting floorboards above. The building is like a living thing, sweating, bleeding, heaving and dying a little every day. *Like all of us*, O'Keefe thinks, following Just Albert as he mounts the patchwork staircase, their way dimly lit by second-hand light from the few remaining gas lamps on the lane. Halfway up, they are forced to step over a sleeping child, wrapped in what appears to O'Keefe to be a burlap sack. The child shivers and flinches in its sleep.

As they reach the first-floor landing where they have been told the Byrnes keep their room, more children lie asleep, a huddled bunch of bodies on the floorboards outside a one-room flat with a torn sheet for a doorway. There is barely enough space to pass them by on the landing. One of the children, a girl O'Keefe reckons to be five or six years old, opens her eyes and looks up at them.

'Are yis here for Jerry?' she asks, as if expecting them.

Just Albert appears to soften at the sight of the children. He smiles at the girl in the half-dark. 'We are, pet. Is he here?'

'No. He's gone ages, since the other men gave him a chase after he brought us some spuds and veg for our tea. Uncle John Keegan ate the bacon so we's didn't have any of that, so we didn't.'

O'Keefe wonders who Uncle John Keegan is and whether or not he will meet him. He hopes, vaguely, that he will.

'What other men?' Just Albert says.

'The other men Mam said was like Peelers but wasn't Peelers. Men in smart clothes like yis'rs. Are yis Peelers?' There is an innocence to her voice that cuts through the gloom and sour, stale smells of the landing.

'No,' Just Albert says, looking up and smiling without humour at O'Keefe. 'We're not Peelers, darling.'

'And when was it these men gave the chase to Jerry, pet?' O'Keefe asks.

The girl thinks for a moment. 'Some days ago, at tea time. Do you have any grub, Mister?'

Sadness chucks against O'Keefe's ribs. 'I've no grub,' he says, reaching into his pocket, 'but here ...' he comes out with a fistful of coins, 'take this and get some ray and chips and peas for you and the rest of the kids.'

The girl eyes the coins but makes no move to take them. 'And do you want to touch my fanny for the scratch, Mister?'

'Ah, jaysus fuck,' Just Albert says. He turns for the curtained doorway to the Byrne flat.

It takes a moment for the words to register with O'Keefe, and when they do, he recoils. He has to force himself to lean back down and press the coins into the girl's hand. 'No, Jesus, no, pet. And don't be ... doing things like that, right? It's not good for a young girl ...' He hears how lame and frail his words sound. *Like pissing on a tenement fire*, he thinks, and then regrets that his mind has summoned the common saying. There is no humour in it here, standing in this crumbling hallway filled with sleeping, hungry children.

O'Keefe tells the girl to go for food, and as he turns to follow Albert into the flat a scream shears the air, followed a second later by the dull impact of fist on flesh and bone. He yanks aside the curtain in the doorway.

In the weak, flickering light from a paraffin lamp, O'Keefe sees Just Albert standing over a naked man entangled in soiled bed clothes. The man's mouth gawps open in a desperate search for air as he tries to rise from a mattress resting on pallets. A woman, naked as well but for a tattered shawl thrown round her shoulders, stands behind Just Albert, and she screams again and moves, lifting the room's single wooden chair and swinging it at Albert before O'Keefe can reach her.

Just Albert steps inside the arc of the swinging chair and it bounces harmlessly against the wall, sending chunks of damp plaster cascading across the room. He grabs the woman by the hair as she stumbles past him and shoves her head first into the wall. There is a sickening thump and her skull leaves a deep, bowl-shaped dent in the soggy render. She slumps to the floor.

'Jesus, Albert, that's a woman,' O'Keefe says, moving across the room before Just Albert can do any further damage.

The doorman's eyes flare with threat. 'And I give a fuck?'

O'Keefe stops and swallows back the words that rise to his mouth. *You should give a fuck. Only an animal wouldn't.* But there is nothing he can say to him now, this woman likely not the first Just Albert has manhandled. Not in his line of work.

Just Albert crouches down to the man who is gathering the bed-clothes around him to cover his nakedness. 'Where's young Jerry?'

The man shakes his head but still cannot find the wind to speak. Just Albert stands up and kicks him in the ribs. 'Where is young Jeremiah Byrne?' He kicks him again and O'Keefe hears something crack. The man yelps in pain.

'Tell him, for the sake of Christ, John, tell him,' the woman says, dragging herself away from the wall, tears shining in her eyes, pulling the shawl over her ghost-pale nakedness.

O'Keefe says, 'What's his name, Missus? Your fella here?'

The woman stands and darts towards the doorway, quicker than O'Keefe thinks possible. He catches her by the arm and tosses her as gently as he can down onto the mattress.

She rears up to sitting and spits at O'Keefe. 'You fucker, you fuckin' cunt!'

'Now, there's no need for that,' O'Keefe says, wiping the spittle away from his jacket, hoping the woman does not have consumption or jail fever. 'Just tell us his name. Is he Jerry's father? Is he father to the kids in the hallway?'

The woman's eyes fill with defiance now, sensing in O'Keefe someone who will not harm her. 'You should know his fuckin' name, yeh thick piece of Peeler shite. Yis lag him every fuckin' week for something, leavin' the likes of us with nothing on our plates at all.'

O'Keefe remembers the girl in the hallway. He pushes past Just Albert and grabs the naked man by the hair, lifting him to his feet and shoving him roughly against the wall. The man is larger than he'd thought, heavily muscled around his shoulders and thighs, a soft paunch around his middle that tells of beer and meals of bacon the children in this house never see.

He had meant to intervene, to keep Albert from doing such damage to this man that he unable to answer their questions. But something inside him has shifted. The thought of the girl in the hallway—of all the children in the hallway—going hungry because of this thing in front of him. He shields his mind, for the moment, from what else this man may have done.

'Are you John Keegan?' O'Keefe asks.

The man looks into O'Keefe's eyes and looks away and nods. O'Keefe can feel Just Albert's breath hot on his shoulder behind him.

'*Uncle* John Keegan?' Just Albert says.

Again the man nods.

'Where's Jerry? Are you his father?' O'Keefe asks.

'No, I'm not his fuckin' da, I'm his fuckin' uncle. That cunt's his mother, but.'

'So you're not Jerry's da and you're riding his ma. Where is he?' Just Albert says.

239

Petulance slips across the man's face and into his voice. 'How in fuck am I s'posed to know? The little git only comes round here lookin' for grub and bringin' grief on his poor mother. I'd love tell yis where he is but he's not fuckin' here.'

There is something about this man that reminds O'Keefe of so many he had lagged as an RIC man. It is the voice, perhaps, or the cast of face that so readily warps from tyrant to victim.

'When was he here last?' Just Albert says.

'Day before yesterday, I think … when your mates were here. And then he legged it when he saw them, not leaving a penny in the pot for us at all or anything for the childer.'

O'Keefe leans in and puts his forehead against John Keegan's forehead, pressing him back into the plaster. The man's breath is rancid with beer and dead teeth. 'He brought potatoes and veg for the kids, didn't he, Uncle John?'

Something shows in O'Keefe's eyes, and Uncle John Keegan cannot bring his own to meet them. 'How should I know?'

Without taking away his forehead, O'Keefe reaches down and knocks the man's hands away from where they are shielding his genitals. He grips the man's testicles in his fist and squeezes, not hard but hard enough to give this man an idea of the pain that is coming if he does not answer his questions.

'I heard you ate all the bacon, John. Did you eat all the bacon yesterday and not give any to the nippers sleeping in the hallway? Did you do that, John?'

'What are you on about?'

'Did you eat all the bacon and not give the nippers any?'

'No, I …'

'Did you?' O'Keefe's voice is a strangled grunt that sounds rough and foreign to his own ears. He squeezes the man's balls harder.

'Yes! Jaysus fuck! What's that to do with anything?'

It is the voice that triggers something in O'Keefe. The whinging, pitiable victim in it. 'And did you fiddle with that little girl out in the hallway?'

'Jaysus, no!'

O'Keefe squeezes harder and tugs down on the man's scrotum.

'All right! Jaysus fuck, all right! Only when her mother's not able is all. Jaysus, she likes it!'

Something red floods O'Keefe's vision and he cocks his head back and drives his forehead into Uncle John Keegan's face, the man's nose shattering under the blow, blood spraying over his chin stubble and onto his chest in a fanlight splatter.

The woman screams. 'You're after killing him!' She makes to stand and Just Albert turns to her.

'Get out in the hallway and mind your babbies for once in your life,' the doorman says.

The woman's mouth opens to speak but closes again. She pulls the ragged blanket from the bed and wraps it around her as she exits the room. O'Keefe moves back a step, rubbing blood from his forehead with a handkerchief.

Just Albert says, 'You tell me where we can find young Jerry. D'you hear me, bigfella?'

Still clutching his face, blood streaming through his fingers and pattering onto the floor, he nods. His voice is high and muzzled when it comes. 'He works down the laneways by the fruit and veg markets, gaming punters, the quare youngfella. Tha's all I know. I swear on the eyes of my …'

'Don't say *children* or I'll kill you myself,' O'Keefe says.

Uncle John Keegan goes silent. He looks away from O'Keefe back to Just Albert and sees something in the doorman's eyes that starts him pleading. 'Yis can lag me, for fuck sake. Lag me, take me in. I'll leave here and not come back if yis lag me.'

A brief, brutal smile flashes across Just Albert's lips. 'Lag you?'

'Look … *please* … there's no need to bate me more. I already told all this to your mates who came yesterday. Just fuckin' ask them.'

'Oh we will, bigfella. *Uncle John*,' Just Albert says, and there is a bite in his voice that makes O'Keefe uneasy.

Just Albert gently pushes O'Keefe aside and grabs John Keegan by the scruff of the neck, his vice-like hand half lifting, half guiding the man across the room to stop in front of the tall sash window, empty of glass.

The doorman leans in close to the man and O'Keefe can only just make out the words he speaks. 'You're never to touch one of them kids again, Big John, right? Do you get me?'

Uncle John Keegan nods, eager to convince. 'Never again. No word of a lie, will I ever touch them, I swear to fuck.'

'Can I believe you, but? Can I trust you, Uncle John?'

'You can, I swear it. You …'

Just Albert smiles and grips the man by the neck and under his arm and lifts him easily into the air.

O'Keefe blinks as if awaking from a dream, a nightmare, and takes a lunging step towards the two men.

Before O'Keefe can reach them, Uncle John Keegan is airborne, Just Albert releasing his hold with a grunt, the man's feet clipping the ledge as Albert propels him out of the window. A short scream is snapped silent by the broken thudding of meat and bone onto the cobbles some twenty feet below.

'Jesus …' O'Keefe says, and Just Albert turns to him.

'You'd have done it yourself if you weren't so fuckin' … *civilised*,' the doorman says, passing out of the room and onto the landing.

O'Keefe follows him out and waits while he gives the girl more coins, her siblings stirring now and waking as Uncle John Keegan begins to howl in pain on the street outside. There is no sign of the woman, and O'Keefe does not know if he should be glad of this.

'Here, and go get more bacon with that, in the morning, pet. Your uncle won't be taking it on you now, he won't.'

The girl smiles up at them. 'Is he dead? Did yis kill him?'

'No, pet. We didn't kill him,' O'Keefe says.

The girl is silent for a moment, listening to her uncle's cries. 'Well why didn't yis not?' she says, her small, bony fist clenched tight around the coins in her palm. 'Now yis've only gone and made him cross.'

33

Half past three in the morning. They make their way across the city in silence, the Bentley's smooth purr masking the drumming of O'Keefe's heart, his adrenaline-sweat sour and sharp in the car, his hands shaking, the sound of Keegan's screams still plaintive and shrill in his ears. The sight of the filthy bottoms of the man's feet as they bucked over the window ledge. A shudder passes through him.

'Albert,' he says.

'We're here, so save your talk, Mr O'Keefe, for them that need it.'

Ginny Dolan's man brakes the Bentley on Capel Street, pulling it up onto the footpath, and they make their way down a laneway to the Chancery Street fruit and vegetable market, where they pause to watch lorries and horse wagons being unloaded.

O'Keefe says, 'The early house pubs aren't even open for another few hours. There's hardly likely to be any lads around we can question.'

They wait as a horse cart carrying heads of cabbage passes into the market and then move on, Just Albert leading them, over his shoulder saying, 'There will be if you know where to look.'

'And you know where to look, then?'

Just Albert turns to O'Keefe, cocking his head and squinting, but all trace of the rough smile is gone, rubbed out by what he had seen on the slab in the morgue.

'There's not much in this city I don't know, and what there is is hardly worth knowing.'

O'Keefe thinks of telling him that there was more to the city than Monto and the darkened lanes and the sweating tenements but stops himself. *No gain in it*, he thinks. Things are in motion. He is riding the train that Albert engineers through the heart of a city, a country, at war with itself. He wonders where or when he could have got off and cannot think of a time or a place.

They enter a lane running behind the markets. One side of it is high, barb-wire fencing bordering the market and the other is backed by the broken-bottle topped walls of tenement gardens and several pubs.

A fire burns in a barrel halfway down the lane to the rear of a pub called Quinn's, and around it stand a loose mob of boys. Five or six lads. More in the shadows beyond the firelight. They stare warily at the approaching men and one of the gang sets down a tall glass jar of clear liquid next to the barrel.

Methylated spirits, O'Keefe assumes, mixed with cordial or sugar syrup or nothing at all. Hands are jammed in pockets and sunken eyes peer up from under rough cut hair and tattered cloth caps. One of the boys suddenly turns and sprints away from the barrel into the darkness, his bare feet padding down the laneway until only the crackling flames in the barrel can be heard.

'He late for an appointment, wha'?' Just Albert says, getting sullen silence in response. He stands close to the fire, holding out his hands as if to warm them, and stares each of the boys in the eyes until they look away. 'Business slow tonight, lads?'

'Business is business, is wha' it is,' one of the boys says, a tall lad with skin stretched tight over high cheek-bones and missing teeth. He could be fourteen or twenty-four, O'Keefe thinks, wondering at the degradation mirrored in the faces of the lads huddled round the fire.

'And we done nothin',' the boy continues, 'and stole nothin', so's there nothin' to pinch us for an' anyway.'

'Pinch yis? Do we look like coppers, do we?' Just Albert says.

The boy tilts his head and considers the question. 'He does,' he says, pointing his chin at O'Keefe. 'You look like ...' The jibe dies in his throat under the dark light in Albert's eyes. '... You don't look like one, but.'

Just Albert nods in acknowledgement of the boy's implied respect. In Dublin, withholding a barb often counts as much. 'Yis can relax then. We need ask yis a few questions is all.' At this, he jingles the coins in his pockets for the first time this evening, but in a perfunctory way, none of the doorman's usual blithe charity in the sound; the clinking coins merely signal that there is payment in the offing for questions answered.

'We're looking for a lad,' O'Keefe says.

'I bet you are,' the tall boy says. 'Sure, you wouldn't be the first Peeler on the hoof looking to have his bottle washed by the likes of me.'

O'Keefe is taken aback by the boy's boldness, the mocking smile on his face. 'You're joking.'

The boy winks in the firelight. 'You're the fuckin' joke, me auld flower.'

'Give it up, you,' Just Albert says, and the boy turns back to him and touches his cap brim. There is no mockery in the gesture, the boy sensing the simmering violence in the doorman. All the boys appear to sense it now, averting their eyes and suppressing vacant, methylated smiles. Their awareness of danger, O'Keefe thinks, is sharpened by their lives on the street to the point where words hardly matter and airs and auras—of menace, weakness, need—is what they have learned to act upon. Still, O'Keefe is amazed by the respect the boys show Ginny Dolan's man.

'Sorry, Mister,' the boy says.

'Jeremiah Byrne,' O'Keefe says. 'Jerry Byrne. Blond lad. White blond hair, he has. Does he work with ye lads?'

The tall boy snorts out a laugh, and the laughter leads to a fit of deep consumptive coughing. Furtive smiles edge the lips of the other boys in the group. Finally: 'Work with us? You *are* fuckin' jokin', Peeler. That lad wouldn't set foot near us, once we was together in a mob, like. He only comes up on a fella when he's on his tot, and then only to rob him of what he's on him. Sure, to fuck, didn't he reef the shoes off Damo there, only last night.'

'Night before,' a small boy says. 'They was too big an' I couldn't fuckin' leg it from him, I couldn't.'

O'Keefe looks down at the boy. Hardly older than the children asleep on the tenement landing, he thinks. At least those children have somewhere half dry to bed down, despite their neglect and mistreatment. The small boy runs a filthy sleeve under his nose.

'Whatever night it was,' the leader says, 'he put a broke bottle to Damo's t'roat and whipped the brogues righ' off him.'

Another boy pipes up, unable to meet O'Keefe's or Albert's eyes, but angry and wanting his speak. 'And I never even got a shot of them.' The boy stares down at his bare feet as if just now noticing their existence.

'You share out the shoes?' O'Keefe asks in disbelief.

'Of course we bleedin' do. What'd you think? That Damien'd land a brace of smashing leather boats for hisself and not gi's a go in them? No fella goes short and no fella hungry if one of us has scratch or bread. Tha's why Jerry Byrne's a dead boy once we lay eyes on him. He waits on us til we's on our own, we waits for him til we're not and he is.'

'And then we'll get our brogues back,' the small lad says.

O'Keefe smiles. The boy cannot be more than ten years old. His smile collapses around the knowledge of what this young boy must do to eat, let alone for a pair of shoes.

'We'll open his poxy loaf with a brick,' another boy says, a dark smile on his face in the firelight.

Just Albert withdraws a handful of coins from his pocket. 'Here,' he says. 'I don't want a hair on his head touched until we've talked with him, right?' He looks each boy in the eye until they nod assent. 'Here's something to keep you going now and there's a pound in it for the lad who finds him and lets me or Mr O'Keefe know about it.' He hands a few coppers to each of the boys. 'Yis can leave word for us at Mrs Dolan's gaff in Foley Street. Yis know it?'

Again the boys nod. 'In Monto?' the older boy says.

'That's the one.'

'Or you can get me at twenty-four Leinster Road in Rathmines,' O'Keefe says, hoping against hope that they might come to him first and he might be able to prevent the hell Jerry Byrne has coming if he's had anything to do with harming Nicholas Dolan. He doubts that they will be able to remember the address.

'Rathmines?' one of the boys says. 'Jaysus, tha's like …'

Another boy finishes his sentence. '… Like another bleedin' country, tha' is.'

And it is, O'Keefe thinks. Only two miles away from the lanes in which these boys live, and most likely will die. Barely two miles and another world away.

34

O'Keefe hires a jarvey hack at the corner of Sackville Place and O'Connell Street and drifts into a restless sleep as the driver flets his horse, clopping the silent streets of Dublin, shades of pale purple dawn beginning to leech into the night sky. Nightmares of boys in laneways and a Turk soldier swinging his bayonet lance his slumber, and he kicks out as the jarvey wakes him in front of the Cunningham house.

'For the love of God, Mister, only you're bleedin' home. Don't be playing the mick now.'

Blinking away sleep, O'Keefe pays the man, unsure of what he has done but tips him too much anyway. He stands at the top of the steps down to his flat listening to the fading chucking of hooves as the hackney heads back to town. Silence then, on the street. He half expects to hear the din of gunfire, revving engines, drunken singing—the music of a city at war—but there is no sound at all except his breathing, and for a moment O'Keefe has the impression that he is the last man alive in Dublin. As if he has been spared from some great cataclysm that has taken the people of the city and left him alone. He grips the iron railing at the top of the steps, his breathing shallow, knowing the feeling is merely an echo of the nightmares he has suffered since the war, his thinking tainted and catastrophic. He pities and hates himself in equal measure when he is like this. An image of the Keegan man sailing out the tenement window flares in his mind and he hates himself even more.

'Mr O'Keefe.' The voice is a loud whisper, and he looks up to see Mrs Cunningham, standing on the top steps, the front door to her house open. 'I've been waiting up for you. Are you … are you all right?'

O'Keefe swallows and forces himself to smile. 'I am. I was only lost in thought, Mrs Cunningham. You shouldn't have … why did you wait up for me?'

The woman comes down the steps to where O'Keefe stands on the footpath, her dressing-gown clutched tightly around her.

'Your mother,' she says, taking hold of his forearm, 'sent a boy round earlier. You're to go home at once. The boy said it was urgent.'

Panic wells again in O'Keefe. What could his mother want with him this late—this early? 'Did he say …?'

'He said nothing but to make certain you got the message.'

Minutes later he is at the door of his parents' house on Fumbally Lane. His mother looks tired, O'Keefe thinks, but not distraught.

'Mam, is everything all right? Is Da …?'

'We're grand, son. Come in. It's not us at all. It's a friend of yours. Your father is with him upstairs. Solly has been to see him, and thinks he'll live, and of course Solly would never report …'

'Report what? Mam, tell me what's happened.'

His mother reaches out and touches his face. 'You go see for yourself. I will say you've interesting friends, Seáneen. But I'm not one to judge.'

O'Keefe makes his way to the stairs, and mounts them with growing dread.

His father sits in a halo of candlelight, morning seeping slowly through the curtains.

O'Keefe enters the room, and is about to speak when his father shushes him with a finger to his lips. Again, his father's face

249

is troubled and blank for a long moment before settling itself to a warm smile. 'He's sleeping. Let him have another few minutes.'

'Who is it?' For a panicked moment, O'Keefe thinks that it is Peter in the bed, and memories from childhood crowd into his tired mind. He blinks the memories away and sees, in the dim light, exactly who it is.

'Holy Mother of God. Jack Finch. He's a friend of mine, Da, from the Peelers. I'm sorry about this. I gave him the address when we demobbed from the Peelers …' He turns to his father. 'When did he come?'

'Around nine. There was a knock on the front door and there he was, slumped down on the steps. Back from the war, thank God. I was worried about him. And you. Peter is no scrapper, doesn't like a fight …'

'It's not Peter, Da,' O'Keefe says, sadness replacing the fear for the moment. 'Peter's …' He cannot bring himself to say it.

The blankness returns and in an instant is gone, and this time annoyance, anger. 'Of course it's not Peter, Seán, for the sake of God, Peter's long dead. Do you not think I don't know that? Jesus, boy.'

'And who brought him, Da?'

'I've no notion who brought him. He was just there, half dead from the look of him. Good thing it was dark or the neighbours would have wondered at it. A bleeding man on the front steps like this was some kind of field hospital.'

'What happened to him?'

'Gunshot wound and some cuts around the face and eyes. The bullet went through and out the other side, the doctor … you know …' Frustration on his father's face again. '*Solly!* A clean wound, Solly said, and lucky for him it was. It was a big bullet.'

O'Keefe leans down over the bed and places his palm on Finch's forehead in the same manner as his mother had touched his face moments before. 'Will he be all right?'

His father shrugs. 'Solly said time will tell. If no infection sets in, he'll be grand in no time. If it does … Sure, you know yourself.'

O'Keefe did know. He had spent nearly a year recovering from blood-poisoning after being shot and bayoneted in his two weeks of fighting in Turkey. 'And did he say how he got it? The bullet?'

'No, he only said that he was a friend of yours, and that this was the only address he had in Dublin for you and that he was sorry to cause us the trouble. Then he handed us a fistful of banknotes to pay the doctor and passed out. I put what we didn't need back in his pockets. Sure, Solly wouldn't take any money. There's over twenty pound in bloodstained notes in those pockets, along with the tenner odd I put back in there.'

Laughing softly, O'Keefe takes his hand away from Finch's forehead. It is clammy and warm but not yet feverish. O'Keefe knows this means nothing, depending on when he got the wound and how well the doctor had been able to clean it. Infection keeps a schedule of its own.

'Solly left fresh bandages and iodine solution to keep it clean and freshly wrapped. "There'll be all sorts draining out of it in the next few days," he said. He said someone else had already bandaged him up and stopped most of the bleeding. Most likely saved his life, whoever it was.'

'I can only imagine,' O'Keefe says, thinking how strange it is seeing Finch so vulnerable. There has always been something so indestructible about the man that it is difficult for O'Keefe to be worried for him. Finch had been through hell in the trenches of the Great War, and another hell of its own kind in Cork, and had survived both with barely a scratch. He had told O'Keefe how many bullets he'd dodged in Flanders, sniper rounds passing through his helmet brim, bullets striking him in the armoured vest he had bought at home on leave from a fella who'd left his arm at the first battle at Ypres. A bullet that had struck a grenade in his pocket once, the grenade scored by the bullet but the fuse staying blessedly intact. O'Keefe had been in more than one gunfight alongside Finch in Cork, and for a man who seemed to value his life so little, he had seemed invincible; as if minded by an overly vigilant guardian angel. And yet here he is, O'Keefe thinks, suffering a bullet wound in a war he has no place in; in a country he was supposed to have left five months ago. *What have you been up to, Jack Finch, since I saw you last?*

As if he'd spoken the words aloud, Finch opens his eyes.

'All right, Sergeant, still velvet then, mate?'

O'Keefe smiles through his weariness. 'Grand, Finch. Better than you look anyway. And I haven't been a sergeant in a long time and you well know it.'

'Odd calling you anything else, innit?'

'So, you've been in some scrap, have you?'

'You could say that. Finally took a proper bullet for my troubles.'

'In one side, out the other.'

'So the doc says.' At this, he tries to sit up and winces, laying back down. 'Facking 'urts … sorry, Dads. Forgot you was there.' He tries to smile and winces again, pain etching lines on his forehead.

'I've heard worse,' O'Keefe's father says. He folds the newspaper he has been reading by candlelight and stands now. 'A few words downstairs, son?'

O'Keefe nods to him and tucks the blanket around Finch again. 'I'll be back in a minute and we'll get you sorted, Finch.'

Night's darkness is giving way to milky morning light through the curtains and O'Keefe's father blows out the candle and leaves the bedroom, his boots heavy on the stairs.

'You rest for the moment, Finch. You'll be grand. There's no killing the like of you, there isn't.'

'There's trying, though.'

'There's that.'

O'Keefe follows downstairs to the kitchen, where his father and mother sit at the table with mugs of tea. His mother rises and pours him a cup, sets it in front of him with the milk jug and leaves the kitchen.

His father takes his time filling his pipe. O'Keefe takes out his cigarettes and lights one, holding the match to the bowl of his father's pipe.

'How are you feeling, then?' he asks, to break the silence.

'Oh, I'm grand, nearly ready to take over that job, if you've had enough of it.'

O'Keefe looks away. 'What job is that?'

Anger flares in his father's eyes. 'I'm not thick, son, so don't act like I am, right?'

O'Keefe nods, shame warming his face.

'But I'm not well,' his father says, leaning back in the chair and talking around his pipe-stem, the anger leaving his eyes. 'Not well in the head. Solly's explained it to me. And your mother ...' his father smiles sadly, '... your mother couldn't keep a secret from me if she was paid to. When she told me she'd taken care of the job, I knew what she meant.'

'She's looking after you.'

'I know. And I ... I'm grateful to you for taking it off my hands. I get ... I get so's I can't remember where I've been or what I'm supposed to be doing betimes. Other times, I'm grand. But I owe Ginny Dolan.' He looks up at O'Keefe as if seeking permission to tell O'Keefe the reason for his debt to the woman.

'It's grand, Da.' O'Keefe interrupts him before he can continue. He does not want to know what ties bind his father to Ginny Dolan. There is nothing to be gained from it. 'I'm happy doing it. A job of work. Keeps me off the gargle by nights.' He smiles and his father smiles back and O'Keefe notices how small his father suddenly appears. His illness has diminished him physically somehow, his broad shoulders now stooped, his head bowed.

'The job's going all right. Ginny Dolan's man, Albert ...'

'... Ah no, not that fella.' His father looks away. 'She's not landed you with him has she?'

'She has, but it's no bother. He's a grand fella, most of the time. Sometimes, not so grand a chap.'

Worry clouds his father's face. 'He hasn't … he hasn't said anything to you about …' His father's eyes turn away and he busies himself relighting his pipe.

O'Keefe says, 'No, we only talk about the job of finding the boy. That's all.'

His father nods and puffs on his pipe. After some moments, he says, 'You're friend is welcome to stay, Seán. You know that don't you?'

'Of course, but it'd be bad news for Mam if a mob of soldiers came bursting through the door looking for him. Tracking muck on the carpets,' O'Keefe says, as he stubs out his cigarette in the ashtray. 'I thought he'd gone home to London months ago, to be honest. Still, I'm glad he came here. He saved my hide more times than I can remember down in Cork and I owe him.'

His father nods. 'He's a pal of yours and that's what matters. You'll take him with you so?'

O'Keefe nods. 'What will you tell the troops if they come? Someone might report him, might have seen him dropped here.'

'I'll tell them I'm not right in the head, tell them we went to sleep and he bunked off in the night.'

'Grand so. I hope he can manage riding pillion.'

'He'll be grand. And let us know, son, if you need a hand on that job.' His father is smiling, and O'Keefe forces himself to smile back. 'Before the lights go out altogether.'

Finch clings to O'Keefe on the Trusty, and O'Keefe can feel him shuddering with pain on the short ride to his flat at the Cunningham house. Finch breathes through gritted teeth as O'Keefe helps him down the steps and onto his own bed before going back up to stow the bike. When he comes back down, Finch's eyes are closed and his breathing is laboured, a sheen of sweat on his face.

'Right,' he says, and Finch opens his eyes and tries to smile.

'A good skin, Sergeant, you are.'

'Enough of that, Finch. Let's get you into bed.'

Finch is undressed and tucked under the blankets, and O'Keefe sits down on the floor with his back to the bed. He smokes, and waves of fatigue crash over him. He glances at his watch. Seven a.m. He should eat something. Instead, he smokes a final cigarette and closes his eyes. Just for an hour, he tells himself. Or two. *Tired … Jaysus-tired, I am ….*

35

The morning streets are crowded with delivery lorries and dray horses hauling beer kegs and coal. Trams full, men hanging on to railings on conductors' platforms in suits and hats reading folded newspapers, swinging gently with the curve and jolt of the tracks. People making their way from the southern suburbs of Ballsbridge and Donnybrook by horse and trap, motor car, foot. Perfect cover, Stephen Gilhooley thinks, his Morris Cowley butcher's van full of meat and money.

He turns onto Dartmouth Walk and comes to a stop in stalled traffic at Leeson Street bridge, the canal water below brown and still as glass. Waiting, he thinks of the fourteen thousand pounds in the bag in the back of the van and what a man could do with it. Start a new life, he thinks idly, revelling in the sheer fantasy of it. Head out for California, US of A, and buy a house with its own swimming baths and a soft, fat blond girleen to swim with; tall whiskey cocktails and gin and vermouth, drinks with all manner of fruits in them, jaysus, the sweet taste of one of them and the big round-arsed doll in her bathing costume ....

There is a rapping on the passenger side window. Gilhooley starts, and his hand goes into his white butcher's coat. Too late, he thinks, as the revolver snags on his shirt and tangles in the folds of the coat coming out.

'Stephen!' A smiling face at the window, the door opening.

Gilhooley's hand releases the grip of the revolver, relief washing through him. 'Jaysus fuck, Nicky Dolan. Here's me, thinking I was dead.'

'I'm alive and well, I am,' the boy says, misunderstanding Gilhooley's words. 'Starving, but. I've hardly eaten a crumb since Monday evening.'

There is a damp, musty smell to the boy that Gilhooley catches now, his face smeared with what appears to be soot or ashes. He wears no coat, and his long trousers are torn. But he is smiling, his teeth white. *A big lark, the whole war is to these lads*, Gilhooley thinks. And why not? Sure, half the reason he's in it himself. Keeps him away from the slow death of arguing with auld ones over cuts of offal for the rest of his days. In it for the craic as much as the cause. A lorry sounds its claxon behind, and Stephen pulls the van forward and turns left over the bridge onto Leeson Street.

'What happened at the hotel, so?'

'Fuck it if I know, I'm tellin' yeh. We came out and were jumped by two gougers first. And then—you wouldn't believe it— weren't we jumped by Free Staters with a Talbot motor. One of the gougers stuck one of the Free Staters with a knife and didn't I take off running …'

'And Robert? What happened young Robbo?'

'No idea. He was behind me and then he wasn't. But he knew nothing about the message, only that it was for Murphy and he doesn't know where the gaff is. Does he?' The words rush from Nicholas Dolan in a boyish flow, as if he is recounting some schoolboy's prank.

'No, Robbo doesn't know the way any more than you do.'

'Then he'll be grand so. Maybe he got lifted, but even so …'

The boy looks eagerly at Gilhooley as he drives.

'So where'd you hide yourself these past two days, then?' Gilhooley asks. 'Back to mammy's with you, wha'?' He smiles to mask the true meaning of the question.

'To fuck I went back there. Anyone could be on the house. I slept in a burnt-out cowshed in James' Street, by the brewery, the first night, I was trying to find McKinney's safe house, but fuck if I could. Last night I kipped in an alley off Pembroke Street. I went to the meet up spot about twenty times yesterday, and then just now was on me way there again. That's when I saw you in the van here.'

Stephen smiles. Not a fool for fifteen, fourteen, whatever age the fella is. Taking precautions, not heading home at the first hint of trouble, returning to the set rendezvous point confident that someone would show for him eventually. Even more, the boy had not come back to the butcher shop.

'Will I get in the back of the van, so, Lieutenant?'

Gilhooley smiles again. Only the young lads addressed the other men by rank. 'Call me Stephen for Jaysus' sake. And no, stay up here with me. We're not going back to the house yet. We've a job on first.'

'What is it?'

'Going back to Burton's Hotel to drop the gun monger the money we scored in Newbridge. You can mind the van for me while I'm inside. Throw on that coat there …' The gunman nods to the white butcher's coat folded and set on the bench seat between them. 'Nothing more natural than a butcher's van in the lane behind a hotel of a Wednesday morning.'

Nicholas smiles. He's a handsome lad, Gilhooley thinks, and no doubt the boss is sweet on him.

'Jaysus I could eat the meat in back raw, I could.'

'You mind the van and I'll fry you a chop or two when we're done, right?'

The young boy, beaming. 'Grand, so.' Then closing down his smile as if it is not something serious soldiers do.

Nora is at her post in reception when the call comes in.

'Front desk, how may I help you?' She assumes, at first, it is the usual request for drinks or sandwiches. Inquiries about laundry or suits to be pressed or messages received. She is thinking, as she picks up the phone—as she has been all morning—about her evening with O'Keefe. She has resolved that it will be her last with him. She will tell Carty that she can get nothing from the man and that he is not worth wasting a shadow on. She can do that much for Seán O'Keefe at least.

'Yes …' the accent of the voice on the line is English, and at first Nora does not recognise it. '… Murphy here in room thirty-four. I'd like to order up some drinks, if I could. Brandy and a bottle of ginger ale, please. Yes,' the order is repeated clearly, 'brandy and ginger ale.'

Nora's heart leaps to a gallop as she recognises the code. *Brandy and ginger ale.* O'Hanley—or his men—are in the room with Murphy. Part of her mind, as she turns to the switchboard to place a call to the Flowing Tide and her colleagues waiting there, wonders if the code is too obvious. *Who orders up brandy and ginger ale at half ten in the morning?*

The line to the pub is engaged, and she unplugs the cable and jams the socket in its hole to try again. Nothing. She drops the earpiece and runs now, first for the lift and then, pausing in front of it, for the stairs, passing Michael the porter to throw open the door, mounting the stairs two at a time until she hears a door, a flight above her, slam closed. She stops, breathing hard, and listens to footsteps descending. *Move up or down, girl*, she thinks. *Do either but do it now.* She decides on up and begins to mount the stairway at a more regular pace, matching the footfalls above, trying to control her breathing and thinking of her bag beneath the counter at reception. Thinking of the Webley revolver she has left inside it. The footfalls halt above her.

Nora has a sudden urge to stop as well, but wills herself on, knowing that to do so will invoke suspicion in whoever it is descending. She continues to climb, takes the turning of the stairs and looks up. Waiting by the door that opens onto the second-floor hallway is a young man—eighteen, nineteen—in a white coat and hat. A butcher, she thinks, relieved for a second—there is a regular flow of butchers and bakers making daily deliveries to the hotel—and then thinks how out of place a butcher's delivery boy is on the second-floor stairway.

The young man appears to relax as Nora comes into his view, and his hand comes out of his coat. He smiles and tips his hat, waiting for her to pass, and Nora smiles back at him, her face hot and flushed pink. She continues on up the stairwell to the third floor, sweat prickling under her arms and on her forehead, knowing she should have said something to the man. A proper employee would have castigated or questioned him for being where he should not be. She resists the urge to look back at him, and sighs in relief when she hears footsteps below her, quicker than before, descending.

Without thinking she opens the door to the third floor and runs down the carpeted hallway to room thirty-four. She should have brought the brandy and ginger ale at least, as a pretence. She decides, if it comes to it, that she will tell him that they have run out, and would he care for something different. Not great as cover but it will do.

The door opens a crack, and one of Murphy's thugs peers out and, seeing her, opens the door wide to let her inside.

'You've missed him, love,' the bodyguard says, smiling.

'Mr Murphy said …'

'He was here, and now he's gone. Mr Murphy?' the guard calls into his boss.

'Was he wearing a butcher's coat? A young man?' Nora says, her heart pounding.

Murphy enters the room from the adjoining bedroom suite. 'He was.'

'He …'

'… Butcher's coat and a butcher's van, look,' the second bodyguard says, standing at the room's window. He points down to the lane behind the hotel. Nora joins him at the window and looks down to see the white-coated man open the driver's door to a black lorry, three stories below, with incomprehensible writing on its side.

'He was only requesting another meet. Wanted me to go to the zoological gardens in the Phoenix Park this time.'

But Nora is gone, sprinting down the hallway and back down the stairs. Again, she passes Michael as she runs through lobby.

'Mind the desk, Michael. I'll be back when I can!' she shouts over her shoulder as she bursts through the hotel doors and out onto the morning street, temporarily blinded by the sunlight. She runs to the corner of the hotel and peers down the lane. The butcher's van is gone. Her head swivels as she scans the busy street in front of the hotel. *There!* Turning onto O'Connell Street. Left, towards the river. She makes out '… oy's Fine Meats' but nothing more.

A tram clangs its bell and she leaps across its path, trusting only God that there is no tram passing in the other direction. A car brakes hard and she is onto the footpath on the opposite side of the street, aware that her hair has loosed itself and become a red banner in her frantic wake. She has not run like this since school, and is breathless when she reaches the pub. Throwing open the door, she shouts into the dark interior.

'Dillon, they've been at the hotel … a van … a butcher's van …'

Her eyes adjusting to the dim light, she does not see Dillon until he is at her side.

'Are they still there?'

'No,' she gathers her breath, 'the van's turned onto O'Connell Street, towards the quays.'

He grabs her arm and drags her to a Ford Tourer parked halfway up on the path. A man is asleep at the wheel, and the stench of stale alcohol assails Nora as she bundles into the back seat, Dillon, cranking the hand starter and sliding in up front, shouting the driver awake.

'Left onto O'Connell Street and put the boot down, Jimmy, for fuck sake. O'Hanley's boys are in a butcher's van.'

'Something "Fine Meats", on the side. A dark van,' Nora says, leaning over the front seat.

O'Connell Street is jammed with horse, motorcar and tram traffic and Jimmy the driver takes the Ford up onto the footpath, weaving off it and onto the bridge. Nora and Dillon rake the street and quays for the lorry and eye any number that could be it. *Navan Finest Furniture. Johnston Mooney & O'Brien Baked Goods. Oxo Meat Extract.*

'There it is!' Nora shouts.

Turning up D'Olier Street is the van they seek, just visible in the lee shadow of the Irish Times building. Nora is certain of it. Gilhooley's Butchers and Purveyors of Fine Meats. It halts behind a slow-moving tram, and Jimmy weaves through the sluggish traffic on the bridge, settling in three cars and a horse cart behind the van. In an instant their pursuit has slowed to a crawl in the Dublin traffic, and Jimmy coughs and covers his mouth and retches loudly, cranking down the window glass to spew a stringy jet of bile into the road. He gags again and wipes his brow with his hand, his hat tipping back on his head, the boozy miasma dissipating through the open window. Nora has not met the man before but this is not unusual, the short-staffed CID adding men by the day, some sent away to outlying areas of the country, others taking up desks in Oriel House. And all of them drinking too much, rarely sleeping, hunting and hunted and nerves hardened, then shattered by waiting and war.

Nora winds her hair into its French knot and sets it with pins. Dillon takes out his Luger automatic and ejects the clip before slotting it home again in the grips of the gun. He snaps back the toggle-lock of the pistol, chambering a round, and slips the gun back into the holster under his jacket.

'I'm not armed,' Nora says, watching as the butcher's van begins to move forward, picking up speed.

'There's a tommy-gun and a Winchester in the boot,' Dillon says, his eyes on the van. 'Jimmy can take the Thompson and you take the shotgun. You've fired one before, haven't you? In training at least?'

'Are we planning on shooting them or following them or what, Charlie? Or taking them in? I'm not planning on blasting anyone with the Winchester.'

Dillon smiles at this but does not turn around. 'I don't imagine you'll be blasting anyone at all, Nora. We'll pinch them when they stop. There's only the two in the van that you know?'

'Two? I only saw the one get in.'

'There's a young lad in the passenger seat anyway,' the driver Jimmy says. 'Look.' His voice is weak and crackles with phlegm.

And Nora sees a flash of a young man, a boy really, on the passenger side of the van as it turns onto College Green. Jimmy cuts off a Chevrolet taxi to the angry squawking of its claxon.

'We'll take the two of them then. We're bound to get something out of them if we sit them down for a chat.'

Nora has never seen one of Dillon's "chats", but she has heard of them. They are held in the outbuildings, the former officers' quarters, at Wellington Barracks. But she has heard the pained braying from the basement cells of Oriel House when her fellow CID men staged their own. Chats. She pushes the thought of what awaits the two men—boys—in the lorry from her mind.

'Would it not be better to wait and follow them? Put men on them and see. I mean, can't we just follow them and see if they lead us to O'Hanley?' Nora is nervous suddenly. This is an end of the job that she has not seen. She is a watcher, and these men are takers. She knows what Dillon will say before he says it.

'There's been enough waiting round, and sure they're sending our lads all over the country along with the army. We've not the bodies to be sitting on these boyos for days on end. Our vigil at the pub is up tomorrow as it is.'

Nora had not heard this. If Dillon and the others are standing down, she would be stood down as well. Murphy would return to England and O'Hanley would still be out there somewhere, planning his revolution, orchestrating the murder of his former friends. Friends like Dillon. She stays silent and watches the van as they follow it up Dame Street, their pace improving as the horse and tram traffic thins.

Left at George's Street, heading south. Onto Aungier and then Camden Street, where they are only two cars behind the van.

'The Dardanelles,' Dillon says, almost fondly.

'Pardon?' Nora says.

'What the Auxiliaries called this street in the Tan War for all the abuse and shite their lads got showered down on them in their Crossleys. More than piss-pots and rotten eggs was thrown from these windows, I'm telling you. Conor Hogan, a lad on the run up from Clonmel at the time—a mate of Danny Breen's—chucked a Mills bomb from three stories up a tenement … there …'—he points up at a building of carbon-blacked brick and missing windows—'… dead on into the back of a Crosser mashed with Tans. Blew two of them to hell and sent five others home missing fingers and feet.' Nora cannot see Dillon's face but she knows he is smiling.

'Here we are, lads,' Jimmy says, and they watch the van pull up in front of a shop with a red and white awning, and on its window is painted: Gilhooley's Butchers and Purveyors of Fine Meats.

'Drive past it, so. Pull up by the Bleeding Horse, Jimmy.'

'The wha?'

'The pub, on the corner there. We need to be close enough so we don't have their friends picking us off as we march them to the car. You've bracelets with you?'

'I do,' the driver answers.

'Two sets then,' Dillon says. 'They'll do us.'

Nora says, 'Look, if we take them here, O'Hanley will find out about it. You know that, don't you? He'll scarper and we won't get him.'

Dillon turns this time. His eyes burn under the sharp brim of his trilby. 'You're not making the shout on this, girl. Is that clear?

We're taking them now. They'll tell us what we need to know and we'll pinch O'Hanley to-fucking-day, before he hears of it. If it will calm your nerves, go into the pub and ring CID and have them send a watcher to see who leaves when we're gone and where they go. Otherwise, stay here or come with us, I don't give a shite.'

Nora nods, trying to hold Dillon's stare but finding she cannot. Her eyes flash to Jimmy, who is turned in his seat and watching the exchange. His eyes are rheumy and bloodshot, and in their own way, sad.

'I'll go with you.'

'Fine, then, let's shift it. We'll put a bead on them, put them on the tiles and cuff them. Then we're off, right?'

Jimmy and Nora nod, and the three exit the car and gather at the Ford's touring trunk. Dillon opens the trunk and hands the Thompson gun to Jimmy, who detaches the drum magazine and taps it against his thigh and replaces it. Nora takes the Winchester 1897 pump shotgun and it is heavier than she remembers. Her training comes back to her. *The Yanks called it the Trench Sweeper in the war.* Dillon shoves a handful of shells from a box in the trunk into Nora's fist and she opens the gun's breech and fingers the shells home as she had been taught. When she is finished, she attempts to rack a shell into the chamber and finds the pump action thick and resistant. She tightens her grip, uses her whole arm and the pump slides back, the shell slotting home with a hollow thack. Only now does she scan the footpath and see the men gathered in the open doorway of the Bleeding Horse pub. She glances at them for a moment, and en masse they turn away from her gaze and drift back into the pub. A bright flare of elation flashes in Nora's heart at this. The power in her hands. Knowing she could walk into that pub and …. She lets the thought die, and notices now that the footpath around them has emptied of passers-by.

'Right so,' Dillon says.

Without speaking, they cross the road, Dillon with his side-arm hanging at his side, Jimmy the driver holding the tommy-gun in the same way, and herself, with the shotgun carried across her chest as if she were on a parade ground. There is a giddy lightness to her step, and she narrows her focus to the front of the butcher shop, a chauffeur-driven Rolls–Royce braking hard and letting them pass, a horse in blinders and its cartload of vegetables obscuring the shop front for the moment and keeping them from the view of whoever is inside. They round the horse cart and a woman pushing a pram gasps and hurries forward, one hand on the pram, the other dragging another small child behind her who cries out in surprise at his mother's sudden violence.

Low autumn sun between tenements across Camden Street reflects off the front window, and Nora tries to peer through the glare and into the shop. Nothing.

Dillon enters first, Jimmy following with Nora behind them. Again her eyes dilate in the interior light of the shop and she is startled by the sound of Dillon's voice, a sudden roar.

'You! You! Get down on the floor to fuck, right now, you!'

He is pointing the Luger at the young man from the hotel. He and a younger boy stand at the back of the shop in front of a curtained doorway leading into the rear of the building. The walls of the shop are white tile, and the meat under the glass is a garish red in contrast. Two men in their twenties in blood-smeared white smocks are frozen behind a thick butcher's block, which is bowed in the middle from years of daily sanding, scored with dark purple grooves from the running of bloody knives. Next to them stands an older man holding a sheaf of newspaper blossomed open around a cut of beef. The older man is Gilhooley, and the two at the block are his sons, Nora assumes. A customer, a woman of middle age in a black shawl and headscarf, drops her wicker basket of shopping, onions bouncing out and rolling into corners and under feet. The woman begins to mutter, and Dillon turns to her.

'Shut it, you!' He waves the pistol in Nora's direction. 'Get her out of here.'

Nora tucks the Winchester under one arm and grips the woman by the shoulder with her free hand. She is turning the woman towards the door when her eye is drawn to a flurry of movement, the butcher's boy from the hotel darting through the curtained doorway into the rear of the shop, followed by his young passenger from the van. Dillon swings his gun back around and fires two rounds blindly through the curtains. Two brassy shell casings clink and spin on the floor amidst the sawdust and loose onions.

'Stay here, hold these here!' Then Dillon is gone through the curtain in pursuit. Heavy footfalls, more shots from the rear of the shop, the sound of a door slamming and Dillon cursing, clanking pans and breaking dishes.

Nora shoves the woman out the open door, the woman stumbling onto the footpath where she falls and cries out. A passing pensioner stoops to her aid and looks into the shop. Nora takes the Winchester again in both hands, and levels it at the pensioner through the open door. She waves the gaping barrel at him as he helps the crying woman to her feet and takes her away, his face a mixture of fear and disgust, and in this moment Nora knows she will never forget the look he gives her for as long as she lives.

She re-enters the shop where Jimmy holds the Thompson gun on the older man, and his two younger assistants, one of them holding a pink and white concertina of pork ribs, the other a heavy cleaver. The older man's mouth hangs open as if the words he had been about to speak are frozen in his throat. Acrid gun smoke hangs in the air making lazy spirals above the glass cabinet of meat. The smell is sharp to Nora's nose, and a memory of her brief musketry training flashes in her mind and then is gone, her eyes flitting between the three silent men. She notes the Adam's apple of the man holding the cleaver rise and fall and for a second. It is the only movement in the small shop.

The youngest of the three men, holding the rack of ribs, is the first to speak. His voice is soft with rage and his eyes drag back and forth between Nora and Jimmy.

'What right have you to come in here? Who in fuck are yis bastards? Chasing youngfellas. Them lads have done nothing, they haven't, so yis can fuck off out of here. Me da's only tryin' to run a business and you barging in here firin' guns at youngfellas …'

His voice is rising in anger as he speaks, and Nora brings the shotgun to bear on him, moving it next to the young man beside him, then to the older man and back. She wonders should she tell the second lad to put down the cleaver but does not, thinking it not her place, thinking that he might refuse and leave her and Jimmy in a position where further, more drastic action might be their only option.

She turns her eyes to Jimmy and notices the barrel of the Thompson gun is shaking, darting from one man to the next.

'… like yis Free State fuckin' cunts own the place now, haring round with yis'r guns and harassing the dacent people of Ireland!'

Jimmy says something above the young man and Nora only catches part of it. '… quiet you down, now. There's no need for that.'

'Fuckin' hard man with the big gun, without it you're nothing, are yeh? And bringing a bint in with yis? Who do yis think yis are?'

Nora watches the senior man set the newspaper and meat onto the counter behind the glass and lift a long carving knife from a magnet on the wall. Nora's voice is dry and brittle in her mouth. She licks her lips and says, 'Put that down, sir. Please …'

There is a hint of pleading in her tone and the senior man catches it, disdain flashing in his eyes. 'You do what you like, young miss, with your shotgun there. I've work to finish.' He lifts a heavy, de-boned shoulder of beef from the glass cabinet, slaps it with a fleshy thud onto the butcher's block and begins slicing it with a vigour and violence that Nora knows is a show for her and Jimmy.

She lets her eyes go to Jimmy and sees him swallow then cough and hack at the phlegm in his throat.

The young man with the pork ribs continues. 'I'd gut you soon as look at you without your gun, yeh big loaf of shite, yeh.'

Nora realises for the first time that Jimmy is a big man. Big and lumbering, with flat feet and a large arse under the tail of his suit jacket. He is speaking again and Nora can hear his words more clearly, his voice rising to compete with the young man who is shouting now, his face as red as the meat behind the glass.

'If yis touch a hair on that lad's head, yis'r fuckin' dead, yeh hear me, you too, you poxed cunt …' This, directed at Nora.

'… Shut yer mouth, I'm telling you, boyo, you shut your mouth …' Jimmy's face flushes red then white.

Nora watches a rivulet of sweat bead its way down Jimmy's cheek, and sees the twitching of muscle under the boozy jowl and a sudden burst from the Thompson gun—a half-second long eruption in the confines of the shop that sends a stream of lead smashing through the rack of ribs in the young man's hands and on through into his heart and lungs, his white coat blooming a bloody garden, the young man stuttering back to the white-tiled wall behind him, as if the machine-gun fire were music he would dance to. For a moment he rests there, his back to the wall, before sliding down, red wash on the tiles like someone had applied it with a brush.

And Jimmy's voice high-pitched with manic chatter: 'I told him to shut it, I fucking told him to shut his hole!' He turns to Nora now. 'It just went off … it did …'

There is a second of stunned silence before the young man with the cleaver cries out. 'Dinnie! Jesus, you've shot Dinnie! Da, he's shot Dinnie!'

The older man lets loose a bellow of such animal rage and sorrow that gooseflesh ripples up Nora's back and for an instant she is frozen and watches as the young man with the cleaver turns and brings back his arm as if he will hurl it at Jimmy. As he does this the older man pulls the carving knife from where it is wedged in the fibrous folds of the beef and reaches as far as he can over the glass cabinet to swing the knife. He is suicidally out of reach, and Jimmy fires another burst and keeps firing, stippling the glass meat cabinet, shattering the tiles on the wall behind the men, taking splintered chunks from the butcher's block and ripping into the older man and the younger, the cleaver dropping with a clank over the sound of the tommy-gun before it can be thrown, the butcher now, like his son, jigging under the hail of bullets and then falling forward to smash through the glass case and onto the meat below.

'Stop! Jesus, stop, Jimmy!' Nora hears herself now, her voice futile and shrill in the sudden silence as the Thompson's magazine empties, smoke rising from its barrel, cordite thick in the air to mingle with the viscous metal scent of blood.

Jimmy turns to look at her and his face is white, his eyes red and bloodshot from booze and gun smoke. Dillon bursts back through the curtains from the rear of the shop, his Luger levelled at Jimmy first, then Nora. He sees the butcher and his sons, sprawled on the sawdust and draped over the shattered glass meat cabinet.

'Fuckin' Christ, Jimmy.'

One of the younger men on the floor moves, his hand flopping on his chest, his other sifting limply in the sawdust for the cleaver. He makes as if to speak and blood runs from his lips. Dillon steps around the cabinet and fires one round into his chest and he is still.

'Right, let's shift it, to fuck. Out to the car and mind we're not given the jump. I couldn't find the other lad but if he's brother to these and he's heard the shooting, he'll be back if he's any kind of man at all.'

Nora swallows and her throat is dry, scorched with smoke and terror. She follows Dillon and Jimmy out of the shop, but instead of scouring the street and surrounding windows, she lowers her head, fearful of being seen.

But the street and footpaths, for the moment, are empty. No men gather in the doors of the Bleeding Horse as they pile into the car, taking their weapons in with them. Nora watches Dillon, the Luger in his hand, resting on the bonnet as he hand cranks the Ford's starter.

The motor rumbles to life, and Jimmy's hands are shaking and he grips the wheel so tightly to steady them that his knuckles blanch white. Dillon slams the door.

'Move, it. We were never here.' He turns in his seat to Nora. 'We were never here until I find out who them boys you shot up are. No doubt they're bent rebel boys, so no need to worry.'

He is smiling as he says all this. 'There was nothing you could do,' he says, turning to Jimmy, clapping him on the arm. 'Was there, Jim? A lad moves on you with a knife … isn't that right, Nora? How it happened? I didn't need to be there to see how it went. Clear as day, a clever man shoots first, asks questions later, wha?'

They are rounding Stephen's Green when Nora shakes Jimmy's shoulder. 'Stop the car,' she manages, before flinging open the door in time to vomit onto the footpath.

36

It is the same dream O'Keefe has had since he was in the army hospital in Cork, septicaemia souring his blood. He is on the deck of the HMS *River Clyde*, the cargo ship converted to troop carrier and run aground at V Beach, the Turkish rifles and machine-guns grinding to life, like some infernal engine, a mechanical clanking rather than the stop-start stutter of the guns of reality. He is there with Peter as always, but in this version his father is with them in the navy blue uniform of the Dublin Metropolitan Police and holding a photograph of Nicholas Dolan to his chest. Each of them urges the other on, to march down the pontoon bridge to shore, as the men in front of them fall, machine-gun rounds harrying the air like bluebottles over a sheep's carcass. And now in the dream, the Cunningham boys stand beside O'Keefe and his father and brother, urging them on towards the beach, the water bloody red and bodies floating in the soft wash of waves.

He is awake with a start before the knocking starts. It is the front door this time, but the same voices as in his dream.

'He'd hardly be sleeping now, sure, we've already had our tea and all.'

'What'd yis have for tea?' This voice is unfamiliar to O'Keefe, and his bones and muscles ache as he rises from where he had been sleeping on the floor beside his own bed. He remembers why he has slept on the floor and bends down to Finch, who is

272

still unconscious in the bed, feeling his forehead. It is clammy but not hot. Perhaps his fever has passed in the night—in the *day*, he realises. They have slept since morning and O'Keefe checks his wristwatch and finds that it is seven fifteen. From the quality of the light edging through the side gaps in the blinds, he judges it to be evening.

'Eggs and Bachelor's,' O'Keefe hears the youngest of the Cunningham boys say.

The new voice now, older than the two boys' says, 'Wha's "Bachelors"?'

'What you mean, "what's Bachelor's"? Sure, they're beans, aren't they?'

'Are yis mockin me, are yis?' There is aggression in this new voice, and O'Keefe crosses to the front door of his flat and opens it. Standing with the two Cunningham boys at the bottom of the steps is another boy, of roughly the same size as the older of the brothers but much thinner and, by his face and voice, older. His clothes are thick with street grime and grease and one leg of his trousers is cut shorter than the other over filthy, road-hardened feet. His cap is the cap of a grown man and it swallows his head down to his ears, the back of it resting on a frayed and hole-riddled knit jumper. His pallor is sickly pale and his cheek-bones jab out under dark-ringed eyes that have seen too much. For a moment, he cannot place the boy.

'Lads, what is it you want?' His voice is thick with fatigue, and his words come out harsher than he had intended. The Cunningham boys look up at him, and for the first time since he has known them he sees uncertainty in their faces. They look young and wary.

'This fella ...' Henry says, his eyes going to the new boy and then back to O'Keefe, '... he says he's a message to give you but I said you were sleeping.'

Young Thomas says, 'He doesn't know what Bachelor's beans are, he doesn't.'

'I'll fuckin' batter you,' the capped boy growls, and O'Keefe realises where he has seen him.

'Now, now, lads, none of that. Sure, there's loads of people who've never eaten Bachelor's beans and so why *would* they know about them?'

'I've eaten beans before, by fuck!'

'Of course you have,' O'Keefe says, hunger flaring in his own stomach. 'And you've a message for me, have you?'

'Yis said yis'd gi's a pound if we laid eyes on Jerry Byrne, yis did. Last night in the lane …'

'We did, did you find him?'

The boy's hand comes out now. The lines of his palm are creased deep with dirt.

'Does Just … does my friend, Mr Albert, know ye've found him?'

'Me scratch first,' the boy says, jabbing his open palm at O'Keefe in the doorway.

'Give us a minute while I fetch my wallet.'

'Who's in yer bed, Mr O'Keefe?' Thomas Cunningham says, poking his head inside the room.

'A friend is all. And he's very sick at the moment so don't be knocking him up, right?' O'Keefe returns to the doorway, cursing himself for his carelessness. Mrs Cunningham is as kind a landlady as a man could ask for, but she would hardly stand for a man sweating out his fever from a bullet wound in her rented bed.

'Here,' O'Keefe says to the boy. He places a pound note on the boy's outstretched palm and the fingers snap closed around it like a mousetrap.

'Now then. Does my friend know you've found the lad?'

'How should I fuckin' know? I'm only here and not every-where, amn't I? And maybe there's more than ye lookin' him.'

Remembering the dead boys in the morgue, a bead of fear runs down O'Keefe's spine. 'And who would that be?'

'Who'm I, Madam Zoraster, the fortune tellin' gypo?'

'So you don't know, then, if there's others still looking for the Byrne lad.'

The boy shrugs, the shadow of a feral smile tugging at his lips.

O'Keefe considers this. There may be others looking for Jeremiah Byrne and there may not be. Regardless, if he can get to the boy before Just Albert, he can save the lad some considerable suffering. 'Where is he then?'

The boy shoves the pound note into his pocket and extends the palm once again.

'I just paid you, youngfella. Where's the Byrne lad?'

'Yeh paid me to tell if yer friend knew 'bout where he is. I told yeh tha'.'

'You told me you didn't know.'

'Yeh pay for an answer, yeh get an answer, even if it's not the one yeh want. Another quid for where Jerry's does be laying low, before he's gone from there and yis're none the wiser.'

O'Keefe smiles at the boy. As sharp in his own way as any boy from the best school in Dublin. Two pounds would feed him and his mates for a week or more, but O'Keefe knows it won't go on food. The boys will drink whiskey and cider and gin instead of meth spirits and smoke Sweet Aftons tonight, and tomorrow they will still be hungry and working the backs of pubs and public toilets, dipping bags on Grafton Street under the clouting fists of policemen and hackney drivers. He places another pound note in the boy's hand.

'He's at the Achill. The doss-house back the Smithfield markets, on the lane off Bow Street. One of our lads bunked in to tap the punters in the showers and there the cunt was before him.'

'Thanks for that,' O'Keefe says, and to his surprise, the boy touches the brim of his oversized cap and turns for the stairs up to the footpath.

O'Keefe says, 'Wait a tick, youngfella.' He dips back inside and returns to the boy, handing him a tin of Bachelor's beans.

The boy holds the tin in his hand and stares at the label. 'Beans?' he says. 'Why're yeh givin me beans?'

'They're Bachelor's. You said you'd never tried them.'

After studying the tin for another long moment, the boy touches his cap brim again and says, 'Thanks, Mister.' He then mounts the steps to the footpath and is gone.

'You know that lad, Mr O'Keefe?' Henry Cunningham says.

'I've met him once. He was to bring me a message is all.'

'He's a fierce one for the cursing, so he is,' Thomas says, with more than a little awe in his voice.

'Right, shove off now, fellas. And don't be bothering my sick friend, right?'

'We fuckin' won't, will we not, Tommy?'

'Fuckin' won't, bejaysus.'

'Lads, don't be cursing.'

'Sorry, Mr O'Keefe.'

The boys are halfway up the stairs before the first of them says 'cunt', and they erupt in laughter.

37

… that this sham state be considered the independent Ireland we fought and died for is inconceivable to me and my comrades in the true Republican Army of Ireland. That traitors, hand in glove with their former Crown masters, should so seek to suppress our striving for a true republic, causes me unspeakable grief and fills me and my men—good and true and virtuous young men—with a righteous rage that will triumph. As God is our witness we will take any measures to ensure the birth of the republic that is divinely ordained as ours by right. We will do anything in our power to resist this rotten compromise of a Treaty brought to the nation by men so seduced by power and prestige that they have abandoned the future of Ireland as entrusted to us by our Father in heaven …

It is after eight when the familiar—but this time unexpected—knock sounds on the closet door to O'Hanley's hidden room, and he puts down his pen and lifts the Webley from the table beside his journal.

'Stephen,' O'Hanley says, letting the young soldier in, Gilhooley's face as ashen white as the clean sheets on his bed.

Words rush from the young man in a cascade. 'They followed us, from the hotel. Murphy's in with them, I'm tellin' you. He placed a call, down to the front desk while I was there. He was telling someone, I swear to fuck. And the girl, on the desk, she's one of them. She came with some heavies to the shop. My father …'

His voice chokes with rage and tears well up in his eyes, surprising O'Hanley.

'Stephen, slow down, please. What happened? In with whom?'

'With CID or Free State intelligence. Murphy. I swear to fuck, I was there, leaving the money, like you said when he makes me wait and rings the desk lookin' for drinks. Half ten in the morning, lookin' brandy and lemonade or some shite. And as I'm hoofin' it back downstairs to the lorry, who do I see? Only the girl at the front desk, on her way up. And not twenty minutes later does she and two other fellas, Charlie Dillon and another lad with a tommy-gun, show up at Da's shop and ...' Again, the words lodge in his throat.

'And?'

'And they shot me da and the brothers. All three of them shot down dead!' His voice cracks with emotion and he pivots and raises his fist as if he will drive it into the wall.

O'Hanley places a hand on his shoulder. 'Are you sure it was the same girl? From the front desk?'

The young gunman lowers his fist and nods. 'It was.'

The commandant is silent for a long moment. He rubs his face and his hair, rage stirring his own blood now.

'You left the money, you did?'

'I did. I didn't know at the time it was a set-up.'

'And you weren't followed here? After ...'

'Of course I bleedin' wasn't followed. The two of us legged it and gave them the slip and then waited til dark to make it back. Jesus fuckin' wept, me? *Followed?*'

O'Hanley winces at the obscenity but ignores Gilhooley's wounded pride. 'Two of ye? Who else was with you?'

'Nicky Dolan.'

'Nicky is alive?' O'Hanley's eyes widen with surprise, and a smile comes unbidden to his lips. His favourite has survived. And as he thinks this, he realises that it had been after sending Nicholas and young Robert O'Donnell to the hotel, to deliver the second of the messages, that the two went missing. Murphy, the traitor. The snake. The smile shunts off his lips under this new weight of knowledge: there will be no shipment. No guns, no gelignite and no detonators. None of the promised field guns for the promised future, and without these things he and his fellow republicans will not take back Dublin; and without Dublin, there is nothing for it but to head to the mountains and wage war like tinkers, taking potshots at armoured cars, robbing banks and post offices. Like common criminals, sleeping in ditches and praying for clear nights while Mulcahy and his Free State henchmen bed down for the long marriage of convenience with the King.

'We need to get the money back,' he says. He is breathing hard from his nose. That bag of money being the future of the republic they are fighting for. Fourteen thousand odd pounds.

Stephen nods. 'I'll get it back meself if I've to hunt Murphy and his two goons to Blighty and fuckin' back. The three of them are walking dead already.'

This time O'Hanley lets the cursing wash over him. He wishes he was the kind of man to take comfort in swearing, in blasphemy and hard talk. But he is not. He is a man of action who is left to rot in this room directing others to do what is right and just and proper for the republic that is rightfully, by God himself ordained, theirs.

'Do what you have to, Stephen. Just get the money back.'

Stephen turns to leave.

'And Stephen? Send Nicky up, will you?'

38

O'Keefe shuts down the Trusty and wheels it into the light from the front doors of the Achill Guest House on Bow Street. He has misgivings about leaving the bike unchained in this part of town at a time when fighters from both sides of the conflict are requisitioning transport of any kind. He has heard that a good deal of commandeering is unofficial; that there are Free State soldiers as well as Irregulars taking their mothers to mass in requisitioned Rolls–Royces. He gives the Trusty a long look, says a small, reflexive prayer that it will still be there when he comes out, and mounts the steps of the Achill.

The lobby walls are tiled, the floor a scuffed black and white parquet studded with crushed dogends smoked down to nothing. Along the wall to the right there is a short queue of men waiting before a reception booth surrounded by wire mesh. A small window is cut into the mesh through which the cashier transacts his business. Some in the queue are day labourers and one or two appear to O'Keefe to be dockers or small farmers' sons up from the country. Some of them may only need a bed for one night before returning to wherever they have come from, but most, O'Keefe reckons, know only places such as this as home, where the lobby smells of stale sweat and alcohol and failure. This is a place where men stay when they have no place else.

A man in a torn tweed jacket and oversized trousers rolled up at the bottom stands in front of the caged reception with his cap clutched to his chest, trying to slide two coins through the dinner-plate-sized window to the cashier.

The cashier—a tidy, balding man with a thin moustache, a blue-grey necktie and braces over a white shirt—berates the man in a west of Ireland accent.

'You stink of the road. And you expect us take you in just because you've begged the shrapnel for one night's bed? You stink like a beast of the fields. The whole house'll stink of you. How am I to know you won't shite the bunk you're given for that shilling?'

The dosser's words strain the tiled walls in a high-pitched pleading that is abject and shameful to hear. The men in the queue look down at their feet or away at the walls, knowing it might soon be them begging for a bed. 'But sure,' the man in torn tweed says, 'doesn't everybody reek of the terrible hard times that are in it? I've come for a wash as well as a bed.'

'You've only enough money for a bed and no wash. You may let the rain wash you and not be reeking up the whole of this house with your stench. Now shove off with you, before I have in the police.'

'But I have the money. You told me last night not to come back til I had coin for a bed, and now I have it.'

Anger catches in O'Keefe's throat as he watches. The cashier's threat of the police galls him further. A small man with small power, abusing it on the down-and-outs. As if the police were the muscled arm of his pettiness. He approaches the cage and says to the pleading man, 'How much for a bed for the night?'

The man in tweed turns to O'Keefe, fear dilating dark pupils, his cap clutched in front of his heart like a shield. 'I … two bob.' He turns back to the cashier. 'Jesus in heaven, sir, why'd you call the guards in, you needn't have done that! I've money and all and …'

'I'm not a guard,' O'Keefe says, using the common term for policemen in Dublin. 'And even if I was, I wouldn't be running like a lackey for this jumped-up fucker.' He turns to the man in the cage.

The cashier is standing now, and pointing his finger behind the wire mesh. 'Who do you think you are? Calling me that? I'll have the police in on *you*, I will, for vicious slander.'

O'Keefe senses the men in the queue take a collective step back and, holding the cashier's eyes, he flashes his hand through the cage's window and grabs the man's necktie, jerking him forward so that his face bangs the wire mesh. He pulls at the tie and wraps it in his fist, trapping the cashier's face against the cage. With his other hand, he dips into his jacket pocket and takes out Ginny Dolan's roll of banknotes. He hands it to the man in tweed, turning his head to count the men in the queue.

The man in tweed stares at the roll of notes and back to O'Keefe. 'What?' His mouth sags open in wonder.

'Take two pound notes off that roll and put them through the window here,' O'Keefe says, tugging harder at the cashier's necktie so that the man's cheek extrudes through the mesh in small, fleshy diamonds. The man is grunting, unable to open his mouth to call out.

'Then put the roll back in my pocket.'

Tweed looks to his fellow dossers in the queue, and O'Keefe can see one or two of them nodding and cracking small smiles. The man takes two notes and slides them through the window, carefully avoiding touching O'Keefe's fist wrapped in the cashier's tie.

'There's rent for two nights' bed, bath and feed for these men,' O'Keefe says to the cashier. 'You're to give them the tickets they'll need, and if one of them, so help me God, is abused by you, and I hear about it, I'll come back and pull you through this window and batter three shades of shite out you, d'you hear me?'

The cashier gives a small, painful nod and O'Keefe releases him.

'Now, where are the showers in this place?' he asks the cashier, who slumps back into his chair, the imprint of the wire mesh an angry red grid on his face.

'Through there, sir,' the man in tweed says, stepping behind O'Keefe, eager to help and pointing to the door leading into the main hallway of the doss-house. 'And down to your right, down the end of the hallway. Then downstairs and past the canteen. And bless you, sir. God bless you and yours.'

'Good man,' O'Keefe says, patting the man on the arm. 'Sleep well.'

Men loiter in the main hallway of this former hospital under the gas jets, and O'Keefe stops at one group and asks have they seen any lads of Jerry Byrne's description in the Achill. The men shake their heads and will not meet O'Keefe's eyes. He had not expected more from them and does not attempt to buy the information. Gone is the terror of informing from the days of the Tan War, but very few men would accept payment for information in front of other men for the age-old shame of it.

He follows a yellowing, handwritten sign down cellar stairs to the canteen and scans the few remaining diners there, seated at long benches with arms shielding steaming tin plates piled high with cabbage and potatoes and small, fatty morsels of greying bacon. No boys are among them. He thinks to ask one of the serving women—older, thick-bodied women whose faces are carved into permanent frowns—but decides against it. Boys under eighteen years are not permitted to stay in the Achill, and a kitchen woman would hardly admit to serving one for fear of losing her job and ending up in the female version of this place. He leaves the canteen and makes his way down the long hallway to the swinging doors marked 'Showers'.

39

Jeremiah Byrne hands his last three pence to the bored attendant in the booth at the showers' entrance and strips off his
clothes, carefully folding them and placing them in a wire basket on the shelf of the changing-room.

Wrapping himself in a towel—the only thing he has managed
to steal since coming into the Achill the day before—Jeremiah
enters the communal showers. They are as empty as his pockets
and he curses his luck. He had managed to meet only one man
willing to part with coin for his company in one of the curtained
dressing stalls that run one wall of the changing-room, despite
spending the better part of the previous night loitering in the
steamy air, and so today he has a hacking, liquid cough that is trig-
gered by the few remaining cigarettes in his possession.

Rum luck. Rum fucking luck and worse hope of filching a
knife from the canteen, though he has managed to buy a heel of
stale bread from one of the harpy cunts working the serving line.
Knives are another story, the men have to rent them for two pence
per item of cutlery—fork, knife or soup spoon—and are especially
careful of them. After buying the bread he had lingered at a table,
gnawing on the bread for over an hour, hoping one of the diners
might accidentally forget his knife, until he was chased from the
canteen by one of the women. Not wanting to test his luck and be
thrown out of the Achill, he had come to the showers and had no

luck here either. If he stumbled into a paying punter, he might rent his own knife and fork in the canteen and simply keep the knife, sharpening it to a lethal edge and point against the brick wall in the toilets, jimmying up a handle grip from strips of torn lining from his jacket. No luck, to fuck, but.

He showers, hanging the towel on a hook on the tiled wall, standing under the hot and constant spray that comes from the ceiling fixtures under the command of a rusting button on the wall. The water feels wonderful, scouring away the dust from his hidey-hole under one of the Achill bunks in the far corner of a dorm room, where he'd slept the day away in the emptied hostel while its paying patrons tramped the streets until the Achill opened again at five. Jeremiah lets the water beat away his cares; his fears for his sisters; fear of the men who are hunting him. It has been what? Three days, four maybe, since he'd stuck the fella in the laneway off Abbey Street. Surely them lads would be after some other poor sap by now and have forgotten auld Jerry Byrne, him with enough troubles of his own. Bygones be bygones. And maybe he hadn't killed the bastard, and anyway, no harm done.

A shadow warps the light through Jeremiah's closed lids and he opens his eyes. His luck a-turning? See now, a fella there, and one he can tell by the spark in his eyes is as bent as a dray's shoes, surely. The man leans in the doorway to the changing room, staring at Jeremiah. A frisson of fear laces through Jeremiah's blood. The man is blocking the only exit from the showers. He is wearing a cap and labourer's clothes but he does not have the look of a punter or a doss-house sleeper. And his eyes, Jerry realises, are alive with something more than lust.

'Young Jeremiah,' the man says, and the icy fear becomes a shudder. *How does he know my name? I've told nobody me name ....*

'Who's that, when he's at home?' Jeremiah croaks, just as the water cuts out, leaving him dripping and naked and suddenly cold. Goosebumps pepper his flesh in the humid veil of steam.

The man laughs. 'Jig's up, boy. Come here to me now and don't be messing. There's lads want a word with you.'

Lads like the mates of the fella he'd stabbed in the laneway. 'I don't know what you're on about,' Jeremiah says, making his way as casually as he can to his towel, drying himself before tying it around his waist. *Rum fuckin luck is wha' I have and that's no word of a lie ....*

'Ah, young buck, you do know what I'm *on about*,' the man, who is from the country by his accent, imitates Jeremiah.

'I fuckin' don't so's unless you want yer bottle washed, fuck off with yeh and let me get dressed.' But his voice betrays his words, sounding young and frightened as it echoes off the dripping walls of the showers.

'You know, young buck,' the man says, rubbing the stubble on his chin, adjusting the cap on his head, 'I don't need bring you in at all. The bossman would be just as happy with you bleeding out into that drain there, boy, so don't make me come in and drag your nancy arse out of here.'

Jeremiah swallows. *Jig's up all-fuckin'-right, but there's life for a fella. You're cold, you're hungry, you're beaten down and then you die. Fuck it, for a game of jacks.*

'You'll let me get me bags on, wha'?'

'Of course I will, young buck. I'd hardly have your shitty arse on the seat of my motor without a pair of breeches on it, would I?'

'No.' Jeremiah walks towards him, his footsteps sucking on the wet floor. Something—someone—passes behind the man in the doorway.

The man turns, seeming to sense the presence, and as he does so his hand goes into his jacket and comes out with a boxy, long-barrelled pistol. The man says something and Jeremiah only catches the last words of it. '... *out of here. We're busy* ...'

He cannot hear the muffled reply from the other person inside the changing-room, but the man in the doorway turns back to Jeremiah, pointing the gun at him, and says, 'Stay there, you. No, sit down, there, now. Now!' before turning back to the unseen figure.

O'Keefe is moving down the hall when he hears the shot. It is muffled and flat from behind the swing-doors of the showers, but he recognises it for what it is and breaks into a jog. Instinctively he pats his belt—as if it still holds the side-arm and baton of his days as a Peeler—and finds it empty. He has a flashing thought that this is what his father must feel as he searches for memory and finds only the mist of incomprehension: the nakedness that comes of being unarmed around armed men. He pushes through the swing-doors into the showers.

The attendant's booth is empty and O'Keefe hears a scuffle from the adjoining room—rough grunting and the sliding of boots on tiles. He moves into the changing-rooms and comes upon Just Albert standing over a man who is slumped on a bench, halfway between seated and supine. Just Albert swivels round and points a Mauser automatic at O'Keefe.

'Jesus, Albert it's me!'

'Took your sweet time of it coming.'

The man on the bench moans, his leg swinging out as if to find purchase on the tiles, and Just Albert turns back to him, putting the pistol into his coat and coming out with his club. Before O'Keefe can stop him, he begins to beat the man on the bench with the club, the sound of it against the man's skull like a wooden door slamming in the wind.

O'Keefe grabs his arm as he brings it down again.

'Stop! Albert, for God's sake, you'll kill him!'

Just Albert does not resist, and O'Keefe releases his arm.

'He shot me, the bastard.' He tilts his head to show an angry red welt on his neck above his collar. O'Keefe is stunned by how lucky Ginny's man has been. A mere graze when one-tenth of an inch either way would have killed him.

'Lucky boy, you.'

'Luck's nothing to do with it.'

'Still, he missed.'

'Lucky for him, then.'

O'Keefe doesn't try to decipher what Just Albert means and steps over to the man, digging through his pockets, coming out with a wallet with several ten-bob notes in it and nothing else. In the inside of his jacket pocket, however, he finds a badge.

'Jesus, Albert. You've done it now. This fella's CID.'

'And I'm to piss meself over a badge?' He turns away from O'Keefe and sticks his head into the showers. 'All right, Jeremiah. You ready to come with us?'

'He's in there? The Byrne boy?'

Just Albert nods and turns back to O'Keefe. 'And this lad, this CID fella, was looking for him same as we are. Who are CID anyway?'

'Detectives, Albert. Mick Collins' own hand-picked lot of gunmen turned into a detective department and protection squad for government men. They're a hit mob more than policemen, so the word is.'

'Well he's the one hit this time isn't he?' Just Albert smiles.

'These are killers, Albert. They aren't the lads for fannying around.'

'Do I look like a lad for fannying round, Mr O'Keefe, when our Nicholas is missing these past weeks? Do I?' His voice is raised and the smile is gone. 'I let *this* lad take *that* lad in the showers there and we get nothing of what he knows about our Nicholas. This fella was as ready to kill him as take him in, I heard him say as much.'

'No, Albert, you don't look like one for … look, here.' O'Keefe's voice is low, calm. 'You can't bludgeon your way around the city and expect not to pay for it.'

'You'd want to be some man to collect what I owe, wouldn't you? This fella tried it.'

O'Keefe replaces the wallet and badge. 'I don't doubt he had it coming somehow, Albert, it's just …'

Before O'Keefe can finish, there is a flash of movement from the shower-room entrance and the boy clad only in a towel darts between them, a pale fury of pumping legs and arms. He makes it as far as the changing-room entrance when Just Albert throws his club, a low, spinning missile that racks off the boy's ankle and sends him sprawling on the wet tiles, slamming into the bath attendant's empty booth. Just Albert steps around O'Keefe and grabs the boy by the hair, lifting him and dragging him back to the bench and seating him next to the bloodied head of the gunman.

'Now,' Just Albert says, 'you get your kit on and hurry up about it, right?'

The boy's eyes are wide and his nostrils flare, as if reacting to the coppery fug of blood in the air. He nods under Just Albert's grip.

Ginny's man releases the boy and watches as he takes a wire basket holding ragged clothes and a new pair of shoes—the shoes he had taken from the lane boys, O'Keefe thinks—and dresses. His hands are shaking, and O'Keefe feels a welling pity for the lad.

O'Keefe's eyes go to the gunman. He wonders should he feel pity for him as well, but cannot muster any. He reaches down with his index finger and feels for a pulse, finding it after a moment, his finger coming away smeared with the man's blood. He wipes his finger on the man's coat and turns back to the boy.

'Are you Jeremiah Byrne?' O'Keefe says.

The boy looks at him and seems to notice him for the first time.

'Blondy lad. Of course he is. Aren't yeh, youngfella?' Just Albert says, walking to the attendant's booth and cracking the swing-doors to peer out down the hallway to the kitchens.

The boy nods. He is so thin that his ribs run like wheel ruts under the snow white of his skin. His arms are strung with the youthful beginnings of lean muscle and his face is handsome and young under the vigilance of ancient, dark blue eyes. Another boy who has seen too much of the world, too early, O'Keefe thinks, knowing there are thousands more in the city who have seen as much.

'How old are you?' he asks.

The boy, still looking at Just Albert as he shrugs on his jacket, says, 'Fifteen, I think. Or Fourteen.'

'You don't know?'

'Sure, how would I fuckin' know? Nobody told me an' anyway, did they?'

O'Keefe shakes his head. A child who matters so little no one had bothered to tell him how old he is, when his birthday is. Like one of a litter of pups to the mother.

The man on the bench moans again and Just Albert turns to look at him.

'Don't,' O'Keefe says. 'We need to shout him a doctor and we need get shot of here in case his friends come looking for him.'

Just Albert nods. 'Right youngfella, you see this?' He takes the pistol from inside his coat and shows the boy and the boy nods.

'Just you make a move to run and you get one in the head and then one in the bollix when you're down, got it, Sonny Jim?'

Jeremiah nods.

O'Keefe and Albert lead Jeremiah out of the showers, past the kitchens and up the stairs, where O'Keefe tells the cashier to ring for a doctor—that there's a fella injured in the changing-room of the showers. 'An important man,' he says to the cashier, 'so do it now or you'll be for it when his friends find him out.'

Out onto the street.

'I've the Trusty,' O'Keefe says.

'And I've the Bento, round the corner. We'll take him in the motor. You can collect the bike later,' Just Albert says.

Down May Street to Smithfield Market square, the scent of blood and rotting meat hangs in the cool, damp night air. Fog softens the lamplight. Tramps and old women scour the cobbles and pub fronts for dropped coins or scraps of meat the dogs might have missed, thick in their rags, like mumbling ghosts in the mist. Whores linger by the pubs and closed shopfronts. Candles burn in tenement windows on the far side of the market square, and horses whinny from an unseen stall. The gang of boys from the lanes is there, leaning on and milling around the Bentley. One of the lads, jumping up from his perch at the bonnet, shines the spot where he's been leaning with his sleeve, leaving a greasy spot on the black paint.

'There he is,' one of the boys says.

'Yeh fuckin' thievin' cunt, Jerry Byrne,' another shouts. 'You're only lucky them fellas wanted yeh or yer guts'd be hangin' out of yeh like ribbons from a tart's wig.'

'All talk, you are,' Jeremiah says. 'The fuckin' lot of yis couldn't gut fish.'

'Come back round and find us when them two lads are fin- ished with yeh and we'll show yeh, Jerry. And here, Mister,' the lad says to Just Albert. 'Where's the other pound you says was in it if yis found him?'

'Pay the man, Mr O'Keefe,' Just Albert says, opening the door to the Bentley. 'They've done good work tonight.'

O'Keefe peels a pound note from the roll in his pocket and hands it to the oldest boy. Behind him he notices the messenger who had come for him at the Cunningham house.

'You eat those beans, did you?'

The boy says nothing, but holds up the Bachelor's tin, unopened.

'We'll eat them when we're ready,' the oldest lad says. 'And remember, you, Jerry Byrne, you're as good as dead if these two don't kill yeh first. Are yis gonna kill him, Mister?'

'We'll see how he behaves and then decide,' Just Albert says, holding Jeremiah by the arm and guiding him to the rear door of the Bentley.

The gang leader is about to speak when a smaller boy approaches him and whispers into his ear.

'Here, right. Them shoes he's on. Can we get 'em back off ye when yis're finished with him?' the oldest boy says.

A pair of shoes a matter of life and death on these streets of his city, O'Keefe thinks. He says, 'You,'—pointing to Jeremiah—'take off those brogues and give them over.'

Jeremiah Byrne shoots O'Keefe a look of disgust, but bends and removes the shoes, making no move to hand them to the boys. One of the smaller lads skips forward and takes them. As he hands them to his leader, he turns back and spits at Jeremiah's feet.

'Fuckin' dead, you are,' he says, his voice high and young.

'Get in the car, Jerry,' O'Keefe says, 'I'm not sure how long I can hold this mob off you.'

'You'd not hold us back one tick of the clock if we wanted him now, Mister,' the leader says, and O'Keefe, looking over this wolf pack of boys, thinks that he may be right.

They pull away in the Bentley, O'Keefe in the back seat with the boy, and drive onto the river quays, past the blast-charred ruins of the Four Courts, east towards O'Connell Street.

After a long moment of silence, Jeremiah says, 'Where're yis takin me?'

'We need to ask you some questions is all,' O'Keefe answers.

'And you'd better answer them right or there'll be only bits of you left to hand back to your mates,' Just Albert adds, his voice cold.

'They're not my mates.'

They continue on in silence, and O'Keefe thinks they are going back to Ginny Dolan's house in Foley Street when Just Albert turns the car left at Liberty Hall and onto Store Street, pulling up in front of the morgue.

O'Keefe is torn between admiration for Just Albert and worry that this is the wrong thing to do. The boy is too young to see what is inside on the slabs. He decides to let things play out, thinking that there is less chance of Just Albert threatening the boy injury if the boy is shocked into telling them what he knows by the sight of his dead comrades inside.

'Right,' he says, holding him by the arm, 'let's go.'

Just Albert leads them into the building, and down the main hallway through the sets of swinging double doors. He appears oblivious to the chance they are taking of being caught and having to hand the boy over to DMP detectives, batting through the doors as if he owns the place.

Through the final set of doors and they are in the morgue proper, the room several degrees cooler than the hallway, the cement floor damp and the slab in the centre of the room empty and clean. The same attendant O'Keefe had bribed the evening before is there at the desk eating a cream bun and drinking tea.

'What's this, you can't be in here …' He recognises O'Keefe and lowers his voice. 'Jaysus, Mister, you can't be barging in like this and with a boy and all? Jaysus. I could lose me job over this.' He makes no move to rise from his seat, and O'Keefe peels a pound note from his roll and tosses it onto the desk beside the bun.

'You'll be rich before the week's out. Now stand out in the hall and keep an eye out. If anyone you can't refuse entry to is coming, you let us know and we'll head out through your office there, right? Anyone else, you stall until we're finished.'

'Well, since we've had no bodies today and the post mortem on your boys there,'—the attendant points to two trolleys against the far wall of the room, on which rest sheet-covered bodies— 'was finished this morning, a quid's worth the risk, but mind you be quick about it.'

'What were the post mortem findings?' O'Keefe asks, as the attendant makes to leave.

'Dumdums to the back of the head for the both of them. There is nothing left inside the boys' skulls at all.'

'Jesus. Any idea what calibre round?'

'Oh yes, the sawbones here, he used to be with the Royal Army Medical in the war. He says it looks like nine by nineteen millimetres, by the size of the entry wound and from the look of the flattened slugs.'

'Luger Parabellum?' O'Keefe says, trying not to match the attendant's enthusiasm but finding it difficult. How many times had he stood as a Peeler speaking in rooms such as this in the past, with men like this one?

'Most likely. Some of the newer sub-machine-guns are using nine millimetre, but it's rare enough here in Ireland so far. At least as far as we see. Still 7.62 and .353 mainly. Some .45 calibre. The Thompson handheld machine-gun loads .45. A fierce big hole it makes too.'

O'Keefe nods. He had seen men with the Luger, had even lagged one or two in Cork during the troubles there. It was a well-respected gun by men who had fought in the war, known for its reliability. He would wager that the IRA had had their share of them brought in from various sources, but they are rare enough, as the morgue attendant had said. It isn't much, he thinks, but it could be something. He has heard that there has been progress matching bullets to individual guns in the laboratory. Kevin Barry himself had been hanged on the basis of this new science of ballistic evidence.

'And the other bodies you've seen,' he says, remembering his previous conversation with the attendant, 'the ones with the same trauma and bullet wounds ...'

The attendant answers before O'Keefe can finish. 'Same-o, same-o. Point nine rounds, contact wounds, back of the head.'

'Is there any chance it's the same gun?'

'Ah now, what I think and what I'd be able prove is a-whole-nother story.'

'Look,' O'Keefe says, taking another pound note from the roll, 'I know we're putting you in a hard place. We need five minutes is all, to ask this lad a few questions.'

'And you thought this was a good place to do it?'

O'Keefe shrugs. 'You never know what seeing his pals laid out under a sheet might do to motivate a lad towards the truth.'

The attendant takes the note, reverting back to the compromised morgue sentinel that he is. 'Now be quick about it, Mister. Two quid's grand for a piss up or a fortnight's grub and rent, but it won't feed the family come winter if I'm out a job.'

'That won't happen if you keep proper sketch, right?'

The attendant leaves and O'Keefe crosses the room to where Just Albert stands with Jeremiah Byrne before the two sheeted forms on the trolleys. He nods at Ginny's man and receives a nod in response. Without pausing he whips back the sheet from the first body, the sheet billowing and wrapping itself around Jeremiah, the sour, sweet scent of decay wafting forth like Dublin fog. O'Keefe had not intended for this to happen but it has the desired effect of shocking the boy, who begins a panicky flapping of his arms in an attempt to shrug free from the sheet. Just Albert grabs Jeremiah by the back of the neck and forces him down until his nose is nearly touching the corpse's cheek.

By chance, it is the body of the boy found wearing Nicholas' jacket, the rough skin of his feet marking him for Jerry's friend. Visible now on his skin, running from his sternum to pubic bone, is a thick, forked trail of stitching from the post mortem. Under the dead boy's hairline, O'Keefe can just make out the stitching of the cranial cut, where the skin of the boy's face had been peeled back and the top of the skull sawn off to reveal the desecration the dumdum nine millimetre had done to the boy's brains. Thankfully, the corpse's eyes are closed, but the cigar burns and terrible bruising are still evident.

'Your mate, is it?' Just Albert says, and Jeremiah nods, still trying to work himself free from the sheet.

'Why was he wearing Nicky Dolan's jacket?'

'Whose jacket?'

'Nicholas Dolan's jacket,' O'Keefe says. 'A black schoolboy's coat. Where did he get it?'

'I don't …'

Just Albert presses down on Jeremiah's neck, burying the boy's face underneath his dead friend's chin, his lips pressed tight to the stitches. Jeremiah struggles but Just Albert's grip is too strong.

'Take a good sniff, young Jerry. You smell that? That's what you'll smell like by morning if you don't start giving me answers.'

The boy grunts and yelps, the sound halfway between a sob and a shout, and O'Keefe begins to wonder are they are being too hard on the boy. He has given his share of slaps as a copper, has taken the hard line once or twice, but rarely with someone so young. And a slap was one thing. Pressing a boy's face into the corpse of his friend another.

'Tell him, Jerry. Where did you get the jacket?' O'Keefe asks, his voice softer and more reasonable than the doorman's.

'Let me up, jaysus fuck. Let me up an' I'll tell you for the sake of holy God.'

Just Albert lets him up, keeping a firm grip on the back of his neck. 'Well?'

'He stole it.'

'Stole it from Nicky?'

Jeremiah nods, and looks to O'Keefe as if for mercy. There is a pleading in his eyes that moves something in O'Keefe.

'And when was this? Where?' O'Keefe says.

Before Jeremiah can answer, Just Albert leans into the boy's ear and says, 'Did yis hurt Nicky? If yis hurt our Nicky you're a …'

'Albert, leave off him.'

'We didn't hurt him. We only wanted his shoes and jacket.'

Just Albert tightens his grip on Jeremiah's neck.

'And any shrapnel, any coin, he'd on him. I swear on the life of me sisters, I do.'

'Let the kid go, Albert. For fuck sake.' O'Keefe and Just Albert lock eyes for a long moment before the doorman reluctantly releases the boy.

'Look, Jeremiah,' O'Keefe says. 'We'll not hurt you, but we need to know what happened. How'd your mate end up dead here? And this other boy.' O'Keefe removes the sheet from the second body, but gently this time. 'Do you know this lad?'

Jeremiah looks down at the second corpse and nods. 'I think … I think he was with the other one who went in the hotel, the one whose jacket we … *Tommo* nicked. They must have lifted him as well.'

'The other lad … Nicholas, you mean? He *was* in the hotel? Show him the photograph, Mister O'Keefe,' Albert says.

O'Keefe takes the photo from his jacket and hands it to the boy. 'Who lifted him, Jerry?'

Jeremiah looks back up at O'Keefe. 'You know the man he battered back in the baths there, at the Achill?' He indicates Just Albert with a nod.

O'Keefe tells him he does.

'Well, I think it was his mates lifted him. They wanted all four of us.'

'But they didn't get you?'

'Nor the other lad.'

'Nicholas?' Just Albert asks again.

'Sure, how to fuck would I know his name? I was robbin' him not ridin' him.' Some of the brashness of the streets, along with colour to his face, has returned to Jeremiah Byrne.

'Mind your tongue, youngfella, or I'll cut it out,' Just Albert says, and O'Keefe frowns at him and signals to go easy.

'And what, did these men come up on ye when you were robbing this boy and his friend?' O'Keefe taps the photograph in Jeremiah's hand. 'This boy?'

Jeremiah studies the picture. 'It was dark. It could be him but I don't know. Sure, it wasn't him I was worried about once I stabbed …'

'You stabbed Nicholas?' Just Albert's voice is a low rasp that sends an icy dagger of panic up O'Keefe's spine.

'No, no. I didn't stab no youngfella, no fuckin' jaysus way I didn't not! I swear on me sister's eyes. I stabbed one of the trench-coats, I did. I'd say that's why yer man, the man he bate,'—Jeremiah indicates Just Albert with another tilt of his head, still afraid to look at him—'is lookin' for me. And why, I'd reckon, they're lookin' for your lad as well. I done the stabbing, but sure, they might think the four of us was together. Maybe that's why Jerry and this lad are dead, but. I'd say it is.'

O'Keefe thinks for a moment. 'Stand over there for a tick, Jerry. I need talk to my friend. And don't think about legging it, right?'

'I won't. Any chance of a smoke?'

Jeremiah takes O'Keefe's proffered Player's Navy Cut and a light and steps over to the sink, some feet away from O'Keefe and the doorman but farther still from the exit. He takes in the welcome burn of smoke and turns, the cigarette pinched between his lips, to the sink to scour the smell of death from his hands and face. He turns on the water and looks down into the deep basin, and for the first time in several days, smiles. Miming his ablutions, his back to the two men, he reaches down and slips the long surgical scalpel into his trousers, covering the handle of it with his shirt.

Across the room, Just Albert says, 'Nicholas went into the hotel. He was running messages and that fucker Murphy knows who for and how to contact him. He has to.'

O'Keefe considers this. 'It seems likely all right.'

'Then why are we still standing here? The hotel's a five minute walk away and we need to have another chat with Mr Murphy.'

'Remember his minders, Albert. They're not men to be trifled with.'

'Neither am I, am I?'

'No, you're not, but I'm asking you, right? No more violence, Albert. We'll not be lucky every time.' O'Keefe points to the angry welt the CID man's bullet had carved in Just Albert's skin.

'Luck's nothing to do with it,' Just Albert says for the second time this night before turning, pushing through the swing-doors, leaving O'Keefe with Jeremiah in the morgue. O'Keefe covers the two bodies with their sheets.

Jeremiah takes a final pull on the cigarette and drops the end on the floor.

'You'd better go,' O'Keefe says to the boy. 'Now, while he's forgotten about you. And stay away from the lanes. Those boys want your blood and won't be as gentle as we were.'

The boy sneers and laughs. 'That sorry fuckin' gaggle? Once they don't cough on me I'm not afeared of them, I'm not.'

O'Keefe shrugs and crosses to the doors, holding them open for the boy. 'Suit yourself, so.'

'I always do, don't I?' the boy says, passing through the doors, the blade of the scalpel warming to the heat of his skin under his shirt.

40

They take the Bentley, Just Albert driving. A short jaunt, four streets away to Burton's Hotel.

'These fellas are armed, Albert. You remember that.'

Just Albert looks at him.

'They are professionals and they're armed. We're not.'

'Fuck them,' Just Albert says, stepping out of the car, leaving it parked at the curb in front of the hotel's entrance. 'Are you coming or not?'

O'Keefe gets out of the Bentley. 'Let me do the talking, Albert. Will you let me do that at least?'

Just Albert cocks his head and squints in the lamplight. 'If there's any call for talking, you can do it.'

They enter the hotel and are greeted by a young man in his twenties at the reception desk. O'Keefe thinks of Nora Flynn, tucked up at home, a book on her lap, tea on a side table, her fags within easy reach. He wonders will this desk man remember their faces and will Nora learn that he has been back to her place of work. How long ago it seems since he kissed her, there on the footpath in front of her digs. He licks his lips, as if he can taste the memory of her, his tongue finding only the tinny essence of fear and flooding adrenaline.

'Can I help you, gentlemen?' The night man has a smattering of acne on his chin, bright, trusting eyes, sleeves rolled up over thin, pale arms in the heat of the hotel lobby.

'Mr Murphy, the Englishman. What room number is he?' O'Keefe says.

'It's quite late, gentlemen. Is he expecting you?' As he speaks, the telephone in the small closet behind the desk begins to ring, small lights on the switchboard igniting to indicate calls coming in from several rooms simultaneously. The night man glances over his shoulder at the switchboard and frowns. 'If you'll excuse me for the moment while I ...'

Just Albert ignores the night man, the squawking phone and switchboard with its blinking lights, and walks behind the desk and through to the small closet housing the switchboard. There he rips a fistful of connection plugs from the board, silencing the ringing and extinguishing the lights. As Ginny's man wheels around, the ends of the cables in his hand lash out at the young night man's legs, forcing him back against the reception counter, fear in his eyes now, hands out, palms raised.

'Sir! Sir you can't!'

'The room number,' Just Albert says. 'Now.' He does not raise his voice, moving in on the young man, leaning into him and crowding him against the reception desk.

'Stop,' O'Keefe says.

'The room.'

The night man turns his head away from Just Albert, his back arched away and over the desk. 'Thirty-four. Jesus, Mary and Joseph, it's thirty-four, for the love of ...'

Just Albert grabs the night man by the shoulders and spins him around, pushing his head down on the desk. He takes up one of the loose phone cables and wrenches the young man's wrists behind his back, looping the cable around them and jerking it tight. He kicks the legs out from underneath him and ties another cable around his ankles, then pulls the night man's tie from his collar and over his head. Taking a handful of hotel stationery from a shelf under the desk, he crumples several sheets into a ball and says to the young desk man, 'Open your mouth.'

'Leave off, Albert,' O'Keefe's voice is hard as he leans across the reception and grabs Just Albert by the arm. 'Leave off him.'

Just Albert shrugs free of O'Keefe's grip and leans down to the night man, shoving the wad of paper into his open mouth and securing it there with his necktie. 'Don't you so much as move a finger for ten minutes. If you wiggle free before that and ring up and warn them, I'm coming back. You understand me, youngfella?

The night man, face down on the ground, nods, terror in his eyes.

O'Keefe circles behind the reception desk, takes out Ginny Dolan's roll of cash, crouches down and stuffs a pound note into the young night man's pocket. He is about to rise and follow Just Albert when he stops and takes out the photo of Nicholas Dolan, holding it front of the night man's face.

'Have you ever seen this lad? Delivering messages, anything? Looking to visit Mr Murphy?'

The night man shakes his head in the negative. O'Keefe is tempted to take the gag out of his mouth but does not, thinking that there is no gain in a small kindness if it results in dead men.

He follows now, taking the stairs two at a time, and he is halfway between the first and second floors, Just Albert one flight above, when the door leading to the second floor hallway slams open and a young couple hustles out into the stairwell. The woman's hair is in disarray and the man's head is bare, his tie and collar loose. Panic is alight in both their eyes, though the woman turns hers to the floor as soon as she sees O'Keefe below her on the stairs. O'Keefe's heart is pistoning in his chest and his hand instinctively goes to his hip for a side-arm that is not there.

'Did you hear the racket of the …' the young man begins to say, but stops when he gets a closer look at O'Keefe. He puts a protective arm across the young woman's stomach and presses her back against the wall of the stairwell, pressing himself in beside her to let O'Keefe pass. Terror blanches the man's face, though whether at the sight of O'Keefe, or at whatever has driven them out of their room in such disarray, O'Keefe does not know. *What racket?* O'Keefe wonders and considers turning back to ask the man, but as soon as he passes the young couple begin to skip down the stairs as if in flight. He continues on up after Just Albert, stopping with him on the landing outside the door that opens onto the third floor hallway.

'Thirty-four,' Just Albert says.

'Let's not get ourselves killed this late in the game, Albert, is all I'm asking, all right?'

Ginny Dolan's man turns and squints up at him. 'I'll not let anything happen you until you find our Nicky, Mr O'Keefe. Then you can die or shite for all I care.'

'Thanks, Albert. You're a gentleman.'

Just Albert opens the door onto the hallway. He begins to walk, his footsteps silent on the carpeted floor. Thirty-eight, thirty-six. Beside thirty-six there is an unmarked door before the numbering resumes again at the door they seek. Thirty-four. O'Keefe grapples Just Albert's forearm and hauls him to a stop in front of thirty-four.

He whispers, 'Do you smell that?'

Just Albert frowns and sniffs the air, the smell of it reaching him but elusive.

'Cordite,' O'Keefe says. 'And that couple on the stairs … they were running from something.'

Ginny's man goes into his jacket pocket and comes out with the Mauser he'd taken from the CID man in the doss-house baths.

'Have you ever fired a handgun, Albert?'

'I've done things you wouldn't like to think on much, Mr O'Keefe.' Just Albert steps closer to the door. He is about to grasp the door knob when O'Keefe stops him, one hand on his forearm, and points to the door jam. The door, Albert sees now, is not firmly shut. He turns to O'Keefe and shrugs.

'Gently,' O'Keefe says, and Albert eases the door part way open until it meets an obstacle and stops. Just Albert turns sideways, and leading with the Mauser, enters the room. O'Keefe waits for a moment and follows. An upended table lamp on one of the bed-side tables casts the room in a harsh puzzle of shadow and light. He looks down behind the door in search of the obstruction and it takes his mind a moment to register the body of one of the gun dealer's guards. The tall, blond one. The one with the smirk, dressed only in undershorts and a white vest saturated with fresh blood. He scans the room, spotting the other guard, a bloody mass in a tangle of bedsheets on the floor beside the bed, part of his skull missing and a spatter storm of brain and blood on the bullet-pocked wall behind the bed.

Just Albert steps farther into the room with the gun raised, the same vigilant calm about him that O'Keefe has come to expect. O'Keefe looks back to the body behind the door and sees the Colt 1914 automatic in the dead man's hand. He crouches down to take it, smelling its barrel, noting that the gun has not been recently fired. He draws back the gun's slide and finds, as he'd expected, a round in the breech. Releasing the clip he finds eight more rounds. He thinks to replace the gun, but a dark part of him holds on to it, feeling a certain comfort in its heft and weight. Out of habit more than anything, he places his fingers at the man's neck and finds no pulse. *Dead before he'd got off a shot.* He considers the pock-marks on the wall and the grouping of wounds on the dead man's chest. Grouped and ascending like bights of a chain. *Like machine-gun fire.* He rises with the Colt, noticing another door ajar beside the second dead man's bed. Adjoining room, linking rooms thirty-four and thirty-six.

'Albert ...' he whispers.

Just Albert turns to O'Keefe, and there is a flash of movement in the adjoining room. Albert senses it and swings the Mauser around, drawing a bead on a young man in the doorway, eyes wide with surprise, a leather satchel in one hand, a Thompson sub-machine-gun in the other, barrel pointed at the ceiling.

A distance of less than ten feet separates O'Keefe and Just Albert from the gunman, and for a long moment the three men stare in silence at each other. O'Keefe is about to speak when the

304

gunman lowers the Thompson and Just Albert's free hand flashes out to send O'Keefe sprawling over the dead man beside the bed.

Just Albert fires the Mauser as the Thompson gun erupts. Smoke and showering plaster and splintering wood. As O'Keefe stumbles to his feet, flicking off the safety on the Colt, Just Albert is still standing. The machine-gun dances in the lad's one hand, too heavy and unwieldy as he struggles to bring it to bear. Just Albert's shooting is no more accurate, the doorman squeezing off rounds, also in a single-handed grip, in the general direction of his enemy, gun hand jumping wildly with the recoil of the pistol.

O'Keefe looses off three rounds into the doorway, and there is a sharp scream and the lad is gone, darting back into the adjoining room. Just Albert begins to follow but O'Keefe grabs him by the collar and jerks him back as a final burst of machine-gun fire rips across the room, punching a pattern of holes through the far wall. Just Albert regains his balance and fires again, wildly, his final two rounds clipping the door-frame and ceiling. A ringing silence descends as O'Keefe makes his way to the wall beside the door, the Colt held up in a two-handed grip. Movement, and muffled sound from behind the wall at O'Keefe's back. The clacking of hollow metal. O'Keefe spins into the room. The gunman is hunched in the corner by the door to the hallway, trying to ram the drum mag onto the Thompson with his forearm. O'Keefe takes this in, the blood on the young man's hands and the leather bag at his feet and realises that he has shot the lad in the hand.

'Put it down!' he shouts, aiming the Colt at the Thompson gunner.

The gunman smiles, and O'Keefe hears the solid click of the drum slamming home, the Thompson's bolt drawn back with a bloody thumb and the barrel rising, machine-gun rounds sweeping the room from floor to ceiling, shattering the overhead chandelier lights, throwing the room into darkness as O'Keefe dives behind the bed, his fall cushioned by the bloody body of Mr Murphy.

O'Keefe reaches up and over the mattress and squeezes off six rounds from the Colt, and abruptly the Thompson goes silent. O'Keefe rolls away from the arms merchant's body, rises to a crouch. For a moment there is acrid silence in the room. Then bright, flaring light as the door to the hallway swings open and the Thompson gunner bolts from the room, the leather satchel in his functioning hand catching on the rebounding door as he exits and jerking from his grip. O'Keefe fires at the hand that comes back around the door-frame in an attempt to claim the bag and is then gone. He pulls the Colt's trigger again and the gun's slide pops back over an empty chamber. Gun smoke hangs in the shaft of light entering the room from the hallway. O'Keefe tosses the gun aside. 'Albert? Are you all right?'

'I'm grand, I am,' Ginny's man says, entering the room with another Colt in his hand, blood running from a wound to his forehead and into his eyes. 'A bit of splinter from the door-frame caught me in the loaf as I was coming through the door behind you. Sure, Mrs Dolan's girls have done me worse with their finger-nails. Did you plug him?'

O'Keefe gets to his feet and feels around the second bedside table until he finds a lamp and switches it on. 'No, he scarpered. I think I clipped him in the hand, which is why we're both still breathing.' He crosses to the doorway and edges a look out into the corridor. Finding it empty, he reaches down and lifts the leather bag dropped by the assassin. 'Fella was fierce anxious not to let go of this anyway.'

Just Albert takes the bag and sets it on the bed, unfastens the buckles and looks inside. 'You can see why.'

Peering over his shoulder, O'Keefe attempts to whistle but finds his lips too dry. 'A knockoff do you think?'

Just Albert shrugs. 'Them three dead fellas were hardly hand-ing it over. But even now, young stroke artists are hardly robbing hotel guests with tommy-guns, even if the guest is the likes of Mr Murphy there,' he nods down at the bloody, gape-eyed corpse of the arms dealer on the floor, '... and his pair of goons.'

'That money is republican gun money, Albert. You know that don't you? Murphy was meant to be dealing guns to the Irregulars. That money is payment for arms I'd imagine.'

'Not any more it's not,' Just Albert says, and the phone jangles on the desk and O'Keefe jumps. Just Albert appears as untroubled as ever, O'Keefe notices, his hands not shaking, his speech level and his shoulders at ease.

'We need to make a move, Mr O'Keefe. I'd wager there's guards on the way, what with all the shooting. And more probably soldiers from both sides.' At this, Just Albert smiles and closes the bag. 'And if that happens, sure the plasterers and glazers will be busy tomorrow.'

O'Keefe nods and leads the way to the door. 'We'll need to talk about that money, Albert. There's nothing but trouble in that bag and we've had our share of it lately. We won't keep getting lucky.'

Just Albert follows O'Keefe out into the hall, holding the bag by the straps in one hand, the newly acquired Colt 1914 in the other.

'Luck's …'

'Luck's got nothing to do with it, I know, Albert, but there's heavy men who'll be wanting that money back and won't stop til they get it.'

They reach the stairwell and begin to descend, jogging down the steps so that O'Keefe does not hear Just Albert say, 'That's exactly what I'm hoping for, that is …'

O'Hanley sits on his chair and tells Nicholas Dolan, who closes and locks the outer and secret door to the room, to sit on the bed.

'Nicholas,' O'Hanley says. 'I thought we'd lost you.'

The boy smiles brightly, young pride and mischief in his eyes. 'Sure, it was ropey enough, it was. Meself and Robert got jumped by two gougers outside the hotel after I gave the message to Murphy. And then didn't ourselves and the gougers get hit up by a great shower of Free State spooks in fine hats and trenchcoats.

Only for one of the lane boys stabbed one of the Free Staters did I get away.'

'And what about Robert?'

'What about him, so?'

'Did he get away with you?'

Nicholas' smile fades now. 'I … I don't know. I … I thought he did. He's not here?'

'No,' O'Hanley says, but he is smiling still, as if not overly concerned.

'Fuck it if I never asked the boys downstairs … I should have asked after him, but I thought he'd be back.'

'Don't curse, Nicholas, it's vulgar. You are an educated young man. A soldier of the republic. It does not suit.'

'Sorry.'

O'Hanley breathes heavily and lets silence descend. He holds the boy's gaze until the boy looks away. O'Hanley reaches across the space between them and pats Nicholas on the thigh, squeezing the taut muscle beneath the tattered woollen trousers.

'Don't worry, Nicholas. You're a fine boy. And a fine soldier.'

Nicholas smiles, and casually shifts his leg from under O'Hanley's grip. 'Here,' he says, holding out a sheaf of papers in his hand. 'I got up to some good while I was wandering the streets. I stripped these from wherever I saw one.'

He hands the papers to O'Hanley, who recognises his own face on them. They are 'Wanted' posters announcing his name and age, stating his crime as murder of Free State forces, offering a reward for information and warning the public against attempting to apprehend him. That he is armed and dangerous. It is, he realises, the same photograph that the British Army and the RIC had used in their 'Wanted' posters during the Tan War. More evidence of collaboration between the Free State and Crown spies.

He smiles ruefully, unable to be truly angry with anything brought to him by this boy. 'I had heard about these. I must send the lads out tomorrow to pull as many down as they can.'

'And here, look at this one.' He hands O'Hanley another poster, and at first O'Hanley does not recognise the face in the photograph.

'You and me, on every lamppost in Dublin!' Nicholas says, laughing like the fourteen-year-old boy he is.

The photograph is of Nicholas, the poster offering a reward for information of his whereabouts.

'But don't worry. It's only me mother who's had them posted. She's worried is all, but I never went near her, like you said.'

O'Hanley looks up. 'You're a grand boy, Nicky.' Again he pats the boy on the thigh, and leaves his hand there.

The boy looks away. 'I should be getting down. Mrs Dempsey is going to mend my trousers and run me a bath.'

'Not at all, Nicholas. Stay with me here, for a time.' O'Hanley is breathing heavily now, his pupils dilated in the candlelight, the musky smell of river and sweat and youth rich in the small room.

'All right,' Nicholas says, and sits back down on the bed. 'Can I help you with anything? I don't know … drafting plans or records or something? Shall I write up a report of my stunt in the laneway?'

'Nicky, please. *Stunt*? We're not common jump-over men. We are republicans,' O'Hanley says, but he smiles as he says it. 'But yes, of course,' he continues, 'a record of your operation. Here, sit at my desk.'

The boy smiles and seats himself, and O'Hanley opens his Ops Log to a fresh page. 'Here, write it here.' O'Hanley leans over Nicholas's shoulder and points at the fresh, white page.

The boy dips the pen in the ink pot and begins to scratch out the date and time of the entry, his commanding officer standing over him, resting a hand on his shoulder. He begins his account of the action, writing several sentences before O'Hanley tells him to stop.

'Nicholas, oh Nicky … How did you ever manage to stay in Francis Xavier's with penmanship like that.' For the moment,

O'Hanley is back in the classroom, the place he thinks he was most happy. 'Here, let me show you something.' Leaning over Nicholas, his face entering the glow of the low-burning candle, O'Hanley takes the boy's hand in his own and begins to guide it in the shape of the letter S. He does this several times, the musky scent of the boy's hair like an intoxicant, inches away from his face.

Laughing, Nicholas looks over his shoulder at O'Hanley. 'Jesus, Commandant, I know how to write my letters.'

The sound of the boy's laughter is lilting, sweet to O'Hanley's ears, and with his hand still on the hand holding the pen, the commandant leans in and kisses Nicholas on the cheek. His free hand goes to the boy's back and slides under his shirt to the ribbed heat of his chest.

The boy pulls away and stands, knocking the chair over behind him. 'No, sir, no … Jesus, I'm not …' The boy backs into the corner of the small room, his eyes alight with fear, confusion.

'I'm sorry, Nicky, I don't know what …' O'Hanley rights the fallen chair and steps over to the boy. He crosses to the inside door and throws it open, only to hear the frantic rapping at the outer false door.

'Sir! Sir!' the voice from outside the room is shouting. 'Open the door, please. I've Stephen Gilhooley here and he's hurt badly, sir. Sir?'

'Let him in, Nicholas.' O'Hanley busies himself removing the medical kit from under his bed.

'And Nicholas …' the commandant says, something bitter about the turn of his lips now, '… not a word of this to anyone, boy. I'd fear for your safety, if ever you were to speak of what you've done here.'

41

The Triumph Trusty is where O'Keefe had left it in the alley beside the Achill, and soon the Dublin streets unwind beneath him, cobblestone and hard macadam, past Trinity College onto College Green, down Dame Street, passing a loose platoon of patrolling Free State soldiers, swinging left onto South George's Street.

The evening assails him in memory. The lifeless, machine-gunned bodies of Murphy and his men. The tortured, sheeted corpses of the boys on the surgeon's gurneys. The smashed and battered skull of the CID man in the doss-house baths, Just Albert's bloody club rising and falling down like a blacksmith's hammer. Bloodsoaked regret and the humid storm cloud of depression he has known since the war, gathering in the dark corners of his mind.

He should never have let Just Albert take the money. No good will come of it. A black assemblage of word and thought clatter in his mind, the Trusty's pistoning four-stroke distant and muffled under this oppression, his eyes scanning the racing shadows and darkened windows of Camden Street as he rides. The flashing nightscape set-dressing his growing despair. Midnight urchins huddling a hackney stand's barrel fire. A late-opening Italian shop, newsprint chip-and-ray wrappings flowered open on the footpath in the margins of its window light. Aging street whores in the maw of an alley, pimp keeping sketch for coppers. O'Keefe's mind keeping grim pace with the bike.

Never should have taken this job in the first place. Nicholas Dolan more than likely up in the Wicklow hills under canvas playing bivo'ed soldiers, and here I am, as if born to it, up to my elbows in blood. And no way to know if the deaths of the boys in the morgue or the men in the hotel are linked to Nicholas's whereabouts. And all to pay a debt incurred by the auldfella. A debt he may have already forgotten.

He curses his father, and regrets it, and then does not.

A light burns behind the curtains in his flat and O'Keefe shuts down the Trusty, leaving it for the moment on the footpath in front of the Cunningham house. He pauses at the top of the steps down to his rooms—a fresh surge of readiness flooding his nerves, heightening his senses—wishing suddenly he had thought to bring the dead man's Colt with him. Then he remembers Finch, sweating out his wounds in his bed. His heart slows as he descends the steps and keys open his door. Instead of Finch, it is Mrs Cunningham sitting in his desk chair before a low coal fire in the grate, a book splayed open on her lap, the weak light over her shoulder from a paraffin lamp on his desk. She starts awake at the sound of his key.

'Mrs Cunningham.' His face flushes with the heat of embarrassment, and he looks to his bed, and beneath a thick welt of blankets is Finch, steadily breathing, lightly snoring. The source of his shame, he is relieved to learn, is still alive. 'I should have told you about my friend. He's …'

The woman smiles, rubs her eyes of sleep then closes the book on her lap. 'It's grand, Mr O'Keefe. His fever's down in the past few hours. And I've changed his dressings. Healthy-looking wound, that is. A bullet if I were to guess.' But there is no malice or suspicion in the words, and O'Keefe nods.

'It is. I'm not sure how he came to get it, but he's a friend I owe my life to. I should have told you. Asked you.'

'Only so I could have tended him, Mr O'Keefe. He's a man in need of medical attention, and medical attention I can provide. I'm happy for the chance to do it again, really. A holiday from the ironing and sewing, it makes me feel young again, and God knows I need to feel that way now and again.' She laughs lightly, and seeing the question on O'Keefe's face, she says, 'I was a nurse, Mr O'Keefe. Before I married, before the war.'

'You're very kind, Mrs Cunningham. I'd like to pay you …'

'Don't be daft, I'm only happy to do it. Sure, somebody needs mind him so Henry and Thomas don't take it upon themselves to do it. They'll mithre the poor man to death if we're not careful. He sent them to shops for whiskey, if you can believe it, and paid them in penny sweets. He wasn't able for much of it.'

O'Keefe smiles back, wondering briefly how long it had taken after he had left for the two boys to sate their curiosity about the man in his bed.

'Will he make it, do you think?' he asks.

Mrs Cunningham stands, strands of her dark hair escaping from their knot at the back of her head and framing her face in the lamplight. A kind face, lines at her eyes that speak of a life spent smiling. Or weeping. Recent weeping, fresh lines carved by the grief of losing her husband, but still a woman more prone to happiness, bitterness not sitting naturally with her.

She is older than O'Keefe by half a decade, he thinks, and her body soft and round, a mother's body under her skirts, her bust stretching tight the blanket she has wrapped round her shoulders for warmth and O'Keefe has a sudden urge to have her take him in her arms and hold him. Change the dressings in his heart, his head. Tend to him. His shame returns as he feels a tightening in his gut, a limning warmth in his balls. He flushes again, guilty and amazed in equal measure with how a body functions. Violence and shame and lust in the space of an hour. And his mind lurches now to Nora Flynn, her lips on his and body pressed against his body, the swell of her breasts against his chest, the heat rising from her

313

skin beneath her shirt collar; Nora Flynn not half a mile away in her digs and his cock twitches, as unashamed and madly sovereign as any inmate in Bedlam. Mrs Cunningham smiles at him as if sensing his need, and though not recoiling from it, guiding it deftly, gently away.

'There's less discharge in his dressings this last time I changed them. I think he'll be grand but tomorrow will tell. If the fever's not worse, then let's hope he's dodged a proper dose of infection. When was he shot?'

O'Keefe squeezes his eyes shut on his yearning. Forcing his mind to speech, rational thought. 'Two days ago. Three maybe. The doctor saw him …' He must pause to think, and with it his desire is stilled, leaving a vague, reassuringly normal wraith of guilt. '… Yesterday, or two nights ago … the days are blending together for me at the moment, I'm afraid. The work I'm doing …'

She closes her book and turns down the lamp to a low gutter. 'I should get back up to the children. What your friend needs is sleep. Nature's nursemaid.'

'*King Lear,*' he says, smiling, surprising himself that he has remembered.

'Who? Oh, I don't know only that the sister who trained me in swore by it. Sleep the healer. And you should sleep, Mr O'Keefe. And don't work so hard,' she says, patting his forearm as she passes him for the door. 'I can't be tending two men at the same time.'

She leaves O'Keefe standing in the centre of his room, his eyes on the slow rise and fall of Finch's breathing under the thick counterpane. *Get well, me auld mate*, he thinks, willing it but unable to pray.

The lamp flickers and dims, running low of oil. Hunger grips his stomach, and O'Keefe tries to remember when he last ate and cannot. Fatigue wrestles with his hunger and wins. Sleep now, he thinks, and takes Finch's bloodstained trenchcoat from the hook by the door. He intends to use it for a blanket, but stops when he feels the unmistakeable shape and heft of a bottle in Finch's coat.

He shoves a hand in and comes out with Dewar's finest Scotch whisky, Finch still preferring the Scotch to the Irish, still loyal to the old trench rumour of Scotch whisky's purity over the rebel distilleries of Ireland. O'Keefe had tried many times, in the year and a half they served together in the RIC, to convince him of the superiority of Irish whiskey, but had never succeeded. But O'Keefe is not picky now, sleep and hunger lost for the moment to thirst. He uncorks the bottle and drinks.

He lowers himself to the floor, covers himself with the overcoat; lights a cigarette and pulls at the Dewar's. When his cigarette is finished, he corks the bottle and blows out the lamp. Tossing restlessly on the draft-rife floor, his mind races and sleep retreats despite the whisky. He thinks of rising and drinking more, but an image of Nora Flynn again rears in his mind. *Don't be a fool, O'Keefe*, he thinks. *Don't be a bloody fool.*

A rushed bath in tepid water, and five minutes later he is for the door.

42

Nora too is sleepless, the shooting in the butcher shop still fresh in her memory, the scent of blood still ripe to her senses despite the scalding bath her temporary landlord had begrudged her. The angry, living faces of a father and two sons. A father and two sons, bloody and dead amidst the sawdust and shattered tiles.

She swallows down sharp bile in her throat, and at each rare passing car on the Leinster Road she pushes back the curtains and expects men to come for her. Someone must. A crime had been committed, and someone would have to answer for it, surely. Three unarmed men dead. Bad men perhaps. Killers themselves, she has told herself, more times than she cares to count since arriving home. Just as Dillon had said as they had fled the scene—and no mistake, that is what they had done: fled, begging the question that if what they'd done was the right thing, why had they run? Why Dillon's instruction—order—to say nothing of what had happened? Their story, sorted between them that the brothers and their father had killed many men, Brits, and more recently, Free State men. They were no innocents, the Gihooleys. Shots had been fired at them as they had entered. They'd had knives. God would judge the butcher and his sons. Jimmy had done what he'd had to do and no more of it, Dillon had insisted. Sure, he'd said, these things happen in our line of work. Still, not a word, to Carty especially. Put it down to a robbery, a dispute among rebels. A revenge killing, one of the Gilhooley brothers riding some other fella's mot and no one would be the wiser, when men were murdered every day of the week in Dublin. Let God judge them. *Like He will judge us*, she thinks.

Her stomach is a hard coil of nerves, her skin flaring hot and chilled with guilt and worry, her mouth sour from cigarettes and vomiting that had stopped, mercifully, some hours before. But sleep will not come, and she sits upright in the hard-backed chair by the window of her squalid room and wonders did the Gilhooley sons have wives who were now widows. Children? *Stop it, Nora. You'll eat yourself alive from the inside out ....*

Something strikes the window-pane and she starts, panic blanching her skin, heart galloping. She takes the Webley revolver from the bag at her feet and pulls back the curtain.

Seán O'Keefe waves up at her from the footpath, his motorbike on its stand behind him on the road. She hasn't thought of him since the butcher shop, or dared hope he might come. *Why would he?* But here he is waving at her, gesturing for her to come out. Her face, of its own volition, breaks into a smile and she mouths the words, 'One minute.'

'You frightened the life out of me!' she says, smiling up at him like an idiot on the footpath. There is safety, somehow, with this man. Respite. In his size and competence. In his warm scent, hard, lean muscle and sad, lovely eyes. The war-scarred face.

'I was only praying you were awake,' he says. 'I couldn't sleep.' He is elated and the words rush out before he can catch them. 'I wanted to see you. I needed to see you.'

And without warning, without restraint, Nora steps forward and takes him in her arms, clinging to him.

'I needed to see you too. I ...' She stops herself. There is comfort to be had with this man, but not in what she can tell him of her day, her work. Her life. Of how she has come to be with him. She steps back, guarded suddenly, but he seems not to notice, an indulgent smile on his face.

'Fancy a spin?' he says, taking a half-full bottle from his pocket and holding it up to the lamplight. 'And a drink?'

'Jesus, more than anything, I would. Will I get my coat?'

'Here,' O'Keefe says, shrugging out of his trenchcoat, 'take mine.'

She sits side-saddle on the Trusty in O'Keefe's coat, her arms clasped tightly around him, and O'Keefe can feel the soft swell of her breasts against his back.

'Where to, Madam?'

'Anywhere, Seán. Jesus, anywhere.'

O'Keefe is startled by the vehemence of her words, but smiles and lowers his goggles. She presses her face now sideways against his back and closes her eyes.

They ride the empty streets, up Leinster Road and down through Harold's Cross, the canal, running Clanbrassil Street to swing onto the South Circular and into Portobello, and back to the canal, rousing nesting swans on the grassy banks.

'Cross the canal and double back, there, that bench,' she shouts over the Trusty's engine noise. 'I love that spot.'

Urgency and giddy abandon this time, and O'Keefe wonders was he the only one who'd been drinking. 'The one under the tree there? Under the willow?'

'Yes,' she shouts, and he swings the Trusty onto Leeson Street bridge, doubling back along the canal under the broken-bottle-topped back walls of Georgian houses, under intermittent ash and oak trees still fat with yellowing leaves waiting for the first autumn storm to strip them.

He shuts down the Trusty and the night city's silence is sudden and mighty in their ears. Nora dismounts and he pushes the bike under the low branches of a massive willow that overhangs the canal and path alike, its tendrils brushing the mirrored stillness of the water. He lifts the bike onto its stand inside the shelter of the willow's reach and beneath this willow is the bench.

'I was only praying there was no one on it. There's sometimes …' she stops before she says the word 'lovers'.

The bench is canted slightly, one end of it raised up by the roots of the tree, and it is dark under the canopy of branches but for the pale lamplight that filters through the row of trees on the far side of the canal. He slips off his goggles and hangs them on the bars of the Trusty.

'Sit with me, Mr O'Keefe,' she says, edgy laughter in her words.

'*Mister?* Now you've made me feel like an auldfella.'

In the willowed half-light he can see her smile. 'And how old are you then, sir? Sure, I've never asked you that.'

O'Keefe steps over to the bench and sits, leaving space between them, but not so much that it can't be breached. 'You'll have to guess. I'm supposed to say that, amn't I?'

'You are. You're very good at this whole business, Mr O'Keefe. I'd almost think you were a professional rogue, casting pebbles at my window and whisking me away for an assignation. A Valentino type and all.' Her words are girlish to her own ears, and behind them she cringes at how forced and jolly they sound, but cannot help herself, desperation driving them.

O'Keefe laughs. 'Hardly. Not even before I had this,' he says, pointing at the scar on his face, and realises that she might not be able to see the gesture. 'No, so go on then. Guess, Miss Flynn. How old do you take me for? And be gentle, mind.'

She turns to face him on the bench, leaning forward. One side of her face is washed in the frail yellow light, and O'Keefe can see the dusting of freckles on her nose, her eyes wide and shining like the surface of the canal.

'Forty,' she says.

'*Forty?* Jesus, do I look forty?'

'All right, all right. Thirty-five.'

'No.'

'Tweny-five?'

'Callow youth, next.'

'A moment.' She leans across and takes his face in her hand, turning it this way, that. Her fingers are hot on his face, scalding and blessed. 'You're old enough and up late is what you are, *Mister* O'Keefe.'

'And you too, Miss Flynn, past your bedtime surely.'

'No rest for the wicked.' The smile fades on her face.

'What is it, Nora?'

'Nothing, really. Just …' She is silent, her mind churning. *Stop it, girl. This is your work. Your job of work. This man ….*

O'Keefe says, 'I meant it when I said I needed to see you.'

There is a long moment of silence between them before Nora says, 'So why? Why did you need to see me?'

O'Keefe is unsure of how to begin. He has never been clever with words, and his mind is too tired for banter. 'I think you're beautiful is why. And good, and kind …'

'No …'

'… and I'm not sure what might happen tomorrow. With this case I'm working. Probably nothing, but … maybe something. Bad things.'

'What bad things, Seán?' she probes gently, surprised by his candour.

He doesn't know why he tells her but he does. 'The boy I'm looking for … the one in the pictures …'

'Yes?'

'I saw his friends, his friend and another boy, last night after I took you home. They're dead, Nora. They were shot, executed. And we found another boy who was with them. A boy who was robbing them when they were "jumped" as he put it, by men in hats and trenchcoats. CID men. Serious men.'

'Jesus, Seán,' she says, but her mind is working. The boys he speaks of are the boys she and her colleagues are searching for. One of them had stabbed Kenny to death, and now two of them, probably three of them, are dead. She has seen what Dillon can do, can justify. But surely not young boys. No, she tells herself. This cannot be.

'And tonight, I was in Burton's again. Things happened.' He looks away, as if ashamed somehow of revealing this new information. 'You'll hear about it at your work tomorrow.'

For a flashing moment, terror grips Nora's throat—*How does he know about my work?*—before she realises he means her cover at the hotel.

'Myself and my colleague Albert. You met him. We came upon a murder in your hotel. More than one. Mr Murphy and his two men.'

'Mr Murphy is dead? Murdered?'

'Yes. The killer was still in the room and there was more shooting.'

Panic crashes in again and Nora's face goes hot then cold. 'Were you ...' She does not know how to ask him.

'I was there, and I wounded the man who killed them. He got away. We ...' He is about to tell her about the money, but something stops him. She is safer not knowing. 'We, my colleague, wasn't kind to the young lad on the desk.'

Nora tries to picture which of the men he means, which of the several hotel staff who are not CID but who are paid a stipend to monitor telephone calls and visitors to the hotel. Glorified touts, she thinks, not minding what kind of a going over the night man had received, but the back of her mind working all the while on the ramifications of Murphy's death. It must be linked to the dead boys in the morgue, but that is not important. What is important is that O'Keefe will be blamed. Heads will roll.

Where were the duty men? Sinking jars of stout in the Flowing Tide, no doubt, while someone waltzed in and gunned down the arms dealer and his men? Maybe, she thinks, panic again swelling in her chest, O'Keefe himself *is* the killer. Maybe he and the brute he travels with—his *colleague*—shot Murphy and his guards. *No.*

321

Please, no. No matter if he did or didn't, the night man will give his report and her department will put a name to Seán's scarred face, and innocent or not he will be made pay for the loss of such an asset as Murphy. Or perhaps not. There are more than a few veterans of this or that war with scarred faces on the streets of Dublin. Maybe he'll be lucky. *Please God*, she prays suddenly, surprising herself with the prayer, *let this man be lucky.*

'Are you all right? You weren't hurt?' she says, all the while thinking: *I'll have to log all this. Report it to Carty. The butcher shop. Murphy dead. I'll have to ….*

'I'm grand, not a scratch. But I'm gutted. Sick with it all.'

'How?' She touches his face again, her palm resting there on his cheek, warm against the cold rope of his scar.

'I thought … I thought I'd left it all behind. Killing, shooting. I thought it first when I left the army, after the war. And then when I demobbed from the Peelers. All I wanted was a quiet life. A bit of peace, but it seems I'm destined not to have it. And then I met you and thought I … Jesus, listen to me, I'm getting ahead of myself.' He smiles, and she smiles back at him.

'You're not.' Her hand still on his face.

'Not what?'

'Not getting ahead of yourself.' She slides closer to him on the bench and she knows she will not say anything to Carty about this man. This good man. Her man, she suddenly thinks. 'I want you to have it, Seán, that peace and quiet life, I do.'

He smiles, her breath warm on his neck, and says nothing. If only life were so simple. He turns to Nora and takes her in his arms.

Nora brings her lips and tongue to his, and his hands now, moving from her face to her back, pulling her closer. She swings herself off the bench, all rational thought abandoned but to make this man her own, and to belong to him if only for an autumn night, and fuck tomorrow and fuck the war and fuck the whole of the Free State. She straddles his thighs and fumbles the buttons of his shirt, his sweat and the smell of soap and oil, the hot wetness between her legs a smell of its own, commingled in the shared air they breathe between kisses. She presses herself against the hardness there, her hand goes down to it, urgency and desire, her fingers tugging the buttons of his trousers, his fingers at the buttons of her shirt, his own coat she wears pushed back on her shoulders, and her breasts free and his kisses down her neck, over collar-bone to her breasts. She offers them up to him, his mouth on them now as she reefs her skirt in a bunch around her hips and guides him inside her, moving forward on him, to make him her own, to make herself his own.

Her face is in his neck when they are finished, his hands resting now on her bare hips under her skirt, the air cooling the sweat on her thighs, where his mouth had been on her breasts, and the light from the lamps across the canal is a gently shifting mesh on her back as the willow limbs stir their leaves in the canal water in thrall to a new soft wind. They are silent for a long moment, and the only sound over the gentle wind in the branches is the soft, hot wind of their breathing. He is still inside her and she does not want to let him go from her, their bodies joined and sated and for once, in what seems like years, her mind is free of thought and only in this moment.

O'Keefe leans forward and kisses her on the top of her head, her hair damp and cool in the night air now. He leans his head back and watches the undulating branches above him, listens to the ancient creak of the willow trunk as the breeze gathers in its branches.

'Thirty-three,' he says.

'Hmmm?'

'I'm thirty-three. My age.' He smiles in the dark.

She lifts her head from the hollow of his neck and smiles, and there is such beauty in the smile, and such sadness, that he thinks he would like to stay here, on this bench under this willow tree inside her for ever, growing old as one with this woman, as old as the tree. She takes his face in her hands.

'Old enough to know better, so.'

'And young enough to keep trying all the same,' he says, smiling sadly in the half-dark, knowing, knowing, this will not last, this peace.

'Yes,' she says, not believing it, feeling old, ancient in her deception. Images of dead boys in a morgue, dead men on a butcher shop floor stealing away the blissful oblivion she has briefly found in O'Keefe's arms.

43

O nly hours after parting from O'Keefe, Nora stands on the sloping cement floor of the morgue and wills herself to lift the sheet. The body beneath it is small, and she realises that she does not need to lift the sheet to prove to herself what she already knows; to prove to herself that what O'Keefe had told her is true.

The mortuary man lingers behind the swing-doors as she has instructed him.

'I'll be forced to ring the guards if you don't take yerself away out of here, Miss,' he'd said to her as she pushed through the doors into the cool air of the morgue, demanding to see the bodies of the two boys. 'I will call for the police, so help me God, miss.'

'I am the police,' she'd told the man, holding out her CID badge. 'So help *me* God.'

I have to see for myself because, though I know it is true, know what Dillon and his men are capable of, I must see it with my own eyes. Because I saw the boy—she lifts the sheet—*yes*—confirming it—*this boy, one of the two who had come to me at the desk of the hotel that night nearly a week ago. This is the boy who'd waited in the lobby while his friend had gone up to Murphy's room to deliver his message.*

And not as a boy then but a young soldier, a small cog in the wheel of war, was how she had seen him, kicking his heels while he waited, his face fixed in a surly scowl. His face now purple and grey and misshapen with the bruising that comes from a bullet to the back of the head.

You had a part in this, she thinks, and swallows down a wave of nausea. *Like you had a part in the killing of those men in the butcher shop. You are the pointer. The pointer bitch directing Dillon and his hunters in the way of their prey.* How many dead men had she marked for execution? And boys now. She notes the red welted burns visible on the soft underside of the dead boy's arm and knows they are the marks of torture. Dillon's work. And she had been part of it. Even before Seán had told her, she'd known something terrible had happened. And O'Keefe, she knows, will probably never find the boy he seeks alive.

Holy mother Mary forgive me, she prays, a reflex, as she struggles to arrange the sheet over the body. Like tucking in one of her younger brothers when they were little. The image rears unbidden, and sorrow knots in her throat, tears welling in her eyes. She lifts the sheet from the other body, forcing herself to look. This one younger. Thinner. Hollow around the cheek-bones, downy-skinned. Again the bruising on the face like someone has punched it from the inside. *This boy is too young for a bullet.* Tears run down her cheeks, the image of her brothers as young boys, snug in their bedsheets, a savage mockery of the memory of love and family and goodness that she feels is now gone from her life for ever. Shot out of it in a war she wants nothing more to do with.

'Wake up, you fucker! Wake up, you Tan bastard!'

The words are bellowed only inches from his face, and O'Keefe registers them from the distance of sleep. He opens his eyes, and the light from a single hanging bulb assaults his senses and he slams them shut again and scrabbles for the solace of unconsciousness.

'No more of that, you sly cunt. Wakey, wakey, Peeler.' The words softer now and followed by a hard slap across O'Keefe's face. His eyes wide open this time, and the man hunched above him mercifully blocks the harshness of the light.

With consciousness comes the pain, the back of his head a fusillade of agony that blinds O'Keefe and sends him turning to the wall, willing his hands out so that he may rise to his knees, but finding them bound behind his back. He rolls, straining against the pain in his head, half on his side, his legs doubled under him, to vomit—thin, yellow streams of bile and the last whiskey he'd drunk—against the whitewashed wall beside him.

Black stars wheel in his vision, and over the sound of his retching he can hear one man tell another that it won't be himself mopping it up, and the other man telling the first that it won't be himself either, seeing as it wasn't he who'd clattered the Peeler so hard when they'd pinched him.

Peeler. To O'Keefe it seems a lifetime since he has been called this, and with such disdain. And with this comes the realisation of who these men are. He struggles to focus on them, slumping his back against the wall, shuffling his arse under him and away from the glutinous pool of his sick. He hacks and spits into the pool, a bloody streak of mucous, and takes in the men standing above him.

Two men in suits, one with a striped tie loose like a noose around his neck, the other with his tie a tightly knotted triangle as is the fashion, both of them hatless, hair slicked with pomade and combed back from the forehead with a roguish flip. Young men, younger than himself. Early twenties. They are both lean and tall, Dublin accents. One of them is strikingly handsome, with blue eyes and angular, almost Slavic features, and he takes off his jacket and hangs it neatly on a hook beside the door. He then begins to roll his sleeves up his forearms, and O'Keefe knows what is coming.

There is a single chair, bolted to the floor in the centre of the room.

And it is not a room but a cell, O'Keefe realises, taking in its dimensions and windowless, subterranean aspect. He has been in such rooms many times in his life, but never on the floor, never in the chair under the hanging bulb. What he cannot remember is how he has come to be here. He recalls dropping Nora back to her digs and stepping off his Trusty and then, nothing. He has an absurd pang of worry for his motorbike, as if it were an unminded child. If these men are who he thinks they are, he's seen the last of his Trusty.

'Get him up,' the man in shirt sleeves says to his colleague, 'into the chair.'

'We'll not wait for Charlie, so? He's on his way from Wellington barracks.'

'We will, but no harm in softening him up a bit, wha? This cunt battered Micka O'Shea half to death. He's it coming anyway.'

'What about the lads upstairs? They won't mind, will they not? He's their pull, their case …'

'Charlie's the bossman on this, sure. This fella bate shite out of O'Shea and plugged the gun merchant and his men full of holes. They're happy to let us have a go at him.'

Awareness dawning, O'Keefe thinks back to the CID man Just Albert had beaten in the baths of the Achill doss-house. No name on the badge but only a number. *Battered half to death.* The CID man isn't dead yet, he thinks, and that's something at least. He blinks and tries to focus on the men. 'Any chance of a cigarette, lads, before we start?'

The man in the shirtsleeves laughs. 'Cheeky fucker, looking for a fag. Well, fair play to you, Peeler.' He turns to his colleague. 'Give the man a burner, Robert. It'll be his last for some time I'd imagine.'

Dragged up and sat in the chair, O'Keefe takes the proffered Sweet Afton and accepts a light from the suited man. He takes a deep pull on the cigarette and begins to cough, the cigarette falling from his mouth onto the tail of his untucked shirt, smouldering there for a moment. The man takes it up and waits until O'Keefe's coughing subsides before placing it back in his mouth. Then he lights his own and Shirtsleeves' smokes and leans back against the wall. These men are prepared to wait, O'Keefe thinks. Their anger held in check by their respect for protocol. Or perhaps they hadn't known, or liked, the man O'Shea well enough. Still, he had seen himself what men did to those who hurt or killed their colleagues. He'd seen it in the Peelers in Cork and it hadn't been pretty. He has no illusions now.

There is silence as they smoke before O'Keefe says, the cigarette pinched in the corner of his lips, 'If it means anything, I battered nobody. I've no idea who your man is, O'Shea. How did you even know to look for the likes of me?'

'Big fella with a scar and a yardbrush moustache on his mug, the desk man at the Achill says. And the lad yis left tied up in Burton's Hotel. That's not you at all is it?' Shirtsleeves says, smiling.

'It sounds a match, but why me? What made you come for me when you got the description?'

'I go where I'm told and I lift who I'm told lift and no one tells me why or wherefore, Peeler. Yours was the name and address I was given.'

O'Keefe shrugs and smokes, relishing the bite of the smoke in his throat, thinking how this could be his last fag, as the man had said. *How had they known about me?* he wonders, but not with any real vigour. Had someone recognised him? Or Just Albert? Had they lifted Just Albert? He cannot imagine Just Albert touting him to men such as these in return for a reprieve from the same torture that awaits him, but O'Keefe knows, as certain as night follows day, that every man will talk eventually, if the pain is applied properly and over a long enough time. Just Albert is unique but he's human. He decides it doesn't matter, but that he would have liked to have found Nicholas, if only for his father's sake. His mind turns to his father and his mother. Another son, lost to war. And what a stupid fucking war to be lost to. One he could have avoided altogether.

He pulls again on the cigarette, and a finger of ash drops onto his shirt front, his jacket nowhere to be seen. The smoke is harsh and wonderful. Last pleasures. Like a man in front of a firing-squad. Nothing certain in this life, he thinks, and maybe they will not kill him, but he wouldn't give odds on it. Not if they think—not if they know—he was in the Achill doss-house or Burton's Hotel. Their very professionalism, in defence of a colleague, would demand it.

'And you're a fuckin Tan,' the suited man adds, mildly, as if this explains everything O'Keefe has coming to him, 'the Tans killed my brother in his bed. In front of his kids and his missus, two year ago.'

'I was a Peeler but I was no Tan. And I never shot any man who wasn't shooting at me first, and no man in his bed,' O'Keefe says, but without conviction, knowing that what he had done or not done during the Tan War does not matter to men such as these so much as what side you fought on and what your side had done to their side. O'Keefe has no doubt the man is telling the truth about his brother, and that Tans or Auxies—or even Peelers like himself—had shot his brother in his bed in front of his family. And now he would pay for it.

'You broke up O'Shea,' Shirtsleeves says, 'and that's enough for me. Whatever about the Brit gun dealer and his men. Either one's enough, and Charlie's got the right hump over the gun seller. Crown spooks are demanding a head for him and it looks like yours fits the hat. You've finished that?' He points with his cigarette before dropping it and crushing it under his brogue.

O'Keefe nods and savours a last drag. The suited man comes and takes the butt from his mouth, and O'Keefe has a flashing memory of Nora Flynn, her hands on his face, her face close to his. Sadness wells up in him at what he has lost. God knows, if they do let him live, what state he'll be in when they're finished. He allows himself a final memory of Nora and then shoves the memory away.

Shirtsleeves takes off his belt and wraps it carefully around his hand to protect his knuckles.

O'Keefe says, 'Right so, lads, mind the face. I've a portrait scheduled for Thursday.'

44

The Foley Street door is opened by the young, mute girl and she admits the two men. The interior of the brothel is dark in contrast to the afternoon light, and Charlie Dillon and Jimmy Boyle wait until their eyes adjust to the dim hallway before following the girl into the parlour.

The room at first appears empty and smells of stale perfume and whiskey soaked into faux-Turkish carpets. Jimmy takes the odour of the whiskey over all other smells and his mouth fills with saliva and his hands begin to shake. He shoves them in his trouser pockets to still them.

'A drink, gentlemen?'

Dillon and Boyle turn to the silhouette of a woman seated on a *chaise longue* in front of the parlour window, the outside light a harsh white through the lace curtains, making it difficult to see the woman's face.

'Don't mind if we do,' Jimmy says, and the driver slips behind the bar before Dillon can stop him, taking a bottle of Paddy from the shelf behind and glugging a generous measure into a glass. 'You want one, Charlie?'

Dillon stares at his driver. 'No, I don't, Jimmy.' This is not how he had wanted to begin.

'A seat then, please,' Ginny Dolan says, indicating two chairs across a low table facing the *chaise longue*.

Boyle refills his glass and follows Dillon to the chairs, setting down the whiskey and taking out his packet of cigarettes. He offers the box around and has no takers, the brothel madam smiling, he thinks, as she shakes her head, but it is hard to tell, seated as she is in front of the window.

'What can I do for you, gentlemen?' the woman asks, directing her question to Dillon. 'You said it was urgent business in your phone call.'

'I'll not beat round the bush, Mrs Dolan,' Dillon says, leaning forward, hands on his knees. He squints and tries to hold her eyes against the light of day behind her. 'We're looking for your man, Albert. You said on the ringer he's not here.'

'He's not, you're welcome to look if you care to ...'

'Missus, if I wanted to search this ... *house* ... for him I'd have twenty detectives and soldiers in here in a minute and you'd not have so much as a plate unbroken when we left. So save yourself the bother and tell us where your man is.'

'I didn't get your name, sir.'

'Captain Charles Dillon, Free State Army Intelligence,' Boyle says, setting down his whiskey, 'And I'm Jimmy Boyle, CID.'

'Ah, a spy and a copper. I feel so much safer now.'

Boyle nods, reaching into his jacket for his badge, and Dillon tells him to leave it.

Turning back to Ginny Dolan, he says, 'This is not a friendly visit, Mrs Dolan. Your man is wanted for the attempted murder of a detective officer and the murder of three men in the employ of the Free State. I will have this house in shreds, I will, if you choose it.'

'Twenty odd years I've run a business in these streets, Mr Dillon, and never once did a single serving soldier of the British Army ever threaten me. And now with the Free State of Ireland only a wet week old, I'm already threatened by an Irishman.'

The woman smiles pleasantly as she speaks, and this enrages Dillon. 'You tell me where he is, whore, or I'll burn this fucking

stew to the ground. See how long it takes for your doxies to jump
ship to one of the other houses …'

'Captain Dillon, tut tut, sir.'

'Do you think I'm having you on, Missus? Do you?'

'I think you'd do well to ask your masters first before you
threaten Ginny Dolan with burning, Captain Charles Dillon of
the Free State Army Intelligence.'

'My masters give me reign to do what I need do in the pursuit
of enemies of the Free State.'

'Including the destruction of Irish businesses and the harass-
ment of loyal, Irish citizens?'

Dillon smiles a cruel smile. 'Your loyalty isn't worth a ride on your
sorriest brasser, Missus, to the people and government of Ireland.'

'So you're threatening me, a poor, widowed woman, on behalf
of the people of Ireland then, Captain Dillon?'

'I'd mind my mockery if I were you, madam. Good whores are
hard to come by if they've no house to tup in.'

Ginny Dolan pauses and turns to Jimmy Boyle. 'Mister Boyle,
why don't you make yourself another straightener there like a
good chap while I speak to Captain Dillon here?'

Jimmy Boyle looks to Dillon, and Dillon, flummoxed for the
moment, pauses. 'There's nothing … he can hear anything you've
to say.'

'I'd rather think you'd hear what I've to say yourself first and
then decide.'

Boyle shifts his gaze from Dillon to Ginny Dolan and feels
a chill wash over his back. There is something about the woman
that unnerves him. She is not afraid of Charlie and certainly not of
himself. He stands and crosses the room to the bar for more whiskey before Dillon can stop him.

'Now then, sir, will I tell you why you'll be taking your threats
away and leaving me be, will I?'

'Go on, then, tell us. You've backbone, I'll give you, for a pimp-
ing whore madam.'

'Oh, I've more than backbone, Captain Dillon, believe you me,' she says, her smile fading. 'I've friends among your masters and among the departing Crown.'

'And what friends are these?' Dillon asks.

'You're an Irishtown lad, aren't you, Captain?'

For a second Dillon is thrown. 'I am, though what's it …?'

'Forty-five the Strand Terrace, is it? And your dear mother and two sisters and poor invalided grand-da live together, snug as bugs don't they, in that lovely Irishtown terrace house?'

His face darkens. 'And what of it?'

Ginny smiles again. 'Oh, nothing of it, sir, only it would be a shame if any fire started here should send sparks down Irishtown way. Life's terrible hard for a family with no home and young, pretty sisters such as your own. It can be fierce dangerous on the streets what with the type of men that will do just about anything to a young girl for the price of a jug or two …'

'You whore, are you threatening my family!?'

'Now, now, Captain Dillon. I do nothing of the sort. I've a mind to find my missing son Nicky and will have nothing or no man stop me. That's all. Perhaps you might care to look for yourself. There's a substantial reward in the offing should you find him.'

'You rickety bitch. I should put a bullet in you right now, and then you'd be no harm to any upstanding man or woman.'

'You're calling yourself upstanding, Captain?'

He reaches into his coat, comes out with his Luger pistol and slaps it down onto the table with a clatter that makes Boyle spill his whiskey at the bar.

'Put that away, for the love of God. Do you not think I've done my sums and paid who needs paying already? Just in case something ill should befall me? Let's call it Ginny Dolan's life assurance, shall we? There is no reason for us to be enemies, Captain Dillon. Grander men than you have benefited from my friendship.'

Dillon stares hard at her for a long moment, unable to believe how this meeting has turned on him. The notion of finding and killing this madam's doorman is gone, leaving only fear in its place. *Not mad*, he thinks. *Dangerous*. There is a part of him that would just shoot the woman, solve this problem as he has solved all others in the past years. But there exudes from this whore a menace older, darker than those he has encountered in the Crown forces or in his former colleagues now aligned against the Free State. Her threats, he feels, are utterly real, and her malice boundless.

He takes the gun back from the table and holsters it. 'Come on, Jimmy, he's not here ...'

'I've enjoyed your visit, Captain Dillon. Really, I have.'

The madam is smiling as they leave.

45

Again O'Keefe awakes on the floor. His nose is swollen closed and his mouth is clogged and metallic with coagulating blood. Gingerly he tests his teeth with his tongue and finds them loose but miraculously intact. He takes shallow breaths to hold off the pain in his ribs. If they are broken, he knows, breathing too deeply may puncture a lung. He straightens his legs, slowly, and gathers the blood in his mouth to spit. The breath he takes to eject the blood and sputum does not hurt as badly as he thought it might and he risks sitting up.

He is alone in the cell, the single bulb still burning brightly, and he has no idea of how long he has been unconscious. Only now does he notice the blood splatter on the whitewashed walls and floor, some of it fresh and no doubt his own. Other stains are older and dried, and some are smeared in arcs of dark wash, as if someone had attempted to clean them with a rag or sleeve, but they are unmistakeably blood. O'Keefe remembers hearing that Jurys hotel in College Green had been forced to strip and redecorate many of its rooms after British Army intelligence had finally returned the hotel to its owners after using it for a headquarters and interrogation centre. And now the Free State has its own torture house. The cellar of Oriel Street, CID headquarters.

The beating had lasted ten or fifteen minutes, he thinks, and he is perversely proud for having stayed in the chair, conscious, for as long as he had. In situations such as these, fists are preferable to feet, and it pays to remain upright. Administering a beating is hard work. Men tire of hefting a man over and over again into a chair and will happily resort to booting a prisoner around the floor to spare the effort of lifting him.

Having manoeuvred himself to an upright position against the wall, O'Keefe listens to the footsteps on the floor above him. Shirtsleeves and his mate hadn't asked him any questions. 'Softening him up' is what they'd called it. But the questions would come and he would answer them truthfully and try his best to leave Just Albert out of it, if Ginny Dolan's man hasn't been pulled already. And his answers would be the truth. He had not beaten the CID man O'Shea and he had most certainly not killed Murphy and his men. He is trying to decide whether or not to admit being in the hotel and coming across their killer, when the sound of footsteps descending the stairs becomes louder, and shortly the latch on the outside of the cell door is slotted back, the door opening outward.

'Get up, you, now, in the fucking chair,' the man entering says, in a grey suit, his hat tipped back on his head, suit jacket open. The two men from earlier follow this man into the cell. 'Get him up.'

Shirtsleeves comes to O'Keefe and hoists him into the chair, O'Keefe wincing at the pain in his ribs and abdomen. He cannot feel his hands behind his back for the tightness of his bonds. 'He's well ripened up, Charlie.'

Without waiting for Shirtsleeves to finish his sentence, the man called Charlie steps across the cell and drives his fist into O'Keefe's face, shattering his nose. The blow is so hard that O'Keefe falls from the chair and the boots come next. O'Keefe tucks his knees to his chest and his head down to meet them, using his feet to try to slide back across the floor to the wall. The kicks come hard and fast, and this time O'Keefe hears the ribs crack, a dull, muffled snapping in his chest. And this man called Charlie is grunting and cursing as he swings the boots in, O'Keefe conscious of only some of the words. *You fucker, you cunt, whore madam, threaten me? I'll break every fucking bone in your murdering body, Peeler ....*

He is conscious of one of the young men speaking. *Charlie? Charlie go easy, man, you'll kill him before he can sign the confessions. Charlie, for fuck sake.* A lucky kick connects under O'Keefe's jaw and slams his teeth together with a sickening clack. Blood fills his mouth again and O'Keefe swallows and chokes on it and splutters, half-spits, half-vomits the blood and a tooth from his mouth. This Charlie's voice rising above the others: *Leave off? I'll fucking kill him I will. Go away from me!* O'Keefe senses more than sees one of the younger men bundling Dillon away, his arms in a bear hug around the man's chest, his booted feet flailing.

The blows stop, and one of the men has lifted him back into the chair. He realises he is still conscious and wishes he wasn't. Minutes, maybe hours pass. The cell door opens, voices outside the cell, closes and opens again. O'Keefe is out of time now, existing only in a long, jagged, moment of hurt.

'Stop this, now, Charlie. He's done nothing,' Nora Flynn says, standing outside the cell with Dillon. 'Nothing at all.'

Charlie Dillon laughs. 'And you're the one ordering the likes of me about now, are you, girl?'

'You've gone far enough.'

'I've not gone half as far as enough, *Detective*. Now, you'd want to fuck off upstairs to your typewriter and keep your snout out of things that don't concern you.' The smile is gone from Dillon's face and his voice is low and mean.

'It does concern me, *Captain*.'

'How is that?'

'I was shadowing him.'

'Fine fucking job of it.'

'I know he didn't kill Murphy and his men.'

'How? How do you know that?'

'Because he was with me the whole time, last night,' she lies, without thinking.

'Was he now? I've heard about what happens to lads who spend the night with you, girl.' The smile is back, but it is vicious, and instead of frightening Nora, it enrages her.

'I saw the bodies of those two young boys you tortured. Murdered!'

The smiles goes from Dillon's face. 'What boys?'

'The cigar burns on their arms and feet and …' She reaches out, without thinking, and grabs the cigar box from Dillon's shirt pocket. 'Was it these cigars you used on those boys? What, fourteen years of age, were they?'

'You'd want to watch your mouth, Detective Officer Flynn. It's leading you to places you've no mind to be.'

'What are you going to do? Shoot me, Charlie? Torture me?'

'You'd be so lucky.' And Dillon steps nearer to Nora, bringing his face close to hers.

'You stop hurting him right now and I won't go to Carty with what I know about those boys.'

'While you're there, why don't you tell him about how you and that fat *dah*, Jimmy Boyle, shot up them lads in the butcher's shop? Cut them down in cold blood. He'd like to hear that wouldn't he?' His warm breath on her face is like an illness.

Nora takes a step back. 'I might tell him, Charlie, because I don't care any more. I don't give a passing damn for any of this. I'll swing for those men in that shop if it means seeing you done for those two poor boys.'

'Go on then, tell him. He hasn't the pull he once had when Mick Collins was alive. I've nothing to fear from him at all.'

'We'll see about that.'

Dillon turns back to the cell door. 'Go on then, you silly cunt, let's see …'

'Give me the papers,' Charlie Dillon says to one of the men as he re-enters the cell, and through swollen eyes O'Keefe watches as the young man takes a sheaf of folded papers from inside his jacket.

'We never questioned him, Charlie.'

'We don't need to, he done it and he's confessed.' Dillon walks over to the coat hooks on the wall and takes hold of one of the hooks. He tugs down on it and then, oddly, grabs it with both hands and uses the hook to support his whole weight, his feet coming off the floor for a second. 'Give us your tie, Robert.'

'My tie?'

'Your tie. The tie round your neck, for the sake of Christ.'

'What're you doing with it, Charlie?' Shirtsleeves loosens his tie, lifts it over his head and holds it out, but Dillon ignores it.

O'Keefe watches all of this and knows the end is coming soon. He is aware of a distant anger that his death will appear a suicide, but then he does not imagine his body will be released to his family anyway, so they will never know. Sadness wells within him to douse the anger, but it is not a great one. More than anything, he feels tired and wants the pain to stop. He thinks of his mother, the rest of her days to be spent tending her husband's dying mind, and wonders will she even get the solace of a funeral, a body to bury, or will her second son end up in a common grave or a tout's hole in the Wicklow mountains. *One son in the rocky soil of Turkey and another in a boggy ditch.* And he thinks of Nora Flynn and her lovely face; the deep green of her eyes and the full, soft heft of her breasts. He thinks then of his brother Peter and wonders will he see him in heaven and decides that he won't.

46

Nora stands outside the closed door to Carty's office. She is conscious of all activity in the office having stopped, conscious of the eyes of Mary Whyte on her, heavy and spiteful. The weight of her future, her freedom maybe, is the weight of her hand about to knock on the Detective Superintendent's door. Guilt drives her to action and she knocks, and without waiting for a response enters the office.

'Nora…?' Carty is at his desk, looking tired, his glass eye appearing slightly askew in its socket.

'You have to stop Dillon. He's torturing O'Keefe. He won't stop.'

'I've no authority to stop him, Nora. Murphy was as much his operation, the Army's operation, as it was ours.'

'This is our building, sir. Our office. We do things our way here, don't we? Or does Dillon do things his way wherever he goes in the country? Are we working his way now, in our cells?'

'We do our share of it, Nora, sure, you've heard it yourself.'

'It has to stop. Seán O'Keefe has done nothing to deserve what he's getting. You must stop it. It's not right.'

'He's done nothing, then?'

'He hasn't. I was with him all night, watching him, like I was assigned.' The lie comes easily to her this second time.

341

'You were watching him.' The words are flat and stagnant with a truth Nora has not foreseen.

'I was. He was with me, last night, he couldn't have done what Dillon thinks he's done.'

Carty says nothing and the silence gathers around Nora like a rebuke.

She says, 'You know that Charlie killed those two boys, in the city morgue. Tortured them first, like he's doing to O'Keefe right now. On your watch, sir.'

'I know he probably did, Nora, but there's little I can do about it even if I could prove it. Just because you saw the bodies does not mean you can prove he killed them.'

'I …' Nora stops. 'He as much as admitted it to me.'

'You weren't with O'Keefe *all* night, were you, Nora?'

Fear rises in her and she knows she has been caught in her lie. 'I was.'

'You weren't. You were seen meeting him, seen …' Carty appears sad, saying this. 'We had another man on him. He was seen coming out of Burton's and our man took the initiative to shadow him. He … watched … saw you two. Together.'

'Oh.' Something collapses inside her and her legs feel weak, hollow, as if they will not hold her upright.

'Look, our man's a good sort and won't say anything. You'll be grand, Nora.'

She swallows, knowing that it is not true, lies set upon lies, and decides that it doesn't matter any more.

'You have to stop Charlie, please. We're supposed to be detectives. Political crimes. It's a crime, Terence, what's happening down in that cell. Please.' Tears begin to run down her cheeks and she swipes them away, choking back the urge to weep in rage, in shame, in sadness. 'Please,' she says.

For a long moment, Carty says nothing. He blinks hard as if to dispel some horrible vision, and his glass eye rights itself. Finally he stands, his chair creaking under him. 'Wait here,' he says, and leaves the office, the door half-open, typewriters clacking back to life in his presence.

Dillon leaves Shirtsleeves holding his tie and comes to stand over O'Keefe.

'Give me a pen. A pencil, whatever, give it to me.' He takes O'Keefe's jaw in his hand and holds his face in front of his own. 'Now you sign these papers, Peeler, and that'll be that. D'you understand me? Nice and easy and this will all be over for you.'

O'Keefe's vision is blurred with blood and tears, but he is able to see, as Dillon looms over him and his jacket falls open, a Luger pistol hanging in the holster under the man's left arm. Anger flares and lights in his gut and some small, futile joy with it. It does not matter now but at least he knows. He mumbles and is not sure if his words can be understood through the bloody mass of his teeth and tongue.

'What's that?' Dillon lets go of his jaw and O'Keefe's head slumps down onto his chest.

Fighting the black comfort of oblivion, the pain in his head and chest, O'Keefe raises his head and forces the words out more clearly. 'A Luger.'

'A what?'

'Your gun,' O'Keefe says, a smeared grin coming to his lips. 'It's a Luger.'

'Yes, what …?'

'Is that the same one you used to shoot the two youngfellas?' O'Keefe says, still smiling, black sleep edging his vision, fighting it.

'What are you on about?' Dillon says, turning to look to his two men. 'What's he on about?'

'The two young lads in the city morgue. You shot them. The two boys …'

'How …?'

'That's why you and your men have been hunting the young blondie fella … and Nicky. You left two witnesses alive … two other boys who can identify you.'

'You're fucking daft. I've kicked all sense out of him, lads.' He turns back to O'Keefe. 'And even if you're right, you've no proof. A murderer, sitting in a murderer's chair, accusing me? Prove it, Peeler. You're not in the police any more, are you, so? No way for you to stitch me up now, is there, you fucker.'

'The way you're trying to stitch me up, battering me into signing those papers of yours? So you can hang me with your man's tie from the coat hooks and close the whole case out with a suicide.' Blood and spit leak from O'Keefe's mouth onto his already blood-soaked shirt. 'I'm surprised you haven't lit up one of your cigars by now … like you did to those two young boys.'

O'Keefe sees the look exchanged between the two younger men before the blow comes, Dillon's fist lashing out and knocking one of O'Keefe's loose teeth back into his throat. O'Keefe tries to bring his knees up in the chair as Dillon works his body with punches. *At least*, O'Keefe thinks, *I know now. At least I know who killed those boys. A shame, but, I never found young Nicky. Shame I didn't find him before this lot did.*

The last words he hears are Dillon's, saying to the younger detective, 'The tie, Robert, give it here.'

Blessed black unconsciousness falls and O'Keefe slumps off the chair onto the hard floor of the cell, his blood bright red under the harsh light of the hanging bulb.

Carty keys the cell door and Dillon turns, the tie taut around O'Keefe's neck, O'Keefe's eyes beginning to bulge, spittle and blood in stringy webs from his lips, his feet jigging and scraping the cell floor.

'Leave off him, Charlie. For the love of God. You're a bloody savage, you are.' Carty's words are spoken softly.

'This is none of your business, Terry,' Dillon says, the necktie still taut in his fist, O'Keefe's face going from red to blue, his tongue bulging from his mouth.

'It is my business, Charlie. The courts are up and running, proper courts martial, and we'll run him through them, but I'll not have someone murdered here under my command.'

'Murdered?' Dillon laughs. 'How many men have you *murdered*, Terence, for the sake of all that's holy? Jesus. *Murdered*? By fuck, you've some cheek.'

Carty's hand goes into his jacket and comes out with his Mauser. He levels it at Dillon and then the two other men. 'Ye two shift it. Out!' he barks, and the two younger agents look to Dillon and then to the gun. '*Out!*'

Reluctantly, the two pass in front of Carty and out of the cell.

'You're fucking finished, Carty. Know that, like you know nothing else. My brother …'

'Fuck the brother, Charlie. You'll be just as finished if I choose to investigate the killing of those two boys.'

'You wouldn't chance it. You wouldn't dare, not with what I know about you, how many dead men you signed off on. How many dead men you fuckin' shot yourself with your Mauser there, before you went so high and mighty behind a desk.'

O'Keefe's feet lash out and straighten and his body goes limp.

'Let him go, Charlie.' Carty raises the Mauser.

Dillon smiles and shakes his head. 'You've gone weak in the head, man.' He lets go of the tie and O'Keefe slumps out of the chair and onto the floor, a bellowing intake of breath and then wracking, coughing exhalation. His eyes flare open, terror in them, ruptured capillaries making his pupils blood-red, blood in a fine coughing spray from his mouth.

'We won't be working together again, Charlie.'

'No, Terence, we fucking won't.'

Dillon turns and takes his suit jacket from one of the hooks before turning back. His face is flooded with rage, and Carty thinks for a second that Dillon will go for the Luger in its leather holster. But the man smiles instead. There is something vicious and unhinged in it, and Carty wonders is the man sane at all. Wonders for a passing second if he himself is.

'Is it the bint upstairs you're saving him for then?' Dillon says. 'Are you jockeying her, Terry? Is that what this is all about, wha'?'

'Fuck off away, Charlie, or I'll have you up for those two boys.'

'You would in your hole, have me up, you soft bastard.'

Dillon leaves, slamming the cell door shut with a din that echoes through the CID offices.

O'Keefe has a faint recollection of a man standing over him, of voices raised, and then water in his mouth, the coolness of it running out over his lips, unable to swallow, and down his neck onto his chest. Rough hands moving him from the floor, his bonds loosened and untied.

And now he wakes to the sting of a cool sponge on his forehead, his face. He tries to open his eyes and finds one of them sealed shut with blood, the other so swollen he can see only a narrow slit of the world. It is a moment before he hears the sound of sobbing over the ringing in his ears. Words spoken, softly, gently and then the crying. He is lying down. A mattress of sorts. But his head is held and supported, his shoulders resting against the firm, round warmth of a woman's thighs. A blissful fog buffers his consciousness. But through this, he is aware of a woman. The low, sweet tones of the woman's voice felt through the contact between their bodies, his back and shoulders on her thighs, his head held against her stomach, this woman. His mother?

Struggling to open his eyes. It is her. Nora. And she is speaking to him and the words she is saying are, 'I'm sorry, Seán. I'm so sorry.'

But he is unable to open his eyes, and is soon submerged again in the nothing-scape of unconsciousness.

47

Nora holds O'Keefe's head in her lap as she wipes the drying blood from his face. The sawbones they brought in—a Free State army doctor known to say nothing to no one about the condition of the men he often attended to in the Oriel House cells—had said he should live. He had dosed O'Keefe with morphine and recommended that someone at least check in on the patient, now and again, if he is not to be removed to a hospital. Carty had looked at Nora and Nora had looked away, but she had stayed, and strangely no soul had come down the stairs to the cells, either to exit the building or to bring down further prisoners for questioning.

And he has survived, Nora sitting by him on the horsehair mattress Carty had insisted on being brought in before he had left.

Only by the sheer grace of God had the team who had snatched him from in front of his digs been led by a CID man who insisted on bringing him back here to Oriel House, for all its horrors, rather than Dillon's cells in Wellington barracks. Thank God for small mercies, Nora thinks, dabbing at the clotted blood around O'Keefe's eyes. If he had been brought there, she knows, Seán O'Keefe would not have survived yesterday, never mind the night.

Now Nora's eyes burn with fatigue, her mouth scorched by endless cigarettes. O'Keefe's head is a dead weight in her lap and she cannot help but think of Detective Kenny, dying in her arms on the lane off Abbey Street, his death kicking all of this into motion. One death begetting more deaths. How many? Nora does not dare count.

Please, God, let him be all right.

'Nora,' O'Keefe says, his voice rough with sleep and blood and morphine, his swollen tongue unwieldy in his mouth. 'Is that you?'

'Yes, Seán, I'm here, it's me,' she says, wiping his brow with the wet cloth.

'How long?'

'Shhhh,' she says, 'try to sleep. I'm here. I won't leave you.'

O'Keefe does what she tells him, nodding his head in her lap, giving her a trusting smile before falling back into healing sleep.

It is the trust in the smile that breaks Nora's heart, and she begins to weep.

Two days pass and Nora keeps her vigil over O'Keefe in the cell, joined once more by the doctor who administers more morphine and tells her again that the man might live and be grand and he might not, but there's not a lot one can do for him now, as it is, but wait. And pray, if she were so inclined.

Carty has left her to it, not questioning her whereabouts, not asking after O'Keefe. The cell has remained unlocked and Carty has passed her, unspeaking, gazing at her in a sad way when he has seen her at her desk or brewing tea, forcing down shortbread biscuits and slices of bread in the room where the CID's waiter and chef prepare meals for the staff. But he has not questioned her or assigned her to any other work. It is as if she has been left alone to atone for the sins of the CID, of Army Intelligence. An angel sent to mop up after ghouls.

As far from angel as it's possible to be, she thinks, nearly dropping her tea as she enters the cell to find O'Keefe sitting up on the mattress with his back against the wall. His eyes are a dark outrage of blue and brown bruising, one of them refusing to open for the swelling. The ragged bolt of his old bayonet scar is barely visible under the bruising but it twitches, like a live wire embedded in his skin. When he sees her, he gives her the faintest of smiles.

She cannot understand him at first, so soft and morphine-thick are his words.

'Is that tea for me?' O'Keefe repeats. There is terrible striated bruising on his neck that will take weeks to disappear.

'Of course, Seán, here,' Nora says, carrying the tea to him, kneeling down beside him on the mattress to help him drink, but O'Keefe reaches out and is able to take the mug himself.

'It's hot,' she says, 'be careful.'

O'Keefe says nothing but raises the mug to his lips and winces, tears welling in his eyes at the pain as the hot liquid contacts the cuts on his lips. But the tea is beautiful to taste, he thinks, his mind waking lucidly for the first time in how many days. It is the taste of life, of healing. *I am going to live*, he thinks.

Nora watches him drink, and driven by the habit of the past two days, brings her hand to his forehead, letting the heat of his waning fever run under her palm.

'You make a grand nurse, Nora.'

She takes her hand away and cannot hold his gaze. 'Oh no, Seán, no. I'm ... I'm sorry.'

'Sorry? What do you mean?'

'For lying to you ... about everything. About how we met ... you ... you were my assignment, Seán. I was ... I was your watcher.'

He is silent for a long moment. 'Your assignment? None of it then ... between us ...?'

'No,' she says, turning back to him. 'No. That was real, Seán. I swear it was.'

It is O'Keefe's turn to look away.

She reaches out to take his hand and he pulls it away. 'I never meant for this ... for any of this to happen to you. Or to that boy ... those boys.'

'Of course you didn't.'

Nora hears the dark sarcasm in his words and almost relishes them, the words savaging her heart and her heart delighting in the hurt of it.

'It's what I do, Seán. I'm a detective officer here with CID. I was only meant to watch you.'

'You work here, so?' There is sad scorn in his voice.

'I do. I have done for ages. First in the Castle for Ned Broy, and now here. I'm only a watcher. And a typist, a shorthand typist …' Her words sound high-pitched and vaguely hysterical to her own ears. *A typist.* 'I'm a pointer … a pointer bitch,' she says now, giddy with the madness of guilt. 'I put the dogs on you, Seán. But then I fell in love with you, and …'

Tears shine in her eyes and O'Keefe sets the mug on the blood-stained cement floor beside the mattress.

'… And you couldn't call the dogs off.'

She shakes her head, guilt a solid, choking wedge in her throat. 'No.'

'I could have loved you, Nora.'

'Stop.'

'You were what I thought of, when they were beating me. When I thought I was going to die … your beautiful face. I was so sad at the thought of never seeing you again …' O'Keefe is aware of the pain his words are inflicting and feels, under the fading haze of the morphine, a malicious bite of pleasure.

'Please stop.' She is weeping now.

'And here we are. Here we fucking are.' *What did she call herself? A pointer bitch. Whore.* His mind registers the hate in the words and in his thoughts. *To think I have never called a woman a whore. Not even whores. Hateful ….*

The bitter pleasure is short-lived, leaving him with only a vast, hollow loneliness, and for a feverish moment he has the urge to reach out and hold her, to take her in his arms and console her and tell her everything is grand and fine and nothing will stop them from loving each other and living together and making a life, a home. Together. But as quickly as it comes, this feeling too is lost to the morphine and shame; the thrumming pain in his battered body. He does nothing and watches as she weeps.

After a long moment, O'Keefe says, 'Am I still a prisoner here, Nora?'

She shrugs, and the gesture makes her appear younger than she is, vulnerable. 'I don't know.'

O'Keefe nods, shifts himself and rises unsteadily to his feet. He looks around the cell and spies his jacket, hanging from one of the coat hooks beside the door. He collects his boots and tries to put them on and a wave of vertigo surges over him.

Nora is on her feet, furiously wiping at the tears on her face. 'Here, here, don't be daft. Sit down here.'

She guides O'Keefe to the chair and kneels at his feet, putting on his boots as if he were a small boy and she an attentive mother.

'I'll take you out through the basement,' she says briskly, lacing the boots. 'There's a way out through the building next door. We use it ourselves.'

O'Keefe stares down at her head as she works, at the neat parting, the tidy combs anchored in the thick waves of red. 'You say you're sorry about those two lads, the boys …?'

She looks up, as if slapped, her eyes wide. 'Oh, Jesus, of course I am, Seán. How could you think I wasn't, I …'

'Your man's side-arm.'

'What?'

'Your man, Dillon. His side-arm is a Luger … a German gun. Not so common.'

'What of it, Seán?'

'I've read it's possible to match bullets to the guns they were fired from.'

Nora delivers O'Keefe into the back of a Ford taxi.

'You should go into hospital.'

'No,' O'Keefe says, not looking at her. 'Home … I need get home.'

She gives the driver the address to O'Keefe's digs, and watches as the car moves off into traffic.

She raises her arm to hail the next taxi for herself, but decides to walk instead, setting off across Westland Row into traffic, hoping a coal lorry, a team of drays, a butcher's van—she laughs, and tears begin to run her cheeks again—will obliterate every bit of her, leave her a wash of bloody meat, of shattered bone and pale, abraded skin on the street. And if this should not happen, and she makes it to the Dublin City Morgue, she will do her best by those two dead boys. It is the least, she thinks, she can do for Seán O'Keefe.

Half an hour later, the morgue attendant tells her she is too late by a day or more. Three fellas, detective lads, he tells her, have come already to collect the bullets the surgeon had taken from the boys' heads.

'And sure, anyway, love, there's not much you can tell from dumdums. They flatten out and there's no reading anything in slugs that have flattened out inside a lad's skull, not yet anyway.'

48

Just Albert follows the priest into his oak-panelled office.

'Sit, please, Mr Albert,' Father O'Dea says, crossing the room to a crystal set of whiskey decanters and glasses. 'Can I offer you a sup of something, sir?'

'No, thanks, Padre. I've a question to ask is all and then I'm on me way.'

Father O'Dea sits behind his desk and gestures again at the chair in front of it. Just Albert remains standing.

'Mr O'Keefe is not with you today, Mr Albert?'

'No, he's … detained.'

'In good health, I pray?'

'Your guess is as good as mine, Father, as I've not laid eyes on him these past three days.'

The headmaster nods, and his brow furls in concern. 'And are you still searching for Nicholas Dolan? Yourself and Seán?'

'We are.'

'And are you any closer to finding him?'

Just Albert smiles, a hard, shark's grin that barely reaches his eyes. 'That depends, Father, on whether you're able to help us.'

The priest leans forward and rests his hands on his desk, Francis Xavier and Ignatius Loyola gazing down at Just Albert over his shoulders. 'Of course, Mr Albert, what can I do for you?'

'You remember how you said you've contacts in the Irregulars? Past pupils, the like?'

'I do remember. And I do have some. Not as many as I would in the Free State forces, but some.'

'I need you to get word to them for me. And this word needs get to Felim O'Hanley.'

'And if I can, what is the word you'd like me to give them, sir?'

'Tell them to let O'Hanley know I've got his money. And that O'Hanley will get it back if he delivers up Nicholas and bars him from the Irregulars. *Persona not grata*, wha'? Here, will you write it out for me in finer words? And don't say "money" in your message, Father. I can't be having half the Irregulars looking for a cut. Just say, "what you lost in Burton's Hotel." He'll get the meaning well enough.'

Father O'Dea nods then dips his pen in the ink pot on his desk and begins scratching words onto a page. After a long moment, he lifts the page, blows it dry and hands it to Just Albert.

The doorman hands it back. 'You'll have to read it to me. I can read numbers but I'm no scholar with the letters, I'm not.'

The priest reads what he has written, and Albert nods in approval. 'That's grand, Father, much obliged. Now if you can deliver it, there's a nice, lovely big donation for your fine school here. Or for the black babies in the wilds of Africa. Or a touch for yourself, whatever ye'd like, Padre.'

'We Jesuits take a vow of poverty, Mr Albert.' The priest smiles as he speaks.

'Like meself, Father. You'll be able get it into the right hands?'

The smile fades from Father O'Dea's eyes. 'I can deliver your message, I'm sure, but there's nothing I can do to stop O'Hanley or any of his men from coming to you directly to get it. You're a well-known fellow, working for a rather well-known establishment. I'd be concerned for your safety, Mr Albert, and Mrs Dolan's as well.'

'You just tell them that if so much as a hair on Mrs Dolan's head is touched, they'll not see a red shekel. Me, Father, I can look after meself.'

'You're a confident man, Mr Albert.'

'You'd be confident as well, Father, if you were me and you had your paws on the amount of money I have.'

Word comes to O'Hanley of Just Albert's offer from Commandant Desmond Manning, chief engineer in the Dublin Irregulars, and one of the few men who know how to contact O'Hanley. A good man, Manning, O'Hanley thinks, unfolding the message on his desk, and one of the last real republican bomb makers not interned or dead. Trustworthy and true to the cause, and as angry as O'Hanley is himself at this sham of a Free State and the whores who serve it. Manning has told O'Hanley that if he can get enough gelignite or TNT, he'll blow a crater in the country so big you could fit the whole of the six Crown colonies of Ulster in it, just to spite the Free State bastards and the sheep's herd of Irish people who support them.

And it is just the procuring of such explosives to which the message alludes. The message is about the money. O'Hanley's eyes widen as he reads, and instinctively he blesses himself.

… *what you had taken from you in Burton's Hotel will be returned to you in full ….*

All that is wanted in exchange is one Nicholas Dolan.

O'Hanley's face burns with shame as he thinks of the boy. *Proof*, the letter demands, *that the boy is with you*. He picks up the 'Missing' poster from his desk and gazes at it for a long minute, his finger tracing the lineaments of the boy's features on the page, his mind sifting through options, considering force and guile and any means there might be to take back the money while holding on to the boy. Any way at all, before deciding that fourteen thousand pounds is worth more than any one soldier, even a special favourite like Nicholas. And the boy's feelings for him are hardly likely to be reciprocal, a small, vicious voice in the back of his head tells him. What good such a boy?

O'Hanley decides that he will, indeed, exchange the boy for the money. The future of the sovereign nation of Ireland demands it.

And if it is proof the collaborating whore-madam wants that her son is alive, then it is proof she shall get, he thinks, by *fuck*. The rare curse is a sweet, hot comfort whispered to himself.

'My … finger?' Nicholas Dolan's voice is high and boyish and he raises his hand as if to consider the fact of his fingers for the first time, staring for a second at them under the weak glow of a paraffin oil lamp that rebels against the musty gloom of the Dempsey woman's wine cellar. 'But why?'

'Because orders is why, youngfella. Because the bossman says it is why. Look at me, I've two of mine blown off me fuckin' hand and I'm tickety-bleedin'-boo about it,' Stephen Gilhooley says, his hand in fact throbbing with pain, the whiskey he has been drinking to stave off the horror of it making his words slur and making him feel sorry for young Nicholas. How O'Hanley comes up with his ideas Gilhooley will never know, but if it means getting his money back—Gilhooley has begun to think of it as *his* money, and has begun again to imagine the life he could make with it away from this horrible kip of a country—and getting a go at the bastard who half shot his own finger and thumb off in Burton's Hotel, well, then it will just have to be and hard luck to the poor lad.

'And it's only the little one anyway. The one you hardly ever use,' he says, watching the tears well in the boy's eyes. 'And I'll cut it clean. Sure, amn't I fuckin' butcher and all?'

'But why me, Stephen, why'd he pick me?'

Gilhooley is tiring of this and lifts the heavy knife from the table. 'Because he thinks you're worth fourteen fuckin' grand is why. Now put your bleedin' hand down here now or I'm taking the arm with it.'

Nicholas Dolan's little finger arrives in the morning post two days after Just Albert had asked Father O'Dea to get word to O'Hanley, and now it sits on the cherrywood table, tucked in its bedding of newspaper in the small box in which it had come. Ginny Dolan wipes away the tears that only Albert has been allowed to see.

'It's all go, Mrs Dolan. I've been told to expect instructions on where to hand over the money in exchange for Nicky. Don't be worrying. They want their bundle back more than they want to hurt Nicholas. He'll be grand.'

Just Albert stands over the table, unable to take his eyes from the severed little finger. It is most definitely Nicky's. There is no doubt about this in his mind. He is surprised by this instant recognition, and has an urge to examine his own hands, his own fingers. Would anybody recognise his, he wonders, the way both he and Mrs Dolan had instantly known that the finger in the box— though the flesh is waxy and a nub of bone extrudes from under the furl of neatly sliced skin just below the knuckle—belonged to their beloved Nicholas?

'These men ...' Ginny begins, and tears again well up in her eyes. 'He was fighting for these men? He trusted these men, and they're willing to trade him for money and ... take off his finger like a pork rib on a plate.' Her voice chokes with a sob and she clears her throat. 'You'll take care of everything, Albert, won't you?'

'Of course I will, Mrs Dolan.'

She is silent for a long moment, staring up at the man she has known since she raised him up from the grit and grime of the street where she had found him. 'You're a good boy, Albert. You've always been so good to me ...'

'Not half as good as you deserve, Mrs Dolan.'

She smiles warmly at him. 'And when you're finished, when you've Nicky back, the men, who did this ...'

'I'll tend to it, Mrs Dolan, you know that.'

O'Keefe's door opens no more than six inches, and an unfamiliar face peers out, causing Just Albert to question for a moment whether he has somehow knocked on the wrong door.

'Mr O'Keefe. Is he in?'

Wary eyes weigh him. Bloodshot and only recently wakened in a pale, sickly face. Hard eyes, but eyes that have seen a thing or two and aren't afraid of Just Albert, who fingers the chequered grip of the Colt in the deep pocket of his trenchcoat. He will shoot through the pocket, if needs must, and the man who has answered the door appears to sense this.

'No, mate, 'e's out. Who's calling?'

'Where is he? This is the third time I've called these past two days. He's not in there having a kip? Sleeping off a skite, is he?'

The pale-faced man opens the door wide with one hand, exposing to Albert that he is dressed only in a long nightshirt. 'Take a butcher's for yourself if you like, my friend, but 'e ain't 'ere.' The offer comes as more of a threat than a kindness.

Just Albert does not step into the room, but makes a show of peering past the man into the basement flat. There is something familiar about the man but he cannot place it. 'You can put away that shooter you're holding behind your back now.'

The man at the door smiles with his mouth but not his eyes. 'And you can stow the one you're fingering in your Lucy, there, chum.'

'London boy, wha'?'

'Shoreditch born and bred. I didn't get your name, mate. So's I can tell the Sergeant you've been 'ere.'

'A friend of Mr O'Keefe's, are you?'

'Who wants to know, then?'

'Albert is who.'

'Albert …?'

'Just Albert's grand.'

'Look, mate, I've been laid up these past three, four days. He's been back—the lady of the 'ouse has told me that much, but I don't know when or for how long. You're no old bill, I can see that, so who are you?'

'Mr O'Keefe is doing a job for my boss, he is, and I need to find him. The job's not done.'

Finch appears to consider this. 'Why don't you step inside and I'll make us a brew. But I can tell you right now, mate, Sergeant O'Keefe will be doing no work for no man for a while, says the Jew sawbones we had in to see him.'

The man in the nightshirt steps aside and allows Just Albert into the flat. He sets the Webley revolver he has been holding behind his back on the desk beside the bed.

Just Albert looks down at the sleeping O'Keefe, his face a swollen mass of blue and dark grey bruising.

Finch joins Just Albert at the bedside. 'A taxi brought him yesterday. And 'e could barely make it down the steps, barely standing when I opened the door. You any notion who done him like this?'

Just Albert nods. 'A fair notion.' He turns to look at Finch, studying him for the first time. 'You don't look well yourself, Mr ...'

'Finch, Jack Finch. And don't you fret about me. Fighting fit I am.'

Albert smiles. 'So you say.'

'So I am. Right, you sit down there and I'll put the billy on the ring for tea. Then you can tell me who done the sergeant like this. Right?'

'He'll live then, Mr O'Keefe?'

'Should, the doc says. Nothing broke up too bad on the inside,' Finch says.

Just Albert studies O'Keefe for a long moment then turns to Finch. 'And how do you know Mr O'Keefe, if you don't mind my asking?'

'Don't mind at all. We was coppers together, down in Cork,' Finch says, with some small pride in the words.

'You were a copper?'

Finch smiles at this. 'Of a sorts.'

'A Black and Tan?'

'Right you are, my china.'

'And that makes you a veteran soldier from the war?'

'Four years of mud and blood.'

Just Albert studies him for another long moment, and Finch says, 'You'd want to paint a picture or ask me to dance, Albert my friend, or fuck off with the eyeballs.'

'You've been in the shop. That's where I know you from. With the other English lads. Flashing it, spreading the coin round.'

'What shop you on about, mate?' Finch's eyes darken and go to the Webley on the desk and back to Albert.

'Ginny Dolan's gaff, in Monto.'

'Ginny what's gaff?'

'Dolan's. Corner of Foley Street. The sweetshop, pal. The knocking-shop.'

Finch appears to think this over and then relaxes. 'Look, if there's a knocking-shop in the 'ole of the country I ain't been in, you'll 'ave to show me it some time, so I'll take your word for it. But you'd want to keep buttoned up about where you know a man from and who 'is mates are, all right?'

'Schtum is me second name.'

'I don't give a fuck what you call yourself. But you can be right sure they'll be no more splashing the silver about for old Finchy. Stony broke as the day after demob, I am.'

Again, Just Albert studies Finch. 'You fit enough for a bit of a stunt, then, Jack Finch? There's a few quid in it for you and a chance to give your mate, Mr O'Keefe here, a hand in his time of need.'

'Fit as a corn-fed pigeon, me, mate. And I could use the bees and honey.' Finch smiles.

'I'll take that cup of tea, Mr Finch,' Just Albert says, taking out his box of short cigars and offering one to the Londoner, 'and we'll sort something out between us.'

49

Five days pass before word comes from O'Hanley.

Just Albert spends the morning sparring in the John of God's Boxing Club, waiting for Finch to come with what he has asked him to bring. He stands naked, drying himself with a thick Egyptian cotton towel that no one in the gym would be foolish enough to touch when Ginny enters the club, crossing over to the sink, amidst the racket of gloves on pads, the leathery syncopation of galloping speed bags, the nicking whir of skipping-ropes. The noise dies, the sparring in the raised ring slows to a halt, when the training men and boys see her. No women have been known to enter the club, and at first this is why they stop, but then Ginny Dolan is no ordinary woman. She is well known and both man and boy alike tip fingers to forelocks as she passes.

'Are you ready, Albert?'

Just Albert clutches the towel to cover his nakedness. 'Jaysus, Mrs Dolan, the state of me.'

Ginny smiles. 'Nothing I haven't seen before, pet. I wiped that arse of yours when you were only a whip, don't you forget.'

Just Albert smiles back and ties the towel around his waist. He looks past her, and his look is enough to send eyes to the floor, men and boys back to the labour of training. The sounds of the boxing gym slap and patter back to life.

'I'm ready. Once the fella comes.'

'Mr O'Keefe's friend?'

'He seems sound enough. And he's been in a scrap or two. He'd an arsenal the IRA'd be proud of stashed in a shed behind an auld doll's lodgings in Harold's Cross.'

'And how is poor Mr O'Keefe?'

'Poor nothing. If he done what he should've done to one or two of the fellas we met along the way, he'd be in no state like he's in now. He done his part, I'll hand him that, but too soft by half, our lad O'Keefe.'

'Not at all like his father, then.'

Just Albert contemplates this as he dresses, climbing into his smalls under the towel, his socks and trousers and shining brown brogues. He remembers how O'Keefe had looked this morning when he had called for Finch at the Cunningham flat to nail down the final details with the Shoreditch man; how O'Keefe had insisted he be included in the exchange. The doorman recalls how he had told O'Keefe that he would be more hindrance than help but had taken no pleasure in saying it.

'Maybe more like his auldfella than you'd reckon,' Just Albert says, buttoning his shirt and tucking it, sweet and neat, into his trousers, hoisting his braces up over his shoulders. 'He can soak a beating like the father.'

'The mark of a man,' Ginny says, Just Albert left wondering whether she means this or is being sarcastic. 'When will you go?'

As if she has summoned it with her words, the door to the club opens, and this time it is Finch, carrying the leather bag that had held the money when Just Albert grabbed it at the hotel. Some of the boxers look up but quickly resume their training.

''Allo, love,' Finch says to Ginny, doffing his trilby. 'Fine morning for it.'

Ginny does not smile. 'It will be if you get my Nicky back.'

'All things going well, missus, and we'll 'ave 'im back by tea, ain't I right, Mr Albert?'

The doorman ignores Finch, inwardly wincing at his bravado, willing his demeanour to match the gravity of their mission. In this he is without success.

'And sort out the men who've been holding him,' she says.

Finch, still smiling, says, 'All things going well, missus, all things going well.' Turning to Albert, he says, 'Bootlace worked a charm, if I do say so myself.'

Albert shoots him a hard look. 'Not in front of Mrs Dolan, Finch.'

Finch touches his hat brim. 'What was I thinking? Apologies, right, love?'

'Just get my Nicky back,' Ginny Dolan says, and Finch's smile fades, a chill blanching his back.

50

Finch and Albert are about to board the number thirty-one tram to Howth at Nelson's Pillar—as they have been instructed by the message from O'Hanley delivered by morning's post—when they see O'Keefe, limping towards them in the remarkable Indian summer sunshine.

'What are you at, then?' Finch says. 'You're in no nick for a jaunt you aren't, my son. 'Ow did you even know to find us?'

'Never assume a man is sleeping when he's only got his eyes closed, Finch.'

'He's right, Mr O'Keefe,' Just Albert says, 'you're no good to us.'

'I'm grand, Finch, Albert. Nearly a week in bed is enough for any man…' But there is pain in his eyes at the effort it takes him to say this. 'I'll be grand.' He stands next to them, and indicates for them to board the tram. 'After ye, lads.' He attempts a smile, and a woman with cloth shopping bags who has been waiting steps back and appears to decide on a later tram.

Finch smiles at O'Keefe.

'Fack off, chum. Age before beauty.'

O'Keefe attempts another smile, and the pain of it is so intense that stars erupt in his vision. He drowns the pain with a naggin of whiskey he takes from inside his suit jacket.

Just Albert takes O'Keefe by the arm and guides him up onto the back conductor's platform. 'We can't miss this tram, boys, so stop the messing and shift it.'

The tram pulls off with a lurching roll, and O'Keefe has to cling to the overhead railing to keep himself from tumbling off the open platform and out into the street.

'You sit down there, Mr O'Keefe,' Just Albert says, and for once, without argument, O'Keefe obeys him. There are only four other passengers on this lower deck of the tram, and Finch climbs the spiral stairs to the upper deck to check the number of passengers there.

'Just two old girls with a picnic lunch and the conductor,' he says when he returns. O'Keefe notices that he speaks only to Just Albert, as if his presence has been noted and forgotten.

'I'm not armed,' O'Keefe says, taking the whiskey again from his coat as the conductor comes down the spiral stairs from the upper deck of the tram. The conductor takes a long look at O'Keefe, before turning to Finch and Albert.

'Tickets please, gentlemen,' he says, but without the usual jaunty authority in his voice. There is something about these men that makes him wary; a look in their eyes, their steady attention to the street outside the tram, the heavy trenchcoats in the rare weather.

'Three,' Just Albert says, 'for Howth.'

'Plenty of seats to choose from…' the conductor says, as if to break the silence, taking the proffered coins from Just Albert and tearing three tickets from the roll hanging from the dispenser on his belt.

'We'll stand,' Just Albert says, turning away from the conductor and facing out into the street. Finch joins him there, hanging from a hand bar on the platform, scanning the streets around them as they roll eastward, the tram running more smoothly now as they pick up speed down Summerhill approaching Ballybough.

The conductor has moved to the front of the tram to stand by the driver, and Finch says, over his shoulder to O'Keefe, 'You all right, there, Sarn't?'

'I am,' O'Keefe says. He stows the bottle back in his coat and heaves himself to standing. He takes his place behind the men, hanging from a strap. 'What are we looking for then?'

'For Nicky,' Just Albert says, still scanning the footpaths as the tram makes its way through Fairview and Marino, through Clontarf and onto the coast road, the water at their backs, on the opposite side of the tram to where they stand on the open platform.

'All Albert 'ere was told is be on this tram and 'ave the bag of money with us,' Finch explains.

O'Keefe thinks about this for a long moment. There would be few passengers boarding this tram at half-three on a Wednesday afternoon. Howth is a small fishing village, popular at weekends with daytrippers eager to climb the hill above the harbour and overlook Dublin bay, but on weekdays, the trams are infrequent and lightly travelled. There are long stretches of empty coastline between Dublin and Howth as well, which would allow O'Hanley to control the conditions of any exchange. Various scenarios run through his mind, but he has trouble following any one idea to its conclusion. The morphine has made his thinking hazy, as has the whiskey he has been drinking since he boarded the tram in Rathmines in pursuit of Finch and Albert.

'There're no other instructions?'

'None.'

'What happens when we get to Howth? If we get to Howth and we haven't been contacted?'

'Don't know, Mr O'Keefe ... now will you shut your gob, to fuck, and stop asking questions I can't answer?' Just Albert says, still scanning the road beside the tram tracks, now and again leaning out of the tram to search fore and aft.

Shortly, the tram clatters to a halt in front of Doherty's Coast Bar, and two passengers disembark, leaving only the two upstairs and an older man and what appears to be his grandson sitting behind the driver.

'We should get those people off … the passengers,' O'Keefe says.

'Get them off then,' Just Albert says.

O'Keefe considers doing just this, but dreads the pain inherent in the effort and drinks more whiskey instead. He watches through the window as a Wright's fish van passes them on its way into Dublin. The tram lurches forward, tilting drunkenly as it gains speed, and O'Keefe feels nauseous with the movement. He closes his eyes in a vain attempt to damp down the illness, and as quickly opens them. His complexion is deathly white but for the fading mottle of bruising around his eyes and neck.

'You shouldn't be here, Mr O'Keefe. You'll do yourself harm.'

His words are spoken with some small compassion, but O'Keefe is deaf to this.

'I'll be grand, I will.'

'Albert, mate, 'ere we go, 'ere we are, chum,' Finch says.

Just Albert turns back to the open platform to see a Ford Tourer keeping pace with the tram. They are on a long, straight stretch of more than two miles before the tram reaches Sutton and must slow, and the Ford and tram are making a steady twenty miles per hour in the summer heat, side by side. The roof of the Tourer is slightly lower than the height of the three men on the conductor's platform, and Just Albert crouches down to look into the car. As he does, the Ford's driver—a young lad with a bandaged hand and a Thompson machine-gun resting across his forearm, barrel jutting from the window—waves and winks. It takes Just Albert a second to recognise the driver as the lad they had shot at in Murphy's rooms in Burton's Hotel. He is about to dive back into the tram, thinking that the driver will fire on them, when Nicholas appears in the seat behind the driver.

'Nicky!' Just Albert says, smiling despite himself.

A man in the rear seat with Nicky leans across the boy and stares out at the men on the tram, locking eyes with Just Albert for a second.

O'Hanley, O'Keefe thinks, remembering his face from the grainy 'Wanted' poster in his RIC barracks during the Tan war. O'Keefe watches as O'Hanley appears to decide something and turns to speak to Nicholas.

O'Keefe, Finch and Just Albert look on as the boy shakes his head and O'Hanley says something else. He sits close to the boy, and it is impossible to make out what he is saying, but all three men can see the commandant's pointed index finger wagging in a universally understood gesture of authority. There is a long pause while the boy appears to contemplate the coming action—the tram rattling at speed, the Ford pacing it along the empty coast road, the barrel of the tommy-gun like an amputated limb extruding from the driver's window. It is now that Just Albert notices the bandaging on Nicholas's hand, and rage quietly ignites within him. *Just get the boy first.*

As he thinks this, the Ford accelerates and overtakes the tram, and when it is one hundred yards ahead, the car swerves, bouncing up and onto the tram tracks. The tram driver clangs his bell, shouting in disbelief, and begins to slow the tram down as the car reduces speed in front of it. The conductor, standing next to the driver, looks back at Finch, Albert and O'Keefe. There is fear in his eyes. He summons the two remaining passengers seated behind the driver and takes them up the front stairs to the tram's upper deck. A quarter of a mile and two minutes later, the driver brings the tram to a halt behind the idling Ford.

'We can't do it on board 'ere, mate,' Finch says to Just Albert.

'Why not?' A wave of nausea washes over O'Keefe, and he would not hear the answer to his question even if Finch were to answer it.

'Come on, we'll do it outside,' Just Albert says, stepping down off the conductor's platform, his gun drawn. Finch follows him with the bag, and then slowly, painfully, so does O'Keefe. He catches up to them at the front of the tram, his body flaring with pain with every footstep. He watches as O'Hanley and the gunman from the hotel emerge from the car and begin to walk towards them on the tracks, the gunman with the Thompson across his chest, O'Hanley with a Webley pistol held at his side.

'Bring Nicholas out of the car,' Just Albert says, as they close the distance.

'Give us over the money.' O'Hanley and the Gilhooley stop ten feet away from them on the tracks, the wind rustling the sea grass in the dunes beyond.

'Give him the bag, Finch.'

Finch looks at Albert, and then walks forward and sets the bag at O'Hanley's feet.

O'Keefe watches as Gilhooley steps forward, crouching down to open the bag, rifling through a few of the packets of bills on top before standing up and nodding.

His eyes locked on Albert's, O'Hanley shouts over the wind and the distant shushing of the tide. '*Nicholas…*'

The boy gets out of from the car, and walks past O'Hanley and Gilhooley without looking at them.

'I'd send the boy on a long voyage away from here,' O'Hanley says, undisguised bitterness in his voice. 'The new republic has no place for the likes of him or any of you in it.'

With his eyes still on O'Hanley, Just Albert says, 'Get up on the tram, Nicky.'

The boy is crying as he passes O'Keefe, tears streaking his face in the Indian summer sunlight.

'You're lucky men, you two,' Just Albert says, turning to join the boy. 'Lucky men…'

O'Keefe follows while Finch covers their return to the tram, his pistol held loosely at his side, a half-grin on his face that O'Keefe makes no effort to understand. He tries to mount the conductor's platform and finds that he can't. Finch and Albert take him under the arms and haul him aboard.

'Might be best if we made our way up to the top deck, if you can make it, Sar'nt…' Finch says, looking down the length of the tram and out the front glass at Gilhooley and O'Hanley as they climb back into the Ford. A moment later, O'Keefe hears the Ford's engine revving and turns to watch the car bump off the tracks and swing around on the road to head back towards Dublin. He turns then to look at Nicholas standing silently next to Albert, his eyes too following the Ford as it leaves. *I hope you were worth it*, O'Keefe thinks.

Inside the Ford, O'Hanley takes the bag from Gilhooley. It weighs the same as he remembers, and as he opens the mouth of the bag, he sees the bundles of notes wrapped in paper bands marked Bank of Ireland. He smiles, and begins to root through the bundles. His smile fades. He takes one of the packets of notes and flicks through it and does it again, his eyes widening in disbelief.

O'Hanley digs deeper into the bag, and begins to reef the wrapped bundles of banknotes from inside, tossing the worthless sheaves of newsprint topped with single, genuine bills onto the floor of the Ford's back seat.

'Turn the car, Stephen,' he says. 'Do it now.'

One of the packets appears wedged at the bottom corner of the bag, and O'Hanley frees it with an angry tug. With it comes a length of leather bootlace, to the end of which is tied the safety pin of a hand-grenade.

It takes something less than a second for O'Hanley to realise what he has done. Time stops for him, but does not stop, and some ancient impulse drives him to open the bag wider, to confirm what he knows suddenly to be true.

The grenade detonates in the confines of the Ford, the car's roof bursting upwards like an inflated paper bag, streaks of fire and scorched air and a million tiny fragments of shrapnel tear through O'Hanley and Gilhooley, the blast smashing bone, lacerating shards perforating the panelling and shooting out the open windows of the Ford, the car slowing and veering across the road where it hits the tracks and comes to a stop, smoke and blood pouring from its blast-bloated doors.

51

Nora Flynn hears the doorbell and listens as the serving girl, Martha, answers it. She hears Martha tell the caller to wait a moment please and she will ask her.

She rises to her feet, her back sore from sitting, hardly having moved from the chair by the window since she returned to her family home more than a week before. She is a worry to her mother, she knows, but there is little she can do about it. She refuses to answer her mother's questions and her mother, mercifully, has stopped asking them. One of these days she will have to take one of her brothers and move out of her rooms in Ballsbridge, but she has decided she will leave the few bloodstained items of clothing in the room on Leinster Road for the safe house owner to dispose of as he sees fit.

'Miss, it's a gentleman caller,' Martha says, barely able to contain the excitement in her voice. 'And he's after asking for you!' She smiles wickedly and Nora's heart pounds. It couldn't be, she thinks.

'Did he give his name, Martha, or did you bother asking?' she says, her voice harsher than she has intended.

'No, miss.'

It can't be … oh please, God, please let it be Seán ….

She opens the door, and her heart skips a bit and then slows.

'Carty,' she says.

'Nora.' Carty touches the brim of his hat. 'You look well, you do.'

'I don't, and you know I don't.'

Carty smiles, appearing nervous to Nora. *Imagine, Terence Carty, the hardened gunman, nervous.*

'You're keeping well, then?' he says.

'As well as can be expected. And you?'

'Grand, Nora, grand.'

'And all at Oriel House?'

And here, Carty looks away, scanning Nora's mother's rose bushes, the neatly clipped grass. 'Not so bad, I reckon. Two men, Killeen and Ahern, got theirs last week. Found dead in a car in Waterford without a notion of who shot them.'

Nora blesses herself. 'God save them.'

Carty nods. 'And you know O'Hanley's dead.'

'I read it in the papers. Blown up in his car?'

Carty shrugs. 'There was talk of banknotes snagged in the gorse and dune grass for days afterwards. The Howth tram was black with people on jaunts to hunt for wind-blown tenners.' He smiles at Nora and looks away again.

There is a long silence between them. A tram passes on the Ranelagh Road in front of the house, and when its clanking rumble has passed, Nora says, 'I'm not coming back, Carty. If that's what you've come to ask.'

'It is why I've come, but there's no hurry. Take your time. You're needed but you need take the time to get over … things.' He examines her face as he speaks, and in his one-eyed gaze, Nora is aware of affection. She is surprised by it, having always thought of herself as more of a burden to Carty than a help, but she is almost certain it is there now. Is it more than general, this affection? She cannot decide, but knows there is nothing for it. She could no more bring herself to love a man like Carty than she could the man in the moon.

'I don't need time, I've decided already. I just can't do it. Not any more. Never again.'

Carty's good eye flashes with anger, and then it is gone, replaced by something resembling contrition. 'Look, Nora, do you think I like the things we must do? I don't, I hate it. I hated shooting every man I ever shot. I pray to God that I did the right thing and leave it to Himself above to decide if it was right or if I'm damned, but in my head, I know it was the right thing. That chucking the English out of Ireland was the right thing. That the Free State is the right thing ... for now, anyway. And that achieving what is right requires ...'—he scans the roses again as if in search of the words—'... that we do what would be otherwise wrong in peace time.'

'Wrong is wrong, Carty. Beating and torturing a man can never be right, I'm sorry. How can a people ever trust a state that would sanction such things? Are we to be like the English masters we evicted? Ruling by force and threats and fear?'

Disgust overrides the contrition in his good eye. 'Jesus, Nora, do you want the British back? Do you?' His voice is momentarily raised, and he lowers it just as quickly. 'Because they'll step right back in if the Treaty fails, if the Free State isn't made to work. The last thing they want to do and yet they'll be back if we fail. Why do you think they're giving us so much help to fight the Irregulars?' He pauses to light a cigarette and pulls angrily at it before continuing.

'And don't talk to me about the *people*. The fine, brave *people* of Ireland want peace and they don't give a shite how it's got or who has to be hurt to get it once it's not themselves. No one will remember the wild things done in the name of the Free State once the Free State is preserved and the good people of Ireland can get back to earning a living in peace. And it's the likes of me, of you ...'—he points a finger at Nora as he would a revolver—'... and even Charlie Dillon, who are tasked with doing the nasty things to achieve that peace. It's not pretty, Nora, but it's the way of things. I thought you were wise enough to know this and here you are running on like any other woman, like some bloody Quaker.'

Nora absorbs the insult. She disagrees with him, but feels worth every slander any man would cast at her as payment for the things she has stood witness to, has done.

She says, 'And what happens when men like Dillon and his lads get so used to doing the nasty things in service of this Free State that they've no way of knowing what's right at all any more? Killing young boys is never right, Carty. Torturing men. Lifting them, killing them and leaving their bodies in ditches for the rats and dogs is *never* right. It can't be.'

'Dillon is a blackguard and a headcase, but every nation state needs men like Dillon, Nora, and don't you forget it. You trained with many more like him. And there was little complaint from you when it was English lads he was plugging and leaving in ditches. Men in the files *you* pulled and copied in Dublin Castle and handed on. Who do you think was on the sharp end of all those pilfered dossiers, Nora? Or have you gone precious on us because of what he did to your Seán O'Keefe? "*Can't do it any more*", you say? You seemed to enjoy the work well enough when you were shadowing Seán O'Keefe.'

Nora flinches at his words, but cannot feel any more shame than she already feels. Part of her mind marks the disdain in Carty's voice and decides that it *had* been real affection she'd seen in his face, because only affection turns so quickly, so cleanly, to hate. She says nothing to him but does not look away.

Carty shakes his head, turns and walks to the gate. He gathers a rosebud in his fingers and tugs it from the bush, bringing it to his nose to smell. He turns back to Nora. 'I'm sorry, Nora, that things had to come to this. I'm sorry if I've spoken out of turn or ...'

'Go away, Carty,' Nora says, opening the front door behind her to step back inside the house. 'Just go away. You've your work to be getting on with.'

52

'It's not your bleedin' turn, yeh thick flitch of shite, yeh.'

'It bleedin' *is*. Uncle Jack went first and I …'

'Now, lads, don't fight over cards. One of the things my old dad told me when I were a lad. "*Never fight over cards.*" 'Course them wasn't words 'e ever lived by 'imself, they weren't, but the truth of 'em stands, in my book.'

'What book is that, Uncle Jack?'

'Book?'

'What's your book?'

'*In my way of thinking*, lads. Christ on a crutch, you could ask questions for the King of England, you two blighters could.'

'No we couldn't.'

'Why's that?'

''Cause the King of England hates Irish youngfellas, doesn' he, Henry? Roger O'Brien in school told us.'

But Henry is not listening. 'Look! Mr O'Keefe is awake, he is. We didn't wake you, didn't we not, Mr O'Keefe? Did we?' He is smiling, and his brother turns and sees O'Keefe attempt to raise himself up on his good arm.

'I don't think I'm able for the cards yet, fellas.'

'You lads shove off for the moment,' Finch says, 'and let me get Mr O'Keefe up for a piss and a shave and then we'll 'ave some more cards later on, right?'

'But I've three trumps! Please, Uncle Jack, can't we play this hand?'

O'Keefe smiles. 'Go on, play the hand. These lads are demons for the cards, Finch. You should never have let them in.'

'S'all right, Sergeant. Great company, bosom chums, we are. They've taught me Twenty-five and I've taught them Pontoon and we're best pals, aren't we boys?'

'Can we play this hand?'

'I don't want to play it, it's not fair, I've no fuckin' … sorry, Uncle Jack,' the boy apologises.

'You stow the naughty talk and lead it out, mate. We'll play this 'and and then you two fack off, right?'

'You said "fuck".'

'Shut it.'

When they are finished and the boys gone, O'Keefe says, '*Uncle Jack?* How long have I been out, Finch, that you've become family now?'

Finch smiles, but it is sheepish and not at all like his normal brazen grin. 'You've been in and out for the past two days and nights.'

'Where have you been staying then?' O'Keefe says, searching the room for signs of Finch's bedding and clothes and finding none.

'Well, I been staying upstairs, 'aven't I?'

'Can I have some of that water?'

''Course you can, let me get it for you.' Finch pours water from a glass pitcher on the desk next to the bed, and holds the glass to O'Keefe's lips while he drinks.

'Prop me up, here. I can drink it once I'm raised up.'

Finch helps his friend settle against the pillows and headboard and watches him drink.

O'Keefe sets the glass on the desk again and wipes his chin. 'So, upstairs is it?'

Finch smiles again. 'It is. A finer woman you won't meet, Sarn't, and in need of a man about the place.'

'*Uncle Jack*. Jesus, Finch, you're quick over the hurdles.' O'Keefe smiles. 'They're good lads, those two.' And as he says it, his smile fades and an image of the two dead boys on the gurneys in the morgue rises up in his mind.

Finch senses his disturbance. 'You should be sleeping, mate. Your pal Solomon, the Jew doctor, says have more broke ribs than straight ones. And a punctured lung. Here.' As if reminded by mention of his lung, Finch offers O'Keefe a cigarette. O'Keefe takes one and a light. 'You've us to mind you now, me and Mrs C and the nippers.'

Inhaling the harsh smoke, O'Keefe begins to cough and his ribs erupt in pain. He hands the smoke back to Finch, who shrugs and smokes it himself.

When he has stopped coughing and the pain has receded, O'Keefe says, 'I'm not going anywhere, Finch. And thanks for minding me.'

'Don't talk about it, mate. Who minded me when I was shot? Who was the one person I could go to in the 'ole of this God-forsaken country … no offence … but you and yours?'

'And the boy, Nicholas, and Just Albert, what's happened with them? Was the boy all right? Is he all right?' O'Keefe remembers leaping from the tram and then nothing else.

'The boy is grand, and so is my china, Albert. Gone to Blighty, a nice, posh public school for the lad, and Albert in digs nearby to make sure 'e don't get too 'omesick. 'Til things cool down. Bad things 'ave been said about the boy by them Irregulars, and no doubt the Free Stater lads still have eyes out for him. Mrs Dolan thought, we all thought, it was best he be out the way for a time. We were going to 'ave a go at the boys who served you up, but Mrs Dolan said to leave it out. That Albert needed get the boy out the country for the while, back into school where a young lad of his class should be. I'll still 'ave a gander for them if you tell me who they are.'

O'Keefe considers this. Considers going after Charlie Dillon himself when he has healed properly, and realises that though he knows Dillon killed the two boys—tortured and killed them—there is no way that he can prove it. He could kill him, he thinks. Justice would be served if he plugged Charlie Dillon. *But no, no I won't. No more killing.* There is enough of it about in the country.

'No. I don't want that, Finch. I mean it.'

'Whatever you say, Sarn't, who am I to go against what you want? Anyway, this'll compensate, look …'

Finch, smiling again, gets up from the chair and goes to the small closet to rummage through O'Keefe's suit jacket. He comes out with something and tosses it onto the bed beside O'Keefe.

'What's this?'

'Payment for services rendered, Seán. Mrs Dolan's not one to forget who done her a good turn. You'd think there'd be more of it out of fourteen grand, but there was any number of folks needing paying. And we 'ad to blow some of it up, obviously, so the bag would look real enough for them lads to take it.'

'Who's idea was it to rig up the bag with the Mills bomb?' O'Keefe asks, knowing the answer.

'Mine,' Finch says proudly, never thinking for a moment how dangerous the booby-trapped bag had been to Nicholas Dolan. 'I done it more times than once in the war, me. Under tin cans, books, bodies, I can rig up about anything given a grenade and a bit of twine.'

O'Keefe has no doubt he can. 'You kept enough of it back …'

'Of course we did. I got my cut—and well I might, seeing as it's money I likely as not laboured for in the first place, say no more. And I done sent an 'efty share of it already to Bennett's missus and the mums of the other boys in my old mob whose tickets got clipped to get that wonga, again, say no more. You remember old Bennett from when we was in Ballycarleton? Mind you, Sar'nt, I've given up some of mine to Mrs C for 'ousekeeping and medical bills, the like, bought myself a new tin of fruit and am looking at a motor today, a nice big, swish Austin so's Mrs C and the kids can go to holy mass in style.'

O'Keefe lifts the wedge of pound notes in his good hand. 'Jesus, Finch, how much is it?'

'A monkey.'

'A what?'

'Five 'undred pound, mate.'

'*Five hundred pounds?* Nearly two years' wages when I was a Peeler,' he says, and as he says it, he knows that he will not keep the money. *Blood money.* He will divide it between the families of the dead boys. Unable to bring them justice, he can at the very least help them to go on living.

Finch is oblivious. 'I know! You get yourself back on your feet, mate, and we'll have a right splash, you and me. A trip out to Leopardstown and Fairyhouse for the ponies. But no knocking-shops, Sar'nt, not me, no more, mate. That kind of larking about is done with me and I with it, what with Mrs C and all.'

O'Keefe smiles. 'Never mind, Finch. I was never one for the whoring myself.'

'Wise man, Sergeant, you always was. 'Cept when you joined me and Albert on that tram … that wasn't wise, mate, it weren't.'

'No, Finch, it wasn't.'

Nor was falling in love with Nora Flynn, he thinks, remembering how quickly it had happened and understanding, suddenly, how Finch and Mrs Cunningham, unlikely a pairing as they may seem, could fall for each other in so short a time. Love is like that, he thinks, remembering Nora's face, her body, her voice. Memory as sharp as reality to him in the wavering after effects of the morphine.

'You don't look so chuffed, now, Sarn't, about the money. Is it not enough or what? You just say and there's more …'

'No, Finch, it's not that at all. I didn't ask for any money from the woman. I don't even want it.'

'But surely you earned it, didn't you, mate? Why'd you take the job on in the first place if it wasn't for the few bob?'

O'Keefe thinks of his father and the debt owed to Ginny Dolan. And he thinks of Ginny's boy, Nicholas, now in England. The lad's eyes, like Peter's. The hair too. The cut of the boy so much like the brother he left forever on a beach in Turkey. Looking so much like him a man could be forgiven for thinking … O'Keefe stops himself from thinking. The debt has been discharged.

'I'm tired, Finch.'

'Well you should be, mate. Well you should be.'

'Has the doc left any of the laudanum, has he?'

'He has.' Finch looks at him.

'Let's have it then, Finch. Let's have another sup of it, so.'

53

In the end, Jeremiah Byrne can think of no other way but to pay in fags for one of the young Sheriffer lads—an eight-year-old with enough bottle to climb those stairs—to lay the bait. To make it so the auld bastard cannot but drag his plastered carcass down into the street, into the night-dark laneway.

While he waits for the lad to return, Jeremiah peeks out from the cover of Hambone Lane and lets his eyes wander the nightscape of Sheriff Street. Lantern light burns in sporadic windows and the wind hums among the mesh of laundry lines that stretch from one side of the street to the other. A barrel fire burns and his old mates surround it, mock-scrapping, throwing digs at arms and shoulders, youngfellas jostling in the way of youngfellas. Ragging. Having a laugh. Able for it and all. Taking time on the cobbles to avoid the bustle of tiny tenement rooms and not because they have no homes to go to or no one to love them in those rooms. These lads are nothing like the lane boys who want Jeremiah's skin to piss on. Nothing like them. Those boys have nothing but meths and petrol fumes for to warm them; no cramped room, no Ma—not even a whore of a Ma—no sisters or brothers to bundle up with on the pallet of a winter's night. No.

Jeremiah's eyes catch movement from the doorway of his own building as the boy he has employed skips down crumbling steps and jogs to the entrance of Hambone Lane.

'Well?'

'Well, wha'? Where's me smokes?'

Jeremiah thinks to Welsh the youngfella, but then realises he will need his silence.

'Here,' he says, 'take all ten.' They had settled on four for the task.

'Ten?'

'Go on, yeh slow cunt,' he places the Player's box in the boy's hand. 'Is he coming?'

'He fuckin' is, he said he'd be down shortly. He's a brace of crutches so he'll be ages I'd say.'

'I've the time, I do,' Jeremiah says. 'Now you're to say nothing to no one, righ'? Yis don't want end up in Artane or the 'Frack, do yeh?'

'Head down, mouth shut, wha'?' the boy says.

'Proper order, youngfella. Now fuck off away from here and don't be minding any business but yer own.'

'All righ', I will. And if y'ever need any more jobs done, Jerry, I'm yer man, you know it, righ'?'

Jeremiah smiles. 'I'll keep yeh in mind, youngfella. Now shift it.'

The boy tips his cap and is gone.

Jeremiah waits, and after some minutes he smiles and backs deeper into the darkness of the laneway.

'Froggy Maughn, I should've known you'd pay me, one day, mate.'

Uncle John Keegan propels himself from the half-light of Sheriff Street and into the darkness of the lane. 'I fuckin knew it, me aul' pal, I always did be telling any manjack who'd listen, *Froggy Maughn'd be back with me cabbage, the day he raised head out of Cork Prison*, I did say.'

'Froggy Maughn's dead these past two year, yeh soft prick, yeh,' Jeremiah says, stepping forward, faint light from the laneway's entrance revealing his face to his uncle.

'*You*? What're yeh at, yeh little bollix yeh. I'll fuckin tan you, yeh little …'

'You'll tan nobody, yeh cripple bastard,' Jeremiah says, and takes the surgical knife from his sleeve.

'Ah now, Jeremiah,' his uncle says, and it is the first time he has called Jeremiah by his given name in as long as the boy can remember.

'"*Ah now*" nothing, yeh cunt,' Jeremiah says, stepping closer and bringing the glinting blade to his uncle's throat, his uncle helpless with his hands bucked under the crutches, one leg bound in plaster and hanging inches off the cobbles. 'You've this coming a long time, y'auld whore's pox. Y'auld dirty fucker.'

'Please, Jerry, I'm sorry, I never meant hurt any of yis …'

Jeremiah drags the razor-sharp blade across his uncle's throat. His uncle's last words emerge as bloody spray, and Jeremiah jumps back to avoid the deluge.

Uncle John Keegan's mouth gapes and he slumps against the brickwork. As his crutches go from under him, he falls and his hands flail at the arterial plume of blood. It takes two minutes before he is still, and Jeremiah watches as he dies.

Before he turns away, Jeremiah spits on the warm corpse of his uncle. 'Save your sorrys for the devil,' he says, and walks down Hambone Lane and out into Saville Place. He stops only to clean his uncle's blood from his hand in a muddy puddle, where he feels for the first time in many years sated, and somehow hopeful for the future.

END